Reaching Montaup

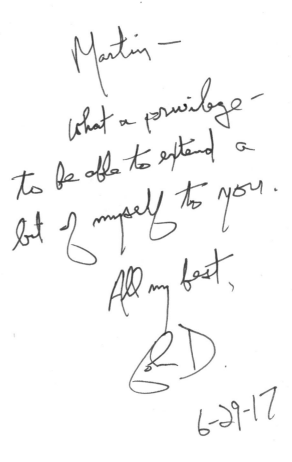

Martin —

what a privilege —
to be able to extend a
bit of myself to you.

All my best,

B. D.

6-29-17

KLX97@outlook.com

Reaching Montaup

a novel

J Dominic

Bay Tree Publishing, LLC
Point Richmond, California

Bay Tree Publishing, LLC
1400 Pinnacle Court #406
Point Richmond, CA 94801

Cover design by Jeff Fuller
Interior design by David Cole
Cover art by Diane Fernald

Manufactured in the United States of America

Library of Congress Cataloging-in-Publication Data
Dominic, J.
Reaching Montaup : a novel / by J Dominic.
Point Richmond, California :
Bay Tree Publishing, LLC, [2016]
Identifiers: LCCN 2016019629 | ISBN 9780996676502 (pbk.)
Classification: LCC PS3604.O4645 R43 2016 | DDC 813/.6--dc23
LC record available at https://lccn.loc.gov/2016019629

Summary: Jate Tavino comes of age when he realizes his twin brother is gay, his best friend has been raped, and his father is complicit in revenge and possibly murder.

Adult Literary Fiction
[1. Regional Fiction 2. Bildungsroman 3. Adolescence
4. Boy's Adventure 5. Friendship]

ISBN: 978-0-9966765-0-2
ISBN: 978-0-9966765-1-9 (ebook)

To
Theo Gund
John J. Sweeney
Robert Hill
and Tom Spanbauer

From perfect grief there need not be
Wisdom, or even memory ...
—Dante Gabriel Rossetti

Contents

MistaCogg says, Tide works rocks. Wears down their rough. Makes them smooth. And then eventual. Fine sand.

Its the eternal process.

MistaCogg says the best place to see the action of this process is the marsh at Montaup. Says the word Montaup means rock shore. Montaup being a word from the language of the Wampanoag and those Wampanoag were just some of many natives living Sowams. Or south of the Plymouth Plantation of the Mayflower Pilgrims in the year 1620. Other tribes living south of the new arrived Pilgrims of England were Pokanoket. They of the Open Fields. And Narragansett. People of the Further Shore.

MistaCogg says, Tides provided all tribes. Everyone. With abundant goodness.

And although the white settlers provided Indians with lots of misery and death. MistaCogg says, Tides always changed death back to life. And then back again and repeated and repeated and repeated. And although the process was. And always has been for the past four hundred years. Vicious in favor of the white man.

MistaCogg says, In the great tide of times. Four hundred years is nothin.

Says, The clear lesson marshes teach is tides always turn and while everything may appear rock solid. Everything. For absolute. Is not.

MistaCogg says, Tidewater changes land. And its not the other way around.

MistaCogg calls tidewater, Tides.

But the Montaup rockshore land? He calls that, TerrorFirmer.

TerrorFirmer is MistaCoggs fancy way of saying sogg that everyone else in our town of Sowams knows is the combined three ingredients. Plants. Animals. And muck.

MistaCogg says not to confuse sogg with muck. Sogg is solid. Sogg is TerrorFirmer. A baked cake. But muck is more the batter. Muck is the early-stages-a-sogg. The uncooked ingredients. The puddin-a-life.

MistaCogg says the puddin-a-life is the slime-a-the earth mentioned in the Bible and although its the begin of the pudding. It has nothin to do with lifes begin but everythin to do with its end. Not the begin. But the began.

MistaCogg says, The begin-a-life has the smell of five and dime perfume. But the began-a-life stinks like wicked foul carryin rot and if you get in the thick of that.

GoodLawd.

And. Not ta say. But. Anyone living near a marsh knows the sure way to remain clear of the bad pudding it is to stay on the solid sogg trail. Usual at the edge of a flowditch. If you dont stay on the ditch edge and you crisscross crisscross. Or you jump the ditch hectic because you dont figure width correct. Might be you could land smack in a grip of razorweed that slices your hands while the muck pulls off your boots with sucking sounds thats earthfarts giving off. WhatHo! Making you gag and puke and maybe gag again all over.

MistaCogg says, Best way to avoid this predicament is walk the straight and narrow.

And I think he means path. Because MistaCogg once said when ZompaGalucci was a boy. Just after Zompas NewYork family moved to Sowams. Poor city kid Zompa ran ever whichway on the marsh ascat-a-Hoogly haunts and got stuck to his waist for almost a full day in such a rank situation and if it hadnt been for MistaCogg fishing nearby from the trestle and hearing Zompas faint calls for help. Zompa would-a-been, MuckleburyFen in a bog ett by fiddla crabs n lopstas.

When I asked MistaCogg if that was a true story? He looked at me full. Poured a slug of brandy. Tamped tobacco in his pipe. And said, Nope. Not true. But should be.

MistaCogg said, Long as pigeonkicked folks act like marshes got the Hooglies. Then those of us who live in such blessed acres. Fott stinks n all. Will have these marshes for ahselves. Most godsome place on earth. Ebb. Flow. Rhythm of time. No one should live where there aint the tides.

MistaCogg corncob.

MistaCogg liquored.

MistaCogg praspective.

I
Stories

1
Bowl on the Head

The first thing you gotta understand is this is a story about me writing my story and getting that thing called praspective.

Its not about bowl on the head.

Or plate in the head.

Its not about days at GreensHillTownBeach.

Or about sailing to Sowams MountHopeShores.

Or the death of Metacomet the Wampanoag Indian chief.

Or the ghosts of the Hindu Hoogly sailors.

Or the way we talked RhodeIsland talk.

Saying preece for priest.

Ott art.

Nuthin nothing.

Hott for heart.

Our father.

Or

Ah mom.

Its not about the way my unexact twin brother Ross and my Portuguese best friend PruneyMendez was queer for each other and how the priest FatherLuis took advantage of that. And how Mikey 2A's. And the other guys. ScarHab. ZompaGalucci. And my Dad. Made a real mess of everything. Especial between our neighbors MistaCogg and GilOwen who were all the time pals till MistaCogg said mean stuff about the white whale MobyDick. And GilOwen.

Both being queers.

And how ZompaGalucci took a hotta. Which every pigeonkicked RhodeIslander knows. Means. Zompa had a bad heart that gave him hot-tattack death and Zompa died.

And it is. Not. Most definite. About Whimpy BugEyes McPherson. Who everyone in Sowams. Even cops. Owed money to. And who. From the steps of his bookie joint said, For the sake-a-the kids. The buck stops here and no police investigation is goin farther than this door.

Yup. Its not about none of those things. Because. Like I just plain and simple told.

This story is about me writing my story after I got truckhead hit and rattled up good. And. As PruneyMendez might say, Long as ya unnerstan that. Ya dont need ta be knowin much-a-nuthin else more.

Unexact twinness was very frustrational for Ross and me.

Not because Ross and me dint look the same. The way twins oughta. But because Mom said Ross and me both had. Inside our heads. What she called, Selfcapricious quirks.

And. For general. No such quirks was visitable for us to see.

And irregardless of that fact. My headscar. The very thing Mom said was the badge of my quirks. That scar was only visitable for a couple of weeks late spring. Because Mom. With electric clippers. Took Ross and me into the yard and buzz buzz buzzed our hair to the wind.

This one spring. 1959. Just before our birthday when we turned seven.

Right after our buzzcuts.

Ross asked me if he could paint my visitable scar red. With his watercolors. I said, Sure.

And while he was dipping and dabbing those watercolors to my head. He was also saying my scar looked like a bent fishhook. And I gotta addmit. While he was painting and poking with his paintbrush. That paintbrush. Like a magic finger. Gave my headpain place a most real feelgood sensation. And what was a lot funny was when Mom saw the paint Ross had painted on me. She got a horror look on her face. And she said Hah raws. Because she thought my redhead was split all over again. And when Ross and me were laughing that we tricked her. Mom said Ross and me was gonna make her hair go gray and she was gonna grow old too fast.

Mom always said that. Hah raws. And the thing about us making her hair go gray. Or making it fall out. And she would always warn Ross that when her hair did go gray and fall out. She was gonna take from Ross. His hair. And wear it on herself. On her own head. And she wasnt giving it back.

Rosses hair. Like Moms. Was brown and straight.

Me? I had Dads dirtblonde curls so I was safe from Mom someday stealing it off me. Not ta say. But. Our faces werent so steal proof. Mom said she was gonna steal them too. When we wasnt looking. And sell our faces to the Indians. Mom said Indians was always wanting to buy. For a good price. A handsome pair of twinbrother faces.

With twinbrother solid bodies to match.

And although those Indians would immediate see by our twinfaces Ross and me were brothers. Why would the Indians want our twinbrother bodies? Our twinbrother bodies dint look like twinbrother bodies. Our twinbrother bodies were different. Rosses twinbrother body bigger. Stronger. My twinbrother body. It was small and shrimp.

If you said, Ross. Show me your muscle.

He'd bend at the elbow and pump a big hunk of bulge that give him shape. Colored his eyes. And made wide his grin.

Mom said we were fish of the same scale. But Dad said we were a lopsided mix of. Land. Sky. Blood and Water.

Mom called Ross a swarty rockfish tautog.

Tautog being fish. And swarty. Mom said, Meant dark skin.

For me. Mom said I was, A fair spinedarter choggy small fry.

Fair is pale. With blonde hair with easy sunburn skin.

Dad just called us, Beachgrit and Sunrise.

And those names are my favorite.

Not that I have anything against tautog and choggy fish because I dont. But Beachgrit and Sunrise was my favorites because when Dad said. Beachgrit and Sunrise. Them words made him think of his favorite time and place. Asquantum and Montaup. Both words Indian words meaning like. Picnic on the rock shore. And that always made Dad smile.

And Mom always smiled too. When she talked serious stuff. To Ross and me.

Mom said when we was born. I came out dancing. And was a beautiful child.

Except she says it, Bew. Dee. Full.

Bewdeeful.

Bewdeeful child.

On the other hand.

About Ross. She talked fancy French and said, Contraire Ross. You were no spinedarter choggy. You took your own sweet time. You were a lollygaggin slowpoke. A tautog. Happy in the deep-a-your own swarty dark.

So. There you have it. Bewdeeful me. The fair skinned spinedarter dancer.

And Ross. The swartydark rocksteady slowpoke.

A pair of fishes outta water.

Unexact twins.

Tautog and Choggy.

Beachgrit and Sunrise.

Both Mom and Dad always said they loved watching the horizon sun and the red trails and pinks and orange glows the low sun left in the sky. Dusk or dawn. Said it was like long faded ribbon strands pulled from their pockets making them feel together when they were apart. Which was plenty and frequent because while Mom stayed home with us kids. Dad worked up and down the East Coast on a big boat. A dredge. For days. And sometimes weeks at a time.

When Dad was home. Especial summertime with us at SowamsGreen-hill Townbeach. Dad would point across the water. Out towards the bay to the tree covered hill and its northeast cliffs and the cobblestone shores. And Dad would tell us how the ancient Wampanoag Indians called the place Montaup. And Dad big grin would say, Let them Massachusetts Pilgrims praise and wup-dee-do their PlymouthRock. We here in Montaup have a much more specialer rock.

The Montaup puddingstone. Just above the shore.

And Dad would always tell how he and Mom. Before they was married. Went to that puddingstone rock. Made a sunset beach fire. And there was stars and moon. Turning tides. Dark sky and distant light. Beachgrit and sunrise.

And then eventual.

You boys. Who.

Forever changed our lives.

When me and Ross was littler.

Sometimes I was Rosses brother.

And sometimes Ross was my twin.

Like when we introduced us to people. Ross would say, Jate is my twin.

Or. I would say, Ross is my brother.

Not ta say. But.

Twin or Brother.

Ross and me. We were always a pair.

Through thick and through thin.

Especial. After Ross and me got caught in the blizzard trying to help PruneyMendez because of what FatherLuis done. But. Im getting ahead of me.

For now. Gotta stick with the beginning.

Not the 1952 Beachgrit and Sunrise beginning.

But. The 1955 beginning when Mom said, Selfcapricious quirks begun to shine.

In the quirks beginning. According to Mom. One rain day. When we was three. One year before my plate in the head. Mom took down from the wall above our kitchen table. The wedding gift made for her by MissusCogg. A framed barnyard picture. With below it. Handstitch.

*How Dear to This Heart are the Scenes of My Childhood
When Fond Recollection Presents Them to View*

Mom called it embroidery. Mom loved that embroidery and so did we.

And Mom said, Lets draw pictures of the barnyard picture.

And Mom put paper and crayons. On the kitchen table.

And the next thing was Ross using the crazy crayon colors and Ross drawing the embroidereed farmhouse. The waterwell. And the waterwell bucket.

Mom said I picked up the black crayon and. On that capricious day. Slow printed.

How Dear.

Never drawed the embroidereed picture.

Just wrote the handstitch words.

And. On many other rain days. While Ross would more draw on his papers. A cat or dog. Six cows. A bullfrog. A weepingwillowtree. Some horses. And. Not ta say. But. A rainbow once too.

Mom said I just slow printed all the embroidereed handstitch words.

That was the quirk beginning Mom said.

The beginning of Ross doing art drawing pictures.

The beginning of me scratchwriting words.

And. Mom always reminded Ross and me. That on a very different day. On Thursday. July 10th. 1956. Front of GilOwens SquarePeg antiqueshop. Ross and me become even way more unexact and different. When. From the sky. A blueshell crabclaw fell into the street and without, Look both ways. Or, Be careful of the machines. I ran direct in the road to pick up the crabclaw and thats when LouieRespeegies fish truck knocked me curbside and I got ambulance rushed to the RhodeIslandHospital where the doctors fixed my broke skull noggin with what they called tietaneium metal but everybody else in Sowams called, Jates plate in the head.

Not ta say. But. That plate in the head thing?

Not fa nuthin.

How did a plate. A actual plate. Fit in my head? And just what kind of plate was it? Salad plate? Dinner plate? Pie plate? What?

And if it werent for Pedro Pruney Mendoza Mendez. Who. One day in the SquarePeg antique store said, Think on it this way Jate. Plate in your head is not fa real a plate. More like a bowl on the head. Bowl. Over your brain. Back-a-your skull. But under your hair. Unnastan?

And I said, Sure.

But I dint. Not for real. Because. Like I been saying. If it was a bowl whyd he. And everybody else in Sowams. Call it a plate?

But Pruney took. From the shelf. GilOwens metal blue enamel speck-led plate and put it on the table in front of me. And he did the same with the old cherrywood bowl.

Next Pruney put the metal blue enamel speckled plate on his head. Which of course. As soon as he moved. It fell right off.

Then Pruney put on his head the old cherrywood bowl that stayed on his head like a good fitting army helmet no matter of how much he moved.

Final Pruney took off the old cherrywood bowl. Put the cherrywood bowl on the table and put into the cherrywood bowl the waxpaper wrapped lunch of fishcakes Mom made.

And Pruney said, Imagine the old cherrywood bowl bein not a old cherrywood bowl like this. But a stainless steel mixin bowl. See? A bowl sorta keepin everythin together and not a plate with everythin all seprate. And when you was on the RhodeIslandHospital operatin table. Four years old with a busted up skull. The doctors took out the brokeskull pieces and in place-a-those busted pieces. Put in a bowl like this. But a whole lot smaller. Like the popes cap. Like a jew hat. Your hair? Was peeled off your head. The doctors scalped you. Just like cowboys n Indians do in the movies. Then afta the operation. Doctors stretched your scalp like those bathin caps girls at the beach wear. Stretched it back on over your skull what was replaced with a bowl. And the old part-a-your skull. The bone? Thats now growin attached to the new part-a-your skull and your hair and everything is growin over that. Over the bowl and skull what is now combined together. Together as one.

Bone. Cranium.

Steel. Titanium.

Scalp. Brainium.

Growin all together. Even stronga than before.

And as Pruney was telling this. His eyebrows knotted and his long eyelashes had crust from not washing his face in the morning. And each part of Pruneys fat cheek face had a look that begged me to understand him.

Pruney poured everything out the old cherrywood bowl. His pretend helmet. My pretend. Plate in the head skull. Poured out our waxpapered lunch on to the antique blue speckled plate. And Pruney said, Tilt a plate back and forth and whaddaya got? Your fishcakes and sauce. All spills right off.

And Ross said to Pruney, Prettgood explanation. Like DoctorKildare.

Then Pruney said, My brother knows this stuff cause-a-his undertaker job.

And GilOwen slid forward in his antique chair said, Here Here.

And GilOwen patted Pruneys fat head.

And GilOwen. From his antique chair. Soft breath gentle said, Bravo Pedro. Bravo. You have a different way of seeing and a finer way of explaining. Indeed you have —

Outta nowhere Pruney said, Praspective?

And GilOwen said, Perspective? Most certain.

And PruneyMendez smiled big.

PruneyMendez smiled proud.

2

TheEecoodeeshKid

Although I got a plate in the head which messes me up my thinking. I always remember. With clearness and with smiles. When Pruney come into our lifes.

We was playing on the railroad berm. Zeebo. WillieD. LilMushGah-doo. Ross and me. In the hillside sand. Above the marsh. And as long as we dint go to the trestle or play on the tracks when the train was passing. Mom dint care.

Sometimes workers for the Providence railroad company would drive. On the rails. In a special made truck. It was like a VolkswagonVan. Except bigger. And for actual had rubber tires that wheeled on the rails but also had braces that locked the whole thing direct to the steel so that the van stayed on the tracks. It was so cool. Quiet too. We'd be on the slope digging dirt holes and all on a sudden. Thered be a humming noise. And the jangling of something. And when you looked up.

The railroad van would be rolling by.

And on this one day. Outta nowhere the railroad van rolled past and slowed. Then stopped. Two guys got out. They was smoking cigarettes. Wore leather gloves and had tools. And one yellow hardhat guy carried a long steel bar. The other guy. Shorter and a bluebandanna tied around his baldhead. Had sledgehammer. And a bucket. BandannaGuy put the bucket down. And HardHatGuy barclawed a railroad spike that popped out the railroad tie real easy. And from BandannaGuys bucket HardHat-Guy took a new railroad spike to the tie. And with his hammer BandannaGuy pounded.

We all stood no talk watching. Final. WillieD said, Whatchya doin?

And HardHatGuy said, Securin the rails. Ties rot. Keepin things tight.

Then HardHatGuy spit.

Ross said, Whatchya gonna do with that pulled out spike?

BandannaGuy said, Use down the line. Less you want it.

Ross said, Sure nough.

BandannaGuy tossed the rust nail to Rosses feet.

Them guys did the same a few ties down. Banged the tracks with their tools. Pried some spikes. Pounded new ones. Tossed old ones. Got back in their railroad van and rolled away.

As soon as that railroad van was outta sight. We scrabbled through the wildrose and raspberry thornbrush and collected eight spikes. They was a wonder. Biggest and heaviest nails any of us ever holded.

Then from the opposite direction the railroad van traveled. We heard it. The trainwhistle.

It was a ways off yet. Probbly just crossing the first trestle over the Quequeshan.

We did what we usual did.

Jumped into the sandpit and waited.

But before Ross come down. He put his head to the steelrail just like Peter O Toole done in *Lawrence of Arabia* and Ross said he could feel the rumbling. Then he plopped beside me.

We heard the bell clanging and another whistle blast.

We looked towards the SowamsRiver trestle and sure enough here comes the big shaking black and yellow locomotive dirt and smoke stained engine with a bright headlight beaming solid like it was night. But it was day.

And as the five of us guys did a huddle there in the side pit waiting for them trainwheels come rolling past not too so far from our heads and crouching bodies the train whistle blew long and loud and the bell clang clang and I looked direct across the tracks. Over them. Over on to CrescentStreet direct in front of the aquablue modern aluminumsided Andriozzi house.

Theres another kid.

A kid coming to a stop on a black bicycle with one wheelrim painted red and another wheelrim painted blue. And on the handlebars of the bike is a steel basket filled with newspapers in a canvas newspaper bag. And that bike kids limping. That bike kids looking at us. And then looking at the train. And now the train is over the trestle and a hundred yard from us. And that bike kids walking his bike to the edge of CrescentStreet direct opposite of us. His blond curly hair and his ripped teeshirt and cutoff short dungaree pants and a belt made outta rope made him look like a real poor bike kid. And on one foot a shoe. And on his other foot a bandage. A dirty bandage so big it covers his entire foot. Just his toes sticking out. Hes limping on accounta his bandaged no shoe foot.

Now the train is twenty yards off and the conductor waving hello out the side window and the bell jangling loud lotsa clangs and the grounds shaking and the train whistles blasting shrill and high. Tons and tons of steel and brown boxcars and flat steel wheels. WillieD and MushGahdoo and Zeebo and Ross and me hunkered in the rust and oil and creaks and clangs and groans. The aqua blue aluminumsided Andriozzi house with high squeals and WillieDunne is blocking his ears and Zeebo is laughing and laughing and Ross is yelling something to LilMushGahdoo who is holding a spike in each of his hands shouting something back to Ross. Instead of laying there in the sand. I stand. The shade of each passing boxcar yellow and the aquablue aluminumsided Andriozzi house yellowbrown and aquablue is the opening between each car with flashes of sunlight in between each boxcar gap blonde curly fat face kid is big eyes of wonder and looking hard to see us seeing him. Instant train caboose chunking past with little sounds and delicate clinking.

And then the aquablue house.

With the blonde bike kid and his cockamaney bicycle.

And nothing.

Nothing but train tracks.

The noise going distant.

Going soft.

Going fade.

And then Ross Zeebo WillieD and MushGahdoo chase after the passed caboose. Throw stones that dont hit and wave to caboose guy standing on the deck rear. CabooseGuy handwaves back and the train clanks past KellyStreet. Past the cemetery and disappears SouthEnd of Sowams towards MountHopeShores and Bristol.

Five kids on one side of the tracks. Opposite one curl blonde haired bike kid with his blackredblue bike and ripped dungaree short pants with a rope belt one scuffedbrown wingtipped shoe and one baretoed foot wrapped in a bigdirty bandage.

And bike kid yells like theres still noise bike kid gotta yell over, Eecoodeesh. You guys crazy or what? Not ta say. But. That train coulda run you over it coulda.

And Ross. Zeebo. WillieDunne. MushGahdoo and me immediate step between the rails towards the EecoodeeshBikeKid.

We all just look at each other.

LilMushGahdoo says, Coulnt not-a-got killed les that train fell off its tracks and anyways we do it all the time. Sometimes even flatten money.

And Eecoodeesh says, Flatten money? Whaddaya mean?

LilMushGahdoo says, Pennies. Dimes. Nickels. Put em on the tracks. Let the train roll over em. Dont on usual do quarters. Did a halfdollar once.

Blonde curl and blue eyes Eecoodeesh says, No way.

And WillieD says, Woulda done it today if I had me one.

WillieD pulls a teardrop copper slug out his pocket and says, See? Used ta be the face-a-AbrahamLincoln one side and WhiteHouse the other. Heads and tails. Now nothin. Cant even see the date. Smooth ice.

And WillieD hands it to EecoodeeshBikeKid who feels the smooth between his fingers and flips it sideways. Holds it so he looks both sides. And long eyelash EecoodeeshBikeKid says, Its not the WhiteHouse. Its either wheatstalks or LincolnsDeathMemorial.

WillieDunne takes it back and says, Whadda you know?

EecoodeeshBikeKid says, My brother told me all about how the penny got made. He read a book by CarlSanbag. Explains how the Lincoln penny was resigned. After Lincoln got ass innated and shot.

And Ross said, Whos your brother?

EecoodeeshBikeKid said, DagamaMendez. Nineteenyears old graduated highschool and reads lotsa books. Sees movies. Gonna be a undertaker someday. Bury the dead. Sunday mornins before church. I help him rinse embombin bottles at MobyDicks funeral parlor. Also got me a job. FidalgosBakery deliverin hot sweetbread. Wanna hunk? Its reggala cold now. But its good.

EecoodeeshBikeKid reaching into his canvas newspaper carrybag pulls out a huge loaf of bread. Brown crust shine and rips of cream color white pieces and holds them out.

Giving him the tight eye. Ross takes a chunk and Ross says, You Portuguese?

And EecoodeeshBikeKid said, Yep. NewBedford. Since I was two. Now moved to Sowams accounta movin in with AuntJovita. 186MathewsonStreet. Eastside-a-town. Go to ChildStreetSchool.

And Ross says, We go LibertyStreet. Here in the NorthEnd.

And Ross then hands me his chunk of uneated bread.

I smell it.

Look hard at it.

Put it in my mouth.

And EecoodeeshBikeKid. He just stone face wide eye looks at me.

Delicious, I tell Ross. Like Moms Easta egg bread.

EecoodeeshBikeKid fatface redcheek thicklip smiles and the other guys reaching for piece hunks that hes giving.

Zeebo stuffs some in his mouth and said, Whats your name?

Eeccoodeesh said, PedroMendozaMendez. People call me Pruney.

WillieDunne says, Why?

Pruney says, Dont know. Just do. Ever since NewBedford firstgrade.

What division?

Fourth.

Retard class huh? Why you got the bandage?

I got MistaPotatoHeadseyeinmyfoot.

What?

Mista Potato Heads eye in my foot.

How?

How? Stepped on its how. Cousin playin and MistaPotatoHeads eye on the floor and dint see it and you shoulnt oughta say that.

What?

Aint a retard.

And Pruney stuffed the sweetbread back in the canvas newspaper bag. Stood straight and gripped tight his handlebars.

WillieD slow chewed his crust treat sogged. Did a slouch and a sideways laze look and said in a friend way, Dint say you was. Just said you was in the retard class.

But then WillieD shmirked and said, Probbly on accounta bein a stupit portagee.

And on the sudden the handlebars of Pedro Pruney MendozaMendez bike was free of hands that was making fists popping WillieDunnes eye and flying over the falling bike and flopping newspapers into the crumpling WillieDunne and the two a them tripping bodies was stumbling over the traintracks and tumbling down the sand berm with WillieD, Ow Ow Ow. He hit me. He hit me. Charging down the rest of us the hill and Pruneys arms. Fist bam bam bam on WillieDunnes screaming red face and Pruney pummeling flying feet wham wingtip into WillieDs jaw and thud side of Pruneys bandaged foot thumping WillieD headside and WillieD Auuuugh drops deadstill in the sand and Pruneys, My foot my foot my foot and Ross wrist grabbing Pruneys arms. Pinning them arms together and pulling Pruney off WillieDunne and Ross hollering Knock it off Knock it off and Ross drops to WillieDs side and Ross pulling Pruney away and holding Pruneys arms and Pruneys flopping thrash kicking. Zeebo MushGahdoo and me just standing there mouths open saying,

Jeeze.

Cripes.

Eecoodeesh.

And I gotta addmit.

Not ta say. But.

The following week. In school. WillieD wore his two black eyes like a shy sheep rather than a sly raccoon. Least ways. Thats how Ross put it. Ross said, WillieD done a humble thing. WillieD had immediate apologized to Pruney and then Pruney and him together had gone back up the steep. Crossed the railroad tracks as a pair. Picked up the smushed breadloaf and gathered fallen newspapers to the bikebasket and canvasbag.

WillieD reaching into his pocket. Pulled out his squashed penny and told PruneyMendozaMendez, You can have it. I'll make me another.

Pruney got big eyes and a full face of wrinkles and he broke off another chunk of bread. Stuck the slug in the dough. Shoved the penny sandwich in his shirt and done it with a big, ThankYou.

When Pruney had rode away. WillieDunne said of himself, Not ta say. But. I got a big mouth. My mother always tells me.

And from that day on. No one gave WillieD no noise about his messup.

At the LibertyStreetSchool I couldnt be like Ross in the wunderkind prodigy class. After my plate in the head truck accident. My thinking dimmed. And if Ross was explaining about me to other kids. He'd say, Jates all right. But sometimes. He dont get things.

Guess the teachers felt the same because. The year before. In June of 1962. At the end of the school year when my fifth grade class for smart kids got done. The teachers said the only way I was gonna be allowed to pass into sixth grade in September was by getting took out the class for smart kids and instead be put into the sixth grade class for dumb kids next to the lowest level class. Fourth division. Or get held back and remain low level grade five.

Mom. Dad. And Ross. Thought none of that was fair.

They said anyone who could sound out and write the words vundakid prodajeeze on his own without no one telling him how to do it correct was way more smarter than a whole bunch of kids with gift brains in the high better classroom.

But. Irregardless of vundakid prodajeeze. Mom and Dad dint want me kept back.

So into the lower not so good sixth grade class I went.

But. It coulda been worse.

At least it wasnt the basement room next to the toilets like at Pruneys ChildStreetSchool. The lowest level room everyone called the youknowwhat class.

Everyone except Ross. Zeebo. LilMush. Me.

And WillieDunne.

The official name for the not so smart low level was called Fourth Division.

Pruney was fifth. Fifth Division. The lowest.

Not that Pruney had a plate in the head because Pruney dint.

What Pruney had was being from a place called the Azores and a mother who died and a father who speaks just Portuguese spit talk. And slobber. Not opera. Like Italian. Or military. Like Polish. Or flowers like French. But growly grunty and what the other kids at school say is gross portagee talk. Thats why Pruney got stayedback twice. And also cause of his not too so good English neither. Leastways writing English. He couldnt write English. Not fa nuthin. But. He sure could talk it. Pruney could talk talk talk America talk like nobodys business. And he did it too without a accent. PruneyMendez talked AmericaEnglish like he'd been talking AmericaEnglish all of his America life.

Except Pruney said something I only heard Portuguese people say. Whenever Pruney. Or any Portuguese. Got full of steam and excitement. He would flat hand smack his head. And outloud say, Eecoodeesh.

When I asked Pruney what Eecoodeesh means. He said, Eecoodeesh is Portuguese Wow.

And I gotta addmit. Eecoodeesh was prettfunny and I told Mom about Eecoodeesh and Mom said, Wow is cool. But Eecoodeesh is wordmusic.

And. Not fa nuthin. But. Thats exact what life was when Pruney was around.

Wordmusic.

Pruney telling stories about his HolyGhost church. With feastdays. Eating bread and drinking wine thats for real. But not for real. The flesh and blood of Jesus. And pracessions. His brother. His cousin. His aunt.

His father.

Pruney who never had any money even though he earned a whole bunch that he all gave to his dad. Saying, Thats what us Portuguese do. Take care-a-our families in the old country.

Me and Pruney seeing each other only when Pruney was on Crescent-Street delivering papers. Him taking a break. Running down the railroad-hill in hardsole wingtip shoes. Them fancy shoes all beatup. Pruney playing football with Ross and the other guys. Or sometime just watching with me. Or taking turns at being the ref.

Pruney never did delivering a paper to our house because Mom said she dint care about the news and Dad was never home to read it. But Pruney was always delivering his news to Mom about him being chased by MissusEngels German shepherd dog that bit him in the leg and he got the bite marks to prove it. And the rabies shot marks too on his arm. Or telling Mom about MissusAndriozzis clothesline being filled with beautiful flower pattern dresses with all kind of colors. And. Not ta say. But. Some womanladys underwears too.

Pruney delivering the paper to MistaCogg and GilOwens. But not at their KellyStreet homes. Instead. Always to their WaterStreet shops. And gift leaving not only the ProvidenceEveningBulletin but also smelly fish fins. Hacked swordfish swords. Cooked out lopsta claws. Hairy conks. And long pointed horseshoecrab tails.

One day in front of theSquarePeg when Pruney and me was afterschool putting the chain on his bike cause the chain slipped from the pedal crank and Pruney was hand turning it while I lifted the back wheel in the air. Ross come along carrying his art sketchpad and books.

Why MendozaMendez, I said. Why two last names?

Pruney said, Mendozas my mothers name. May she rest in peace with the Father Son and HolyGhost and apostles cept for Judas and may she always be with the VirginMother Mary AhLady-a-Fatima sayin the blessed rose ree in the glories-a-heaven on the sir-a-bums and the chair-a-bums with the other angels and the saints and the sacred hott-a-Jesus.

Pruney doing on his self what he called, The sign-a-the cross.

That means shes dead, I said to Ross.

And Pruney said, Eecoodeesh.

Then Pruney said, I prefer my fathers name. Mendez. Just hate when someone calls me a stupid portagee.

Well. Sometimes Ross calls me a stupid prodigy, I said.

Pruney tilted his head to the side. Scrunched his nose and closed one eye like Popeye the Sailor. Looked direct at Ross and said, An you bein a twin. That kinda ignorant cant none help Jate or his plate in the head.

And Ross said, Wasnt. On intention. Bein hurtful. Just sayin what the teachers said cause they was gonna stay Jate back to help him get ahead.

Pruney said, I'll knock. Like I done WillieD. Anyones head ever says again such a thing.

Pruney stood straight. Blonde curl hair and blue eyes. The longest babycomb eyelashes. The reddest sunset cheeks. The fattest sturdy face that wrinkles like a prune when he breaks into that thick prune lipped smile. Two years older and the same size as seventy pound me. But Pruney way more solid. More solid than all of us kids.

Ross said, I get your meanin.

And from then on.

Pruney was my best pal.

Pedro Pruney Mendoza Mendez.

PortugeseWow.

3
SweetSweet Lands

EastBay RhodeIsland is made most of bay.

Water.

TheNarragansettBay.

We dont have the Atlanic ocean like the rich kids in Newport. But what we do have is two rivers and all the marshes them rivers can hold.

We have bridges too.

One bridge crosses the SowamsRiver and the other bridge crosses the Quequeshan meaning falling or tumbling and everyone in these parts says correct as Kwik-a-shan but strangers often pronounce wrong as Kwee-Kwee-shan.

But. Correct or uncorrect talking. Living here is good.

In the NorthEnd of Sowams. Our neighbor GilOwen lives direct across from our only other neighbors Mista and MissusCogg. Both the Owen and the Coggs houses are over the railroad track at the bottom of Kelly-Street where the pavestreet ends and becomes crushed quahogshells.

Our house. TheCoggs. And GilOwens are the only three houses past the railroad tracks on the railroad berm. And if you dont turn left at the Coggs house and go down our real long dirt driveway to what MissusCogg calls the true BaggyWrinkleLane and park your car or turn around under the giant weepingwillow tree. Youll end up being on the marsh because the real bottom of KellyStreet leads straight in the water of KingPhilips-Cove.

And. Not fa nuthin. But.

Who'd wanna be there?

In the days before we knew PruneyMendez.

What was for real cool was the railroadtrack and the sandy hillside slope was where. Lotsa times. Ross. Me. Our friends. WillieD. Zeebo. And LittleMushGahdoo. Caught prayingmantises. Got snakes. Made sandheaps. We built forts and dug foxholes. Played army. And in the wintertime. Even sledded that east facing drop.

Mom said the sand part of the railroad slope was our backyard. But it wasnt for real our backyard. It was just close.

About a quartermile away was the red brick AmericanLuggageMill. Just before the traintrestle and the two NorthEnd bridges. And even plate in the head me knew all the names of the streets and all the names of the peoples houses. Starting with the streetlight at LandStreet and WaterStreet. Then DavisStreet with Zeebos house and the alley where LeoDriggs and his hobo buddy Bundles lived. The cottage of LilMushGahdoo next to WillieDunnes three decker. And FatFingerPetes corner store. And then Sippons bar. GilOwens SquarePeg antiques. And the StoneFleetTavern with thirteen parking lot millstones. The stretch of shady chestnut trees. MistaCoggs shack the Port n Starboard Shop across from the cradled drydocked boats. MannySousas Shellfish. And the EastBay Shipyard. With the welders archglow we werent suppose to look at cause it would burn out our eyes but it smelled good like gunpowder after fireworks so we looked anyways.

All that.

All of that is what we'd see each day Ross and me walked to the beach or to go visit MistaCogg at his Port n Starboard Shop. Direct on WaterStreet. MistaCogg built and repaired lopsta pots and pot buoys. And he also made fakewood harpoons and traded scrimshaw.

And no walk to the beach. Ross and I knew. Was complete without stopping in the place and letting MistaCogg to buy us a Nehi soda. Which we never had to pay for from his icebox that was a old refrigerator out in back.

Sometimes we'd just drink our sodas and watch MistaCogg work.

But more than usual. Wed listen to about when he was a boy in Penobscot Maine and how. When he got older. He had to walk with a limp on accounta him taking a stumble from overboard his ship. OystaMoon. In a blizzard.

1939. Except MistaCogg said it, Nine teen thah tee nine.

Comin down from Glouster through the Stellwagen Banks. Round the Cape. Vineyard. Then Squibbanocket. Newport. NarragansettBay. November. Early gale. Blew out all the sudden from the nor nor east. Cold as a brass monkeys balls. An I washed ovaboard. But not ova ova. Just part way. Tangled in the nets draggin off the stern. Head banged. Sandwiched gainst the transom n the skiff. Half in the water. Half out. Leg broke and twisted behind my back.

No one saw me go ova. An by time they noticed me gone. Where were they ta look? Searched the deck fore n aft. But. Warnt visibl. I was lopsta broke and crushed in unna the gunnels. Course the boys. They were three. They had their hands in the pilothouse full. And no one dared out till we were dockside.

Hours later. Gal-a-one-a-the crew from the bark in the slip behind us saw my yellow slicka. Then my head. An twisted leg. Out the net they fished me. Called me the luckiest bastid EastBay and probbly Easten seaboard for that matter. Said twas my daily cod liva and my woolens that kept me from bein froze drown dead.

But twarnt neither. Twas my brain and my lungs workin two tagether. My lungs knowin when to breathe an when to hold tight.

My brain sayin, Live you somnabitch. Live.

With MistaCoggs leg gimped. His fishing days ended. Him and his wife. They started a new life in a new house EastBay at the bottom of KellyStreet just up from Grampa and Grandma Tavino on the corner of BaggyWrinkleLane.

MistaCogg worked for the Pokanoket County WaterAuthority and he told all the history about how the rivers. The Sowams. The Quequeshan. And the Kickamuet. How they three begun as fresh water streams reaching way up in the red maple forests of nearby Massachusetts.

If MistaCogg got yammaring while smoking his corncob and drinking brandy or burgundy hed tell about, Pilgrims and Puritans. KingPhilip-MetacomsWar. The massacree days. Abb original Pokanoket Wampanoag and Narragansett. Colonist times. SarahHaagsBunktown tide meadows. Marsh hay. SwanseaSchooners. Colonial hog farms and swamp areas where grist stones were quarried and further down. On streambanks. Millwheels churned and flintcorn was ground and johnnycake journeys were begun. Places where. In springtime. Blueback herrings jumped earth dams and breach-a-ways spilt into brooks mixed brackish deep rust colored channels twistin bendin cuttin swellin and roilin with suckamouthed lamprey flowin through RhodeIsland saltmarshes and gut mill ponds thick with rainbow smelts. America eels. Crabs and mussels. And freshwater fishes. Into the Narragansett with the brine bed-a-quahogs. Oystas. Scallops. Rockcrab and flounder. Stripebass. Lopstas. And the big pond.

The Alanic Ocean.

And although he never said At lantic like the right way we learnt in school. MistaCogg sure knew water. Marshes. Rivers. Inlets. Mill guts. Gut ponds. And such.

Mista and MissusCogg never had children.

And 1958. MistaCogg retired. He said, Two years short a fulltime pension compensated by disability from cast iron water main repairs and dip nettin riprap spill away spawns.

Whatever that meant.

Think it had to do with fishing. Whether water being good or bad. Something MistaCogg called, Pollushun.

But dont know. Not exact.

Anyways.

In his yard. MistaCogg had built. One of those glider swings any number of people could sit on together. And one of his favorite enjoys was rocking beneath his arbor. And because MistaCogg had his own way of talking. When he said arbor. I thought he said harbor. The way he'd rest on his swing. Smoking his pipe. Watching the cove. Usual with his wife. Or with whoever stopped by for a visit. It was the same way people in boats did at docks and slips.

So arbor or harbor. Both made sense to me.

On many of those summer and autumn evenings. After we roasted chestnuts or caught fireflies. When Dad might be home from working on the dredge for a few days. We'd all sit beneath the grape arbor. And do a thing Mom called pablabberatin. We'd tell stories.

The Coggs would tell about knowing Mom. ClaraLeeRossi. And her sister. BenedettaRossi. When both Mom and AuntBeni was little girls and then they quick become teenager grownups.

And MissusCogg would tell about what she called the chestnut burgundybrown magic in Moms eyes in them days.

And MistaCogg say about Montaup ancient Indians doing things called rituals.

Mom would get blushed up and Dad would hold me or Ross would snug in close. Both Mom and Ross had them same chestnutburgundy brown eyes.

And MissusCogg would give MistaCogg a look and say, Now Jack you mind yourself.

And MissusCogg would look direct at Ross and me and say, Your Mom and Dad loved each other very much the way all good and decent people do.

Mom put her hands to her face and MissusCogg would get giggleshine eyes and her cheeks would shake and MissusCogg would tell about Mom and Dads secret December wedding no one was suppose to know about. Theyd all tell of when Ross and me were born. June 9. 1952. And about how. AuntBeni, like a Eyetalian Paul Revere. Ran house to house in the whole NorthEnd-a-Sowams. Spreadin the news yuh Mom had twin boys.

All of us. Underneath the grape arbor. Sitting in the deep of our dark. And Mom would tell about how. Six months after Ross and me was born. AuntBenedetta went vacationing to Italy. And for a while. Because Dad was always up and down the coast working. All who Mom had to look after her on the day to day was Mista and MissusCogg.

Mom told me, While Dad was workin off LongIsland at the VeranzanoNarrows on the dredge and AuntBeni had gone to R-O-M-E to R-O-A-M. Ross and you were so fortunate to have the Coggs in your lives.

What would we do without the Coggs? Mom always asked.

MissusCogg said she thought it was sweet for Mom to say that. That we lived in, Sweet sweet lands because we had each other.

But MistaCogg said, Sweet sweet nothin. Them boys is unexact twins and no matter what. They are kids none the anyhow.

Like all kids they gotta learn obedience.

To mind, is how he actual put it.

And when he said a thing like that. And he did all the time. He'd make a monster face which was more fun than it was scary.

MissusCogg would knuckle her index finger. And cuff him on the side of his bad leg saying, Oh my sweet lands. You hush.

Mom said this behavior was what she expected from MistaCogg. Him always wearing. What Mom called a thin billed. Short visor. Greek fishing cap.

Mom saying MistaCogg was, No way. A-E-G-E-A-N. Just a pretend old sea bird.

Playin the fool, is how she said it.

And it made him, Dear to her hott.

Of course. Mom and AuntBenedetta had their own parents were more dear to their hearts. Only thing was though. Two years before Ross and me was born. Grandma and GrampaRossi got killed in a carwreck on the Barrington highway. When Dad drove us to Providence we'd pass the place. Just after the white church along the RunningRiver. Where. In 1948. During the early of a February blizzard. Grandma and GrampaRossis car went on black ice. Spun around into the other lane. Did a headon with a snowplow. And Grandma and GrampaRossi got killed dead.

Dads parents got dead too.

Not in a accident dead.

But dead from being real poor dead.

Dad said, Nonno and NonnaTavino were old country people.

But. He hardly ever talked about them.

They died.

Way before Ross and me were born. As Dad always said, Before the war. 1941.

And the little I know about Nonno and Nonna Tavino. Im gonna save for telling later. However. For now. Whats important to understand is. For Ross and me. As far as anyone like grandparents was concerned. There was only Mista and MissusCogg. When MissusCogg died. Old bird CapnJack was all the fake Grampa we had to call our own.

4

A Lok Ascendin

The afternoon MissusCogg died. GilOwen come over and got Mom.

We was seven years old.

Before PruneyMendez.

August 1959.

GilOwen said since the Coggs had prepared well for this day. He would go to the funeral parlor and see to their final wishes. GilOwen called those wishes in turn mints. And GilOwen said he would let Mom know if there were any in turn mint changes and, For Jack to worry about nothin.

During that long August afternoon Mom sat with MistaCogg under the arbor on the swing. And from where Ross and me was front yard playing. It looked like all they was doing was talking. Mostly MistaCogg did all the talking. Mom did lotsa listening.

Grapes were hanging dark purple direct over their heads. Would any of them grapes fall and get squidged under their feet? None did. Couldnt hear none getting squidged neither. Just late in the day voices mixed with the afternoon katadids and crickets. And although Mom and MistaCogg sat in the swing for over a hour. The swing never moved until Mom stepped off the footdeck and then the whole swing moved the wrong way and Mom held on and dint let go until it quit wrong and was hanging good all over again.

When Mom was halfway back to Ross and me.

Thats when I heard MistaCogg cry.

It was the first time ever I heard a man cry.

Ross too.

First MistaCoggs crying sounded hardly nothing at all. Maybe a faraway seagull gliding low on the water. But then the crying become the sound of that same gull on a mooring. Wings moving back and forth but the gull going nowhere. Beak open wide and a kree gone cloud.

Way up.

High.

High. And lonesome.

Mom stopped solid in the long BaggyWrinkle driveway.

She. Just for a moment. Stood tall.

And Mom again walked forward. Getting to Ross and me. Putting her arms round our shoulders and saying, Lets go to the garden and see what needs to get done.

For a while thats what we did.

Got stuff done.

Got stuff done in the garden.

Late afternoon.

In the garden by the marsh.

Mom picked lavender and pink gladiolas and QueenAnnes lace and arranged them in a basket. Then she picked some nice ripe figs.

Them figs was dark purple and soft and I just know real juicy.

Ross found cocoons.

Two cocoons.

With the spoutcan I did some watering but stopped to watch a praying-mantis eat a white moth. Moths head was all gone and one wing hanged like that wing would fall any moment.

The garden was behind our house and you couldnt see MistaCoggs house from there.

Or his yard.

Couldnt see GilOwens house neither.

What you could see. And hear though. Was the marsh with sometimes swans and sometimes Canadagoose honkers and Moms all of the time other favorite birds she was always seed feeding. Finches. Sparrows. Rock-doves. And homingpigeons.

And those birds. They were okay. Ross and me liked them fine. But we dint pay much attention to them. Not like we did prayingmantises. Snakes. Crickets. And cocoons. One time Ross brought some cocoons into our house. Put them in his chest of draws. Then forgot about them. A week or so later. We had a million baby mantises praying ever which where. Mantises praying in our room. Praying in our beds. Praying in our closests. Praying in our hair. GilOwen. He said those mantises wernt praying but P-R-E-Y-I-N-G.

He tried to explain the difference by folding his hands and then doing pretend knife stabs saying, Keeping them praying is just fine because the world has too much preying.

Had to think about that one for a long time.

But anyways.

Praying or preying. Mom used the vacuum cleaner to get rid of what she called, A Biblical plague-a-locusses.

And Ross said, Theyre not locusses. Theyre mantises.

Mom said, Hah raws. From now on promise me to always leave your cocoons outside. Promise me to kingdom come.

We did. We promised her to kingdom come. But Ross still loved them. Loved cocoons. And as much as Mom dint. Ross couldnt help but show Mom his two cocoons and ask, Wheres MissusCogg goin now shes dead?

Mom said, Thinkin about MissusCogg are you?

Ross said, Uh huh.

Mom said, Dont know exactly. But most people would say shes goin to heaven.

Ross asked, Is she gonna go direct or will she still be around for awhile?

Mom said, Dont know that either. But suspect MissusCogg will go however she wants. Direct probbly. Why?

Ross said, Dint say goodbye.

Mom said, You? Or her?

Ross was tight lip. Then Ross said, Both.

Mom said, When people die. Friends have funerals. Its everyones chance to say goodbye.

Then she looked at me and asked, What you think Jate?

And I asked, Is MistaCogg still cryin?

Mom said, Maybe. But thats what needs to get done.

Why?

Mom said, To lose some-a-his sadness.

How much sadness does MistaCogg have?

Mom said, Lots.

Did you and AuntBeni cry when Grandma and GrampaRossi died in the carcrash before Jate and I were born? Ross asked.

Mom said, Yes. But friends helped with the hurt. And cause we are MistaCoggs friends. We are goin to help. Like he and MissusCogg helped AuntBeni and me.

How?

Well, said Mom, Tonight we will take him some food. And bring him this bouquet. And during this next week or so. We'll look afta him more than usual.

Can I bring him my cocoons? said Ross.

Mom tucked her lower lip under her upper teeth. Pushed back some dangling hair. Gave a long breath and said, Of course. He would like that very much.

Does Dad know MissusCoggs dead?

No. Dont think so. But when he comes home we'll tell him.

Will Dad be home tonight?

Hope so, said Mom. For certain hope so.

Late afternoon what drifted clear over the water of KingPhilipsCove was a FM Boston radio station. The radioman said the concert was recorded live. From a place called Tanglewood. And the music was. *Hansel and Gretels Evening Prayer.* And I liked that a lot. Next. *Tales of Hoffmann.* Which Mom said was her favorite. Then final. *The Lark Ascending.*

And Mom said, How fittin.

Dint exactly know what Mom meant by that so I asked, Whats ascendin?

Flyin, Mom said. Up. Goin up.

The music was soft and pretty. A violin mostly. Slow. Quiet.

And Mom was slow and quiet too. Occasional she tucked hair behind her ears. Or sometimes try and blow it outta her eyes with a huff. Or wipe it fast with a sideswipe of her wrist. Sometimes she would hum with the radio. And other times. If she was looking in the cupboards. She'd say in almost no kind of voice, Now let me see.

No pans banged.

No things dropped on the table.

Just Mom placing and slicing.

Whispering and whisking.

Arranging and pouring.

The smell of garlic and olive oil.

Sound of eggshells cracking.

The sight of flour dusting above a bowl then floating haze through the air. And I touched the scar place at back of my head and wondered if that larkbird did its ascending to the sky as beautiful as Mom did her cooking in the kitchen.

Mom made MistaCoggs favorites of her summer recipes. Mom did the preparing and the cooking so everything seemed beginning and ending all at the same time. Waterpot being set to boil. Fennelstalks trimmed of their fuzzy greens and sliced at the bulbs. Artichokehearts dusted in pepper flour then dipped in beat up egg and fried gold. Pasta into the rolling boil. Mom letting Ross sprinkle the smallest amounts of salt over the finished artichokes while she cut lemon wedges and placed two in the center. Mayonnaise and tarragon mixed in a bowl. Strainer into the sink. And the linguini waggled from the kettle and slithed into the strainer. Then into a deep platter with the white clam sauce with the quahogs MistaCogg had give to Mom the day before. And lotsa fresh parsley picked that afternoon special for the occasion. Mom with her woodfork fast motions. Tossing up the pasta. Clams and the juice. Parsley in the platter. And of course. Quick. Outta the oven bruschetta. Or what MistaCogg called garlicbread. Or sometime. If he was drinking way too much. Eyetalian toast. He loved it. Especial if it had some black on. Not just melt butter gold. But dark crisp brown. Crust all around. And bits of parmesan cheese.

Specked and baked to crunch all over.

When we brought the supper platter into MistaCoggs house the food was still steaming and MistaCogg was seated with GilOwen who immediate took the supper platter from Mom and set the supper platter on the table.

GilOwen fussed big with lotsa OOOs and AAAhs. His oysta white teeth glowing like they always did. His straight hair falling to the side of his face. And his bay rum cologne smelling fresh in the August humid.

Mom took the artichoke dish from me. And the fennel finocchi strips with tarragon dressing. She set those on the table too. Then she turned to Ross. Gathered the lavender and gladiolas. Put them in a vase from the cupboard and placed the entire bouquet on the small table direct across the doorway we come in from.

GilOwen set the dishes out. Fast dipped the raw finocchi into the dressing. And he started crunching immediate.

Ross walked over to MistaCogg who hadnt moved from his rocker.

Ross stared until MistaCogg asked real soft, Whaddaya lookin at?

Ross said even softer, You.

Well, said MistaCogg. Ya like whatchya see?

No, said Ross.

And whaddayasee? said MistaCogg.

A grouch, said Ross.

A good grouch or a bad grouch? said MistaCogg.

A old one, said Ross.

Ya got that right, said MistaCogg.

And they both shook hands like all three of us done a hundred times before.

Next morning the chatter of voices and the strong smell of coffee had Ross and me downstairs faster than. As Mom would say. Three shakes of a lambs tail.

Dad, I yelled and jumped into his arms.

Its about time you mushheads got outta bed, said Dad. His cheeks the tiniest prickle of thorns. My face. Thorn stings?

AuntBenedetta had Rosses cheeks smeared with lipstick before Dad even thought of putting me down because, Youre gettin too big, he said.

AuntBenies wet kisses put out Dads rough stings. AuntBenies kiss lips had already lost most of their red. And those kiss lips. Both of them. Like old pink roses. But that color fading dint stop her perfume smell from getting stuck on me the way her perfume smell always did. Lip color faded. But perfume smell stayed the same. Maybe got stronger. Who knows.

Dad hugging Ross.

Me climbing back into Dads arms and rubbing Dads whiskers.

You dint shave, I say.

Dad winking at Ross.

Dad giving me again a hundred kisses.

And me all, Ouch. Ouch. Ouch. Doing night crawler squirms with every kiss.

And Rosses face all laughing.

And mine. All stinging too.

But the good sting.

AuntBeni talking Mom about fingernails saying, Garden breaks em you know.

Mom pouring coffee.

Dad saying, Traffic on the parkways awful. So many stops on the turnpike too.

AuntBeni separating cream from the milk from the bottle saying to Mom, Nail polish. Cherry n Webb. On sale. Bought you one there too.

Im saying, Dad. Dad. Dad. Dad Im tryin to tell you somethin. Dad. Listen to me.

My hands turning Dads cheeks.

Room goes no noise.

Dad saying, What son? What? Go ahead. Im listenin.

MissusCogg, I say. Is. Dead.

AuntBenies coffeecup getting put down. That coffeecup sound on the table.

Dad looking hard into my eyes.

And I just know hes thinking about the eggcrack scar looking like a fishhook Ross painted red back of my head.

Mom watching.

Dads face in my hands like before.

Dad saying, I know son. Mom phoned me afta Ross and you were to sleep.

Jus wanted to tell you too, I say.

Then I let go of Dads face and add, You can do goodbyes at the funeral.

Thanks son, says Dad taking a bite off my fingertip. Thanks for lettin me know. We'll say goodbye at the funeral. Thanks for lettin me know.

I climb from Dads arms and sit in the chair next to Ross. I say, Mom said MissusCogg went direct to heaven. Like a bird. A lok ascendin.

The Morris Benjamin & Richards Funeral Parlor that everyone calls Mo B. Dicks is two buildings east of the Methodist Church with its high white steeple across the street from the town common and the pointing to the sky black cannon in the center and Ross and me climb up the funeral parlor stairs and go through the doors to see MissusCogg in the coffin with flowers all around exactly the way Mom said it would be because I never before seen MissusCogg like that. Not dead. Not asleep. Never laying down. Always MissusCogg in the garden. MissusCogg cooking. MissusCogg on the swing. MissusCogg sewing. MissusCogg coloring Easter eggs. MissusCogg poking CapnJack. MissusCogg shoveling snow.

Of course MissusCogg went to bed every night. Sometime she'd be in her nightgown. Or her housecoat in the morning doing coffee with Mom. But I never saw her in bed. Never saw her dressed in her white mole hair sweater. Three pearl buttons. Her blueblouse underneath. Laying down with folded hands on her waist and her eyes shut and her glasses with the sparklechain resting on her chest.

Never saw her like that before.

The red on her cheeks and her lips.

Her blue silver hair. Pinned up.

All that makeup. MissusCogg never wore makeup like that. Her face looking like she was wearing one of those gauze Halloweenmasks that was a regular persons face. Not a monsters. Just a persons. Those masks would give me the Hooglies because I always thought those masks looked like dead people. And now its true.

Even though old MissusCogg was laying there dead in front of me it was strange because aside from thinking about Hooglies and Halloweenmasks. I. For real. Wasnt thinking about her being dead at all. Rather. Was thinking the many times when it was snowing or raining. Only just MissusCogg. Ross. And me. Colored with crayons at her kitchentable. And she stayed inside all the lines. And helped me write words correct on pieces of paper. Instead of.

Sences of My Chidl

She saved thoses pieces of paper in a napkin drawer.

MissusCogg boiling up potatoes and making them thin little pancakes she called lefsa. And eating lefsa plain. Lefsa all by themselfs. Cant say I was nuts about lefsa. Lefsa sorta tasted real blah. But then MissusCogg would spread butter on them. Fold them into a triangle. Sprinkle with cinnamon sugar. And sometimes creamcheese. And I gotta addmit they were prettdelish.

And what was real funny is when sometimes MistaCogg would come home. In his coveralls and boots. From doing WaterAuthority work. He'd say, Ma. Lets see about them lefsa. And he'd grab a lefsa off the plate and shove the whole triangle thing inside his mouth and go big eye funnyface like what he was eating was real good.

MissusCogg would smack his hand as he'd go for another and she'd tell him straight off gentle, Oh my sweet lands. Mind your manners and set both the table and a better example for our young guests.

But my very more favorite than lefsa was MissusCogg making fattyman funnelcakes in her small black fryingpan. Dripping batter through the funnel spout into the hot oil and making all them squiggles till the pan was sizzling up what looked like a doughboy. But tasting like a cake doughnut and looking like somethin got run over by a trucktire then sprinkled with powder sugar and cinnamon. And with sometimes whipped cream and strawberries.

MissusCogg said them fattyman funnelcakes came from her Dutch-Danish ancestors. Funnelcakes was the best. Especial in the wintertime with her telling stories.

She would make us sit on the floor in front of her chair. Straighten her eyeglasses with the palms of her hands until them glasses squared on the tip of her nose and she'd make sure plenty of funnelcake was on the plate between Ross and me and if we spilt any sugar on the floor she'd just say, Oh my sweet sweet lands.

And MissusCogg told us *TheSnowQueen*.

Smaller than sugar crystals. Millions-a-tiny glass splinters got into the hearts-a-people when theSnowQueens hobgoblins crashed a devils mirror to the earth makin prideful children undiffrent and ungrateful.

A girl named Gerta and a boy named Kay promised eternal love sayin Roses bloom and cease to be but we shall the Christ child see.

When Gertas grandmother told about hobgoblin devils and theSnowQueen. Kay laughed and said, If theSnowQueen ever visited he would melt her on the stove.

And at that moment an almost invisible lookinglass splinter went in Kays eye makin him believe roses were ugly and Gerta was foolish.

TheSnowQueen took Kay to the Palace of EternalNorthWinter. But Gerta wouldnt stop lovin Kay. She set off to find him and Gerta met Ravencrow who took her to a prince and a princess who then gave Gerta a royal coachride north.

But robbers and theRobbergirl kidnapped Gerta. And in their hideaway cave Robbergirl was cruel. But Gertas kindness changed Robbergirls heart. And Robbergirl released Gerta with a Buckdeer. And Buckdeer carried Gerta to FinnLap women who helped Gerta use her powers of angels to stop theSnowQueens blizzard.

And finally. In SnowQueens castle. Gerta found Kay. His heart froze solid and thinkin only SnowQueen would make him Master of the World.

Gerta knew such a thing was evil.

Gerta cried.

Gertas warm tears thawed Kays cold heart.

And through confusion. Sorrow. Melting pride. Kay again knew Gerta as his lasting. True. Eternity partner.

And they were so happy.

MissusCogg would snuffle in a handkerchief and wipe away tears and say, Thats just how I feel about my own grouch Jack.

I knew exact what she meant cause *TheSnowQueen* was the first story ever made me think about friends and love and loyalness and all the things good people do when they care about life and stick by each other.

MissusCoggs story was the best.

Never no plate in the head with that one.

TheSnowQueen.

Loved it.

Fattaman funnelcakes.

Oh my sweet lands.

AuntBeni and Mom hugging MistaCogg there in the funeral parlor.

MistaCogg asking me, How you doin?

Wanting to say, On winter cold nights. MissusCogg showed Mom to put marshmallows in baked apples. Then brown sugar raisins. Walnuts and butter.

On rain April days she couraged Mom to handstitch sew and Ross to draw pictures and me to write words D-E-A-R. T-H-I-S. H-E-A-R-T.

Dad and Ross. Kneeling.

Ross saying, Goodbye MissusCogg. Roses bloom and cease ta be. I hope ta Christ that God youll see.

MistaCogg saying, Jaysus. Betta than us all. She saw.

MistaCogg giving Ross a flickered wink with sagged eyes.

Then MistaCogg turning to Mom and Dad. And MistaJackCogg saying, She heard the kids playin. Just before she. She heard em. Her words. She said, So good. Hearin childrens voices. Now.

And MistaCogg crying and slobbering inside Moms hugginmuggin arms.

And Dad looking down at the floor.

And me wanting back outside.

But couldnt stop thinking about people doing love and Gerta changing Kay. And theSnowQueens powers destroyed cause of that love.

Wondering, Who was gonna do embroidrees?

Make fattyman funnelcakes?

Yankee pot roast. With little red potatoes?

And sopping hot gravy?

With MissusCogg. Now. No more.

5

Ouch Ouch Ouch

Ross.

WillieD.

LilMush.

PruneyMendez.

And me.

At the beach.

SowamsGreenhillTownBeach.

Early June Saturday. One of those eighty degree days in town. But. On the beach. Cool of the water with every gust or breeze. Its not yet summer. And spring been rain. And cold.

Because of early heat. The beach is the place to be today and we get there ready to go in. But whos tracking tides? Not ta say. But. Been a long time since last summer. And we havent got our Blounts Eastons Seafood tide charts yet. When we get to the beach and its low.

Lowtide.

Fullmoon last night and wind is blowing from the north and everything heading south with the current and the blow. So its definite what we call low.

Real low.

Chock a block low.

Low.

So low the chock a block low sandbar is outta the water like a beached whale sunning on a CapeCod shore.

A quarter mile stretch of sand. MistaCogg calls it a spit.

We call it a bar.

LeoDriggs and Bundles call it, Clammud. And theyre out with rakes and baskets working their best for what MistaCogg calls, Rotgut wine.

Cold air coming off the water is a bit too much for swimming. But. Tides out. Spits flat. Clams squirting. We're quaggin for quahogs.

Its drop bikes. Kick shoes. Off shirts. And. Whahoo. Long pants dungarees into the water. Tonight for sure. Stuffies and chowda.

Between the beach and the spit water drops deep. And LilMushGahdoo to his nipples working furious his feet. Shoulders back and forth and LilMush grin a frown and before we even reach him hes stooping underwater then breaking back surface prize clam in hand and, Got one.

And its, Way ta go Mushy. First-a-the year.

But weve no basket. No burlap. So. Its into his pants the hardshell clam. And then its Mush wiggling and feetfinding back for another.

Ross, Got one.

Then WillieD, Got? Shit. Shit its just a rock.

Then me, Got one.

And another.

And another.

Into our pants they go.

Into our pants go the hardshell clams.

Bivalves.

Mollusks.

Squirters.

Clam cookies.

Chowdas.

Bulls.

Cherrystones.

Necks.

The Clampers.

The Clappers.

The Quahogs.

The wampum.

The spit is disappearing because tides coming in. Leo and Bundles. About half hour ago. Crossed over shore. Tide is lots higher now and weve worked our way back too. When all on the sudden LilMushGahdoo screams. And the seagulls circle and turn. And Ross yelling, Help. Help. Mush is drownin.

Or something. A toe grinder or horeshoecrab maybe.

And Mush screeching. Going mental now. Seagulls diving. WillieD and Ross weighted down with clams in their pants and neck high water trying to get Mush and Mush keeps going under and surface screams. Leo-

Driggs his cigarette to the ground runs into the water. LeoDriggs runs to LilMushGahdoo and Leo reaches Mush first and carrying spazzing Mush in his arms to the beach and spazzing Mush cant stop screaming or kicking and thrashing. And Leo puts screaming MushGahdoo on the beach. Mush pulling off his dungarees. Unzipping them and flinging clams. Wiggling and screaming. LeoDriggs pulling legs of Mushs jeans. Pulling off those pants like LeoDriggs skinning a eel. Mushs flopping around sand. His underwear bulging clams. LeoDriggs standing Mush and pulling down Mushs underwear. Clams plop plop to the ground. And people way up near the shower looking and start towards our noisemaking. LilMushGahdoo bare ass naked. LilMush. Jumping. Screaming. Yelling. And on Mushs dick. Biggest white chowda bull. Clamped down. Stretching LilMushGahdoos dick looking like a night crawler being pulled from its hole. And Leo calls Bundles and Bundles comes around. And LeoDriggs. He dont even tell Bundles what. Bundles wristgrabs LilMushGahdoos spazzing arms. MushGahdoo screaming. Ouch. Ouch. Ouch.

Bundles, Yare. Yare. Yare. Yare.

Rosses eyes big.

WillieDs eyes bigger.

PruneyMendez his eyes bigger than big.

My eyes. Busting bigger than them all.

And Leo drops knees. And his cigarette stained fingers with black-rimmed fingernails and that dick choking clam back and forth like a Sowams diamondback tarapin turtle doin a Tarzan swing.

Leos hand rubbing his chin.

Rubbing his chin.

Rubbing his unshaved whisker muttering chin.

And Mush is screaming agony.

Pruney grabs the dick.

Pruney grabs the clam.

And PruneyMendez yanks.

Pruney dont yank the frank. Pruney holds the frank and yanks the clam.

And LilMush is free. Just like that.

Jumping into his underwear and pants that Bundles is now offering.

Funny how news travels fast in Sowams.

Because the next day when Im in MistaCoggs Port n Starboard Shop. Theres CapnJack and GilOwen gamming over beers and brandy. All lit up and snookered with a attitude in a cloud of BorkumRiff. CapnJack asks,

Still got yuh whale lance?

Which set both him and GilOwen laughing. To snotting and snorting until MistaCogg again saying, You boys need heed extra special care-a-yuh precious hah poons.

And he yipps and keeps repeating poon between his sniggles.

GilOwen asks, Is it true what happened to your friend?

If youre meanin LilMushGahdoos clamdick. You betcha. Quahog almost bit it off. Till Pruney saved the day.

And that gets them both cracking up all over again.

GilOwen and MistaJackCogg.

As Mom would say, A pair-a-cods.

Them two.

Grown men.

Not fa nuthin.

Behavin like kids.

6

Flying the Colors

GilOwen spoke soft.

GilOwen smelled of bay rum aftashave.

And GilOwen smiled.

GilOwen. Always. Always. Smiled.

Except one time when GilOwen dint smile.

One time when GilOwen dint smile but almost cried. That one time JackCogg called GilOwen, A gottdamned Sodmite. But MistaCogg was drunk when he said that. That Sodmite thing. And as always. GilOwen. Even though MistaCogg made him almost cry. GilOwen just set it and a thousand other bad things people say. GilOwen set it aside. A drunks temper mental without no original intend to hurt, is what GilOwen said.)
And GilOwen let the whole Sodmite thing go.

GilOwen never mentioned it again.

Let bygones be bygones.

Keep the peace.

Thats what GilOwen said.

And GilOwen moved on.

And tidied up his shop.

When she was in high school. Moms favorite English teacher was GilOwen who stopped teaching before I was born. And. For all my life. Up til now. He owned and ran TheSquarePeg antique shop and told Ross and me just plain out call him GilOwen.

So we done it.

Although Mom said, A man-a-his professional distinction should be MistaGilOwen.

GilOwen said, Antiquing didnt require such antiquarian distinction.

He would, Gladly defer deference to Thee Curmudgeon of the Seas. MistaJackCogg.

And all though I knew about seas being big waters surrounded by land. Of antiaquariums defering diffrences and three crahmudgins. I had no) ideas.

Not ta say. But. It dint sound good and GilOwen wanted none of it.

When I was nine years old. Mom. Ross and me was in TheSquarePeg antique shop looking at amber bottles. Blue bottles. Glass cases filled with rings pearls and jewry. Colony crocker cookware. Fancy dressed dummies. A few old suite cases with stickers slapped on them said Seattle. Philadelphia and Idaho. Green painted milk cans each with a eagle decal. Then of course there was the RhodeIslandSchool-a-Design. RISD. Rizzdee art from hanging between old broke clocks. Charcoal naked people but you couldnt see nothing. Watercolor marshes and rivers. Oil still lifes. And acrylic wildshapes and designs. Bigwood benches and highboy oakchairs polished smooth and rich with what Mom said was, The grain-a-character.

While she went over and drinked a glass of wine with GilOwen. Ross and me kept looking at stuff. Old dolls with cracked porcelain faces. Broke toy trucks. And our very favorite. Called StereoVision cards that had double photographs that you put in a wood holder thing and looked through and the pictures popped out. Ross said it was old fashion ViewMaster. Old fashion cause none of it was plastic and you had to do each set a pictures as individual pairs. Our favorite picturepairs were The Eight Wonders of the World. Egypts Pyramids. The Sphinx. The Great China Wall. Victoria Falls. Niagra Falls. Big Ben. And The Snow Covered Alps.

When we got finished we sat with Mom and GilOwen in his NOT FOR SALE red velvet chairs. Direct above GilOwen was a embroidree. And Mom explained the handstitched words.

Two Loves I Have of Comfort and Despair

Mom said them words was mouthspoke by MistaWilliamShakespeare but handsewed done by sewing artist MissLydiaRogers who taught MissusCogg. Mom said MissLydiaRogers lived on UnionStreet not too far away and had sewn the flowers on the seats we was sitting on. And Mom patted the cushion and shared her chair with Ross. I sat alone. Hand stiched red velvet seams soft on the back of my shortpants legs and GilOwen said, Jate. I hear youre writing quite a book.

And I said, Plate in the head. Lots-a-dont know how to spell words.

And GilOwen said, Good writing is not just spelling. Its communicat-)
ing. Communicating ideas. History. Representing lore.

And I said, Huh?

And Mom said, Events. Traditions. History. NarragansettBay.

And GilOwen said, The oceans. Being all about fish. Your Mom says.
You. With mere paper and pencil are serving up a fancy fine feast fit for
feeding a full shore dinner hall. But remember. Just because some rich
BrownUniversity scholar has gormay. With a T. Bait. Excellent string. And
the best hooks. That doesnt mean he has himself a handsome fish dinner.

Not ta say. But. I was plate in the head about that gormay with a T one.
And everything else GilOwen said. And a few days later. When explaining
to MistaCogg what GilOwen told. All I could headplate remember was
BrownUniversity. Fishhooks. And GilOwens long splash of F words.

The only F word come outta me was fish.

I told MistaCogg, GilOwen says we're all about fish.

MistaCogg had himself a fit of laughing coughs he stopped with swig
of the bottle. MistaCogg said, Gormay is fancy French. G-O-U-R-M-E-T.
And if you and me are gourmet fish. GilOwen oughta know cause hes
swish. Man swish and CampbellSoupcan swish.

I thought MistaCogg meant GilOwens swish had something to do with
swish swosh slosh painting pictures for the Eastbay SeafoodCompany. The
outfit here in our small town of Sowams sold clams to CampbellsSoup because Ross later told me about a CampbellsSoup artist named Andy who
did lotsa swish swosh slosh fast painting.

Andy Hole.

Andy War Hole.

AndyHole swish swosh sloshin his paint brushes and paintin labels on
each of the CampbellsSoup cans.

Talk about a big load of work.

But Ross also told me, Swish has nothin to do with swish swosh slosh
paintin lables. Soupcans. Or the Eastbay SeafoodCompany.

GilOwen finally told me how them labels got painted.

GilOwen said, Andy wasnt painting lables. But painting lith o graphic
silk screens portraits of the labels.

Said Andy was his hero. And AndyWarHoles lith o graphic silk screen
art made people slow down and pay attention to the plainer things of
the world.

A celebration of the ordinary, is how GilOwen put it.

But. Me? I was just glad the clams of Sowams. Our dug from the mud clams. Got in the soup.

But. For the most part. GilOwen ignored Sowams clams and pablabborated on the importance of those lith o graphic silkscreen soupcan portraits.

GilOwen loved pablabboratin.

MistaCogg said, Sayin somethin about nothin was GilOwens idea-a-keepin quiet.

Said, GilOwen could talk knit from a sock. Tide off a ocean. Put pastina on a antique.

And I dint understand that one.

Not fa nuthin.

Not at all.

Everyday outside the SquarePeg front door.

GilOwen raised the America United States flag.

Flying the colors, is how GilOwen said it.

He'd fly the colors on a.

Taken from a yacht.

Boatmast.

Cemented.

In the streetcorner.

He'd always remind me and Ross, On land a flagpole is called a staff. But on a ship. Or boat. That same pole is a mast. But because this pole is for real a mast then it isnt a staff. But a mast. And do you understand?

Ross said, Yep.

But I said, Nope. Jus the Merican flag flyin on a pole.

When Ross asked GilOwen why he flied his flag when no one else flew one?

GilOwen said, Soon as the politicians make you believe they have a monopoly on our flag. Then we're in for real trouble. Which this country is in because those guys think they own the world. Viet Nams about to blowup in their faces and those snake charmers are going to learn a thing or two about what this flag is suppose to represent.

GilOwen was so serious. No usual smiles. Nothing reflecting off his eyeglasses. Blue in his eyes so deep. Couldnt get myself to tell him Ross and me yesterday caught two brown garter snakes and we had a Monopoly game we liked just fine. Or ask, Whats a vee ett dam? And hows it gonna blowup the faces-a-them politicians?

So I just listened and let GilOwen be GilOwen.

The friendliest guy in Sowams.

At the SquarePeg. GilOwen bought and sold all kinds of things.

He said, Soup to nuts.

But he never made any soup.

And nuts?

GilOwen said the nuts was us.

Everyone.

Everyone who was always hanging out at GilOwens SquarePeg antique store just down the street from MistaCoggs Port n Starboard Shop. Or as MistaCogg sometimes said, One-a-the many nut houses on the fruit cake-a-WaterStreet.

Dint for real know what MistaCogg meant by that but in GilOwens SquarePeg WaterStreet shop. Under his mast staff pole flying the colors. Aside from bright rainbow cloth bundles. Broke statues. Hunks of green yellow red blue glass. Old photographs. And lotsa antiques. GilOwen and a bunch of Rizzdee ottists MistaCogg called a swish friend or two. Or three. Usual a couple of guys and a gal. Or the other way round. A couple of gals and just a guy. On Friday nights. With Mom. Ross. Me. And sometimes Dad. They played jazz records. Set up easels. Touched shoulders. Drinked wine. Smoked cigarettes. Ate pizza. Oozled blooms. Kissed lips. And spoke fun words like, Scumblin crumblin cool. Yeah man. And, Dig.

During weekdays. Or Saturday afternoons.

GilOwen would sometimes give Ross art lessons.

Them two would sit on different sides of the room with something Ross called StillLife between them. The StillLife was usual a whiskey bottle. Or a wine glass. A few vases with a bunch of phony roses and fake fruit laying around. Plastic purple grapes. Wax bananas. A couple of green wood apples. Rubber oranges.

Sometimes theyd have that not real fruit and things on a nice velvet cloth. Or on a bare board wood table. But the fruit and things always looked prettfancy. Like it dint just drop there. But was put by someone who knew about placing plain stuff good.

There was this one time Ross let me watch him with charcoal pencils sketch. He sketched in a big pad. Rosses left hand. Never left the paper.

Fingers. Pencil. Paper. Lotsa flow like he was tracing what was already on the paper. Thin lines becoming thick lines becoming etches just like youd see in a uncolored coloring book.

Then all zigzag and squiggles. Smudges and rubs and the picture looking no more a coloring book drawing but now like a magazine black and white photograph. No more white space black lines. But lotsa what Ross called grays. Dark gray. And gray white. And blackandwhitegrays. And the words Ross used was. Shades. Values. Tones. And Ross said, Similar to people. To each his own.

What did he mean by that? Ross wasnt drawing people. He was drawing bottles. Flowers. Vases and fruit. But he did more quick lines with the right hand and lotsa brushing and wiping with the fingers of his left. And then pushing the pad away. Then bowing his face towards it. Big cheeks blowing dust from the paper and more finger brushing and a nod of Rosses head and his face no shadow calm and full light and he silent said, So be it.

Which was his own liking for what he done.

Anyways.

Usual after school. What Ross did. Was watch the SquarePeg shop. Mind the pretty cash.

And organize stuff.

During slow time. He'd paint or sketch. And people would enjoy looking at him. And maybe theyd buy something too.

Most of the time GilOwen had to leave the store and pick up or deliver antiques and art. Go to things that were advertised in the newspaper as Artist Estate Sales. They was like when a sick guy or a old lady died or something.

Ross said, GilOwen makes a killin even though GilOwen never does no hurt to nobody. Has to do with earnin money.

And. Because of that. Ross called himself a employee. Said GilOwen was his employer. Which. On the plain and simple meant. Ross had himself a job called Display Ottist.

And both GilOwen and him not only displayed the real stuff. But had their art pictures showing. And I gotta addmit. Their art was good. What was the most interesting thing was even though they would usual sketch the same still life displays. Their art pictures always made that same stuff look different. GilOwen said that was, The guaranteed nature of perspective. Same subject. Different views. Same. Only different. Guaranteed.

And. Not ta say. But. That got me thinking of Ross and me.
Although we was twins.
We too.
Had so much difference.
To each his own.
Guaranteed.
So be it.

7

Breath and Breathe

When GilOwen was a high school teacher. Before Ross and me was born. He got fired from his teacher job because a student at the high school said GilOwen did a indecent thing to him.

And whenever the adults would talk about that. The indecent thing. They always made sure Ross and me werent around. And if we were. They would talk soft. Or fast change the subject. And once when GilOwen come over our house for supper. Mom tapped GilOwens shoulder. And she nodded at Ross and me who were on the floor sketching and writing. And Mom said, Little pitchers have big ears.

When I looked at the lemonade pitcher. No ears were there.

Ross said it had to do with kids listening to stuff they shouldnt.

After GilOwen left. What our ears heard was Mom and Dad both saying the indecent part wasnt true. The whole thing was started by a guy who was angry with GilOwen. Someone. A kid whos now a adult. With a axe to grind. And someone who Mom said she liked a lot. A guy she grew up with but who Mom said, Had lots-a-personal problems of his own.

When I asked GilOwen about what indecent means and why do people grind axes? He laughed. But then got serious. He told me the best way to learn anything. Especial the meaning of words like indecent. Was to keep my mouth closed. My eyes and ears open. Said what I saw would be about as close to the truth as I could probbly ever get. And what I heard was what others would probbly be telling. What I had to understand, GilOwen said, Was others would be telling only parts of the truth. But by writing just those parts each and every day. I would eventually have something would add up to perspective.

GilOwen dint say it praspective the way everyone else did. He said perspective.

And no one seemed to mind. We let him have his fancyway.

His perspective.

And one day. When Ross and him was outside on the marsh. Easels side by side. Doing fancy paint acrylics. Dads upside down boat. Ross was looking down his pointing paintbrush. And closing a eye. Ross asked GilOwen if he gave the word praspective to Mom?

GilOwen put a few colors on his canvas and said, No. It is a word all honest people know and understand.

Then GilOwens stood long before his canvas. He dint do anything. Just stood. Stood and stared. The sunlight doing crinkles on his hair and his shoulders. The canvas straight before him. Not at a angle. But connected to a long thin brush connected to his fingers connected to his hands connected to his arm connected to his body.

Youd think with all of that connecting he mightve been stiff and rigid. But he was full of ease and relaxation. Left hand in his pocket. No effort about him. Like the reeds and the cord grass behind him. Just there. Being in the open. Just being.

And the paint went swish swosh on his canvas in that same ease way.

Criss cross of the brush.

A push here.

A pull there.

Every now and then he would drop his arm across himself to see what things he had just done with the colors. And the colors reflected on his face and on his glasses. In his smile. Or his frown. Then he'd do the brush tip into his pallet and then back on to the canvas. And the canvas colors showed in his eyes. Green. White. Yellow. Black. Red. And blue. Then next. All a blush mix on his face. And. He isnt doing colors. Colors are doing him.

That got me all plate in the head.

Final. GilOwen said, Perspective. Was about all a reasonable man could hope for.

And a person should always be reaching for truth. But be suspicious of anyone who says hes grabbed a solid hold of it.

And then GilOwen stood behind Ross. Looked at the marsh boat. Then back to Rosses painting. GilOwen nodded his head up and down yes. Went back behind his own easel. And GilOwen said, Truth. Just too big for one body.

I looked at the painting on GilOwens easel.

GilOwens painting had the boat showing transom with no bow. Yet

Rosses was mostly bow with no transom and all from the starboard. For the most part. Prapective worked just fine.

I thought, Not ta say. But. What does he mean by that?

And just like GilOwen and Ross saw the same boat different. So did Ross and Pruney think different about our favorite movie star. Ross and Pruney couldnt decide which JulieAndrews they loved more. The *Mary-Poppins* JulieAndrews or the MariaVonTrapp one.

Supercalifrag-a-somethin?

Or.

Doe a deer a female deer?

During that time those two guys would argue and josh about everything on TV and radio. *Combat* or *TheGallantMen*?

AddamsFamily or *TheMunsters*?

TheBeatles or HermansHermits?

Now what you gotta understand. Is. Not Ross or Pruney cared a whole lot about none of these things to actual argue fight about them. But because. When Ross and me helped Pruney deliver papers. Ross would usual bust out a newspaper section and read it out loud.

Rosses favorite sections being the front page.

Then the section called Entertainment.

Real particular funny is how Ross would read outloud the headlines and stories. Like the cancercigarettsmokin death of NatKingCole which made us sad cause we sure did like Nats *MonaLisa* and rolling out those *LazyHazyCrazyDays of soda and pretzels and beer.* Or. Usual about places and things I never heard of before like Selma and Montgomery. Alabama. And that war GilOwen once talked about. Vee Et Nam. And Watts. With riots.

And did he mean warts? From touching toads? And rot?

And. Not ta say. But. Even though none of us never heard this stuff before. Pruney sure did know lots about it. If Ross read something outloud. Pruney could. On immediate. Explain it way better than Ross. Or the newspaper.

Like.

Take for instant.

PresidentJohnsonsWarCabinet.

Acording to Pruney. PresidentJohnson had a cabinet in the WhiteHouse kitchen. Next to the broom closet. Where he kept guns and bullets and armyboots and C-rations. And other stuff for fighting CastroCubans and the Russians.

Pruney knew more than everybody.

Ross said Pruney was MistaSirKnowItAll.

And Ross said it to me private. Like being MistaSirKnowItAll was bad.

And I gotta addmit.

If Ross meant being MistaSirKnowItAll was bad. Then Ross was wrong.

Being MistaSirKnowItAll wasnt bad.

What was bad was being MistaSirKnowNothing.

Like me.

I was MistaSirKnowNothing and was always in wonder and surprise about the ways Pruney. In the schools lowest class. And Ross. In the highest. Was both so smart about all kinds of stuff.

Like for instant.

One rain day.

Pruney. Ross. And me. Delivering the newspaper at GilOwens SquarePeg antique store and waiting. With GilOwen. For the rain stop. And Ross read aloud the newspaper headine. *LBJ Assures Americans Right to Vote.*

Pruney said, Dont see the big deal. If youre a American. You vote.

Ross said, Well. Its not that easy. For Negroes.

I said, Whaddya mean?

Ross said, Well. Down south people make it real difficult. To vote. Some white people dont think colored people plain and reggahla.

Pruney said, Thats why the King. MartinLuther. Whos also a doctor. Is always fightin the police. I seen that piture of the GermanSheperd bein sicked on a colored guy and all he wanted was silver rights to vote. Not ta say. But. They let Italians vote. And Portuguese vote. Why not Negroes? Theyre like us. Plain and reggahla.

And although GilOwen was listening and laughin. When Pruney said the word. Reggahla. For whatever reason. GilOwen got real serious and particular.

GilOwen said, Boys. The plain and simple truth is people arent plain or reggahla. Bagels are. And yes. Some people sure are simple. But reggahla? Save the reggahla for ordering coffee. And do me a favor will you boys? Please? The word is spelled R-E-G-U-L-A-R. Pronounce the word reg-YOU-lar. GilOwen said, Plain and reg-YOU-lar.

And Pruney said Reg-YOU-lar. And so did Ross. And then both busted out laughing. And next thing Pruney and Ross run out the shop like a couple-a-pair of what Mom woulda called gigglin gerties. And then there was just me and GilOwen.

GilOwen closed his eyes and looked like he was thinking hard. And with his fingers he rubbed the sides of his head where his eyeglasses rested on his ears. Then at last he said, Plain and reg-YOU-lar. Life is so much more complicated.

And I said, Thats the problem. Cant ever figure out on complicated life stuff.

GilOwen got wide eyed and said, Not true. Take for instance your writing. May I open to any page in your notebook and read it outloud?

No way.

How about you approve first?

And I still said, No.

But then GilOwen said, Magic happens when words are spoke.

I liked magic tricks. So I said, Okay.

Gill open flipped pages and said, *Gulls*? May I read it?

And there wasnt gonna be a magic trick. So. I said, Yeah. You can read that.

So GilOwen outloud read,

When I first heard the word culls. Thought JackCogg meant gulls. And for a long time. Least-a-ways til Pruney and Ross told me different. Flapped my wings and squawked round the beach in the dash-a-them flocks sometimes tryin to sneak up on em while theyd be restin in the morning. Dozens and dozens-a-them. Like beaked marshmallows on toothpick legs. Me tryin to catch one-a-them gulls that took to the skys and left me on the shore thinkin bout what can and cant done cause I dint have wings. Bein a gull makin me feel special. A special creature but no wings.

GilOwen read them words.

Then he got real quiet. Took his no rim glasses from his eyes and held them eyeglasses folded in his hands. And GilOwen repeated *beaked marshmallows. Toothpick legs.* And then GilOwen said, Vote chya day ragottzee.

The smallest hint of smile curled GilOwens lips and he pointed to my words.

His lips moved with the words he was silent reading. By himself.

As he turned the pages. He looked at me again and again.

And he said, Vote chya day ragottzee. Vote chya day ragottzee.

Though I dint understand Italian because Mom and Dad never taught me and Ross how to talk Italian. I could easy recogonize it when I heard it spoke. So I asked GilOwen, Wheredya learn Italian? Whats vote chya day ragottzee mean and hows it spelled?

He said. We learn what we want. Your mom. Lifes music. Kid speak. Honest words. Poetry.

And long shadows from GilOwens WaterStreet window antiques stretched and filled the place with dark crawlings. And GilOwen. His charcoaled stained fingers to his almost moving mouth. Them earthfingers on his lips. Shadows in front of his eyes the smallest smile curled his lips and he spelted V-O-T-E-C-H-A D-E R-A-G-G-A-Z-Z-I

Then. Like he always done when drinking wine. GilOwen gave a gentle swirl to the wineglass and he again rubbed the sides of his head where his eyeglasses usual rested. That place he called, The Temples. The place where he always rubs.

Again and again.

All the time.

Today and so many days.

And although. Mom. Dad. Kids at school. And now. GilOwen. Said I was a creative in the flesh trans scribin machine. My real plate in the head most difficults was slow understanding what everyone else real fast understood. Especial Ross and PruneyMendez. And like I already said. Writing this book helped me realize I werent dumb stupid. But maybe. As Ross said, Just a stupit prodigy.

Which was way better than what MistaCogg. So often said about others. Them being. What he always called, Gottdamn pigeon kicked idiots.

Now GilOwen closed my notebook. Put on his eyeglasses. Picked up his charcoal and sketchpad and his hands started back and forth and. He looked at me hard and said, Jate? Your plate in the head. Like MistaCoggs limpleg. Its the thing makes you special. You and Jack are culls, he said. Good culls. The priceless kind.

GilOwen one hand charcoal sketching while the other his wineglass. Said, Youre special all right. And made with wings. When LouieRespeegies fish truck drop knocked you to the curb. The doctors with fancy titanium. Remolded small. A patch of your skull. And just when everything looked healing. Along came. Bleeding. Swelling. Mild stroke. And two more months. RhodeIslandHospital. Everybody worried sick. But. You made it. Sure. Now and then. An episode. But for the most part. Indeed. Youve come along. You certainly have.

And GilOwen meant about me having a episode was. He knew. Sometimes my plate in the head felt like it was light and made of air and Id get dizzy. Or a vibrating would start my arm and my fingers clenching like a crabclaw and Id feel a tingling sting like youd get at the beach if you picked up a jelly fish squish side with all dangling tentacles slime full of poison dont kill you but makes you feel rashburn. Sometime the not usual happened. Id close my eyes and see colors and feel dizzy. And sometimes hear the ocean sounds a seashell make. But. There would be no ocean.

Usual the seashell ocean sounds in my head would go away. Fast. And everything would be just fine. Regular quiet. Like nothing happened.

So there we were. In the SquarePeg talking. GilOwen putting down his sketchbook pad. Black fingers picking up his longstem wineglass. Swirling the red around. Wine dripping down the insides. GilOwen said, Youve become a writer Jate.

Wrapping his black fingers around the big part of the glass GilOwen said, You with your plate and JackCogg with his leg. Both given wings. Limpleg. Plate in the head. Wings. Make you reach for where you want to go.

GilOwen took a wine drink and said, Plate in your head helps you reach for things. For instance. Words. For you. Each words a puzzle. An adventure. The hear. The now. The moment. Right. This. Instance.

GilOwen tapped his charcoled stained pointing finger on the sidetable with the speak of each one-a-them last three words. And after a instant GilOwen said, Do you understand?

Nope, I said. Sure dont.

GilOwen put down his empty wine glass. Wiped his hands on a rag. Messed his blonde hair hard. Sat back in his chair. Put his charcoal gray hands behind his head. Looked around. Old bottles. Dolls. Framed pictures. And then. Smile on his face. Gold light glimming off his eyeglasses. GilOwen said, Show me ErnestHemingway.

And I said, Who?

E. Hemingway.

Just you and me whos here is all.

And GilOwen waved to the walls and said, His photograph.

And around us all the hanging pictures. AbrahamLincoln. Old ladies with grump faces. GeorgeWashinton unfinished neck. BabeRuth. Slick haired men moviestars. Women ones too. But big hair. Not slick. Being bewdeeful beauty parlor gorgeous.

Dont know GilOwen. Too many everywhere hangin.

Yes. But only one is bookfamous.

And when GilOwen said that. Immediate I saw. A mustached guy squarejaw handsome. Banging at a typewriter on a wood table. Outside.

Steep background hill. Puffed dark clouds. A grand face. Sharp eyes.

Him, I pointed.

GilOwen said, Bravo.

I said, Thats a prettgood photo.

GilOwen said, There are no bad photos of Ernest Hemingway.

And I said, Well whats Heminway got to do with me bein plate in the head and who is ErnessHeminway?

And GilOwens said, Well. This picture was taken after Hemingway hurt his head surviving a plane crash. You can even see his scar. Yet. Many say. Hes Americas greatest writer. But regardless. God rest his tortured soul. You figured author has to do with writing. You figured it by yourself.

I scratched my forehead. Pulled in deep some air and busted out a big breath and said, Not ta say GilOwen. But what are your talkin about?

On the sudden. GilOwen sat straight in his chair. Slid direct to the edge and said, Jate. Come over here. Do that again.

What?

GilOwen said, That breath. That. Full gathered. Deep breath.

And GilOwen reached out and with charcoal stained hands gripped my clean hand and slipped his hand. Palm down. Between the buttons of my shirt direct on to my thin clean chest. GilOwens soft hand. Strong. And warm too. And he said, Again. Deep breath. This time hold.

And I did.

Drawed that breath. Mouth. Nose. Chest getting swolled. The rush. The thump. My heart bumping my head. GilOwen reaching out his dark hand on mine. His palm skin under my shirt and top of my stomach. And GilOwen saying. Hold it. Hold.

And me no breathing. But in my ears. Distant ringing.

And GilOwen saying, Slow. Now breathe. Make your breath become breathe.

And I did. A long long soft sigh. No trouble. Felt good.

And the soft of his gray hand slipped from the smooth of my white skin.

And GilOwen said, You took a breath. But if thats all you had done. Youdve been dead. A man doesnt just take a breath. A man needs to breathe. A breather. Its just that split second it takes to add the letter e. Time to make the breath count. Time to give breath quality. A breath becoming breathe is life itself. Breath is worth nothing if you dont slow down and take time to breathe. Your plate in the head slows you. Take advantage of it. You. My young friend. Have a gift. A gift that helps make connections others miss. Why? Because they dont slow down. Stop for understanding. But you do. Plate is an opportune connection between the meaning of things and how things relate. Gives you time to walk around a thing and see it from a different side. A different angle. A different point of view. Perspective. Ideas have to breathe in order to grow. It only takes a little time. Time. Time for one word to another. One experience. Then another. One point of view. And another. Time it takes to make a connection. Connect. Dont rush through moments. Pause.

Take a B-R-E-A-T-H.

Add an e.

B-R-E-A-T-H-E.

Breathe.

8
Asquantum

Asquantum always begun with early morning fishing when the sun came up but then stretched to late morning. Late morning became afternoon and afternoon became evening. And what all them hours blending for real into was foods. Friends. Beachfire. Hotdogs. Sausage. Fish. Oystas. Molasses brownbread. Clams. Corn. Watermelon. Maybe rockcrabs. Blueshells. Or lopstas.

And stories.

Always stories.

Pablabborated stories.

Dad telling about KingPhilip and the Wampanoag Indians.

Mom telling about the Greeks. Who she said had the best stories. Myths. She called them. Borialis. The wind god. And Boreas of the north. Zephyr of the west. Notus south. And Eurus from the east. Spelling. Just for me. Each correct.

After late at night. MistaCogg. In his boat. Towing us home.

Sometimes underneath stars. And sometimes through thick solid fog.

The reason why MistaCogg had to tow was simple. Dads quahog skiff dint have a motor. Or running lights. And MistaCoggs catboat did. But most of all. By late night. Current was usual against us.

But Dad dint call himself a sailor. Even though Dad sometimes sailed our skiff on the SowamsRiver. And even though Dad worked the ocean on a dredge. Dad always said he was a dredge oiler. Made sure the dredge engines ran smooth. Said he had a good job because when the dredge engines broke down or werent running right. Someone else did the fixing.

Mechanics. Dad said, Thems the guys who for real got dirty.

But the one thing Dad dint like was. He hardly ever got on deck. Always down below. In the engine room. Listening for trouble. And reporting trouble whenever he discovered trouble. Dad said, Usual the trouble noise was smooth. Constant. Not always loud. But there. Not goin away. A racket. Sometimes a quiet racket. But a racket none the less.

That dint make plate in the head sense to me. But what was perfect clear was. When Dad got his days off and was free of all oiling troubles Dad just wanted home.

Home outta the racket.

Home in Sowams.

On the marsh.

In the quiet.

On the water.

Asquantum.

The river.

The SowamsRiver.

Fishing.

Floating.

Reaching.

Taking it easy. Just the sound of wind and water. And sometimes sail. No racket.

Dad had a eighteen foot quahog skiff he bought off MannySousa.

Dad said, For a song.

What song?

Dad said, *JetSong. WestSideStory.*

Said, MistaSousa was glad to get rid-a-the skiff. It bein so beat up.

But it werent for real. Beat up that is.

Dad said something about MistaSousa owing him favors. But Dad never much more went into it. Dad just sang, *When youre a Jet youre a Jet all the way.*

And, *Somethins comin. I dunno. What it is. But it is. Gonna be great.*

Dad with a face. Mom said came straight out a Rossalini movie she seen in Providence at the Avon theater on Thayer Street.

Mom saying, If MarlonBrando been Italian. He'd be your handsome dad.

Dad the curl of his lip and the hook of his nose.

Dad with his smile would make his face go big and his teeth gleam bright.

Dad his white teeshirt. Swarty skin arms. Swarty skin neck and swarty skin face.

Dont know about Dads legs.

Dads legs being swarty.

Not hardly.

Dad never wore a bathing suit. Or shorts. Nothing but long green workpants. A teeshirt. And a zippertan jacket Dad called a windbreaker. Old green workpants. Cuffs rolled. Mom said, Hightide. Clamdigger style. And always. Dad wore a pair of black moccasins he said, Eastside Wampanoag Indians made.

Dad sure was fun.

Mom said he was, A card. A joker with a touch-a-the king.

And plate in the head me dint get it. Ross did though. And he laughed.

What Dad did was. Wintertimes. Kept the skiff turned over. On three cinderblocks. Two for the transom. One for the bow. But in the late spring. Usual after we uncover the fig tree. Dad did. What he called. Caulk the hull. Then he painted the hull. Turned the skiff over. Put the skiff in the water. Swamped it. Let swell her seams. Asked MistaCogg to bail it. And then. From the dredge. When Dad came home again. Anytime from Fourth of July through Labor Day. He'd gather up a set of three oars. One long one for a rudder. One each for port and starboard. A small Thurston sail stuffed in a duffle. A twelvefoot wood mast. Complete with rigging. And a real smooth tall as me sideboard. Dad called it, A mahogany leedagger. Salvaged from a DyerDhow got rockcrunched in a storm.

We'd load up the puddleduck wagons and lug to the boat. Three beach bags. Two coolers. Two folding chairs. A couple of cheesecloth bolts. A couple of small pans. Rosses pallet. Rosses easel. Rosses paint box. Rosses blanket wrapped canvas. Dads fishingpole. A yard rake. The four of us. And we'd float KingPhilipsCove where Mom said, A Eurus cranberrysky sunrise was bein nudged by a westZeffer breeze.

Zeffer, Mom reminded me was, Z-E-P-H-Y-R.

Dads expert S-C-U-L-L-I-N-G.

He said, Was rowING. Not bonehead S-K-U-L-lin.

Got us easy through the trestle current under the bridge and then direct into the Sowams.

Past the AmericanLuggage. The belltower and the smokestack.

Past the Quequeshan neighborhood with running off WaterStreet BarringtonYachtClub and what Mom called, The confluence-a-the QuequeshanRiver.

Past the DyerDhow Anchorage boat yard sign.

Past the StoneFleetTavern and at the edge of the parking lot down by the wharf. The thirteen millstones.

Count em, Mom always said. Count em.

And we did. Thirteen round millstones set near the water.

Past MannySousas Shellfish Market and behind it ThurstonsSails. Past the EastBay Shipyard to SowamsGreenhillTownBeach. The closed refreshment stand. The beach wall. Tall lifeguard chair. The wide stretch of sand. The outside shower. Little kid swings. Big kid swings. The slides. The merry go round. The monkey bars.

Past the HooglyCoveSwamp.

Past the breakwater danger rocks.

On to KingPhilipStraits and Narrows.

And then what we been waiting for.

PatienceIslandLighthouse. Just over HooglySpit and the cobblestones of MountHopeShores. Where Dad would say, River eddies from the channel.

And we saw the. Off on their own. Whirlpool current swirls. What eddies meant.

Late the night before all this. Mom. Made cole slaw with crispbroiled chicken. Also wine mixed breadcrumb dressing with crushed tomatoes. Parsley. Fennel. Gold currant raisins. Dried figs. Olive oil. All in a plastic bag so after we catched a striped bass from the boat. Mom cleaned the fish. Breading packed the bass. Wrapped the bass in aluminum foil. Then coal baked that breaded fish. Beach fire. Near the puddingstone.

Dad steered. Lotsa whirlpools. Under the trestle and through the dark bridge mouth. And pigeons flew and Ross shouted echoes whirpools sloshed and gulped current skiff rushed from under the bridge into dawn and we waved to topside fishermen always looking down at their lines and us.

Under the morning moon. Once clear of that.

Mom might nod to the absolute calm sky.

Dad says, She'll fill. She'll fill in.

And sure enough a steady Zephyr.

Mom would open the sail duffle. Feed sheetline through the masthead rigging and stand the roundwood post. Lower the mahogany leedagger into the special made sleeve. Carter locked the smooth dagger. Hoist the Thurston leg of mutton sail. Dad holding the clewline and rudder. Making what him and Mom loved.

A reach.

Dad. Would then open the plaid coffee thermos and pour for Mom and he. Ross and me sitting at the bow. Mom center seat. Dad stern. His rudder in a oarlock. Steering.

Us.

Tavinos.

In the gentlest west breezes.

Zephyr slight across the gunnels.

Bow pointing dead ahead.

No engines.

No oil.

Just wind.

Water.

Sail.

Reaching down the river.

Past tide showed danger rocks.

Us.

Reaching Montaup.

9
Seeing Providence

The summer after Ross and me met Pruney. One of Pruneys NewBedford cousins. Had a big throatlump. A thing called a goiter took out from his neck. Well. Somehow that cousin got his goiter operation infected and that cousin died.

Pruney said the cousin wasnt a close cousin but a distant one.

And of course that cousin could not have been a close cousin because the cousin lived in NewBedford. And thats distant. Not close. FallRivers close. But. Even though his father and AuntJovita and her son Edu was gonna go the Monday morning NewBedford funeral. They said Pruney could stay home by himself with his older brother Dagama who had to work early and Pruney woulnt never see him and be alone. And when Pruney blathered this to Mom. Mom said, Alone? Hah raws. Youll not be a moment alone. Youre spendin Sunday night here with the boys and comin asquantum with us Monday dawn.

Pruney. On the sudden got a shocked look. Eyes all big and said, No way. Got my paper route and SousasShellFishMarket job I gotta do.

Moms hair in front of her eyes and she quick swiped it back. Then frowned.

Dad said, No problem. MountHopeShores only a mile and a half by train track. At noon. You and Ross walk back here. Get your bikes. Do your papers. While youre at Sousas. Ross can go SquarePeg. Afta you finish Sousas. Go meet Ross and you guys ride back here with GilOwen who always arrives by car late aftanoon early evening.

Dad with a big grin said, Pedro Mendoza. Youre doin asquantum with our family. From now on. Youre part-a-this tribe. Beachgrit. Sunrise. And Wow.

That evening we helped Dad with the sailing gear. Stuffing duffles and loading puddleducks. Smells of Moms asquantum preparation cooking floated everywhere. Shoodeez Portuguese sausage Pruney give Mom and Dad. There was also lotsa on the floor pillows and folded blankets. Comic books and swapping treasures. Pruney spent his first night. As he said, Over ah house.

August 19. 1963.
A little past dawn.
Everything quiet.
Seagulls.
A bit of luff from the sail.
Moon fading west. East sun rising between SowamsGreenhills and MountHopeShore. Sunrise colors not staying still. Sunrise colors moving.
Pruney. Eyes of wonder. The river stopping Pruneys chat chat chat.
Ross with charcoals soft scratching his open sketchbook.
Sounds moving like wind. Or current. Or my breath.
Faraway sounds.
A outboard on another quahog skiff.
Pruney stands and points and says, That guys movin.
Dad says, BobbyBrayton. 75 horsepower Evinrude.
And wowed Pruney whistles low.
MountHopeShores not too far off and darkgray in some spots. Or a thick blue in others. Every now and then. A skipjack leaps.
Splashes of water.
A drop or two on Rosses pages.
Ross exasparates. And rag blots.
A pogey jumps.
Now a entire school of little fish roiling the slick because one bigger fish.
A blue. Chasing them.
Then.
Splitsplash.
The big fish.
Complete in the air.
Whole thing. Leaping dog glory.
Next. Splitsplash. Back into the water.
And gone.
But Pruney sayin he, Never. Eecoodeesh. Seen a swordfish so up close.

And Dad tells Pruney, For certain. For absolute certain. That particular swordfish jumped out the water to look. Only you. In the eyes.

And why Dad would say such a thing when he knows that pogeyjumper werent no swordfish I cant say.

And. Not ta say. But. No one should ever lie about fishes.

Now unusual gusts of morning breeze blow steady.

Mom saying, Borialis startin early.

Mom and Dad knowing exact how to deal with Borialis. We're sheets full and air tight. But too close to the breakwater rocks jutting from the land.

Ross and me know enough to sit still.

Dad gotta tell Pruney, When I tell you duck. Duck your head. Got it?

Pruney nods.

Dad nods Mom. Mom lets go the kicker.

Dad. Real calm tells Pruney, Duck.

Boom swings hard over head ducking Pruney.

Line twang zip and pop. Muttonleg drops. Dad holding rudder. Dad grabbing and Mom hauling the boom and arms of gathered sail Ross and me are stuffing fast. Back into the bag. Wrinkle duffle ship shape. Dad lifting high the oar rudder and our flat bottom skiff gliding smooth. The rising sandbar. The cobbled shallows.

MountHopeShores.

Lowtide landing sometimes real difficult.

But can be prettyfunny too.

We're wearing old sneakers and carrying everything. Coolers. Easel. Buckets. Beach bags and blankets. By hand. Over the oystabeds. Past the clamflats. Steamers pulling in their necks and mud tight closing. But Pruney has not ever before been here and he dont step careful and on the sudden. A clam is squirting. As MistaCogg would say. Up Pruneys ass. And Pruney jumping.

We're all laughing till we're crying because Pruney grabs his butt and drops his beachbag. And when Mom goes to help him. Big softshell clam squirts her too. And she slips and falls smack in the mud. And when Pruney tries to pull Mom to her feet. He gets squirt again and screams Eecoodeesh. But more long on the high sounding Eeeeeeeeeeeee and not so very too much low coo deesh.

Of course. Even though Ross carried his sketchpads and canvas blanket wrapped over his shoulders. One geyser shoots so long and high. Ross is certain it hit him and ruined his watercolored pictures. So he starts running reckless and that makes more clams squirt. And Ross is hopping one foot the other like hes on hot coals or sharp tacks or broke glass.

And I gotta addmit. If MistaCogg had been there. He woulda said we were, Laughin ah damn fool heads off.

Well. Even though Dad was laughing. He had stayed with the skiff till it scraped bottom and couldnt go no more. Then he ran the anchorline over the beach to the sumac stand where he tied. Tree base clovehitch.

At the puddingstonespot the first thing Dad does is dig a bake pit and line it with cobbles. Ross unwraps his canvas from the blanket. Clamps it to the easel. Lays it down on the cobbles aside. And second what we do is what Mom calls, Puttin Down the Blanket. She tells Pruney, Grab a cobble. Then hands a blanket corner to each of us boys. And us four. On Moms, Go. Open the blanket. Then luff the blanket down. Rock each corner. Gear set center in the middle. Keep from blowing away when we're shore combing. Or swimming.

Third thing we do. Immediate. Is beachcomb sungrayed driftwood. Branches. Boat planks. Sticks. Logs and dock boards. Beach is loaded and in no time we got plenty.

We watch Dad ball up newspaper he brought and then light the bonfire. And as facinating as them licking flames are Ross and me tell Pruney about the footbridge that leads to the railroad tracks. And we leave Mom and Dad for the trail through tall horsetail fragmites and cordgrass chatter that sworls wide at the creeks edge.

Crossing the footbridge when the tides rushing in for the high is better than crossing at dead low. We center stand. Then sit and air dangle our legs over the edge. Lotsa gurgling from marsh draining MetacomCreek beneath.

A clapper rail bird rattles from the rose briars. And Pruney is big eyes and ears everywhere. But he sits. He watches. He listens.

A flitter and a fluster and a bust of seaside sparrows in the horsetail reeds gets Pruney back on his feet. And hes looking this way and that. And a twitter and warble and tweeter and cluck have Pruneys head tilting one way then the other. He nods. Whispers, Them blackbirds got red patches on their wings.

Not ta say. But. Pruneys wonder proves what Mom always says, Theres no mistakin the redwing when its givin song and makin consort.

And Ross jumps to his feet and says, Lets go see the lighthouse.

We run below the upbeach bramble. Then walk. And sit some rocks.

A pair of cardinals overhead. A canary sings tweet tweet tweet tweet. Its yellow body bouncing on a rose. Then gone.

And as we make our way along that crescent beach to the rock exposed HooglySpit. The PatienceIsland Lighthouse grows out the ground. With every step we take that lighthouse gets bigger. And when we finally reach the edge of the narrows. There it all is. The full lighthouse.

PruneyMendez. Mouth open. Speechless.

I tell Pruney, Not fa nuthin. But. Although you see the islands Patience and Prudence. You cant see the others. Faith. Hog. Or Hope. But them islands are out there none the less. Everybody knows it. Now. Even you.

When we get back to puddingstonespot. Dads is knocking down the fire and the cobbles give off blast of heat and Moms got cherryred Kool-Aid and peanutbutter sandwiches. Leftovers from yesterday. Jelly soaked bread. And when Ross sees them. He turns his nose. Mom says hes, A fussbudget. Fast hideous.

Me and Pruney. We must be slow hideous because we just eat them. Ross just takes a KoolAid and then does his usual. Off by himself. Easel and paintbox. A sight Im always glad seeing. Because when fast hideous Ross sets up that tripod easel. His hand over his eyes. His paint brush stabbing. Him stepping back and tilting his head. First one way. Then the other. More paintbrush pallet messing. His canvas. Some slashes. Some swirls. Canvas colors cuckoo. It all eventual. Becomes bewdeeful art.

And Pruney and me distance follow Ross. I tell Pruney, When Ross is doin ott. You gotta let him have to his self.

Pruney asks, Do you do ott Jate?

I say, Dont paint ott. Just write stuff. Stuff I see. Stuff I hear.

And Pruney says he wishes he could do some art. Then adds he dont have time. Says AuntJovita once tried teaching him knitting and he kept getting yarn tangled fingers. Then Pruney says with off distant eyes, She sure does knit me nice sweaters and blankets.

Pruney and me finish our sandwiches. Then its me and my notebook. But Pruney. Like he dint hear a earlier thing I told him. Follows after Ross.

And Dad shouts, You guys gotta leave in an hour. Dont get lost.

Asquantum always means clamming and oystaring.

And the way we do it is split the party. Mom for oystas. Or cockle shells as she likes to call them. On the rocks down by the footbridge. The oystabeds. Eventual. Mom'll work her way to Dad and me who clam the flats. We'll be looking for those small holes showing clams living under. And when we find sufficient enough holes. We'll turn round and face the water.

Dad with his moccasins and me with my sneakers.

Two feet apart.

Bent over.

Seagulls overhead.

A pair of sandpipers behind.

The wood slat basket between us.

Dad calls the basket a hod peck. Says H-O-D means to carry and peck is smaller than a bushel. And hes singing, *I love you a bushel and a peck. A bushel and a peck and a hug around the neck.*

I sing, *I love you. A* hod *and a peck and a hug around the neck.*

We laugh.

And we start digging.

Dad pushing the fork straight down. The steel sound in sand. Steel hitting rocks. Dad pulling on the handle. Dad rolling mud in front of me. Sometimes black muck stinking like egg rot with bloodworms and tiny crabs scattering like theyre sun afraid. But most times slate gray sand. Pure cleangrit. Smelling fresh lowtide. And all the time me picking those white shelled steamers from the gray grit and clay. Those fat little salt pies all swolled vanilla flesh with fresh brine. Closing to my fingers squeeze. Shooting off a gush-a-what goes to show you. Even a clam will fight when push comes to shove. Comes to scoop. Comes to toss. And another. And another. And if none. To the next hole and repeat. Till Dad and me are doing ditch. Two foot wide. Moving ahead of step. Pushing and pulling that hod slat peck. Digging again. Till we're tide edge out. Tired out. And now our backs to the bay going. Tide in. Till we're opposite the ditch we started with the Sowams between our feet and our slat peck packed pile top breaking neath the handle.

A hod peck of hard soft shell clams with a hour to show for our efforts.

Pruney carrying Rosses easel with the clamped on art painting. And Ross with his brushes and pallet heading back towards the puddingstone.

And Mom crossing from the rocks. Carrying a full slat of oystas. Joining us.

Mom and me in our short pants.

Dads longpant legs rolled high ankles and blue bandanna squareknot loose around his neck. No more singing about necks pecks and bushels. But instead singing *WestSideStory, Somethins comin. I dunno. What it is. But it is. Gonna be great.*

Back at the blanket. Mom says to Ross and Pruney, Before you boys leave. Lets all we're gonna need heaps-a-clambake rockweed.

So. With a few rolled dry burlaps. We head below the oystabeds. Down to the bigger rocks jutting above the incoming tide.

As we walk. Mom tells Pruney the squishing and slurping is from, Perrawinkles crawlin. Mussels clatchin. Glued barnacles. And she points.

Although theres broke shell everywhere under our sneakerfeet. I cant hear none of them shellfish on boulders. And although PruneyMendoza nods his head. He doesnt look to where Moms pointing. Pruney just keeps looking at Mom.

Moms face.

Moms eyes.

Mom tucking that dangling hair behind her ear.

Looking with wonder and amazement like he never before seen a woman.

And on a sudden I realize Pruney aint seeing our mom.

But his.

And seeing this makes me have a episode.

I sit.

While everyone gathers armloads of seaweed.

My head is spinning. For definite I am not having a plate in the head episode. Just a aching heart never before had. And I take a breath.

Pruney doesnt have nobody telling him about nature. About the little stuff thats around all the time. About the wind gods. Tautogs and choggies. Beachgrit and Sunrise. Figgy plum pudding rocks. Hah raws. And other funny words to make laughing happen.

Add an e.

I breathe and decide not to be telling anyone why my heart is hurting. And with my fingers do lotsa fat bud squeezing on the rockweed clusters. Some them swolled buds make a excellent snap sound. Or a pop bust. Mixing my tears with saltwater spray just like them buds will do when they get steamed in the fire and bathed their own brine juice on the clams potatoes sweetcorn and little buck worst sausages.

When Mom asks, You okay Jate? I say, You guys. In no time got three sacks-a-rockweed.

And each sack gets carried over someones shoulder but mine.

When theyre dropped at Dads feet back at the bake pit. Dad says Ross and Pruney need to get moving and I can walk as far as the footbridge with them. But hurry back to please help him set the bake.

At the footbridge the three of us once again stand at the bridge center piling and this time watch the incoming tide surge and little whirlpools and ever so long kelp streamers go back and forth back and forth in the current endless into the marsh towards MountHope with schools of minnows. A skuttle of rock crabs. Glimmers of blueshells. And a smack-a-jellies. Big ones. Little ones. Silent.

Pruney and Ross leave to do the paper route.

I hike back.

To the puddingstonespot.

Alone.

Dad has most of the hot coals raked puddingstone side of the bake pit. Moms got the clams and all the other foods in their own cheesecloth bags. Dad grabs a burlap sack. Holds one end and dumps the seaweed that immediate hisses sizzles and pops. Mom rakes it even over the hot cobbles which of course will become the food pile bottom. Both her and Dad start tossing the cheesecloth bags of clams. Buckies. Onions. Lopstas. Sweet corn and some links and chunks of shoodeez sausage. Mom spells C-H-O-U-R-I-C-O. Potatoes on top. Dad says because steam rises. Now Mom is tossing the next bag of rockweed and covering all the food and Dad is unfolding a canvas tarp. Hands me a corner. Dad takes two and Mom one. It billows and settles over the mound and white steam immediate rises from the sides. Venting. Dad and me start laying cool cobbles all around the mounds ring and pack heaps of wet sand to seal the steam. Air smells like burned hay or damp autumn falled leaves in a fire.

A rock explodes with a loud thud deep inside the hissing mound. Mom and Dad open a bottle of wine. And they sit on the blanket while I take another walk with my notebook. Is the PatienceIslandLighthouse still there? And what will I hear on the rocks of Montaup shores?

Im sitting lee side a boulder just above the rising tide. A fidgeting of plovers peck grit and snag a hermit crab. Those birds run circles happy they found something but dont quite know what to do. So they thrash and trill. Leap and screech.

The deep channel and dark current push just a few feet from shore with channel markers leaning with the incoming tide and both the wind and tide is solid from the south. Notus blowing hard. And seagulls high above whirling and diving and the rock is shelter from the warm bluster but all around waves rhythmroll and spraybreak the air.

Southwest is the lighthouse. To the northwest. Blocking Providence from MountHopeShores. Is RumstickPoint. But Mom always says, Nothin without Providence.

And Im not sure what she means. But. No matter where you stand at MountHopeShores. Best youll do seeing Providence is waiting for the black night. Watching how the city you cant see from here. Not fa nuthin. Lights up the northwest sky.

Before that sky show begins. Spine darter dancer. Plate in the head. Choggy. Good ear. Me. Gotta take a nap.

So back to Mom and Dad.

At the puddingstone blanket. Bake pit smoke and steam is huffing. Mom and Dad are wrapped together cozed in their spot. They been watching me my whole lollygagging way. And Dad says, Whats shakin bacon?

Im not bacon. Im Jate.

And Mom opens the blanket and says, Plenny-a-room Jate.

A steady wind blows ocean breeze cool.

Us three.

Nap.

The burned seaweed smell.

Canvas mixed with charcoals.

NarragansettBay.

Floating all around.

10
I Will Fight

The bluster of wind and the chug of MistaCoggs catboat.

And by the time he drops anchor and dingy rows to shore. The tide is higher. Sky dusk and the Notus south breeze sends thousands of beach fire sparks to the sky and Mom is hooded sweatshirt with long leg dungarees and flipflops and Dad is front zip windbreaker. Face and neck tanned. Green workpants. And a pair of black moccasins. Im plate in the head clear fog awake.

Ross and Pruney have returned with GilOwen whos parked his car across the railroad tracks. GilOwens brung along some of his SquarePeg nuthouse fruitcake tribe. Rizzdee friends. A goatee guy StevePaquin. Says hes from Utah. A state out west. And a wrist bangled gal. Veronica from TivertonRhodeIsland. Veronica looks like that Breakfast Tiffany gal on the cover of Moms book at home. And TivertonVeronicas wearing what GilOwen calls a Russian navy teeshirt. A dungaree jacket. And white pants and thin soled sandals. Her hair is real short and her neck is real long and aside from Mom. Veronica is the most bewdeeful woman ever. And she smells. Good too.

And Ross stands his easel at the edge of the blanket and GilOwen and Veronica. Fuss a bunch about Rosses art. Veronicas bangles jangling each time she points.

Pruney gives Dad a grocery bag and says, MistaSousa tol me this is for you.

Delicate. Dads fingers. Pulls from the bag. A small red lopsta. Holds it in his hand. And Dad says to Pruney, Wow.

And Pruney says, Four culls. Steamed a hour ago. Still warm and ready for eats. Just each missin a claw is all. MistaSousa says, Enjoy.

How wonderful, Mom says, Thank you Pedro. MistaSousa too.

Pruneys all big smiles busting proud.

Mom and TivertonVeronica give each other a hello hug.

GilOwen tells goateeguy StevePaquin, Jates a writer.

StevePaquin says, Cool man. Gotta read us sometimes some-a-your pages.

And StevePaquin pats my shoulder and raises his fist and says, Write on.

So I do.

And Mom and Veronica walk down to the shore.

When Dad and MistaCogg toss the cobbles from the tarp edge and they each grab a canvas corner and walk it back and uncover the bake pit and a big cloud of steam rises and a pile a dark brown withered rockweed and the clouds of smells are rolling while they rake and pull the cheese-cloth bundles and place them on the upturned groundcloth. Mom and Veronica return and Mom pours wine in a paper cup.

Theres clams and potatoes steaming. Dad cracking watermelon on the puddingstone and Ross and Pruney grab big pink hunks with their fingers and spit seeds by the shore. Veronica joins them and them three are laughing. I wanna be with her and them guys. But MistaCogg asks me to help him tong the oystas on the open fire. And MistaCoggs going on about how to know when the oysta is cooked and saying, Watch the spillin juices. Steamed flumes. The oystas skirt swellin in the shell.

But I wanna be spitting seeds with the guys and Veronica. And MistaCoggs going on about oysta cackles. Shells splitting. Burning seaweed. Lopstas. Steamers. Breaded wine soaked bass. Onions. Corn ears. Buckworst buckies. Im heave throwin more wood on the spent bake pit cobbles. And MistaCogg says, Place the logs or youll bruise the rocks. Who has newspaper? Lets get this fire blazin. And yes I'll have another Gansett. Please. Thankyou. And. Yourewelcome.

Smoked fish. Clams. And oystas.

And lotsa pablabborating.

MistaCogg taking tongs. Plucking a oysta direct off the fire. Blowing in his hand on the shell.

Opening the shell with his fingers and saying to Veronica, Smoked oysta belly. Cross between crisp bacon and goose liver pat tay.

And he tells the oysta, Time for us to talk-a-many things.

MistaCogg pitches that hot oysta flesh in Veronicas lipstick mouth.

And Veronicas eyes are closed and she goes, Yum. Her hands on Pruneys shoulder and in his curl blonde hair. She hugs Pruney. Wish she were doing that to me.

Pruney got that big Pruney smile and Dad gives him a plate and Moms making sure Pruney has a whole lopsta. But Pruneys plate is piled with breaded bass. Red potatoes. Buckies. And a small cup of melted butter.

Pruneys telling Veronica, My brother Dagama. He got a book says Pilgrims werent first here. Was the Portuguese and they got their own stone bigger than Plymouth called Dite n Rock with higher gliffic piture writin all over it just Wompagansett Indians killed em.

When Pruney says Wompagansetts. GilOwens mouth is full of steamers and onion. Plate in one hand. Molasses brownbread in another. And GilOwen bout near chokes laughin and when he final swallows. He says, Wompagansetts? Never heard that before.

Shoving his lopsta meat from the tail shell, Pruney says, Thems the tribes lived here with the Pokonokets and the Pequags and the Purigrims.

And Veronica winks Pruney and asks, You mean the Narragansett. Wampanoag. And Pilgrims?

And I gotta addmit. And dont know why. But first time since I knowd Pruney I wish he'd keep stuffing his mouth. Who ever heard something so foolish as Wompagansetts?

Pruney. Doing his yap says, Same difference.

Veronica says to Pruney, Then you must be Portalian?

Pruney says, Am not. Im Portuguese.

GilOwen says, Portuguese. Italian. Same difference.

Pruney does a necksnap and throws GilOwen a look.

GilOwen says, Narragansett. Wampanoag. Both names mean something special and distinct.

Veronica says, Narragansett. People on the FarPoint.

GilOwen says, Wampanoag are DawnsChildren. Those of FirstLight.

Dad says, Noble Indians. Helped the Pilgrims.

The Pilgrims helped emselfs, interrupts MistaCogg.

GilOwen says, RogerWilliams cashpaid the Narragansett.

But cash played the Wampanoag, says MistaCogg. R Williams dint know his arse from his shinbone. And if ya ask me. Which ya dint but Im gonna tell anyway. Mista RahjaWilliams wasnt a Christian do gooda. But a Jewfool bastid.

GilOwen says, Must you be so? Off center?

And GilOwen brushes butter on a steaming ear of native sweetcorn.

MistaCogg dips a lopsta tail. Bites a chunk. Licks his thumb and says,

Uncentered my flat flagstone arse. Wheres my brung rum?

GilOwen says, Jack. Youre shut off.

But CapnJack waves off GilOwen and says, RahjaWilliams let all those Jewbastids inna Newport which they woulnt-a-come inna if it warent for Williams actual buyin land from the Narragansett which pissed off Philip cause he was the only smart one in the whole gottdamn colony and Philip knew he had got screwed when everyone else thought KingPhilip had himself a prize deal.

And UtahRizzdee friend StevePaquin asks, KingPhilip? Dont you mean KingGeorge? Englands KingGeorge the Groovy Third?

An ocean away and a groovy hundred years off, smirks MistaCogg, No. I mean Philip. Phil PrettyBoy Wampanoag. Heap big medicine. Pometacom. Feathers in his hair. Me take um scalp. Metacomet. Philip.

GilOwen. Shaking his head. Hands a beer to his Rizzdee pal.

Pruney sits between Veronica and Steve.

Mom wraps her arms around Ross.

I wanna sit the other side of Veronica but Dad pulls me close.

The smoked brine smell. Pine trees and salt air. Butter and beer.

GilOwen says, The king to whom we are referring is Philip. Native son of ChiefMassasoit who aided the pilgrims during their first Plymouth years.

StevePaquin asks, Son of a chief? Woulnt that make him a prince? And how did an Indian prince get a name like Philip?

How. Indeed, says CapnJack.

Must you Jack? says GilOwen.

And Mom says, Palabboratin asquantum. Lie see um. Chautauqua. Bardenay. Call it whachya may. Story time has just begun.

I gotta addmit. Mom is good with them big words. And from Veronicas side Pruney is looking proud of Mom too.

Mom says, Metacomet was Philips Indian name. But bear in mind. RhodeIsland was named afta the Greek mythical Isle-a-Rhodes by the Italian explorer Veranzano. So when the English settle a hundred years afta Veranzano. They called Massasoits son. Metacomet. KingPhilip. As in KingPhilip of Rhode Isle. Massadonia. Its sheer ridicule.

GilOwen leaned close to me and spelled, M-A-C-E-D-O-N-I-A.

Then. Sitting up. GilOwen said, Quite fashionable. White men condescending to red. Did the same to the black. Own a slave. Name him Pompey. Caesar. Cassius. Or Brutus. Et tu?

Indeed indeed, says MistaCogg. And he raises his beer to Gil.

Dad tosses wood on the fire. Clears his throat. Says, Bunktown. North. Up river.

MistaCogg whistles and says, SarahHaags. Boardinhouse. Bore dello.

All the adults laugh.

Not Ross. PruneyMendez. And me.

But. As soon as Dad says, PhilipMetacom begun war with a Bunktown raid.

GilOwen, says, The whiteman began the war stealin Indian land.

MistaCogg said, Trans send dental noble savage crap. Plain and simple. Metacom not humble like his father Massasoit. Philip was full-a-himself. Vain. PhilipMetacom got what he deserved. Theres plenny-a-proof.

GilOwen said, Proof is for fools who cant handle doubt.

Everyone got quiet.

StevePaquins arm rested on Veronicas shoulder. And her hands touched his.

MistaCogg stood. Swagged a drink from a rum bottle. Palm of hand wiped his mouth. And passed the bottle to Dad.

MistaCogg started telling, Proud Metacomet had an Indian advisor. Sassamon. A friend to the whiteman. A convert to Christ. What the colonist called a prayin Indian. There were quite a few actually. And this Christian convert Wampanoag Sassamon. Advised Metacomet to keep the whitemans peace. Was the beginnin-a-the end. PhilipMetacom turned to that Christian Indian. That advisin friend. And with a tomahawk. Dashed the Indians baptized brains. Then Philip bathed himself in dead Sassamons blood.

The kids. For goodness sake, says GilOwen.

MistaCogg looks to Mom and Dad.

Mom tucks hair behind her ear.

Dad. His eyes a dark silent shine.

Nods.

Dad nods. And Dad says, Go ahead Jack.

MistaCogg continues, PhilipMetacom along the banks-a-the KickamuitRiver. Swansea road just above BunktownBridge. Rampaged past Barneys Old Providence RoadHouse. Up to SarahHaags. Killed eight settlers. Eight. And piked their colonial heads n limbs. Next he sent a messenger to a CaptainBenjaminChurch.

Philips message?

I will fight until I have no country.

CaptainChurch. With Bristol militiamen. Lowes. Fowls. Smutts. And Graves. A fine bunch-a-lowlife gallants. And with another Wampanoag Christian convert JohnTauntonAlderman. Brother of Sassamon. A pathfinder. They track coldblooded Philip above these Bristol shores. The Indian scout. Mind you. Brother-a-murdered Sassamon. Leadin the militia. Sneaks upon KingPhilipMetacomet in campfire pow wow.

Raise their ten guns.

Blast.

Not a single bullet hits startled Philip.

Church commands, Kill that bastid now.

And with the one remaining loaded gun.

ChristianWampanoagJohnTauntonAlderman.

Brother of murdered Sassamon.

Fires.

And on August 12. 1676.

Three hundred years ago.

Out from under the gunpowder smoke.

The charging KingPhilipMetacom. Metacomet of the Wampanoag.

Falls dead.

MistaCogg continued, Some-a-the soldiers. Oh they had a good time violatin Philips body. Kickin. Spittin. Singin *What cheer netop?* The very words spoken when the WestBay natives provided Williams providential haven from his Boston exile. What cheer netop? What is the news? What is the news good friend?

Next the miltia hangs Philip from a Montaup MountHope tree.

The soldiers spill his guts to the ravens. Coyotes. Seagulls. And wolves.

An Indian quarters the carcass and each bloodied rack is sent. With scriptured parchment. From one colony to the other.

Philips head remains trophy piked for twenty years at the hallowed gates of Plymouth.

The sanctifying verse? *Genesis.* Chapter 14. Verse 20.

Blessed be God who has delivered your enemies unto your hands.

For a long while we sit.

Pruneys close to Veronica. Her arms on his shoulders.

Ross sitting by her side.

But for some reason I keep thinking about enemies I dont got.

Enemies delivered to my hands.
And eecoodeesh. I plate in the head dont know who they could be.
Dad adds wood to the fire.
Lotsa quiet. Fog rolling in. Bells in the buoys distant.
At last Rizzdee friend StevePaquin says, Thats quite a story.
GilOwen says, Spun spindrift on the open ocean.
And MistaCogg snaps his fingers. Says, Yeah man. Can you dig it?
And cracks himself another beer.

11
BorkumRiff

MistaCoggs Port n Starboard Shop was weather beaten shakes with all colored pot buoys hanging ever which where. A claw anchor grabbed at the middle of the raised flowerbed and a brickwalk led southside to the entrance. And as soon as you walked inside that door. There was on the wall. Another MissusCogg embroidree. Or maybe it was LydiaRogers?

Scout sees warning; Safe harbor in a grove
Sailor in danger; Seeks comfort from the cove.

Although Mom said the shack was now a safehaven CapeCod cracker-box. Before Ross and me was Beachgrit and Sunrise. The building used to be a two car grarage. With doors that opened wide. Swinging to the street greeting no one.

Mom says what MistaCogg did was to take down those swingdoors. And in their place. He framed walls and a large window jam into what he put the front store window with sixteen individual panes of glass. Mom said it was a old fashion store window. Like the shops of NewBedford and Plymouth. Said it was, Quaint.

MistaCogg said, Quaint my arse. Its what was layin round the salvage yard. And if a fella cant make do. He ends up shiddoo.

That always got Ross and me cracking up with Mom saying, Come on boys. MistaCapnJackCoggs in one-a-his moods.

And if we were heading to the beach. MistaCapnJack would toss us a wink and a warning like, Dont get too much sun. Or if we were returning he'd always say something to Mom like, Whats ClaraLee Rossi fixin supper for her boys?

What was funny about that question wasnt CapnJacks different way of saying stuff. It was the fact that after MissusCogg died. Whatever Mom

was fixing us for supper. She was also fixing for CapnJack. Because Ross
or me. We always had to carry down BaggyWrinkleLane a serving of spa-
ghetti. A bowl of soup. A dish of salad. A sausage or two. A stuffed pepper.
Or native sweet corn on the cob.

Lotta times. When Mom had to go shopping. Or if the dredge was in
and Dad was home and needed to catch up on his sleeping. Mom would
say, Go check JackCogg and see if he needs help in the shop. And Id ride
my bike up WaterStreet and sit with the old bird watching to make sure he
dint hurt himself. Just like Mom told me I needed should do.

This one time when I got there. MistaCogg was out front in his pansy
bed sticking a old piece a long snout driftwood into the ground. I said,
Whats up CapnJack?

He said, Heard a commotion. Came out just in time to see this Australian auhnteata messin with the flowers.

A auhnteata? Whats a auhnteata?

Ya know em creatures that eats bugs in the ground.

Ya mean ant eaters?

Yeah. But this ones got more a British oxccent.

And MistaCogg did a right hand sissy wave. Left hand on his hip.
Kinda missy. Prettfunny. Gotta addmit.

This other one time. CapnJacks shop. And hes top on a leaning ladder
just above the front window. Hes lag bolting a big oar by its throat to the
shack. On the blade part of the paddle is the woodburn words. Jacks Oar
House. When I asked him if hes gonna now start selling oars instead of
wood whales and harpoons?

He says, Naw. Just doin up a new sign.

Whats wrong with your Port n Starboard transom sign?

CapnJack come down that ladder. And looks at the transom sign thats
hanging off one of his harpoons and CapnJack says, The way its hangin.

Whats wrong with the way its hangin?

And CapnJack says, Catawompus. Should be a breachin whale. White.
Stead-a-just a ol transom hangin laz horizontakal. We're talkin matchin
the Port n Starboard sign so it becomes MobyDicks angry sister. A feared
spermaspagghetti. Another great white whale. Boldness. The sign gotta
hang white. With black letters. Maybe gold. If its gonna get lady customers. As-a-late theres just been too many gents. Buoys. And what Im chasin
is gulls. Gals. And for gulls a buoys gotta project a different altitude. Been
thinkin about closin down and remodelin. Get out the whazzit business
altogether and open up instead a combination fish market n launda matt.

Whaddaya think-a-that?

Well heck. If ya want more gulls all ya gotta do is feed em. Ya know gulls eat anythin. And if ya dont want buoys why ya keep makin hangin and decoratin?

MistaCogg bites hard on his pipe stem and says, Im talkin male and female here and further more yuh soundin more like a gottdamm NewYawk tourist ever day. Fishermen dont hang buoys for decoratin. Its for dryin em waterlogged suckas out.

But these here have never been in the water.

Thats a secret just tween you and me. And kept secrets is what makes kept friends more better kept.

And that one sticks all over me for awhile. But then Im figuring fine by me. But why the need for hush hush? He makes them plain in the shop front of everyone for all eyes. Dont he?

My favorite times for being with MistaCogg were Sunday afternoons when some rich guy that just moved NewYorkCity to Barrington pulls up in a Mercedes too near the pansies and begins proper improper asking MistaCogg. Excuse me. Sir? I just bought a cottage on the Quee-quee-shan. Want to do some fishing. What might you be getting for your lobster cages?

The guys saying lobster instead of lopsta and that all too proper incorrect way a talking about the river and what MistaCapnJack calls The Impliments-a-Fishin would just set MistaCoggs upper lip to trembling. Not to mention the Mercedes what MistaCogg said was a sea hunt hair too near the flowers. And just what the heck is a sea hunt hair? Something MistaCogg says all the time. Especial when hes measuring wood hes about to cut on his tablesaw. MistaCogg being MistaCogg. MistaCoggs working. Thirty seconds. His lip fore he answers this guy about lopsta cages Jack wants to tell him aint cages but pots. Maybe swig his just cracked pony bottle of beer. Tilt rickety in his canvas back chair. Cross his bone legs all tight locked at the crotch. Bare ankles. Old biscuits. Then Jack might take off his head his Greek sailor cap and scratch. Put his Greek hat back on adjusting at the visor. Final. MistaCogg might say something like, Its not a lopsta cage. Sah jellyfish. A jellyfish cage. This weeks a sale. Low. Real low. Cause. Im gonna be hightide honest witchyah here like I was chunkin for bass. The gottdamm things dont work. All eyre good for is a piece-a-plate glass atop. Which I got plenty out over round back. Plate glass is. Make yuhself a coffeetable. I suppose ya could keep in ya cagetable a pet lopsta. Or two. That is-a-course. Only if theyre the outta water kind.

Everyone would get a laugh.

And CapnJack would get a sale.

Plate in the head is nothin, MistaCogg once told me. Unfortunate? Yes. Stupid? No. Kicked in the head by a pigeon? Much worse.

MistaCogg said, Fer chrice sakes. Four. You wuh four. The world. Way things work. Hows and whys-a-it all.

MistaCogg said, Show me the shame-a-that.

MistaCogg said, Youre Sweet Jaysus lucky a plate in yuh head and not a fetch-a-gottdammed pigeon toes.

MistaCogg said, Youre plenty smart enough to see the difference.

MistaCogg said, Take yuh dog bite. Mos-a-the time yuh average dog is smarter than any person. Anyone. Theres no shame in a dog bite cause yuh dog got a way-a-gettin his way. And a cat scratch? Hell. Mos cats smarter than ten people. Sneaky too. Same with yuh bee. And yuh bee sting. Bees are nasty. Crafty? Yes. Way crafty. Hornets? No shame in a hornet bite neitha. Hornet got the devil. Why a body cant hardly do nothin gainst a hornet. Wasp. Cat or dog. Bee that is out to get ya.

But yuh pigeon. A pigeon. Foolish. Lazy. Noisy too. Not like yuh pigeons gonna sneak up on ya with all its constant pigeon sound-a-looka-da-coo looka-da-coo looka-da-coo. See? Noisy. Who but a fool. A gottdamm fool. Sgonna let a pigeon walk up to im and kick im in the head? Yet people do all-a-the time. Everday. Eyup. Lotsa stupid people. Pigeonkicked. Dont have sense to know. Dont have pride for shame.

MistaCogg said, Worse thing than bein pigeonkicked was gull shit to the brain. And Jack almost never said shit. Usually shite. Like the way he said arse. Always arse.

MistaCogg said, Yuh ordnary person was pigeonkicked. But yuh fancypants la dee da knowledgeiser? Yuh sanctimonious preacher? And yuh career hound politician?

MistaCogg said, Those fellas was gull shites to the brain and those guys dint have sense enough to wipe it from their heads.

Said, Most those preachers and politicians wore their gull shite like a badge and were always spectin someone to say, Thats a might smart badge ya got there.

And so shiny too.

One time CapnJack was out front his Oar House. Setting shop the way he always did.

Hanging pot buoys.

Stacking lopsta pots.

Displaying harpoons.

PassabyEyeCatchas was how he said it.

Scour us up some business. Wink.

Third week of June. Same week LilMush got saved.

Morning. Seagulls circling overhead.

Straight out the sky. A gull turd. Splat. MistaCoggs right Topsider deckshoe.

Little toe. A clam neck. Poking through the busted seam of his usual no socks.

Jaysus H. White shite, says MistaCogg.

Says it plain like hes doing a nursery rhyme been in his head all his life.

Shoe and toe both shite covered white. Bit-a-yellow. Some green. Little glumps.

CapnJack pulls out his red rag bandanna. Workjacket pocket. Blows his nose.

Wipes clean his shoe. Then works nice his clamtoe too. Folds the red rag bandanna and puts it back into his jacket once again. Then Mista-Cogg. He looks at me and says, Howd that gull know to find my brains?

And thats whats best about MistaCogg. CapnJack. Crazed. Sorta. Always saying crazed things. About people most all the time.

But Mom says, If you listen real careful. MistaCogg isnt talkin crazed. MistaCogg isnt talkin people. JackCoggs talkin himself. Him. What he is. Who he is. Us. Everybody. Her chestnut burgundy hah raws twinkles. Mom says, Who we are to all and each and everyone to one another.

This one time. Wind and rain. First week of September. Stahmy aftanoon is how MistaCogg said it. Then added, A Bremuda Tropicana.

I just got finished the paper route with Pruney who then went straight to Sousas and Ross to the SquarePeg. So GilOwen could come to the Oar-House and take a JackCogg tea break. MistaCogg had been carving pot buoys all afternoon and the smell of fresh cut wood was the first thing hit me when I walked through the door. Maybe not a customer though.

For a customer. Maybe it wouldnt be the smell but the sights. The foot pushed lath on the drawshave horse. The woodcurls and pinechips thick to the floor. Or the bacongrease splattered wall above the Franklin. Or the cast iron skillet and the spatula dirty with Kenyon cornmeal crusted flip end spade.

And then the smell of CapnJacks tobacco and late afternoon Johnny-cakes and fried bologna sitting a sop of maple syrup. Vermont honey. Or the pie plate covered pissbucket MistaCogg emptied only when the pie plate was floating. Those might be what would shake a new customer first. But me? I was used to those all the time smells. But it was new cut wood grabbed me all the time first. Smell of forests. Smell of imagined camping. Being in the woods. Loved that smell best.

Then of course. The smell of JackCoggs smoking pipes. He smoked pipes all the time. And he about near owned two dozen. Briarburls carved rootwood. Or mirror shums for ones made from sea foam turned stone. But his very favorite. He said. Was the all American MizzOarRee Mirror-Shums. M-I-S-S-O-U-R-I M-E-E-R-S-C-H-A-U-M-S. Everybody else just called corncobs. But he called them classics, Apple pie America and cheapa than a good date.

Not too quite so sure what he meant. But. Whenever he mentioned corncobs. He called them MissouriMeerschaums.

And the tobacco he smoked. Borkum Riff. It come in a plastic pouch with a sailing ship picture on it. And CapnJack always puffing away one pipe or another. But. The wonderful smell. Something like what I imagined the combine of pine needles and ocean fog. Was always Borkum-Riff.

So. This rainy day. Early September airwarm. And raincool. The wind. Thickbalm. Sky blacks and grays. Some purple. Steel lavenders. Yellows hints and blues. The dark sky summer storms made the Sowams green greener. And more richer. Loved this weather best. On the shelf. Mista-Coggs books all lined straight above the scrimshaw case. *Idylls of the King. Last of the Mohicans. The Brothers Karamazov. For Whom the Bells Toll. Call Me Brick. The Sea Wolf.* And the *MobyDick* I take down to look at the blockprint pictures. And I for real like those blockprint pictures lots. Excepting for the way they make CapnAhab with no beard. Anyone whos seen the movie knows CapnAhab gotta have a beard. And I put the book down and start on my plate in the head writing exercises.

Ever since my. Eight years ago. Plate in the head truck accident. GilOwen he keeps on me about writing to make my memory better. He checks my spelling. Not to make correct because. Hes all the time. Votecha de raggazzi. But he wants to keep things readable and GilOwen goes on about how the printing press ruined it for twelve year old guys like me. Because good spellers get report card A's while bad spellers write books. And no idea what he means. And while writing. Who should the only person in all the world of WaterStreet come passing but dandy GilOwen. Handsome. Mom would say, As a October rose in springtime. Whatever that means. But. No matter of my ignorant. Right off I know the guy is GilOwen because the flash of his yellow slicker. And GilOwens peeling leaves off the window he raps smiles hi at me. But I just nod and keep on writing because he'll wanna check when he walks soon through the door. And without even looking or hearing the thing open. Hes in because bay rum cologne is everywhere. Bay rum. The wood chips. Bay rum. The piss bucket. Bay rum. The blackskillet bacongrease and Johnnycake burn. Bay rum. Floating over everything. Giving all a glorious aroma. Taking away the stale.

GilOwen says, Its some rain. Is the crazy coot outside?

In the back, I say.

And then GilOwens immediate over my shoulder looking at my sketchpad. Checking my writing. Telling about Missouri Meerschaum spelling. Careful getting raindrips to the floor and not me. And from under his parka he takes out two record albums. Some guy sitting on a curbstone looking like he just asked a question and hes waitin for a answer. Big hair. Cool blue shirt. Pink flower print.

BobDylan, says GilOwen.

And even though GilOwen is a old guy. He and his swish friends listen to all kinds of music. Especial anything gets played at one of the Newport festivals which GilOwen every summer goes to. The jazz. The folk. The opera. He and his Rizzdee pals love that stuff and they play records from those festivals at the SquarePeg all the time.

But. I gotta addmit. MistaCogg. He just tolerates anything someone listening to as long as theres booze. And probbly thats why he has a record player. Not because of music. But because the drinking always goes on around it.

So. GilOwen blows off sawdust all over MistaCoggs Victrola record player in the corner and the first thing I hear is the needle down scratch sound then its a drum crack. Then a organ roll and *Once upon a time ya dressed so fine ya threw the bums a dime in your prime didnt you?* And everybody loves that song thats on the radio constant. And I say, Tell again about the harmonica in Newport?

GilOwens casual says, People around us booing Dylan. Yet he comes back and says, Someone got and E? And guy right next me hollers, I do. And throws it to Dylan on stage. Who catches it and sings *Tambourine Man* using the harmonica of the guy right next to me. Cool huh?

And I say, Yeah sure. Youbetcha.

GilOwen. Eyes a sparkle raindrops on his no rim glasses. Changes the record to BobDylan sitting front of a fireplace with a red dress lady on the cover. While putting the first album back in its sleeve GilOwen asks me, What are you writing about?

Pot buoys. And what CapnJack has tol me bout em.

GilOwen is glasses off and squinny eyes and sleepy looking. And wiping them glasses one lens at a time dry with his white handkerchief. Then dry glasses. Big eyes back on his face again. And hes over my shoulder reading aloud my wrote writing—*A sixas what MistaCogg calls the six by six beam he firms in the vice then cuts his blocks for and axe hack. Then a lave shave. Each buoy then whittled in the grip to sich and such. Most lookin like the pin head of a drownin drunk. Then coded with a coat. White base usual. A strip stripe. Ringin round the posy.*

One green. Two red.
Or two red. One green.
One yellow. One blue.
Maybe a stripe and a dot.
Or a dot and a squiggle.
A bloodworm here.
And starfish there.

GilOwen says, This is good Jate. But its V-I S-E not vice.

And remember your "Gs." Your narrative I-N-G.

As for pot buoys. The colors and designs of each depend on one of two codes. First being the family tradition. A coat of arms for lopster men. Second being more important than the first. Captain Jacks weather code.

And I ask, Weather code? Whats that?

GilOwen smiles toothy oysta pearls and spells W-H-E-T-H-E-R or not Jack is in the chowda. Or more to the point, whether or not the chowda is in Jack. You know. B-W squared. Beer. Wine and whiskey. And GilOwen puts his thumb to his mouth. Pinkafinger sticking out. Does glug glug glug.

A plate in the head is not easy. Im glad GilOwens here. Helping me understand. As CapnJack always says, The poetry and words-a-the world and how it all together happens.

And while I write. And BobDylan sings. GilOwen is for the stove. Poker and stirring. Folding those coals. Tossing splits of fir. Chunking up a few fire licked knots. Yellow red blue and orange. Glow sip tongues.

So. By the time CapnJacks back in with his six by four board now a fourteen incher vise tight and sawed off from the beamer. BobDylans way past *Maggies Farm* and GilOwens got the fire going good and hes already relaxing with the *MobyDick* RockwellKent block prints what I before put down. And a burgundy. And what with the rain outside and the wind whipping white caps on the Sowams. We are as MistaCogg says, About as cozy as wet rats in a stateroom bilge enjoyin tea with the Astas and the Vandabilts ceptin they would-a-thrown this nasil whinin Jew boy out on his himey hinny arse bone.

And MistaCogg is reading the backside jacket of *Highway 61 Revisited.*

GilOwen flipping *MobyDick* says, Just paid six dollars for that record. And that album will help change the world.

Dylan blue and pink. Big hair. Waiting for a answer. Staring at me.

MistaCogg puts it with his other records. Cracks open what he calls a pony Gansett and MistaCogg is rough shaping with a hachet his vise gripped pine loaf on the seat end of the shave horse and for a long time its just the sounds of chipping at the wood block. GilOwen turning pages. Rain. Wind. Fire in the stove. And BobDylan. Starting and stopping and laughing. And starting again real cool harmonica and something about riding on the Mayflower and CapnArab being stuck on the whale what gets CapnJack off the shave horse pouring a slug of brandy from his sea chest cut glass sniffers. Pours one for Gil too. Turning down the Victrola low so as to talk over the Dylan doing *MobyDick* that MistaCogg calls cat-o-wall.

C-A-T-E-R-W-A-U-L. GilOwen says to me. Then says, Forget it.

MistaCoggs red in the face. And I can tell. Dog tooth drunk. Or snail lipped with a attitude the way GilOwen sometimes says it. And drunken MistaCogg he pumps the foot push for a lave shave. Snugs tight the handle on the vise grip holding the pine beam. Then stops on abrupt and says, Hell. I guess thats the Jew boy way-a-lookin at *MobyDick* but any Gott damn pigeonkicked fool like me can see straight off taint a book atall about whalin. Its a red herrin ruse about Sodmites. Ya got seamen without a A semen and that aint no haccident. Then ya got yuh heathen redskin bein a Sodmite agent-a-the devil. Out sellin his Sodmite head. Seducin a God fearin Christian. Sleepin in the same bed given to im by anotha Sodmite named Peter. Talk about yuh blatant obvious. And. Not ta say. But. He even uses the word married dont he? This Sodmite Queerqueg aint no ordnary Injeein. He can wield his Sodmite hahpoon so it seeducks the Quaka ship owna. Then ya got all these Smite sailors on board lovin each otha with their hands all squeeze squeeze squeeze squeeze. Lotioned up in the spermaspaghetti vat-a-the lubricant-a-life.

And GilOwen. Not blinking a eye. Is hard staring MistaCogg who got his hand wrap round the neck of his brandy bottle slip his fingers back and forth over the throat.

And MistaCogg continues, Then-a-course ya got the Smite dibble hisself. CapnAhab. Blasphemizin baptism by forgin the phallus ultimate in blood then makin the sailor Smites a alligence to live and die questin the holy grail-a-all grails. The phallus-a-god. Mobys. Need I say? Dick. Ya can do the learniments-a-knowledgizin all ya want. But it haint no haccident Melville died a paupa. And furtha some more. Yuh think that preface in token to Hawthawn was on the up and up? At the end whaddawe get? Ahab a demon-a-the one eyed pants cod. And Ishmael too. Saved by the coffin-a-Peter. Yes. Yes. Its for real Queerquegs coffin. But remember the early scene when Ishmael all a-scat-a-Queerqueg cries out. PeterCoffin save me. Peter. Which. Beside the pigeonkicked obvious. Means rock. And this rock dont sink. Its perpetual up and neva goin down which is what every Sodmite wants for the act what dares not speak its name. And now Ive done my drama which youll soon collapse as foul and the great sea remains in shrouds. Five thousand years ago. Till Rachel finds her notha orphan. Ergo. The dibble in us all.

GilOwen never once looks up from his RockwellKent stays his eyes looking at them and says, Sometimes Jack I swear to God. Youre far more than a pigeonkicked bubble off plum. Make sure you add a B so its plumb Jate, GilOwen says to me.

Then back to CapnJack. GilOwen says, Jacko it aint the things ya dont know what scares me. Its the things ya know for sure what aint so.

Oh? says CapnJack. Me ya question. But yuh Newport Dylan dahlin ass? For that ya give money? That Jew boy bastid aint music. Im glad they pulled the plug on im. They shoulda throwd the gottdammed switch too.

They dint pull the plug. Only booed.

Boo the Jew did ya? Wup-de-do-boo-hoo.

Talk sense man. Must you always jabberwok?

Me? Ott-a-the gam my Sodmite friend. The ott-a-the gam.

Theres no art in it. Youre cruel Jack. Out and out vicious.

Im also the way God attended.

So be it.

Gottdamn Sodmite.

Like GilOwen just been stabbed. GilOwen sits straight. Pushes his no rim glasses from the bottom of his nose to the top. Stands. Eyes like they seen KingPhilips ghost. Puts down the RockwellKents. And GilOwen walks out the Port n Starboard Shop.

And was GilOwen gonna cry? I dint say nothing cause just wasnt sure the why of such a thing.

MistaCogg was. No more in his hands a pot buoy. But instead. Straight on painting the black on a wood harpoon. So I asked, Whyd GilOwen leave so all on a sudden? And whats Sodmites?

CapnJack said, Time to get goin and folks from the city-a-Sodom.

But GilOwens from Sowams. And Ishmael NewBedford. Isnt Queequeg Hawaii?

MistaCogg said, Ishmael was Manhattan. And Queequeg the isle-a-Coco Loco. Somewhere South Pacific.

I said, Well. Is Sodom Coco Loco?

MistaCogg said, No. Bible. But not anymore cause God destroyed it.

Why?

Oh. Cause.

Why, Oh cause?

Cause-a-stuff that flies in the face-a-nature.

Stuff? What stuff?

Stuff stuff, and aint it time for ya to be goin too? Meetin yuh brotha for home?

And when pedaling away on my bike. A mental in my metal was to be asking Ross and PruneyMendez about Sodmites. If anyone knew about Sodmites it would be one of them guys.

And if Pruney dint know Ross would for sure.

Between my twin brother Ross and our good pal PruneyMendez.

Them two knew everything.

And then some.

12

SarahHaagsBunktown

SarahHaagsBunktown was above the OldProvidence and SwanseaRoad junction direct below Route 6. Just past the hanging stop light everyone said was more long on yellow than red and green. And although Mista-Cogg said SarahHaags was the place where KingPhilip piked the colonist heads. MistaCogg also said, SarahHaag dint come to the place till a hundred years after. A good thing too cause she probbly woulda been witch burned. And truth be known. The true cause-a-the traffic between those two streets was more due SarahHaags bein filled with the most. Once upon a time. Roughest toughest seamen. Slavetraders. Pirates. And the honest workin women in all-a-Sowams. EastBay. And West.

MistaCogg said, If this was Europe. They indeed woulda beamed the red lights in her honor. But it bein a tide Puritanical backwater. The yellow light was longated timewise to a caution for all who entered. Were about to enter. Or mere pass by.

And not to say. But.

Except for them chopped off heads. What was MistaCogg talking about?

According to MistaCogg, Those business days were long gone.

Leastaways at SarahHaags.

First fact of the matter, MistaCogg said, Was business. And that I could understand because if it werent for the NorthEnd paper route business of EastEnd PruneyMendez. WillieDunne. LilMushGahdoo. Zeebo. Ross and me. We never woulda got to sail to SarahHaags.

Second fact being. Pruney introduced us something from SarahHaags we liked a lot. Something we couldnt stand life without. When we got the sight. The feel. The smell of these somethings. We just had to have. No matter how many we already had. More. MistaCogg said Pruney put a spell on us and that spell was monkeys on our backs.

Dont know what MistaCoggs monkey spells of Pruney had to do with anything. But do know. Pruney never give us monkeys. And he never taught us spelling neither. But once he give us the thing he give us. These things got firm a hold on us.

And. Not ta say. But. Maybe that hold is what backmonkeys was.

For a while. These backmonkeys was the most incredible things we ever owned. Square. Rectangle. Gold. White. Red. Bronze. Smooth. Flip open lids that was always attached. And on that attached lid was always bewdeeful fancy blackprinted words. And some surfaced raised gold coins. Like the coins was 3D.

The things what Im talking about is cigar boxes.

King Edward Imperials. DutchMasters CoronaDeLuxe. PhilliesBlunt. TampaNugget. WhiteOwl Perfectos. Rose-O-Cuba. ElProducto. HarvesterHorse. And Slendorita.

For us. These boxes were instant valuable. Treasures.

Its kind of weird if you think about it because. As Mom said, Into these treasures went our treasures. Prized cats eye marbles. Swirled patterned chestnuts. Any Topps CivilWar card. Nuts. Screws. Washers. Bolts. And jewry. Rings. Rubies. Diamonds. Broke blueglass. And quahogshell blue wampum.

Kept money in a cigar box was way more impressive than anything envelope deposited in the OldStoneSavingsBank. Especial flattened railroad track coins and a dead dried prayingmantis too.

A good cigar box. When it shut. Closed tight. And always made a soft clup sound. A huffahish whisper that said, Anything saved in these walls is safe. That secureness come with a tobacco hint never like threw away actual cigars smell. But always a aroma making our room go to heaven.

How we got our first cigar boxes at SarahHaags was. WillieD. Zeebo. LilMush. Ross and me. Was doing chalk drawings on the cement patio piazza outside our front door when PruneyMendezMendoza finishing up his paper route come by our house.

A midSeptember chockablock low moon tide rising fast. And we. Being so fixed in our making patio piazza chalk art. Dint even notice till pointing Pruney give a, Eecoodeesh. Looka that high risin surge. Sure hope the boat is tied real good.

That gets us to the bottom of KellyStreet and the marsh is so full of water the sogg all disappeared beneath a swelling KingPhilipsCove. Only thing above the highwater. Tips and strands a cord grasses.

Dads boat. Floating. Its bowline staked in the saltmarsh firm. And that boat clovehitch tied good going no where not too fast.

Except Pruney. He got big ideas.

Its September autumn in the air day. Ross says, Cobalt skies with a few puff clouds. Just the way a Saturday should be.

Pruneys talking on pirates. *The Boy and the Pirates.* The movie playing at the LyricTheater that he wants to see it but dont have time to because Pruney always working. And anyways. Mushy. Who seen it. Says its a stupid movie and nowhere near as good as what he seen on WJAR TV TomMorgans Dialing for Dollars One O'Clock Matinee. The movie *TreasureIsland.* But. Pruney keeps on his blather. And Mushy. Zeebo. WillieD. Ross. And me. Get into the boat.

Pruney says hes untying. Unlashes the clovehitch but drops the line because he trips in the sogg and goes face down into the water and the wind blows the boat out.

Ross grabs the oar and tries to pole but it gets bladestuck mud.

And Pruney. Back on his feet. Dives in after but once hes got the oar unstuck he cant swim to the boat cause now we're fast halfway out the cove.

As MistaCogg later tells, Five guys standin in a boat catchin the NotusZephyr are more like sails than pirates.

Drenched Pruneys back on land running crazed and dropping to his knees smacking his head yelling, Eecoodeesh MotherMary-a-God please help me. Call the police. Call the fire department. Call the rescue squad. Please. Please. Please AhSacredLady help me.

VirginMaryMother of God must be busy and not hearing Pruneys sogged prayer because we're still floating further up the cove but no more any which way the wind blows because now we're pulled firm and current caught.

Moms not home.

And MistaCoggs not home.

GilOwens not at home.

Pruney jumps on his bike and does a dash up KellyStreet.

And Im plate in the head buzz.

The seashell sound.

Jellyfish sting in my arm.

Theres no seashell but that shell sea sound louder in my ears.

Plate in the head coming on strong.

My plate in the head hurting. Jellyfish sting is down my arm making my fingers claw and I hide them behind my back and take a breath. Add an e. Breathe. And Ross sees my hand twitching to a keep hid claw. Sees it and Ross squints and his face is washed out pale because my neck vein what I know is popping out and Ross says, Jate lay down a minute. Close your eyes.

So I do. I lay down.

And in the heat of the sun coming off the floorboards a good feeling against the back of my neck but everything else a clam rake scratching through sand. Sound of steel hitting rocks. The sound those rocks make when you pull them out the mud and the smell of quahogs rotting in the muck. Sandworms appearing and disappearing. Pinchyas. And horseshoe crabs dying on their backs. Sandfleas and gnats. The tide coming in. Seagulls and waves chopping and a skiff going by and the wind in the marshgrass sound. A deep breath. Plate in the head feeling softer and softer and the jellyfish sting fading away and my claw is just fingers again and the warm of the dock boards on the back of my neck and when my eyes open its Ross Mush and WillieDunne staring down at me and all I talk is what Im seeing in front of my eyes and say, Your faces. Why your faces all Hooglied?

Rosses eyebrows together knit.

WillieD fat cheeks. Purple red. Like when theyre coldwinter.

And Ross says, River. Driftin up the river. But everythings all right.

Rosses chestnut burgundies tight on me.

MushGahdoo says, You okay Jate?

And somewhere my head a bit of steel scraping rock and hint rot clams. And my arm? Small shakes. A little unsteady but I manage up the warm boards and say, What we gonna do?

And Ross says. Ride tide and see where we go. As long as we stay in the boat we're safe.

And anyway. Pruney for sure is gonna get help.

We're going past HampdenMeadows to SarahHaagsBunktownBridge because MistaCogg told us about it millions of times. The eel track. The colonial shipyard place not there no more. The fishbarrel factory and the stoppers used to plug them barrels.

Then who knows where next? Once under the BunktownBridge maybe the current will pull us into Swansea. Past Rehoboth to the ShadFishFactory. Maybe Route 44. Possible all the way to Foxborro. Boston. And beyond.

We are fast approaching Bunktown. Low concrete bridge quick coming up. Tides so high. Boats no way gonna make it under the bridge without a crash a tumble and a spill into the drink. We stand mouths open till ten feet Ross yells, Down. Get down.

We drop our backs to the bilge just as bow and gunnels and transom slide beneath the girders and pigeons fly from their roosts. The flap rush of pigeon wings brushing my face and pigeon crap falls and the boat smoothes along the bridge bottom a inch above our twig feathered bird shit faces. Now I know. For definite. What MistaCogg means when he says pigeonkicked.

Once the spit lips sputter clear of the BunktownBridge the river narrows and we're under the Route 6 bridge floating fast into lotsa curves and twists and Route 195 bridge now high above us with cars and trucks and four lanes east and four lanes west and our boat. And we float fast through the pilings. Now silent current. Now around a bonebend with a flooded brackmarsh and some guy in a low pram tending crab pots.

And LilMush yells, Hey its BobbyBrayton.

All start yelling, Bobby Bobby we're adrif. Help.

And big giant redhead Bobby. Hands over his eyes visor yells back, What in hellsgate below heaven you boys doin?

Everybody in the NorthEnd knows Barrington Bobby TheBullRake Brayton. TheBullRake on accounta thats what he uses when clamming. But this far up river Bobbys not quahogging in his usual eighteen foot skiff with his 75 horsepower outboard Evinrude but floating gentle in a eight foot pram and hes gathering blueshells and rockcrabs and his big arms are hauling up a pot from what hes tossing leg wiggling clawcrabs into a bushel. The pram hes in is so small for his big giant body. And youd think with all his redhair his skin would be milkwhite. But its not. It more like splotches of giant freckles and rust and as he drops the crab pot back into the water and as we drift past him a tattooed hula girl on his bicep arm does a dance as he pulls in his starboard oar. Bobby tosses a transom line Ross ties to the bow and as Bobby digs deep both his blades to row forward and our boat does a come around and in but a few splash. Dip. Digs. Heaves. Dip. Digs. And heaves. And its absolute amazing because with each of them arm heaves Bobbys muscles get as big as breadloafs. His chest does too then we're heading back towards the BunktownBridge with Bobby. Dip. Dig. Heave TheBullRake. Brayton.

BobbyBrayton. While hes rowing. Hollers us, Cars parked SarahHaags RoadHouse. BunktownBridge. You boys call your mother soon as we get there and shes gonna call the other moms and let em know I'll be gettin you home quick n soon enough unnerstan?

Yessir, Ross says.

Now tides so high under the BunktownBridge. Less than two feet of space beneath it between the rushing current and girder beams and Bobby ties his boat a bridge cable. Pulls our boat longside the roadbank and hauls. With them giant bullrake arms. Each one of us to the street pavement. Slapping our backs when he drops us on the road.

We all walk together over the BunktownBridge. Water pushing high fast and silent and cant believe halfhour ago we were sliding under this bridge and I ask BobbyBrayton, How you gonna get back your pram to Sowams?

Bobby. Carrying his crab bushel says, Arent. Keep her moored at Sarahs for backwater antic recreation bouts. Beer for crabs. BartendaTweet thinks its a fair trade. People love a crab feed too. Do a damn good boil. Youll see.

We walk to the driveway side of the building and as we turn the corner. LilMushGahdoo screams like a girl and grabs WillieDunnes arm. And WillieDunne screams too. Because stuck on the top of three four foot poles. The tortured face heads of KingPhilips victims stare. Except they arent for real heads. Theyre lopsta claws. Bottom of the claws looking like chins. Top of claws looking like noses. Each head painted with a different face. A face of horror each lopsta claw. One looking like a witch with a black witch hat and straw for hair and cat whiskers under her nose. Another with wire rim glasses. A MissouriMeerschaum and a ragged JackCogg Greek sailor cap. Jutting chin and big nose. And the third. In its wigged skull. A hatchet. A plastic hatchet. Like you buy at the Woolworths five and dime.

Bobby drops his bushel. Nods and says, They once was fine crust stations.

Then he picks up a garden hose and sprays his basket. The greenish bluish beadeye clawclapper crabs scuttle and buttle over each other. He drops the hose. And when he goes turn off the faucet. While we're still staring at the lopsta heads. WillieD gets the bright idea to pet one of Bobbys basket crabs. WillieDunne gets a handshake he wasnt exact expecting. That crab snags him good on the pointing finger and WillieD is screeching like a midnight alley cat. And that crab aint letting go. Bobby just calm as all get go pries apart that clutching claw and then Bobby smacks WillieDunne top side WillieDunnes bawling head and says, Hey. No cryin.

WillieD goes big eye astound.

Then immediate sucks his finger and whimps while doing it.

I gotta addmit. Between the lopstaclaw heads and Willie petting crabs. It was all prettfunny. But we dint say so at the time and while WillieD licks his wound. Bobby shakes the half full basket. Bows to the lopsta-heads saying, Thank thee all brethren for thy sacrifice.

And BobbyBrayton bushel carries through the backdoor calling, Bar-tendaTweet. Get the kettle boilin.

And at the moment we walk through the door. SarahHaags Bunktown Old Providence RoadHouseInn is a place I like. In a lotta ways reminds me of MistaCoggs Port n Starboard. It had wood stuff. Not raw boards and planks. But polished smooth surfaces a dark gold colored wood. The long bar which a bunch of guys was at. The tallwood backrest barseats. The square and round tables on the main floor. But my favorites was the wood booths along the walls near the windows and could easy imagine Mom saying they was cozycorners and we should sit there but Bobby was pointing the bar stools to us and the phone to me which he give him a dime for and Ross dropped it slot in clink ching and then dials.

When Mom answers. I say, Mom?

She says, Jate? Jate you okay? Where are you?

SarahHaags, I say.

And she says, SarahHaags? What are you boys thinkin?

We were just messin round in the boat. An—

Mom cuts me off and says, Pruney and MistaCogg left in his boat. Worried sick. I am so angry with you boys. Ross there? You boys stay right there till MistaCogg arrives. Understand? Put Ross on right now. No. Bobby. Gimme Bobby. Phone please. Now.

The phone goes to Bobby.

And the guys can hear Moms voice coming through the receiver. Mushy and Zeebo are ascat with pity and all eyes on me. WillieD is holding his hand with his claw bit finger shrivel hooked like he wants some ladys kiss and I just know the guys are all thinking about their own Moms and what alls waitin for them when we do get home.

BobbyBrayton says, Lo ClaraLee.

Moms voice is continuing loud from the phone but I cant understand none of it. Just Bobby laughing telling Mom we're fine but when Mista-Cogg gets here. He and CapnJack are gonna yard arm hang us boys. And even though Bobby TheBullRake is laughing. None of us guys get happy till Bobby hangs up the phone. Claps his hands once. And shouts, BartendaTweet! Gansett n a shot for me and orange sodas all around.

And now all eyes go front and center on BartendaTweet. He got on his head a funny threecorner hat like them minutemen wear in the RevolutionWar.

And LilMush says, Grape. Can I have grape?

BartendaTweet says, One grape comin up.

WillieDunne says, Me too.

And Ross hanging up the phone says, Me three.

BartendaTweet finger to me says, You four?

I say fast, Leven. Gonna be twelve in June.

Zeebo says, No. What kinda soda?

Orange. I like orange.

Zeebo says, Same.

BobbyBrayton says, Two outta four aint bad.

And BartendaTweet snaps them bottle caps and serves them sodas fast and plops a shotglass and pours Bobby a brass colored drink and swishes a Ganset mug in front of Bobby who hoists it high saying, Boys to men. May the mother-a-pearls make beautiful girls.

He shoots back his shot. Clacks the empty glass on the bar. Clinks his beermug against our sodabottles and we drink together. Its *The Boy and the Pirates*. And. Not ta say. But. Theres a shout of, Eecoodeesh. Thought you guys was drownded for sure.

PedroPruneyMendozaMendez doorway huggmuggin Ross.

Pruney big eyes all mouth, Me and CapnJack come up river in his catboat.

MistaCogg pushing straight for the men gang at the bar.

And BobbyBraytons saying, Coggs a swab. Aint no captain.

MistaCogg saying, Here here all cheer. A round for the boys cause when their mother keelhauls them and lets the seagulls pick the rawbones clean they will think twice before again hijackin another buccaneers craft.

MistaCogg looks whisker grizzleface hard at me.

Does his wink.

Our bottles clink.

BartendaTweet drops down another orange soda and asks Pruney if he wants anything else and Pruney says, Got any cigar boxes?

And my soda about near shoots through my nose because Pruneys ordering boxes of cigars? And I give Ross a elbow but dont need to because Ross is already giving Pruney both eyes and so is WillieD Mushy and Zeebo.

And one of two guys bar end is staring us. He elbows other guy and shouts to LilMush, Aint you HankGahdoos boy?

LilMushGahdoo says, Yep. Hes my Dad.

EndGuy says to BartendaTweet, Give me each-a-these from the rack a bag-a-popcorn cheddacheese ta the boys.

BartendaTweet snags six cheese popcorn bags. And plops each one alongside our sodas. Says, Gift-a-the BullFrog. Say Howdeedo and ThankYou.

When we do the BullFrog raises to us his glass and smiles.

Not ta say. But. All gratefulness aside. Direct behind and above the cash register a big calendar picture woman fat and chunky and not wearing nothing on. Got redface cheeks. Big smile. And a seethrough cloth wrapped delicate around. Like where her shirt should be. And that seethrough cloth drapes around her waist and her legs. Shes laying on a red couch. She got her arm propped up at her elbow and in her other hand she got a cigar between two fingers. And her arm is holding out like she wants to give that cigar to anyone who takes it. Big letters say, *Take Time. Enjoy.*

And we drink our drinks slow. Real slow. And eat the cheddacheese popcorn slow. And coldsodas and cheddacheese popcorn in a bar sure is good.

That woman.

Take Time. Enjoy.

Im prettsure means the same as GilOwen saying, Breath. Add an e. Breathe.

BartendaTweet comes back to the bar and passes a stack of all different size boxes and asks, Whachya gonna do with these?

Keep stuff in em, says Pruney.

And BartendaTweet says, Okay. But dont be throwin em in the river.

No way, Pruney big eyes says.

Balancing a tower of small boxes. Pruney swerves from the barseat to the windowbooths. And each of us guys follow Pruney to the window-booths where Pruney places his odd perfect boxstack and we watch in holysmokes wonder.

Pruney up holds a box. Flicks with his finger a lid that glides up and over but stays boxattached. And he hands me it. And says, Whiff.

Vanilla? But a smidge of stink that aint really no stink. But. More like a sting in the sweet of it all. Maybe a rootbeer linger.

Pruneys giving each of us guys a box. And we're, Wow. Smelling and sniffing.

And WillieD says his DutchMasters makes him hungry for candy and when he flips open the lid a bunch of guys looking like pilgrims are grinning.

Mush says, Mines *Kiss of the Waves*.

Zeebo says, Mines got a picture-a-MiltonBerle and it says *Phillies Blunt*.

And Ross goes, How much these boxes gonna cost?

Cigar boxes are free fa nothin, Pruney says. All the bartendas in Sowams give em away. Prettcool huh?

I'll say, says Ross.

And Ross outloud reads the words on the top of Pruneys lotsa color box. *El Producto Reproducto Chromolithographic Commemorative Cigar Label Collectible Limited Historic Editions.* And underneath. *Buy Now and Save.*

When Pruney flips his lid. The art is colors of glory. We lean in and stare. The pictures called True Americans and it has dead center a palm tree but way more green big leaf than any palm tree I seen before. And no trunk neither and sitting under these big green leaves is two guys. A spear carrying red robed war bonnet Indian guy. A colony guy with a hat and a musket gun. But the point Im making here is colors. Never I seen art so bright and exact before. Red reds. And yellows bright. But some yellows like brown mustard and warm too. Like on the Indians leggings. Blue lines and red swiggles. And off center of this painting is red white and blue symbol of the American flag. But not looking like a flag but instead a bold shield. The whole thing. Unbelievable like you wouldnt believe and way better than studying a for real good ClassicIllustratedComic. But the point Im making is its a cigar box lid. From SarahHaagsBunktownInn not GilOwensSquarePegAntiques. Its all sortakinda like the KingPhilip story. But not exact. And who on earth woulda ever thought of such a thing? If I owned this TrueAmerican Lithographic ElProductoReproducto. I would put it in the Rizzdee art museum. Or maybe even the art museum in Boston. Or NewYork. Or at least taked it home and laid on my bed and studied it for months and years.

And Ross interrupts our silence saying, Chromolithographic ott is like what AndyWarHole does. Cept this was not silkscreens but first done on limestone slabs.

Sure. Like caveman paintins. My brother got *NationalGeographics* with all that caveman ott, Pruney scrunchin his eyes a bunch.

Just when Ross is about to add something to Pruneys eye blinkin blab.

BobbyBraytons at our table saying, Back to the bar boys. Its crabs.

Zeebo asks, Can we see your tattoo?

And Bobby says, Which? And shows a anchor on his right arm and a hula girl on his left.

And Zeebo says, The hula.

When Bobby make a muscle for to show it. Zeebo for actual. Wraps his thin arms around Bobbys bullrake big arm and Bobby sweeps laughing hanging Zeebo all the way to the bar like Zeebo is the man on the flying trapeze.

And. I gotta addmit. SarahHaags was way better than JackCoggs Port n Starboard. Or GilOwens Square Peg.

Between Bobbys bullrake muscle. Smells of olive oil and garlic clove. BartendaTweet singing, *Cippolini onions. Old maids bunyons. I got a girl from Kalamazoo.* Bobby saying, Did you do easy the hot redpepper flakes? BartendaTweet saying, Used OldBay spices mixed in vinnygah. Mista-Cogg insisting, Wine vinegar gotta be red forget that pale white piss. BartendaTweet asking, You think this the first time I throw a crab boil?

Behind the bar a huge kettle steaming rockcrabs and blueshells. BartendaTweet spreading newspaper over the bar. And them rockcrabs are now orange red with blueshells more like a dark rust with a purple spray. Nutcrackers and crab claw picks. Fingers mushing crab guts and lips sucking morsels of tasty white brine meat. The squish of them innards and the airfloat of beer and men customers coming and going. Cigarette smoke. Cigar smoke. Brandy. Burgundy. Wine. Orange soda. Grape soda. WilleD. Zeebo. Mush. Ross. Pruney. And me. At the bar drinking drinks.

In the mens room peeing in a wall toilet MistaCogg calls a urinal that we gotta stand tipatoe to reach and flush.

JackCogg and Bobby TheBullRake Brayton. Loud and laughing.

Then.

Out the door. Under the hardly any stars.

And MistaCogg singing, *Shine on. Shine on Hahvest.* I mean *Oysta-Moon. Up in the sky.*

WillieDunne. Zeebo. Mush. Ross. Pruney. And me.

The tides now low enough to get Dads boat under the Bunktown-Bridge.

Bobby says, In my boat. Opened up. Be home ten minutes.

MistaCogg says, You take the kids. I'll bring Tavinos about and tow her home.

Then he sings, *I aint had no lovin since January Febuary April May June*

July August October and Septem—

MistaCogg abrupt stops singing and MistaCogg says hes gonna call Mom tell her the plan. And MistaCogg stumbledances to the bar. A invisible woman in his arms.

Bobby opens 75 horsepower full throttle the skiff flat planes with bare a bounce with Ross. WillieD. Pruney at the bow. The rest of us center bench seat and we below the fullmoon on glass and air. And not even a breeze on warm KingPhilipsCove.

And strange how a place you think you know looks so unusual in reverse. Our home from the water. Its all the same. But different. Like GilOwens and Rosses canvas art boat paintings. One bow. The other stern. Praspective.

At the bottom of KellyStreet a small campfire with shadows and bodies moving. And a flashlight beam across the water hits Bobby in the face but a moment. Then that beam is faces in the shadows.

And its Mom.

And Zeebos Mom.

And MissusGahdoo.

And MissusDunne.

When Bobby cuts the throttle and the boat glides in. Mom grabs the bow and steadies it to shore as each of us kids jumps out. And most everyone stands around the small campfire showing off cigar boxes and getting mother told off about foolish antics and just wait till you get home. WillieD disappears into the dark and theres lowtalking a mile a minute and then WillieDs mom from the shadows and WillieDunne in firelight a tightlip grin and shoulders wide.

And MissusDunne says, BobbyBrayton. My boy here tells me you side-a-his head whacked him. If thats true BobbyBrayton theres trouble.

And WillieDs chest goes a rise.

Between WillieDs eyes and lips. WillieD got a smirk.

For a guy as big as Bobby. I never magined Bobby could shrink so small.

Yes MissusDunne. I hit him. Just one tap.

WillieDs Mom a fierce cat shouts, One tap you hit my boy?

Again Bobby says, Yes Mam.

And BobbyBrayton. Throat a clench. Swallows. And says, Probbly shoulnta.

Damn right you shoulnta.

And Bobby does a eye flinch and a lip quiver.

MissusDunne wipes a drip of snot off her what I imagine nosewhiskers and says, BobbyBrayton next time my boy needs one tap. You better absolute make certain you give him two taps. Or three. If I ever again hear my boy needs one tap and you dont deliver at least ten. By god youll pay the dickens.

And with that MissusDunne smacks Willie a crack the other side of his head and says, You pologize to MistaBrayton right now this minute.

And WillieDunne does.

And as MissusDunne and WillieD disappear into KellyStreet night. A couple more cracks and lotsa WillieD bellyaching could be heard.

Pruney also apologized BobbyBrayton for causing the whole mess.

But before falling asleep that night. Nudging my headplate was chromolithographic cigar boxes. Bewdeeful color. KingPhilip lopstaclaw heads. Jutting chins. Witch whiskers and big noses. One with old fashion wire eyeglasses. A MissouriMeerschaum and a Greek sailor cap looking lots like MistaCogg. The calendar *Take Time Enjoy* naked lady.

Pruney wanting to see *The Boy and the Pirates.*

LilMushGahdoo saying, Its a stupid movie.

And nowhere near as good as *TreasureIsland.*

13
FrostFishing and the Hooglies

When the frostfish came in late October was no place better for catching them than the beach at the bottom of KellyStreet that wasnt for real a beach but rather a place where the land just fell off the marsh and spread itself into sogglumps and sandblots with eelgrass and razorsedge and carpets of rottedkelp from the endless lowtides of summer.

What made the KellyStreet bottom particular good frostfishing was. All you had to do was build a driftwood fire on the land bank. Right near the bullrush and horsetail fragmites where Dad kept his boat turned wintertime. And sit in a lawnchair. Or on a woodblock. Or a three legged tripod stool MistaCogg made. And. With a scoopnet.

Wait.

Frostfish. Similar to poggies and blues. Swim together in big schools. They like deep water. Cold. But they get chased by striped bass. And a school of bass will chase a entire school of frosties into the backwater marshes like KingPhilipsCove and with that water being shallow. Frosties wash right in and flop around on shore. Their silver bodies flashing midnightmoon and beachfire. Them reflections advertising where theyre at. The rest of frostfishing is just picking them up and tossing them in the bucket.

Sometimes frostfish dont actually wash up on the beach shore. What frostfish do is they swim in the shallows and when frostfish do that Mista-Cogg. In his highwader boots. Gets off his arse. Goes into the water and scoops them frostfish with a handnet. Three or four frostfish at a time.

But more usual. Just one.

One caught frostfish flopping in MistaCoggs net.

What I for real liked is. When we ate what the frostfish ate. Shynas.

S-H-I-N-E-R-S MistaCogg spelled. Then said, Forget it. Your way is better.

So. These shynas. What we had here was. The bass and blues chasing the frostfish and the frostfish chasing the smallfry. Or the shynas as MistaCogg and Dad called them cause of the way the fish. Minnows really. Would shine a reflection when the flashlight beam or glint of light from anything hit them.

Sometimes. Especial when the frostfish wernt running. Which sometimes on a cold night. For whatever reason. They wouldnt do. We'd scoop up a net full a shynas and without even gutting them or anything have them rolling in flour salt and pepper then deep frying in the beach side Dutchoven before MistaCogg would even have second catch ready. Im talking we'd be cooking them little fishes. Heads. Fins. Tails. Dipping them suckers in olive oil and vinegar. Or mayonaize mushroom sauce. Or Italian sauce made with tomatoes from Moms garden. That tomato sauce was good.

Anyways. Frostfishing was like asquantum but instead of being a long boat cruise to MountHope Shores. Frostfishing was a hop skip and a jump in our own back yards. And since it was such a at home sorta thing. We for real dint have a special name for it. Frostfishing was the best name anyone ever come up with and so just saying frostfishing suited everyone real fine. We all. No doubt about it. Knew exact what frostfishing meant.

One night when there was no moon. Dad come home from the dredge with a bottle Irish whiskey he give MistaCogg and Dad and Mom said something about going bed early be catching up on sleep and would MistaCogg keep a eye on us all night by the fire if we wanted and CapnJack said, Sure.

And he tossed a big couple-a-three more crateboards and skidflats on the blaze.

PruneyMendez had just finished eating a plateful of shynas and with a fat belly smile said, Bottom-a-KellyStreet be best place for NewEngland frostfish fishin.

MistaCogg said it werent always so.

He said maybe it is true now and true long long time ago. Before the PowaHouse. Long time ago before he come down east from Penobscott Maine.

MistaCogg said all through his younger days there, Wernt a frostfish anywheres past the confluence-a-the Quequeshan on account-a-the PowaHouse steam warmin waters comin from the hotbox lagoon and if a guy wanted to catch himself a shiver-a-frosties. He hadda go round bayside all the way to the KingPhilip Strait and Narrows where we do asquantum.

Eyup, MistaCogg said, Was the PowaHouse steam warmin water drove the frostfish away. And-a-course. The Hooglies.

The Hooglies? We said, Whats KingPhilipsCove got to do with the Hooglies? Everyone knows the Hooglies happened KingPhilip Strait n Narrows base-a-MountHope and not our backwater marsh KingPhilips-Cove but bayside. Over at HooglySpit. Mouth-a-the SowamsRiver.

MistaCogg said that story part. The part where the Hoogly sailors got burned alive aboard their very own vessel was, Whachya call. A historical prologue. Just the begin-a-the story.

MistaCogg said, The real meat on the bone. The heart-a-the matter far as any NorthEnder from Sowams was concerned. Happen just up the cove. A flagstone over. And since you seem to bear ignorance-a-the-matter. Its high time for hearin and learnin the importance of lettin the dead rest in peace lest you wanna end up like the immigrant boys. Who. Afta catchin a bad case-a-the Hooglies. Died a horrible death.

And MistaCogg said the right proper way to begin such a story is with the utterance of a incanation. A sacred incanation. And he said all low fire serious,

Doglick breath
Sign o death
Catfish head
Better off dead.

The reason why MistaCogg said he cantated was. MistaCogg said we needed Hoogly protection whenever chestnuts fell. Frostfish swam. Marsh grass turned brown and crab apples hung thick clusters in trees. All these things were sure signs the Hooglies was about. All about and everywhere. Lurking and skulking. Slitherin and crawlin. Beatin and reachin. Wantin home.

What CapnJackCogg told us was after the Hoogly sailors went insane in quarantine and the ship burned moored at HooglySpit those Hindu sailors so far way from their homes in India. The people of Sowams with no identifiable remains to send. Thought it would be proper for to give those charred body parts a decent Christian burial.

MistaCogg told how a plot was donated east the double crypts of Freeborn Sisson and Jane. Wife of Freeborn. Except. JackCogg dint call those above ground graves crypts. He called them cigar for gifts. Said that was, Fancy Greek that meant flesh eatin stone.

And. Not ta say. But. I dint get that one. Not for nuthin. Till Pruney explained the Egyptians invented cigar for gifts for mummies.

But Ross said, Wrong words.

Ross spelled, S-A-R-C-O-P-H-A-G-U-S.

MistaCogg said, You boys gonna have each other a spellin lesson, or let me tell my story?

Which of course made us three-sit straight and shut up.

And MistaCogg scooped his pipe into his BorkumRiff pouch and told how a sarcophagus was erected with six granite posts and fitted horizontal iron bars establishing the plot. Atop the sarcophagus slab in the plot was the inscription—

Hoogly Seamen Lost to Sea
In thy Bosom Eternally
Rest
1829

We knew MistaCogg was telling true because we had seen. A hundred time before. Them words. Everyone in the NorthEnd had. Maybe too. All-a-Sowams.

But. Irregardless.

MistaCogg went on to say, A hundred years later. 1928. A real bad blizzard hit. Ten to fifteen foot drifts. Half dozen dead in the EastBay alone. Lectric poles snapped in half. Trees and limbs everywhere and the Freeborn Sisson tomb was frostfroze open. Snow. Ice. And every kid in the NorthEnd went sneakin round. Seein what was inside Freeborns casket. Out the grave? Clawin fingers. From the cracks? Spillin hair. Gold teeth. Broke jaw. Craze stuff.

So these three immigrant buddies. Two-a-them NorthEnders. One-a-them a rich French Canada kid down from Montreal. Come from school. Stay with his CherryStreet grandparents every summer and Febuary winter vacation. Was the only boy-a-the three that finished his schoolin.

MistaCogg said, The Polish boy and the Wop. They were dropouts. But the Montréal Canook CanadaKid. Stayin with his CherryStreet Memmae and Peppae. Had a social and academic future. He was slated for a tour-a-Europe with a well to do visitin rich aunt from France. She gonna be takin him. Her nephew. Back with her. Early Octoba. Five month tourin expedition. Through all-a-Europe. England. France. Italy.

These three buddies one early September night decide to open the Sisson tomb. They had candles. Lamps. Shovels. And a prybar.

Problem was. The Sisson family. Durin the summer. Had repaired the crypt and closed it. Tighter than a twidget on a she clams dimple.

However. These boys was snoopin round the Hoogly Crypt and one-a-them. Got a idea to try and lift the face slab from the crypt and-a-course the thing was about heavy as rock stone weight should be. But with all three-a-them boys liftin. They not only lifted the heavy lid but they also slid the dead weight thing wide enough to look inside. Course was dark. But they got candles and suchwhat and were able to see and what no one since the funeral party-a-1829 had seen and what no one in town any-more realized. There was no casket. No coffin. No bodies. There was only a cast iron urn. Like a pot bellied spider legged kettle. With a sealed lid. And inside that urn just ashes and charred bones. Point bein. Because-a-no coffin. The tomb was big enough for the Italian boy to writher inside on a dare from his two pals. And the place was crawlin with earwigs. Wart toads. Garter snakes and silverfish and he was no sooner in there then was boltin back out screamin a slime hand just slathered upside the back-a-his neck and sent all three scatcats runnin to the edge-a-the cemetree fence.

Direct before they hit LandStreet. The boys remembered they had left the grave slab open with their tools and jackets layin all round. Hadda go back. Coulnt leave evidence. So they did. The next few days CanadaKid started joshin ItalianKid sayin he had no guts cause there werent no slime hand. ItalianKid dint like bein called chicken. So he tells them he'd lay in the Hoogly flesh eatin stone and the guys can close the lid for ten whole minutes. Said he'd show em who was a chicken-a-the sea.

Followin night the boys went back with. Not only their tools. But also a bottle-a-cheap rum that PolishBoy said was both for courage and a last hurrah sendoff because mornin the French kid was takin the 9:05 to Mon-treal then board the European steamer.

So. All three-a-them seventeen year olds. Liquor up good. Put their efforts to the inscripted vault slab cover. Takes all their collected strength to lift that lid off its lip and shift the thing over so the slab can slide and create a gap enough wide for ItalianKid to slip in. He lays down. Gives the other boys the signal. They slide the lid back. Groove to lip. Off by a sea hunt hair. Then. Thunk. Tight closes. Fits solid. No gaps. Goodbye.

CanadaKid? Hes got a watch. One minute. Two minutes. Three. Not a sound. Just the wind. Maybe some barkin night dogs. Lonesome. Plus ever now and then. A LandStreet automobile. Six minutes. PolishBoy and the CanadaKid. Drunk tooth suckin nervous. Dont hear nothin from their buddy inside the crypt. Eight. Nine. Then. Ten.

Two boys close to frantic. Wanna get their pal out the grave.

Heave lift the lid. And?

Cant move nothin.

Heave again. And still?

Nothin.

Boys dont realize. Took six arms lift the lid.

Twelve minutes.

The two boys crazy anxious now to rescue their pal. Think they can hear kickin and screamin comin inside the tomb. Again they heave. Strain all the chowder in their bones. It jolts. It slides. And before the lid gaps wide. Out that crack openin. Clawin at the midnight sky. Rises a skeletal hand.

The Polack? He screams like a woman and CanadaKid trips over the tools.

Them boys push away from the grave as far as they can.

Then they hear the insane laugh-a-their Italian buddy callin them chicken shites and bird turds and the two scramblin boys finally inch back to the belly-a-the vault. Lantern high. And see a three twigged tree branch scratchin up and down.

When the boys finally slide the lid wide enough for the inside laughin ItalianKid to climb out. Hes pullin on something looks like a spider legged cast iron Dutch oven with the sealed tight lid. Its the burial urn.

You crazy? They holler at him. We're goin to hell uncertain. But youre goin to hell for sure.

Italian kid? His eyes crazed. Says, Stay or leave. Im bustin open this urn.

And he raises high a granite rock and from way across the cemetree. Outta no where. A solid beam-a-light sweeps onto the gravestones. A car from UnionStreet proceedin on LandStreet south to Barrinton. And ItalianKid holdin the urn says, Lets take it down the railroad tracks. Behind the PowaHouse. Hotbox lagoon. Bust it open there.

He hunkers low through the tall grass. Pals on his tail. Tools in tow. They slip through the east fence corner gap near the rail car repair shop. A few workers inside the buildins. No one payin attention three shadows cuttin round the cinder piles followin the discharge pipe to the hotbox lagoon.

Boys finally make it to the edge-a-the planked pond. Got the cold water-a-KingPhilips Cove on one side-a-them. The hotbox water coolin for release. The other side. Water black. Glassflat. Steam vapors risin all round.

Then a rumblin. And tremors. And hot water gushin from the release pipe into the hotbox lagoon. Thousands-a-gallons a boilin water dischargin into the September autumn cool. Noise so loud shouts coulnt-a-been heard.

ItalianKid thinks, Now or never. Hefts a mean cobblestone. Fullmoon light. Steam driftin off the water. Drops that cobble center on the Hoogly urn. Half dozen fractures crack. Those kettle pieces separate like cranium plates cross a hollow skull and bone white ash spills out.

A knuckle here. A jaw part there.

No gold doubloons. Or emeralds and jewels.

Just dust.

The dust-a-sailors long dead.

They that go down to the sea in ships.

And now. Again. The fullmoon disappears. The boys cant hardly see each other save for the PowaHouse through-the-steam lights. And CanadaKid says, Now what?

Without a word PolishBoy is scoopin the ash with pieces-a-the broke urn and dumpin each scoopful into the silent water.

The ash. White on his fingers.

The ash. Risin with the vapors. Spillin to the lagoon.

The ash. White powder on the black mirror surface.

The ash floatin like a map-a-the world on the water.

And then comes rain.

Sprinkles first.

ItalianKid. He cant leave well enough alone. Not only is he scatterin the dust-a-sailors into the PowaHouse hotbox. But too hes strippin off his clothes in the September rain. And hes head first. Bare naked. Divin.

Hes down so long. The hot water surface again goes glass and the up top boys wonder, Whered he go? Whered he go? Then. Softest sound-a-water breaks and swimmer from the black calm dead says, Waters fine. Come on in.

All three-a-these boys jump and dive without the slightest awares they been doin wrong even though two-a-them talked goin to hell. Now? Nothin. As a matter-a-fact. When they get out the water and once again dress. All three sit. Dangle their legs. And start skippin shards-a-cast iron. Then. Soon enough. Partys over.

They walk south up the railroad tracks to CherryStreet. Italian and Polish kid say final goodbyes because CanadaKid will be off next mornin for

Montréal. Then France. And Europe. Careless in the world.

Not a one-a-these boys know about the Hoogly curse.

So. CanadaKid goes for his European tour. Italian and Polish boys pass the autumn doin day shift at the mill. But every Friday night. One boy braver than the other gets someone to brownbag a bottle. A package. At the liquor store. The packy. And one Friday. Guy they get is a sailor passin Providence to Newport. LeoDriggses grandfather. From the packy they go the grave. And AlexanderDriggs tells history with warnin about stirrin up the curse. By ten or eleven. BoswainDriggs goes his way leavin the boys. All three. Stewed in restless curse talk.

ItalianKid aint buyin it. Hes lived in Sowams most-a-his life and he never heard no talk-a-there bein a curse. Plenny-a-Hoogly stories sure. But never no curse ones.

PolishBoy is a bit more cautious.

But. The followin Friday night. Both boys. There they are. Once again. All liquored up. Back at the crypt.

All the time ItalianKid goadin PolishBoy lay in the grave. Says OlMan BowswainDriggs just a dockfront drunk passin through town and there aint no curse and to prove it. Italian says he'll lay in the grave again.

But PolishBoy? He dont like bein thought chicken and he takes the bait.

Into the crypt PolishBoy goes.

ItalianKid is usin all his drunk power to slide the cover shut.

PolishBoy pushin up with his arms and fumblin hands. Leanin back to ease. Delicate. With all his strain. That stone into place.

But then PolishBoy is. On the sudden. Two left hands. And the lid falls shut.

Whole thing falls pah-klunk solid.

And as that face slab locks in place. At the same instant. Italian hears a scream aint a scream. Sound-a-throat breath leachin through stone. Not hardly there. But enough to be somethin. And to double check. ItalianKid lays atop the sepulcher and?

The whole tablet sinks.

Just a bit.

A scrunch?

Maybe.

A schosh?

Most definite.

Italian knows he felt somethin.

Did his weight settle the thing?

Then a sound.

His ear to the stone.

No breathin.

Heart poundin.

Listens again.

Damn. Hes thinkin. Too much booze.

So ItalianKid rolls off the sepulcher and picks up the lantern.

Lamp to the edge-a-the lip and.

What makes his heart stop?

No breath.

No breathin.

Fingers.

Tips a two fingers tween the base and the lid.

He stands there. Pigeonkicked.

His Polish buddys fingers. Blackrimmed fingernails.

Stickin out the grave.

There they are.

Two fingers.

Purple.

Italian reaches for those fingertips.

Two lines a blood drippin down the sarcophagus side.

And it slow dawns his drunk fool brain the lid dropped on his buddys hand.

Italians fingers touchin Polish purples nubbin from the crypt.

And just when the Italians fingers touch the Polish purple nubs.

Polish purple nubs fall to the ground. And wriggle like cut up sandworms.

Smashed at the knuckles.

We're talkin knuckles mashed to a millstone grind.

Knuckle slop.

Knuckle grist mash.

Meat and bone.

His frantic mind. EyetalianKid sees his PolackPal direct beneath him.

PolishBoy layin in the grave.

Arm stretched up.

Thrashin. Wild.
Entombed alive.
And ItalianKid just knows.
Screamin to be freed.
ThePolishBoy.

ItalianKid is now a-scat.
Jumps off the crypt.
Tries to lift the lid.
Nothin.
Prybar? Gottdamn black as night. Sheepgrass tall. Chestnut leaves everywhere.
Rose briars and field burrs. Poison ivy. Stingin nettles.
Gotta run for help.
Stumbles through the cemetree.
Over the fence.
LandStreet.
Stumbles drunk his knees.
His feet.
Arms flailin. Radical.
Car. Chug chug chug. Two cylinder Maxwell. Those days a cars noise gave away the make. Car comes fast round the curve.
Car passin the Portuguese Church what aint there yet. Just a open field.
Car now passin the graveyard.
ItalianKid steps cars dim headlamps. Driver doesnt see. Car grill splits the kids ribs and sends ItalianKid to the Vermont granite curb. Cracks the kids skull. Smacks the kids brain.
Car driver tells the cops, Boy come outta nowhere. Jump right in front-a-the machine. Outta nowhere I tell ya.
Course ItalianKid was gutter dead moment he hit the curbstone. The town-a-Sowams gets prett all shook up. Aint nobody yet ever been automachine killed. First time. Headlines-a-Times Gazette Ledger—

Automachine Kills Sowams Boy
Barrington Driver Reports Tragedy

Towns all a buzz. Especial NorthEnd. But the real shocker un-beknowd to nobody. Only one knows the truth. Deader than a quarryprized curbstone.

PolishBoy in the Hoogoo chamber.

Within a day or two. Parents-a-PolishBoy report him missin.

Sure. Everyone thinks it strange. Might bit off typical. PolishBoy aint round for his Italian buddys funeral.

Meanwhile.

Remember the CanadaKid?

Well. CanadaKid been gone to Europe since late October.

No one connects CanadaKid to Sowams deeds done foul.

But.

A-course his Memme and Peppe. They take it upon themselves to write their boy his two friends. ItalianKid bein killed. PolishBoy gone missin.

But their news is lost abroad and never reaches CanadaKid.

None the anyhow. Febuary. CanadaKid is back. Sowams got a foot-a-snow.

But on that day. On that day. The day CanadaKid arrives back in Sowams.

Weathers blowin rain and sleet.

Memme and Peppe break the news.

CanadaKid bolts out the house.

And. Height-a-the mid aftanoon storm. Makes it fast all the way to Sowams town hall police and rants his suspicions to a desk sergeant who. On the astonished quick. Calls the PaddyMick chief-a-police.

According to MistaCogg.

On Febuary 15.

Five oclock P.M. Rain all aftanoon. Twenty knot wind. Dark. Cold.

Three patrol cars. A fire truck and a rescue squad. Roll along side VitullosPub across the street from the cemetree and park.

No lights.

No sirens.

Someone from the barroom window sees all the silent commotion and in a matter-a-moments the tavern goes empty.

Twenty-a-thirty people to the graveyard. Every one straight for the Hooglies. Seems whole town there and more showin up every second.

The seventeen year old CanadaKid directin the scene like hes mayor-a-Sowams. Everyone jumpin to this CanookFrogs orders. Fire marshal. Police chief. Ambulance driver. Micks. Portagees. Kiltboys and Daegoes.

CanadaKid directs six men. Two centersides. One. Each corner-a-the slab.

And count-a-three. In a drivin sleet and cold. The team lifts.

Clears.

And.

To the outside ground falls.

Minus severed fingers.

The entombed crushed hand.

Rest in peace.

Ever think what the honest to Gott true north mean those words?

Rest in peace.

Well. On that evening in the North Burial Grounds-a-Sowams. 1937. MistaCogg found out what they dint mean.

MistaCogg said he was twenty-five years old in that cemetree on that raw Febuary in the beam a flashlights and emergency lamps. He seen and heard it all.

Yuh weepin.

Yuh wailin.

And yuh gottdamm gnashin-a-yuh drunktooth teeth.

The sleeve. It was danglin from the granite cover like a limp flag directin mortified eyes to the final chapter-a-the Hoogoo hauntin.

When MistaCogg looked into that tomb. PolackBoy was, Ice crystals on a stargazin mudfish. One eye. His left. Sunk. Purple green spreadin low. The right eyeball. Swoll froze. The nostrils. Wide. Both lips deflated blueblack pullin dried bloodgummed teeth jagged rotwood brown. One leg straight. Other all a twist on the straight legs knee. Entire corpse a misshapened bite on a bowline hemp. Mean. Ugly. Horrible.

MistaCogg remembered most PolackBoys shoes.

Toes. Scuffed and complete worn.

Leather gainst stone.

Left shoe hole a toe poked through. Grated black froze flesh.

What MistaCogg said he'd never forget.

Fingers right hand. Curled. Little PolackBoy makin claws. Knuckles.

And-a-course.

The flesh left arm.

Sleeveless. A splayed crushed wrist bone pointin from the tomb.

They scraped the mash of the fallen hand from the lid lip groove.

Sleeve n all.

With a puttknife.
And placed the ice mess.
On the froze contort body.

Hoogly Seamen Lost to Sea
In thy Bosom Eternally
Rest
1829

II
Secrets

14
Goodboost Counts

The way actual we discovered the PowaHouse was Moms fault. And JackCoggs. They were to blame. Not us. Lets face it. Like JackCogg always says, Chrice sakes. Youre just kids.

And Pruney. He actual discovered the power of that place.

So.

One day. Before Pruney.

When we was real little. Six years old. Mom decided we werent beach going our usual WaterStreet way. Said first she wanted to pick flowers for MistaCoggs shop.

Ever since when I was little and got truckhead hit and MistaCogg curbside stood over me helping the men put me in the ambulance. Mom was always dropping off appreciation bouquets at the Port n Starboard Shop.

Usual Mom had her gratitude bouquet ready before we went to the beach. And as we passed by we would leave her appreciations at the back-a-the shack in the scrapwood stacks. She would say,

LeoDriggs and Bundles might get ideas.

These are for CapnJack. Not them.

Yes. Someday we'll leave appreciation bouquets for those men too.

Dont ever say bums. Only bums say bums.

On this one particular beachday. Mom had got behind in her dishwashing and clothesfolding and we left our house late so she decided. Instead of walking straight up WaterSteet. Our usual way. She would instead backway go to the beach by following the railroadtracks. Cut across SowamsGreenhills. And drop off the flowers on the return home down WaterStreet at the dayfinish end instead of at the daystart begin.

A foolish idea because the beach is no place for picked flowers. By the time we got to CapnJacks shack. Them flowers were all windblown and wilted.

Mom said this roundabout way to CapnJacks was the second foolish idea-a-the day because once those railroad tracks crossed over the Sowams River on the trestle,

You boys must promise me.

Never ever go on that trestle.

Once those railroad tracks crossed the wood trestle over the SowamsRiver the tracks passed atop a ten foot berm that separates our house from the aqua blue aluminum sided CrescentStreet Andriozzi house and the red brick American LuggageFactory and the rest of the NorthEnd and past the cemetree curve round the PowaHouse bramblegrove,

Never ever go into those woods. See the NO TRESPASSING signs? Break the law? You go to jail.

Right. Breakin the law is like breakin windows or startin fires or smokin cigarettes when youre too little.

And right before the tracks reached the end of the line end in Bristol. They got widened where the Sowams train station used to be but isnt there anymore. And we asked why? Mom said, *Burned down. Never rebuilt cause now that we have cars no one needs to take the train to Providence. And anyway. You should have Providence in your heart and everyone in Providence lives off Hope.*

No. We are not in Providence.

Thats right. We are in Sowams.

Yes. Everyone should have Hope.

Of course MistaCogg did.

And your Father at work does too.

Thats right. And KingPhilip too.

Of course. I hope.

Hope rains a turn L.

Mom put hope so much in us. Even though we never broke windows. Smoked cigarettes. Or started fires. When we was twelve. The woods. The trestle. And the cemetree. Became our secret places.

The PowaHouse stuff we did was strict after school, Hush hush. Cross your heart and hope to die. And you will die too. Honest ta God. Spit on your mothers grave. Hey. Wait a minute. Pruney. You got no mother. Secret.

In those days our two favorite TV shows was *Combat* and *TheGallant-Men*. Those shows was about army guys in the war of WorldWarTwo.

And each of them television shows was on the same channel. But on different nights.

TheGallantMen was lotsa repeat shows. But they was cool.

Irregardless. At the edge of our marsh. The PowaHouse chimny stack had collapsed around its square granite base. Part of the base was total opened and anyone could easy scramble the outside brick heaps and enter. Its round hollow was like a fort. And in the center of that. On the ground. Was a campfire. We never lit the thing. But kept it looking like a fireplace constant with bricks and rocks and tepees of sticks. Twigs. Newspaper wads. And straw.

Campfire was Pruneys idea.

Pruney said, Since we're *TheGallantMen* who ever heard-a-soldiers without no campfire?

I said, Thought we were *Combat*?

That was yesterday, Ross said.

But anyways, Pruney said, If we're gonna play war for real? We not only need a campfire. But we also gotta have some C-rations.

Whats C-rations? asked WillieD.

Its soldier food, said LilMushGahdoo. Everybody knows that.

Well I dont. And Anyways. Where we gonna get these C-rations?

And Pruney says, Simple. Just take some canned food from your house.

And LilMush interrupts, Cant be just any cans. Sgotta be the square kind. Like anchovies or what Spam come in. With the keys. Gotta have keys.

And Pruney says, Doesnt neither gotta be square. Can be small round ones too. Like tuna fish. Or those little sausagedawgs.

And Ross says, Yeah but tuna fish and sausagedawgs dont have keys.

And Pruney says, Dont gotta have keycans. Can have regular kinda cans long as you got the right kinda can opener.

Yeah, says LilMush, Can opener. The G-I kind like my Uncle Snotty has. Its a kinda hook thing you stick into the can and pry with.

Yeah, says Pruney.

Yeah, says WillieD.

Yeah, says LilMush. Can opener. Gotta be the right kind though.

Then Ross says, Labels. What about labels?

And Mush says, Can openers dont have labels.

And Ross says, Not can openers. Cans. What kinda labels on the cans? Cause. Never once. Not a single time. Ever. Have I seen VicMorrow eatin outta a can has a label on it.

Yeah. But *TheGallantMen.* They have cans sayin COFFEE. And boxes sayin MEAT. And packages sayin CHOCOLATE, said WillieD.

Well this aint *TheGallantMen* This is. How many five times I gotta tell you? *Combat,* said LilMushGahdoo.

Pruney says, No sweat. We peel off the labels. Spraypaint the cans army color green and then use black markers n stencils.

Cool, says Ross.

Yup, says WillieD.

Yeah, says LilMush.

And Ross says, Lets do it.

But thats when Ross sees em.

Thats when Ross sees some magazine ends sticking out the brickhole. One of the chimney pigeon holes. The fort walls. High.

Give me a boost will you Pruney? says Ross.

Pruney cups his hands a stirrup. Ross slips a foot in. And Pruney hefts Ross steady up. And Ross stands steady on Pruneys shoulder.

Ross just high enough his fingers reach the end roll.

Got em, Ross hollers and pulls out the magazine log.

Pruney. Like a elevator. Ross down from his boost. And we all gather and Ross hasnt even separated one magazine from the other yet. When LilMush already grabs the top one and is flipping it.

Whatchya got? Says Pruney.

LilMush wont show.

And Ross divides the found stuff automatic on accounta them best-friends. But also because Pruney gave the boost and it was real good boost. Not everybody gives goodboost. Ross dont. Gets him dirty. And LilMush? Too little. So. Pruney. Automatic. Halfstash.

Goodboost counts.

Goodboost goes a long way.

What goodboost for Pruney got. And all of us? Was four magazines. Brand new. And in a matter of minutes we had all them magazine pages flipping. *Swank. Cavalier.* And *Bachelor.* Lotsa naked lady pictures. But *Playboy* pictures more better. Prettier women. And in color.

Swank and *Cavalier* most black and white with huge big tit women. WillieD says, Some-a-those ladies tits so big it looks like their holdin up two-a-the three little piggies.

Ross and me. We're looking at *Playboy.* And all on a sudden. Ross flips the page. But instead of it just flipping to the next one. It unfolds into his lap. Center page out. Jeeze. Almost big as me. And Ross dont even hold the book no more. Lays it down. Lays down the magazine. Pruney drops *Cavalier*. Mush rolls *Swank*. WillieD shoves hands in pockets. And they. All three. Come over. *Take Time. Enjoy.* Our mouths dry.

Jaws grinding left.

Jaws grinding right.

Arms and legs twitching.

Twitching while we scratch.

Pruney says, I got a boner.

WillieD says, I got a boner.

LilMush says, I got a boner.

And I say, Me too. Got a boner too.

Ross says, MissNovember? Shes got a month for a name. Thats weird.

We all agree. Weird. But we also all agree shes the most bewdeeful woman in the whole wide world. Way more bewedeefuller than *Take Time. Enjoy.*

For real like the army now.

I say, What are ya talkin about Pruney? Never on TV I seen VicMorrow or any-a-TheGallantMen lookin at no clothes pictures-a-girls.

VicMorrows *Combat* not *TheGallantMen* and. These pictures here? Theyre pinup girls. All army guys had em.

Sure. All did. Pruney says, Cept they dont show it on television shows. They show it in the movie shows. Saw a picture called *Yank in Hell* or somethin or other. Cant remember the whole name. But the guys whistlin this gal Betty Cable dressed in a bathin suit and then this bomb exploded and guys hadda rescue her cause her legs was stuck under the piano.

WillieD says, That was *Combat*. LilJohn pulled the lady out the burnin buildin.

MushGahdoo says, No way. *GallantMen*. Three weeks ago. Episode nine—

HEY. Ross hollers. *GallantMen Combat* or *Yanks in Hell*. We cant just take these magazines. We gotta return em. Whoever put em up there is gonna come back. And if they find out we stole em. Theyre gonna come afta us.

Mush asks, Whodya think put em there?

Ross says, Probbly LeoDriggs and Bundles.

WillieD says, Well. Then they wont mind if we just borrow em.

Youre not thinkin-a-takin em home are you?

Sno big deal.

And Ross says, Better not let your mom or dad find em.

Dont matter if they do. My dad got all kinda tittie picture magazines. Even gave me one once. Said, On accounta you dont have a sister to take a bath with.

Whaddaya think he meant? asked LilMush.

Who knows? Answered WillieD. But I took a bath with it. Entire time soakin and lookin at the pictures. Had the biggest boner-a-my whole life. And my mom yellin from the kitchen. Hurry up in there. So started soapin. Next thing. My dick gettin bigger and bigger and my legs like theres pins gettin stuck in em and my heads feelin. Honest ta God. Like its gonna kapow. And. All on a sudden. My entire body spazzin and my boner squirtin whitestuff and Im like driftwood in the current floatin to the beach.

Did it hurt? LilMush asked.

What?

The squirtin.

Nope. Best feelin ever. Asked my dad and he said meant Im healthy. Asked him if boners was a disease cause lately I been gettin boners all the time. And he said no. Just means youre growin up. But. Told me should keep it private. Said shoulnt tell no one cause it can make people kinda mental. But you guys arent mental bout it. Are ya?

Ross said, No.

LilMushGahdoo said, No.

No, I said.

And Pruney said, Its called whackinoff an I do it all the time.

15

PowaHouseStuff

We stared.

Ross asked Pruney, You mean whenever you take a bath?

Whackinoff dont need no bath.

And WillieD asked, None?

Heck no. None. Can do it where ever. Whenever. Trouble is. And WillieDs dads right about this part. Some people for real do take a mental. Specially nuns n preeces. Never. Never tell a nun and absolute never tell a preece. Unless youre in confessional. Then usual theyll ask.

Whachya mean? Ross kicked the fireplace.

Well. You know, said Pruney. Whenever I go confession FathaLuis asks, You ever touch yourself? Touch yourself is preece code for whackinoff. They never say whackoff cause theyre. You know. In a church.

So. Whatya sayin is. Youre sayin you can whackoff anywhere?

Sure. Could do it right here if I wanted.

Right here?

Right here.

Right now?

Right now.

Dare you, said Ross.

And Rosses brownchestnutburgundies looking Pruney straight into his skyblues.

Pruney not a flinch unzips his dungarees.

Pruney reaches into his dungareefly and kneels the bottom Miss Novembers page. Each his knees on each her highheeled shoes.

Pruney takes out his dick.

Dont know why the sight of that dick surprised me. It wasnt like Pruney to keep secrets. But then again. This one. He never told till now.

And even now Pruney werent telling secrets.

Pruneys showing secrets.

Pruney had a Michelangelo.

Pruney come close to telling his secret that rain afternoon last winter. After *Take Time. Enjoy.* Pruney. Ross. And me. In our house looking at *National Geographic* naked pictures. And looking at Rosses art book pictures. Naked people too.

Ross wondering out loud, What if theres a bunch-a-white natives got discovered in Africa? Would *National Geographic* print em naked?

Pruney said, No way. There were rules and rules were colored people okay to be naked cause they werent Christians yet. And it was only a sin for Christians naked cause they got thrown out the Garden-a-Eden.

Ross said, But theres colored Christians. What about them?

Pruney said, Only colored Christians are America ones. It is a sin to be American. And naked. Special if youre white.

Yeah? Well what about these people on the Sistine Chapel? Theyre all naked and white.

Well. Theres a couple a things you gotta consider, said Pruney. First. None-a-those people are America people. Theyre all Bible people. Jews and such. Second. They arent photographs. Theyre painted. And painted picture naked isnt the same as photograph naked. Photographed picture naked is a sin. But painted picture nakeds all right cause its ott. And ott nakeds always okay. In fact its praferred.

Praferred? By who? I ask.

Why the preeces. And the nuns. And the kings and queens and the popes. All those royalty folks praferred naked people paintings. If you go Italy. Them naked people pictures are all over the place. Isnt that so Ross?

Well, said Ross, Its not all like that exact.

Whaddaya mean? said Pruney.

And Ross said, Preference. It has to do with time. Bible time. Way back in Bible time. People had different preference. What they prefer. Feelins about wearin clothes. All these figures painted on this Sistine ceilin. Theyre Bible people. And Michelangelo. He wanted to show the way it was in Bible time. Take for instant. All these nakeds. Look the way Michelangelo painted em. Special. The dicks. Look at the dicks. Michelangelo painted dicks on those guys that way cause Michelangelo bein a ottist and all. Was interested in way people looked when they were like God made em. Not the way some old doctor cut em up.

You mean we looked like that when we were born?

Uh huh, said Ross. All guys do.

Who told you that? I asked.

GilOwen. And Dad. GilOwen told me ask Dad. So I did. And Dad said its true.

Sure, said Pruney, Everybody knows that. All started about a couple-a-three thousand years ago when God told Abraham.

Lincoln? I interrupted.

No. Bible Abraham. A Jew. Way long before AbrahamLincoln. Bible Abraham and God were good friends. Abraham had two sons. One named Ishmael who the MobyDick guy got his name from. And one named Isaac like the gravity guy. Anyway. Isaac always drop his pants. Pee everywhere. Livinroom. Bedroom. Front yard. Back. Abraham asked God how make him stop? And God said, Kill him. Kill the boy.

Wait a minute. God wanted this Abraham guy kill his son? God wanted a father kill his own kid?

Sure, said Pruney. See if he loved him.

See if God loved Abraham? I said.

No. See if Abraham loved God.

So Abrahams gotta kill his kid prove he loves God?

Now you got it, said Pruney.

Jeeze, I said.

Yeah. So. Anyways. Abraham.

Bible Abraham?

Yes. Bible Abraham. Theres no other Abraham. This is the first Abraham. The only Abraham. Eecoodeesh. You gonna let me finish?

Well its complicated, I said.

Pruney giving me the Eecoodeesh look. The look he gives me when he knows Im plate in the head struggling. The PruneyMendez look. Popeye. One eyebrow raised. Other eye closed tight and his nose side scrunched.

Then Pruney takes a sigh. Gets normal again and Pruney continues, Bible Abraham takes Bible Isaac up the mountain and Bible Abraham puts. His son. Bible Isaac. On a altar Bible Abraham built. And Bible Abraham raises a knife into the air hes gonna plunge into poor Bible Isaacs beatin heart.

Whats he doin all this goin on? I ask.

Whats who doin? says Pruney.

Isaac?

Isaacs not doin nothin. Hes tied up and blindfolded. Just layin there.

Just layin there? Ross asks.

Well. Maybe Abraham got him drunk or somethin cause hes just layin there. So. Abrahams got his hand in the air the daggerknife hes gonna stab Isaac with. And as his hand comes down with the dagger. A angel-a-the Lord reaches and pulls the knife from Isaacs hands. And God yells over Abrahams shoulder. Makes Abraham jump a mile. God yells. Hey. Dont do it. Changed my mind. Abraham says, Whaddaya mean you changed your mind? You just about made me take a hotta heartattack. And God says, You dont gotta kill im. Just cut off his precious jewels and give em to me. And Abraham says, Hes not wearin any jewels. No rings. No bracelets. No watch. No nuthin. And God says, Not them kinda jewels. His private parts. And Abraham says, You mean you want me cut off his dick and his balls? And God says, Abraham. When I made men. Put on too much dickskin. Now trim em. Thats an order. I'll teach you. And. For doin it. You become a general-a-my people. Who. From now on. Im gonna call Jews cause-a-you cuttin their jew-els. And whenever a babyboy Jew is born. You do a little family jew-el cuttin. Call it circle scribin. Be proof your people are my people and these people love me. Its no sweat. Offerin up to me a little-a-the best pieces-a-yourselfs. A sacrifice. Not fa nuthin. But. I could be askin for a whole lot more cause. Im God n youre not.

So, finishes Pruney. The cuttin-a-the family jew-els. Thats where Jews come from.

I was total plate in the head because. Did anyone ask where Jews come from? Plus. I had thought. Even though we dint go to church. Ross and me Catholics because Nonna and Nonno were Catholics. I asked Ross. And Ross said, We're sorta Cathlics. But not really. Why?

Well we dont have that dick skin, I said.

And before Ross could answer. Pruney grabs Rosses book. Flips some pages. Says, Look here. And Pruney points to a naked man statue.

First thing I seen straight off. That naked man statue. A uncut dick just like the guys on the ceiling. And the naked man statue is standing sorta showing off his naked man statue uncut dick and he dont care whos seeing. One hand on his shoulder. Other hand. His side. Real handsome. And hair. Real curly. Like mines.

Pruney says, This guy is David. From David n Goliath. And I dont mean that puke Gumbylike Proddastint kid with his stupit ol dog.

I know, I say. You mean the slingshot guy in the Bible.

Right, says Pruney. Afta Abraham. Ishmael n Isaac. This David. He become King-a-the Jews.

How can that be? His dicks not cut up.

Right again, says Pruney. Thats like what Rosses been tellin. This statue is a Michelangelo. And if Michelangelos David is king-a-the Jews with a uncircle scribed dick. You can be Cathlics with circle scribed dicks.

But. What about Gods deal with Abraham?

Exceptions, said Pruney. Always exceptions. For the most part. Circle scribin caught on like gang busters. Thats why us Cathlics go to church on NewYears Day. Thats when Jesus got circle scribed. Become a real big deal. Everybody started imitatin the old Jews. Then long comes Adolf Hitla. And Hitla says, Enough-a-this already. And Hitla tells that Germans trimmin dicks gonna be against the law. And Hitla starts a very strict war called the Hullacoss. This is the whole reason for *Combat* in the first place.

What about *TheGallantMen?*

Pruney gives me another Eecoodeesh Popeye look and says, Same war. Its all WorldWarTwo. Its the same war. Theyre all fightin Hitla. And my brother says if Hitla dint get too extreme we never woulda hadda fight the Nazis. Russians. Japs or Italians and thered be no WorldWarTwo movies or TV shows. No *Combat*. No *GallantMen*. And like I been tryin to tell you. Not fa nuthin. Whether you believe me or not. Every guy is born skin on his dick. And all this Sistine Chapel stuff. Is cause Michelangelos first guy painted dicks the way God for real made em to be. Skin on em. Skindicks. And thats why theyre called Michelangelos.

Ross took the book from Pruney.

Pruney, Ross said. GilOwen teaches me lotta stuff bout art and about the Bible too. No hard feelins or nothin Pruney. But you got a few things wrong. Its okay though cause you tell it prettfunny.

Pruneys eyes big headlights and he says, Whaddaya mean? My brother. Hes studyin to be a undertaker and he knows all about this stuff.

Ross closed the book and said, Pruney. Why dont you give it a rest. How about you stay for supper? Moms cookin baked scrod stuffed with scallops and toasted cracker crumbs just the way you like. And she got a good lopsta bisk steamin in the pot.

Like so many nights Pruney stayed with us and ate Moms cooking. Pruney loved Moms cooking. And Mom loved Pruney. Dad did too.

Dad always said, Whats another mouth to feed? And besides. That kid does us honor. We can all learn a thing or two from the likes-a-Pruney-Mendez.

So now theres Pruney with. In hand. His Michelangelo. And Mush looking. And WillieD looking. And me looking. And Ross looking. And

Pruneys sturdy cherub turning into Abrahams sharp knife right over MissNovembers curved up tits. Pruney sliding his hand back and forth. The next thing is WillieD kneeling and hes pulling on his dick. LilMush. He dont kneel. Just drops draws standing. Pants and underwear knee bunched and both hands jerking and tugging his skinny little finger dick. And my boner. About busting out my pants. Im on my knees next to Pruney and out jacking my dick hard and those pins WillieD told about prickling up my legs and into my head and Pruney eyes closed. Cheeks frost cold red. And him hollering, This for real is *Combat*. Im VicMorrow suckin MissNovembers jugs.

And Ross. The only one not altar praying. Only one not campfire singing. Ross standing like David. But dressed with clothes. Watching each one of us. And all on a sudden. Like Abrahams angel. LeoDriggs. Outta nowhere. Scrubbed face behind Rosses square shoulder.

LeoDriggs and Bundles.

LeoDriggs showered n shaved.

Bundles a wino stink ass.

Leo hollers, What in JesusMary grab ass heaven? You boys skedaddle.

And its us, Oh shit.

Ross gone fast and quick too. Our hands stuffing pants. Pruney walking on his knees straight over MissNovembers belly and her getting all torn ripped with WillieD doubled over and the *Cavalier* flying in the air. LilMush tripping. Leo pulling LilMushGahdoo outta the dirt and *Swank* slapping Mushes bleached white ass.

Its Bundles smashing a empty Mad Dog pint against the round PowaHouse chimney wall shattering a thousand sparkling glass confetti and Bundles yelling, Hahlaylewyuh Hooglies. Gwon home. All-a-yous. Git.

Discovering the PowaHouse for real was Moms fault. And JackCoggs.

They were to blame.

Not us.

Truth was.

We wasnt smoking cigarettes.

We wasnt breaking windows.

We wasnt starting fires.

We were just playing army.

Just making C rations.

Just reading magazines.

We were just being *Combat*.

And *TheGallantMen*.

16
Talking Doing Feeling

Not ta say. But.

After Pruney showing. All we talked about was dick.

Dicktalk always.

Dicktalk constant.

Dicktalk secret code.

No more playing army and just staying focused on football and baseball.

But girls.

No more just WillieD. LilMushGahdoo. Pruney. Ross and me. Names like Lynn. Vickie. Sally and Denise. Leslie. Gail. Monica. And Veronica. Kept showing up in our everything talk. Our everything talk about dicks.

For some reason we never talked about what the girls dint have down there. We just knew they dint have dicks. They had cracks. So we dint pay that place on the girls much attention. Pruney called it their holes. And he said it this way, For girls its sorta like their asses jus curl round to where their dicks suppose ta be. And the reason God made girls that way was. God give Adam. A extra rib.

Ross cut Pruney off and told Pruney, Its got nothin to do with spare ribs. Got everythin to do with eggs. Sperm n women havin babies. And furthamore. What girls have goin on down there is waymore complicated than youd think.

Howdya know?

Cause my mother explained it all me n Jate. A man puts sperm into that hole and babies come out that hole Pruney. Babies. You even went into that hole. And came out that hole too. Everybody does.

And then Pruney blinked his eyes a whole bunch a times. He looked for a splinter in his hand and said he knew. Said his brother Digga told him that too. But also, Bible said Adam was made-a-slime clay. And Eve was made-a-Adams extra rib.

Then. Looking back at Ross. Pruney said he was telling not what girls holes was for. But how theys holes was made.

Then I said Ross and him was both being dickheads because it was a stupid argument.

And then Pruney said he'd, Rather be a dickhead than a dicknose.

Who you callin a dicknose? said Ross.

And Pruney said, You.

And Ross said, Well a dicknose is betta than a dickface.

And see what I mean? Pruney and Ross kept dicktalk arguing all the time everywhere.

There was. Dickhead. Dickmouth. Dickass. And sometimes. Assdick. Dickfingers Dicktoes. Asslickdick. Dickface. Dicknose. Dicklips. Dicktoes. Dickhair. Dickfeet. Dickeyes. Dickteeth. Dickgums. Dickbreath. Dicktalk this and dicktalk that.

And even. Dickweed and Dickwad. Whatever that was.

One time when we were listening to Moms records on the hifi. Ross said, You guys gotta hear this new one Mom the other day bought. He flipped through her collection. *Show Boat. Sound of Music. South Pacific. King and I. West Side Story. My Fair Lady. Camelot.* And one called *The Music Man.*

Ross dropped the needle on the first song and these guys started sing-talkin. Slow first. Then real fast. And then we all flipped because the guys started saying stuff like, *You can talk. You can dicker. You can dicker you can talk. You can dicker dicker dicker. You can talk talk talk.*

We played that over and over. It was a crack up.

But the one that made us go total mental was *Kiss Me Kate.*

The Music Man come close. But *Kiss Me Kate* for real spazzed us good.

One song these guys kept begging this lady to pick one a them to marry. And the guys were Tom. Harry. And Dick. Which was funny enough by its own self. But then the woman starts singing over and over,

A dicker dick. A dicker dick. A dicker dick.

We just total lost it. We must have played that song ten million times.

There you have it.

Dicktalk.

Then there was Richard.

Richard was like Dicktalk. Except it was Dicktalk in code.

Pruney began that one when we were camping with Dad. The Montaup puddingstone. There was Ross. LilMush. WillieD. Pruney and me. Dad had turned in real early and we guys were all Dicktalking around the campfire roasting marshmallows. Pruneys stick hit WillieDs stick and made WillieDs burning marshmallow fall. Into the fire. WillieD called Pruney a dickface. And Pruney said, Yeah, well you got my dick in your mouth.

And Dad sits up in his sleeping bag and says, You boys knock off that gutter talk.

Dad scared us have to death. We all thought he was asleep. And for a while. After he settled back down again. We all thought for sure this time Dads sleeping. So quiet. Just fire crackling. The small waves doing the shore. And somewhere seagulls making long sad crying sounds when theyre nesting for the night. And Pruney figures hes gonna get back WillieD.

You know Pruney.

Just gotta have the last word.

So. In all that real real loud quiet.

Fire snapping. Soft wind.

Pruney says, WillieD. You got my Richard in your mouth.

And we all snort laugh and Dad up again sitting in his sleeping bag. saying, Thats it Pruney. We're goin home.

And Pruneys all, Dint say nothin. Dint say nothin.

And Dads, Knock off that snickerin or else and Im not gonna warn you boys again.

And we allow lotsa quiet settle in. No one speaks. For a real long time its just fire. Just waves. Just wind and the dune eel grass making that whisper sound that sounds like long. Shushes. Shhh. Shhh. Shhh.

Then Pruney.

Through the sound of whispering dunegrass.

Pruney starts to sing. Real quiet.

You can dicker dicker talk.

And trying to keep our laughs in the sleeping bags is tough. But Dads still quiet.

Then Pruney saying, Richard.

Then again. We sleeping bag snort laugh. But into our hands. Into our shoulders. Into our arms. But for real keeping our laughing quiet so we get no stir from Dad. And we dont. Dont get him riled again. For the rest of the night its, Richardhead. Richardface. Richardnose.

We go the whole way round. Richardthis.

Richardthat.

Richardeverything.

And then there was Whoosh.

Sometimes we did whoosh right in front of Mom and Dad.

Sometimes we even did it in front of teachers.

What whoosh was is you curled your hand like youre whacking off. Like your fingers and thumb are wrapped round a fat stick. Or your dick. But the most important thing being your thumb and your pointing finger making a circle and you say, Whoosh.

Whoosh always got lotsa laughs.

Then Pruney told us about blow.

The way Pruney told us was blow was all wrong.

Blow was for real about suck.

Like, Suck my dick.

And suck was as nasty as you could get. So we dint much say suck.

Blow was definite more popular. But the way it all come about was dicktalk first.

Then Richard.

Then whoosh.

Then blow.

Then dicktalkdoing.

We never just said, Hey lets go to the PowaHouse and whack off.

It usual begun with Pruney having to take a leak. And him showing us how far he could wiz. Then. Id take out mine and try to piss farther than him. Then Mush. Then WillieD. Prettsoon we were all standing around with our dicks in our hands. Looking at each other going from soft dicks to boners.

Pruney would jerk and tilt. Bend and bob. One hand doing the whoosh up. The whoosh down. The whoosh back and the whoosh forth. Faster and faster. And Pruney. Now hes on his knees and hes calling Lynn. Michele. Mary. Denise. Sharon. Gail and Monica. Locomotive arm. A back and forth blur. Whitestuff on his fingers. Whitestuffsperm on the PowaHouse walls.

It wasnt like we were all just standing there watching Pruney.

No. Pruney would always start.

Then we'd follow. Follow his begin.

And by the time Pruney was yelling out girls names. So were we all. We'd all be doing a round. Singing with that feeling that kept bringing us back to the PowaHouse to do this thing that we promised each other would always be our secret.

All of us.

Except Ross.

All of us.

Whacking off in the dirt.

Ross would always stand off a ways.

Ross was different.

Ross would just take peeks then look aways. Said, Somebody hadda keep guard cause we dont wanna get caught like we first time did. Leo-Driggs and Bundles.

And no one gave Ross any noise about that. LilMush did once. Said Ross was playin pocket pool.

Pruney told Mush knock it off and leave Ross to be. Leave him alone too. And after that no one never said nothing to Ross as we'd stand from the ground quiet and wipe our fingers off on the brick roundhouse walls. Wipe our fingers off on the inside of our underwear. Our wet dicks back into our pants. No one saying nothing. No one looking each other in the eyes.

Stickywet down the railroad tracks and heading home.

Stickywet when WillieD headed up DavisStreet.

Stickywet when LilMush said, See you. And ran down Land.

Stickywet when Ross. Pruney. And me. Walked up BaggyWrinkle. Hanged our jackets on the wall.

Mom called to Dad, Boys are home and its time for supper.

Stickywet under the supper table.

And remember.

There was dicktalktalking.

There was dicktalkdoing.

What I learnt from Ross and Pruney was there was also dicktalkfeeling.

And about that dicktalkfeeling stuff. I knew nothing.

Till then I got to see what Ross and Pruney did.

That made them different.

Made me different too.

Ross? Pruney? Me?
Difrent.
Diffrent.
And different.
Because I knew what Ross and Pruney did.
When Pruney slept over our house.
Like Pruney would do again tonight.

17

Pruneys Island

Like I already told. Pruney used to sleep over our house all the time.

We liked having Pruney over.

After his first asquantum. We invited him all of the time.

And he'd always come over our house and stay.

It wasnt that his dad dint care about him.

His dad did care.

A lot.

But the old man worked night shift and Pruney was suppose to stay with AuntJovita and his younger cousin Edu who we called SkiffheadEd on account his wide forehead being like a quahogskiff boat bottom.

Pruneys older brother. Dagama. Digga was always doing funerals and dint get home till past midnight. And anyway. One day. Mom alone walked all the way by herself to SowamsEastEnd MathewsonStreet. Mom give Pruneys AuntJovita. Some mint. And basil. And flowers cut fresh from our garden. AuntJovita made coffee and her and Mom did a real long talk. And Mom said. AuntJovita said, It was always gonna be okay. Pruney stayin over.

So Mom put a old mattress underneath Rosses bed. With sheets and a pillow and a handstitched quilt. Just like ours. That she handstitched all by herself. And whenever Pruney stayed over. He just pulled the mattress out from under the bed and put it between Rosses bed and my bed. And thats where Pruney slept.

Mattress.

On the floor.

Middle of our room.

Comfortable and cozy.

We called the mattress Pruneys Island. Said it was the middle of Nar-

ragansettBay next to all the other Islands. Prudence. Faith. Hog. And
Hope. And from Pruneys Island. Pruney would tell crazy stories. Or
would read with flashlights. Batman comics. Or swap cigar box treasures. Study the chromolithographic art labels. Or look at naked natives
in *National Geographic*. Especial in the summer. Window open. Cool
SowamsRiver breeze. Or KingPhilipsCove. Depending which way Borialis.
Wind god. Was stirring.

Mom used to say, If wind smelled clean salt and heavy fog. Weather
was Notus south. Hot and humid. Huggamugga.

On the other hand. Mom would also say. Wind smell-a-rockweed n
kelp. Eurus-a-the east and Boreas-a-the north lazin down from Canada
and lingerin over the marsh.

In thick dead of summer. Boreas strict north made it feel like god
Boreas turned on a air conditioner. And even though it might be late July.
Or early August. It could all on a sudden feel like autumn fall. Mornings
youd wrap in a quilt. And for the rest of the day wear a sweater or a jacket
and always be thinking about how soon was it gonna get hot again.

When we got a breeze. It never for real mattered to me where it was
blowing from. I liked how in NewEngland it could be one day one way.
And complete different the next. Sometimes breezes was all mixed up at
once in a one single day.

What I dint like was when we got nothing.

Nothing but heat.

Nothing but sweating.

Nothing but feeling everything was left sogged from the hugmug day
before.

Sometimes it would get hugmug for a couple of days. Sometimes even
for a couple of weeks. And when it did. When it did get that way in the
day. Of course we went to the beach. But the nights we'd all lay on our
mattresses. Pruney his island. Ross and me our beds. With nothing on but
underwear. No teeshirts. No blankets. No sheets. No nuthin.

Thats the way it was first time Pruney showed us LittleRichard and his
TapDancinDick.

Pruney was telling about this girl named LynnWazzalewski in his low
slow classroom. Who used to go to Miss Annie Pogostamus tap dancing stu-
dio. Pruney said LynnWazzalewski was. For a long time. Real flat chested.
But then. Like overnight. She got big tits that bounced too much. So Miss
Annie Pogostamus. Or as Pruney called her. MissFannie Pogostick Legs.
Said, LynnWazzalewski couldnt dance in the recital.

One day Pruney was delivering papers to LynnWazzalewskis house. LynnWazzalewski was crying on her front steps because LynnWazzalewski for real wanted to dance in the dance recital and Pruney told LynnWazzalewski that, MissFannie Pogostick Legs is a idiot cause anyone can see that LynnWazzalewski is way more bewdeeful than MissFannie Pogostick Legs. Most cause MissFannie Pogostick Legs is a pirates dream. MissFannie Pogostick Legs has a sunken chest and MissFannie Pogostick Legs is jealous.

Pruney said to Ross and me he had heard his brother Digga tell that joke. But not about Miss Pogostamus and LynnWazzalewski. Pruney said when Digga told it. It was about two hores. And I always meant to ask Pruney, Whats hores? And the way I figured. It was girls who hung around with pirates. Not ta say. But. Pruney said that joke made LynnWazzalewski laugh.

And I thought it was a good one too. A good joke. Sunken chest. No tits. Get it?

Anyway. Pruney told LynnWazzalewski he was sure she was the best tap dancer in all of Sowams. And maybe even RhodeIsland. NewEngland and the whole wide world. And then Pruney asked LynnWazzalewski if she'd do a tap dance for him?

And LynnWazzalewski said, Sure.

And LynnWazzalewski went into the house and turned on her record player real loud and came back on the porch.

And LynnWazzalewski tapped *Tea for Two* on the front porch for Pruney.

Right there on the front porch.

And thats when Pruney said, LittleRichard started dancing too.

Then Pruney got quiet on Pruneys Island.

Pruney was thinking real deep.

Then Pruney told Ross. And me. MissPogostamus wasnt a idiot. MissPogostamus was right. Even though LynnWazzalewski could tap dance real good. Those tits could dance a whole lot better. But Pruney said he would never tell that to LynnWazzalewski because Pruney could see by the way LynnWazzalewski counted. Before the music started. One. Two. Three. By the way LynnWazzalewski held out her hands in front of her with her palms flat out. And her red fingernails in the air. By the way LynnWazzalewski bounced at her knees. And kept her legs all springy. And how LynnWazzalewski sang with the record music and her own voice all serious,

Tea for two. Two for tea. Me for you. You for me alone.

Pruney said it hurt in his heart bad how LynnWazzalewski for real wanted to dance. And it just about ached him awful seeing how much LynnWazzalewski wanted to be a dancing star. And it wasnt LynnWazzalewskis fault her tits got in the way.

We all three agreed it was real nice of Pruney for him to say good stuff to LynnWazzalewski.

And then in the dark Pruney singing. Singing to himself. *Tea for Two.* My flashlight. And there he was. Pruney on his mattress. Pruney. His dick out. Not whacking off. Just fingers. Thumbs and dick. Doing the tap dancing dick with a big smile on his face. And some of my flashlight sparkle in his eyes.

Ross was watching Pruney too. So I turned off my flashlight and listened to the dark. The no breeze night. Listened to Pruney as his singing faded into just breathing. And a giggle now and then.

For a long time just lay there in the dark.

Lay there in the dark thinking about Sowams.

KingPhilipMetacom.

The Hooglies.

About LynnWazzalewski crying and how Pruney told a joke made her smile.

Tea for two. Two for tea.

And somewhere out the window a cat made a stretched out meeeow. And the Hooglies did a whisper. And a car over on LandStreet rolled by too. Maybe heading up MountHopeRoad to Bristol. Or even driving all the way to Newport. And the ocean.

Then. The slightest of breezes pushed the window curtains forward. In our dark room the breeze. Was it north or was it south?

The faint outside light. Coming through those drifting up curtains. Made it seem like the dark form of things in the room were moving.

The chair dark form?

Moving.

The bookcase dark form?

Moving.

The Ross dark form?

Moving.

The dark form of Ross moving from his bed to the dark form of Pruneys Island.

The dark form of Rosses hand touching Pruneys shoulder.

Rosses head on Pruneys chest.

Pruneys hand around Rosses hand.

Both hands on Pruneys Michelangelo. The whoosh up. The whoosh down. Except now its not whoosh. Now its slow. Now its just a gentle whoo.

Whoo up. And whoo down.

Whoo. Dark quiet soft.

Whoo. Silent. No darkness breeze.

Whoo. So hardly there. Over the railroad streetlight through the window and drifting past the curtain.

And now its both Pruneys hands and Rosses hands on both Pruneys body and Rosses body and both Pruneys body and Rosses body stretching side by side and now Pruneys body and Rosses body stiff and straight and Rosses hands on Pruneys mouth and Pruneys hands on Rosses mouth and the sounds of Rosses and Pruneys sounds trying hard not to be sounds but being Rosses and Pruneys sounds anyway and then just Pruneys breathing and Rosses breathing. Breathing fast. Breathing long. Breathing slow. Breathing.

Just long. Slow. Breaths.

Breaths.

And no breeze.

Breaths.

And no moving.

Breaths.

No e.

And no nothing else.

The next morning Pruneys Island had disappeared.

Ross was in the bathroom and would probbly be in there a long time because thats how Ross was. Pruney had already gone home to make his father breakfast and I realized this breakfast Pruney was about to make for his father before Pruney went off picking clams at SousasShellfish was gonna be Pruneys fathers supper.

Dad was in NewYork doing on the dredge and Mom wasnt around either. She was probbly weeding the garden. Cutting back basil and tending tomatoes. Or maybe she was doing a wash. But more than likely she was in the garden because it was a beautiful morning and she always talked about. Beside how much she loved being at the beach. Being at dawn in the garden with the lavender and sweetpea blossoms. Sometimes she'd tell about the dawn sky being the sweetpea color and how. If she. Resting on a old crate. Took a moment from her weeding and looked out over the water. Sweetpeas were growing right in the water of KingPhilipsCove instead of around it. And then she'd say prettysoon all the sky and all the clouds would turn from the sweetpea color to the lavender color because the sun was just a bit higher and of course the water would be lavender too. That skychange from sweetpea to lavender reflecting in the water made her feel better than being in a church and about the best gift God could give her. Except for Dad. Her two boys. And all our good health.

So.

There it was.

Just Ross and me in the house. Sweetpea blossoms in the garden. Lavender in Moms dawn sky. And this whacking off stuff between Ross and Pruney.

I poured me a cup of coffee. Put in some milk. Stirred.

All the windows were still open and the marsh smelled strong. But the coffee smelled strong too. And the mix of coffee. Marsh. Sunrise and summer for a kid with a Dad at work. A mother in her garden. My twin brother in the bathroom fussing about himself. Made me. All on the sudden. Realize things were prettgood for us and real tough for Pruney. And even though Ross and Pruney should not be touching each other so private and everything. Sudden I was glad Ross had maybe made Pruney feel happy.

Not that Pruney ever complained about having a tough life because Pruney dint. Dint complain about anything.

Dint put on long faces.

Dint whine.

Dint drag around like the Barrington richkids. Or act a pukey moe moe all the time saying, This blows. Theres nothing to do.

Dint talk about how much he missed his mom and he did because he liked ours so much. The way he talked about our mom. Like she was his.

Dint stay quiet with stuff eating inside of him. The way it was doing me now.

Fact was the only thing ever seemed to upset Pruney and put him in a bad mood was when someone called him a stupit portagee. Or when he saw someone else feeling bad. Like with LynnWazzalewski.

So what could be the bad of it if Pruney and Ross was happy?

Still there was something.

Plate in the head something.

Something about it all what just dint settle in me because Mom and

Dad always said our privates were our privates and only time you shared them is when you fell in love and got married.

And that was my plate in the head problem. Not fa nuthin. How could Ross and Pruney ever fall in love and get married? Whacking off at the PowaHouse or doing it to each other on Pruneys Island wasnt Mom and Dads meaning when they said behave yourselfs and be good. Wait for the right times and the right places.

Time and place.

Sooner or later we would have girl friends. And we'd all be doing that private stuff the right way. Everything would work out just fine. And that was how I decided to leave it. Especial since Ross had just unlocked the bathroom door and also because I had just finished my cup of coffee and was hungry for breakfast and that meant making a omelet for Ross and me because we both. For real. Liked omelets and we always cooked them together.

And then did halfs.

When Ross finally come out the bathroom. Towel around his waist. Hair slicked back. Face all clean. And body smelling bathsoap and new day. I cracked the second egg while Ross watched and said nothing.

Then Ross. Reaching. Took a egg from the carton. Cracked it. Then another. A four egg omelet. He went into the bedroom put on some clothes and only sounds in the kitchen was outside traffic noises from way up LandStreet coming open window through and me doing eggs with a fork in the stainless steel mixing bowl. And that fork clankclankclank against that stainless steel mixing bowl made me for a moment think of my plate in the head. Was Ross thinking that too? When he come out the bedroom wearing a pair of dungaree cutoffs and a teeshirt he was saying nothing. Just watching me pour them scrambled eggs the hot buttered pan. Hisses and bubbling. Firming. Using the spatula. Flipping the omelet. Cutting in two. Turning off the gas and on the sudden Ross asks me, Pruneys dick ever make you think-a-Pruneys eyes?

And that question makes me almost drop the hot pan on the kitchen floor. Im all splats and sputters just like the firming of the omelet. Then no breath.

My mouth open and me adding an e thats more like stutters than breathe-ing and say, No Pruneys dick dont ever make me think-a-Pruneys eyes. I put the hot pan back on top the stove and say, Just makes me think hope we dont get caught.

And Ross said, The PowaHouse?

Anywheres.

Ross said, Already got caught. You guys. PowaHouse.

Well what you guys doin lastnight in ah bedroom wasnt just dickdoin. That was dickfeelin. Bein Sodmites.

And just like JackCoggs stab had harpooned GilOwens heart. So too did my just said hurtwords. And I never meant such a thing. Just came out and Rosses eyes went flinch. Rosses head went quiver. And without another word. Ross took hold the omelet panhandle. Slid his omelet half to his plate. And quiet walked from the kitchen.

Disappeared.

Our room.

Behind the closing door.

Left me total plate in the head.

And I finished my omelet alone.

18
Ah NorEasta

And I gotta tell you.

I was different.

Watching Ross and Pruney made me realize I dint wanna do what they were doing.

Made me different from Zeebo WillieD and MushGahdoo too cause. Up until now. What I knew about Ross and Pruney. WillieD. Zeebo. Mush and me. We dint keep any secrets from each other.

But this Sodmite thing?

Something way inside just told me this thing had to stay my secret. Had to stay inside me. Not so much for me. But for Ross. And for Pruney.

Pruney dint think on things that way. If he acted crazy. Or did something strange. If something was making him mental. He took that thing to confession. To church.

First time Pruney took us in the PortugueseCathlic church. Which was only about a quarter mile from the ItalianCathlic church. Was the Thanksgiving after Mom caught Pruney faking the raw turkeyneck was his dick. Talk about crazy strange.

Early Wednesday evening. Pruney had took the turkeyneck and giblets from out the sink where Mom was thawing the frozen Butterball. Pruney stuffed the neck in his pants. Pulled down his zipper. And whipped out the bony meat saying his dick was the biggest limp dick ever.

See? Pruney. A total mental case. And all three of us laughing so hard we dint hear Mom coming from outside. Because. All on a sudden. The door. Open.

And theres Mom.

A turkeyneck giblet hanging from his pants where should be Pruneys dick.

Mom calm as ever walked over to her knife drawer.

Got out her big old chef knife.

Walked straight to Pruney looking him eye contact direct. And with the slightest jolt. Stuck that knifepoint into the side of that hanging turkeyneck. Pulled the hanging turkeyneck from Pruneys pants. Raised the knife over the sink and wiggled Pruneys hanging turkeyneck so the hanging turkeyneck fell into the sink doing a wet thud splat sound.

Then Mom told Pruney, Pull up your zipper.

And Pruney turned around. Away from Mom. And he made himself right.

Mom said she was raising us better than for us to be showing such low behavior to ourselfs. Further somemore. That poor bird had give its life for each of us and if we were so base with each other that was one thing. But she wasnt gonna tolerate such disrespecting to the turkey.

We said, Sorry

And we were too.

Mom accepted our apologies. But asked, What on earth ever gets into you boys?

Pruney said, FathaLuis says its the devil.

Mom smiled. But then she told Pruney, From now on. When you stay over this house. You best doorstep leave the devil.

She told Pruney, Take the turkeyneck outside and leave it where a cat maybe can have some Thanksgiving too.

That night when we were all laying in our beds. Pruney and Ross got into a argument about the devil. Ross had been telling he heard GilOwen and MistaCogg talking a book by some guy called Milton about Paradise being lost. And how the devil was for real a beautiful ark angel who God called Lucifer. And that the name meant beautiful light.

So I said the light Ross was talking about was probbly like the ark torch welding glow we would always see at Blounts EastBay shipyard when the workers were welding together flat sheets of steel to build a boat.

Ross said ark was Noahs boat. But when talking about Blount shipyard welding boats it was A-R-C. And having to do with angels. It was A-R-C-H. Meaning highest. Top rank. Main.

Did I already say how much I hate doing right spell writing?

I hate it.

No matter.

According to Ross. When God was first thinking about making Adam and Eve. God talked the whole idea with the angels. God said he needed a assistant. God wanted bewdeeful arc light Lucifer to help Adam and Eve behave. Be their guardian arch angels and stuff. Lucifer said, No way. He would only serve God.

When God insisted Lucifer do double duty. Lucifer led a rebel war. And Lucifer got tossed outta heaven by Michael. The other. ArchAngel. Who JackCogg called, Mikey 2A's.

Pruney said he thought it was a real good story. That he had heard it before. But not the name Mikey 2A's. Or the part about Lucifer being beautiful.

Ross explained that Mikeys two A's was for the first letter in Arch being A and the first letter in Angel bein another letter A too. And the two A name. Mikey 2 A's. Was just MistaCogg bein MistaCogg.

But Ross worked real hard explaining the also too being different from the T-W-O-2. But worked more hardest explaining Lucifer dint get ugly until after Lucifer got sent to Hell. Pruney wouldnt have none of that.

Pruney said, Spelling To. Too. And Twos not as important as the ugli-ness-a-the word in the world. And all the worlds ugly begin with Lucifer in heaven. The horns. Fangs. Firey eyes.

And snakebody. It all come before hell. And Pruney said there were a statue of Mikey 2A's and Lucifer. At his church and that statue could prove where ugly begun.

So. Next morning. Which was Thanksgiving. With turkey roasting in the oven. We jumped on our bicycles. Pedaled up BaggyWinkleLane. Up KellyStreet to Land. And parked our bikes. Bottom steps. Portuguese-Catholic church.

As we climbed those steps Pruney said, Mornin mass been over about-a-couple-a-three hours ago and be okay if we go in.

The front door was extra heavy thick and Pruney had to use both hands pull it open. The inside was real dark and I could immediate smell the inside smell of that church was real different from the outside smell.

That inside smell was like the smell-a-pinetrees and smoke. But not exact.

When the door shut behind us. That door made a closed real good wump. And I threw Ross a look. And Ross threw back a look meant, Dont be chicken. Its only a church.

The first thing we saw was a small hallway and immediate to our rights and our lefts was altars. Except they really werent altars. They were candles. Candle racks. Couple three dozen candles on each with kneeler things in front of them where Pruney said you could kneel. Light a candle. And say a prayer to suffering Jesus who was right there on the left. Hanging on a cross being. Pruney said. Roman crucified.

We're looking up into a candle glowed face of Jesus. Those flickers made it like Jesus was groan suffering for real. Werent pretty. Tell you that much. To be high tide honest with you. I was having the Hooglies right then and there but dint want Pruney or Ross to know so I pretended everything was hunkadory and too splendid to be good.

Pruney and Ross had gone on straight ahead. Up the main wide staircase. Through another set a big doors and had disappeared into the church. And with Jesus. Me. And the Hooglies having a regular bit of a get together. I was in no mood to stay and enjoy the celebrating. I was up them stairs and through those doors fast. Whoa but that church was amazing. The artwork was bewdeeful. Almost as beautiful as chromolithographic cigar box lables.

The ceilings were real real high with all kind of them freshca paintings like in that Michelangelo book that GilOwen had gave to Ross. Except none the people on this ceiling were naked. They all had on clothes. Mostly robes and stuff.

As for that pine smoke smell I mentioned. It was candles. Way more candles than the hallway. Candle glass colored jars. Different sizes too. Big jars and little. Big flames and small. Each glowing jar colors. Red. Green. Blue. Real nice. And warm.

Then there was all window colors. Bright colors like a slideshow projected of all different Bible people standing with white pigeons over their heads. And cups of wine getting spilled. And sheep being carried on shoulders. Seagulls flying with angels. Oxes listening while some guy read to them from a storybook. And lions laying down with lambs.

At first I thought that church smelled like campfire smoke and the pine trees outside PeteJanettoes house. But then. For no reason I could figure. That church started smelling like MistaCoggs shop after he be carving wood. Sipping brandy and smoking his Missouri briar burl Meerschaum.

So there we were. All three of us. Standing in the PortugueseCatholic church. Thanksgiving. Sowams RhodeIsland. And lets face it.

Gawking.

Gawking at sights we never before seen.

But not Pruney.

Pruney wasnt gawking.

Pruney was right at home with himself.

Pruney was the boss.

First. Pruney showed us how to holywater bless ourselfs. Dip our fingers into a thing Pruney called a font. A sorta bowl carved into a tall piece of solid rock. And in this bowl was water and a sponge. Not a dishwashing kind of sponge Mom uses. But the kind of sponge Pruney said lived at the bottom of the ocean. Sponges living in the ocean bottom? Whoever heard of such a thing? Yet Ross said it was true. Anyway. Pruney works at SousasShellfish and he should know if anyone knows. But. That holywater fontsponge dint look like a dishwashing sponge. But like a big clump of mermaids hair from some rock off the HooglySpit.

Pruney showed us how to dip our hands in the font and touch the mushwet sponge. I thought the mushwet sponge from a holywater font would feel different than the regular dishwater sponge from a sink.

But the mushwet holywater sponge dint.

Not until Pruney showed us how to bless ourselfs with our wet holywater fingertips while at the same time bending down on one knee. Pruney called that bending, Genuflecting.

And I gotta addmit. When I followed Pruney showing. Bending my knee and blessing myself. A holywater buzz went direct through my plate in the head right down my neck down my back through my hips into my legbones into my shins and into my toes. Maybe there was something special about holywater being different from dishwater. But before my mouth opened to ask. Pruney said, Lets go up the side aisles and see 3D pictures hanging on the walls.

Did he mean like oldfashion ViewMaster photos? Or popout coins on cigar boxes? Nope. Pruney took us below stautes in a picture hanging on the wall. Pruney said, These are stations-a-the cross showin the sufferin of Ah Good Lord Jesus.

Pruney dint know why they called them stations. Said it was probbly like train stations and bus stations but Ross said maybe they were called stations because they were stationary. Ross said stationary meant standing still.

Irregardless. The 3D statue pictures were real sad. Especial the ones where soldiers were hammering nails into the hands and feet of Jesus.

Think about it. Nails big as railroad spikes in your hands are bad enough. But nails almost big as railroad spikes into all that footbone. Who could stand such a thing?

The candle flicker in the hallway on the face of Jesus.

All his gimmacing and anguishing.

We stood in the side aisle under that picture for a while. How soldiers could do such pain to another person was beyond me. A itch on my head and in my hair. And then Ross and me feeling the tops of our hands with our pointing fingers. Feeling the bones them spike nails had to go through. Then feeling palms of our hands with our thumbs.

Imagining where them spikes stuck through.

And while doing that. Pruney went on ahead.

Ross and me. Imagining them Roman spikes cracking through our foot bones. We was hopping one foot to the other and dint realize we were doing it till Pruney inerrupted saying, You auditionin for MissAnnieFanny PogoStickLegs or what? Stop your tapdancin and come on over and see AhWondrous Lady-a-Fatima.

Which we did. Even though it was still imagine painful to walk.

But AhWondrous Lady-a-Fatima made all that imagine pain go away.

Bewdeeful Lady-a-Fatima.

Floating on a cloud and being about as happy as a cloudfloater could be.

Nothin fat about her, I outloud said.

And Pruney forehead smacked himself. Took a sigh. No Eecoodeesh. Said, Fatima dont mean shes fat. Fatimas a place. A Portugal place.

Ross rolled his eyes and said, Everybody knows that.

Excuse me for bein ignorant but I dont know from nothin bout Portugal and AhWondrous Lady-a-Fatima Cathlic statues.

So Pruney then explained, AhLady-a-Fatima was for real AhBlessed-Mother. TheVirginMary. Mother-a-Jesus. Lives in heaven. And about fifty years ago she floated down on a cloud to a place called Fatima Portugal. She visits three Portuguese kids. Helps em get so Russia woulnt be communiss anymore by prayin everyday on their rose ree beads.

And I said, I dint know the communiss had rose ree beads.

Pruney said, They dont. And thats the whole point. What AhLady-a-Fatima wants is for everybody else in the world to pray so the communiss will get rose ree beads and start usin em and in order to make that happen AhLady went to Fatima Portugal and asked those three kids for ta help.

Pruney continued, Not ta say fa nuthin. But. Thats a prettnice thing for AhLady-a-Fatima ta do. Bringin those three Portuguese kids in on the deal.

Deal? What deal? I said.

Again Ross rolled his eyes and Pruney did to him like Popeye. Pruney turned to me real calm like he usual does when Im plate in the head.

And Pruney said, Rose ree beads. Somebodys gotta sell all those communiss rose ree beads. AhLady-a-Fatimas bringin in the kids to do it don-chya see?

Sure. Now I get it. Thats real nice-a-her. Such a good mind for busi-ness, I said.

Ross listened and dint say nothing.

Pruney said, AhLady-a-Fatima is my favorite statue in the church cause how happy the BlessedMother looks on her face and the two girls. Lou-seea. Yahsinta. And boy. Fransisco. They look so happy too.

VirginMary. Smiling. Floating on her little cloud above a tree. Three kids ground kneeling in front of the tree and the holy cloud. Hands folded for lotsa rose ree bead business. Looking up VirginMary like they absolute knew VirginMary was gonna give them all the rose ree bead customers they ever would need.

Then Pruney points the other side of the church. And we passed in front of the altar again. Had to genuflect again. On account of Pruney said Jesus lives in the little tabbanackle box in the middle of the altar.

Pruney pointed to a red candle hanging from the ceiling off three big gold chains and said, That candle burnin means Jesus is right now livin in the altar tabbanackle.

Hooglies in my head.

I said, Thought Jesus lived in heaven?

He does. But he sorta lives in tabbanackles too. When the preece blesses the bread and wine. The bread and wine becomes Jesuses for real body and blood.

And Ross said, Whadaya mean for real body and blood?

And Pruney said, Its holy communion. It looks like bread. More like a vanilla wafer. But when the preece says the confiscated words. It miracle like. Becomes Jesuses flesh and blood. Just cant see meat. Cant taste blood neitha. But it for real is alive Jesus.

Ross said, Pruney. Sometimes you tell some crazy big stretchers. This is the biggest one ever. Who ever heard-a-people in a church eatin Jesus flesh? And. Not ta say. Drinkin his blood?

And Pruney said, Its not exact his meat and blood. Its communion bread and wine that becomes meat and blood. Miracle like.

And Pruney. Quick. Like he was getting away from Rosses pressure. Turns around and says, When the priest says his confiscation prayers. When he confiscateblesses bread and wine in the chalice cup. Sometimes the preece confiscates too much wafer and hes gotta put the leftovers somewhere. Preece always drinks leftover wine. Leftover waferbread goes in the tabbanackle. So. Thats how and why Jesus lives in tabbanackles.

I was just about to say, Then the tabbanackle is sorta like a holy breadbox.

When Ross said, Meat and the blood? Shoulnt it be a refrigerator?

But Pruney. Not paying no never mind to lotsa doubts Ross or me. Again genuflects and crosses over to a little table and grabs. From a velvet envelope. Something looking like a gold flat frying pan with a black wood handle stick. And Pruney. Like he got all the answers. Carries it. Delicate like. One hand holding the tip of the black handle and the other hand. Just using his finger tips. Under the frying pan center. Pruney says, This is the communion plate. One-a-my most important altarboy jobs is hold it at the throat-a-people receivin communion.

Pruney puts the gold flat frying pan right under my chin and the cold of the metal sends a shiver around my neck.

Pruney does the same to Ross and a gold reflection goes all over Rosses face.

And Pruney says, Because communion is the confiscated body-a-Jesus. If ever that confiscated bread. Which is really a host. Falls from the preeces hands or from some persons tongue. I gotta catch it so it dont hit the floor. If it hits the floor. Itd be like deadalive Jesus gettin crucified all over again. And trust me. That aint good.

Pruney does another genuflect and puts away the communion plate. And nailed crucified bodies on crosses and eating deadalive guy flesh and drinking deadalive guy blood has got me all plate in the head. Not ta say. But. Even though suffering Jesus is a hanging bloody mess. This church sure is bewdeeful. And as I turn full to again see all that bewdeeful wonder. All on a sudden. In the close corner of a side altar.

Its *Combat*. Its *TheGallantMen*.

Michael the ArchAngel charging forward wearing a helmet. A armor vest. A cool Roman soldier dress. Leather sandals strapping around his ankles way to his knees. And behind his sturdy shoulders. Spread out wings looking they belong to a topbird seagull. Or better yet. The lake swans at RogerWilliamsPark. In Providence.

And Michael the ArchAngel. Serious look on his face. Is holding a sword high above his head. His other hand pointing like hes sending his dog outside.

Except there is no dog.

Only Lucifer.

The devil Lucifer.

The devil Lucifer horns and all.

And Pruney. Breaking between me and Ross. Says, See? Tol you. He already got horns and hes gettin tossed outta heaven. Look how scared ugly Lucifa is. Nope. Michael the ArchAngels not takin no nonsense from nobody.

And its obvious clear Lucifer looks so mean because as a devil he is real ascat. Hes afraid. With bulging ugly red eyes. His head straining high. Neck bridging back. Hes trying to do push ups refusing to look down at hell. But angel Mikeys sandal foot keeps horned up Lucifer in his place. And that horned up Lucifer is going no place but down. This is what paybacks all about and thats what you get for messing with God. Looks like Pruney was right. Lucifer was ugly before he got tossed outta heaven.

But Ross is not so ready to give. Ross. Arms folded. CombatVicMorrow.

Ross says, Well maybe so. But maybe also its cause Lucifer turned ugly minute he decided he wasnt gonna do what God wanted. GilOwen told it that way. And everybody knows GilOwens prettsmart bout everythin havin to do with ott and this antique Bible sorta stuff.

As we walked down the center aisle Ross pointed the confessions and asked, Can we go in these?

And Ross pulled back a greenvelvet curtain.

Pruney said, Sure FathaLuis aint around. Who cares?

Pruney knelt inside and folded his hands like he was praying and said, Its where I confess my sins. Other side-a-this walls where FathaLuis sits.

I opened the door and there was a very small closet with a polished woodbench with a cushion made of the same greenvelvet as the curtains.

I sat where FathaLuis sits. Left side was a panel. A panel on the right side too. And I slid the left side panel and Bingo. There was Pruney. I could hear Rosses footsteps as Ross went by me outside my preececloset.

Could hear Ross kneeling. Slid open his panel. And Bingo. There was Ross breathing on my right. And I gotta addmit. That preececloset was cozy.

Above the cloth screens the walls felt like they dint have wallpaper but instead were a nice cloth. Soft burlap. Like a good clam bag without the mud. And because the whole closet was lined with peaceful clambag cloth. You couldnt hear none of LandStreet traffic. Just Ross and Pruney. Breathing down my neck.

And. Not ta say. But. Because of that clambag burlap clothscreen separating us. Getting spitjuice in my ears from those guys dint even worry me. No doubt about it. Preececlosets were built JackCogg smart and GilOwen fancy and it was easy to see confessions was serious business. So I whispered, Ross. This is all fascinatin but we best gettin out fore we get caught.

Ross said, Whaddaya thinkll happen we get caught?

Its Thanksgivin morning. Pruney said, Whos gonna catch us?

I said, Our bikes. Outside. Maybe FathaLuises gonna investigate.

Pruney said, NewBedford. His sisters house. Goes there holidays.

I said, Whaddya think Ross?

Ross said, So these are confessions.

Thats right, said Pruney. FathaLuis listens to people tellin their sins. And cause the inside here is so dark. FathaLuis dont know whos tellin him what for. Why he dont know me from my cousin Skiffhead. I tell FathaLuis everythin.

Everything? asked Ross.

Everythin, said Pruney.

What you did with the turkeyneck and giblet. You gonna tell him that?

Sure.

And Ross said, Why?

Just makes me feel a whole lot betta when I do. Knowin if a car hits me. Or somethin. Im goin straight to heaven and not to hell.

How about swearin? And dicktalk?

And Pruney said, Yeah. That too.

Even the PowaHouse stuff?

Yeah. Mosly. Not all. But sure. Most.

You mention our names?

Did once. But usual. Just rat myself out.

But Pruney, said Ross. Thats personal. Dont want anybody knowin that stuff bout me.

Pruneys voice got all serious. Each word. The smack of JackCoggs woodmallets. Do you have any idea would happen a preece told somethin he confession hears? First. God probbly kill im with death right there on the spot. Second. Drop a fat meteorite or somethin on im. Third. Bolt-a-lightnin. Or a car accident. If that dint kill im dead then he'd suffer leppridsee disease. His nose. His ears. And his fingers fall off. Im tellin you Ross. Confessions serious business. If preeces dint keep things secret theyd be out-a-job and everybody be goin to hell.

Ross said, You tellin me when Grandma and Grampa Rossi got killed on the WampanoagTrail it was cause they did somethin bad and God evened up the score?

Maybe. But probbly not. Lets face it. Your grandma and grampa werent preeces tellin secrets. They were just a grandma and a grampa out for a Sunday drive. And anyways. They probbly always confessioned so they dint have nothin to worry about. Bottom line? Confessions good insurance.

Ross said, But Jate and I dont do confession. We dont even do church. My Dad dont believe in it. And Moms not crazy bout it neither. That mean we goin to hell?

I gotta addmit. Ross was pushing Pruney pretthard on this stuff. But hell werent no place I wanted. Especial if. Like Pruney said, Lucifa and them Roman soldiers ran the joint.

Before Pruney could answer. The sound of the church front door opening and the LandStreet traffic noise rolled in real loud. And then as the church front door closed the LandStreet traffic noise faded. Someone was walking up the center aisle and I dint know what was louder. Our dead quiet. Those footsteps. Or my heart hitting against my ribs. I could distinct hear talking. Drip sound of fingers dipping in holywater. Lips saying prayers. And the sounds of footstep walking.

Look out your curtain a crack, I whispered to Pruney.

No. You look out yours, whispered Pruney back.

No way, I whispered. And anyways. Dont got a curtain. Got a door and suppose whoever is out there is standin right in front-a-the door?

Ross said, I'll do it.

Pruney and me just sat there like chickens of the sea. Holding our breaths. Both of us about ready to drown.

And finally Ross said, Just a old woman. Way up the aisle. Shes lightin a candle. Lady-a-Fatima. Lets go real quiet. She'll never know we're here.

Pruney and Ross disappear when I slide the panels in a shush of black. All on a sudden. A mans voice. Then a whooshing sound. A thud and Pruney loud Eecoodeesh and saying to somebody something about Michael ArchAngel. And a Portuguese adult voice. And Pruney voice in Portuguese. I open the door a slit. Its dark church and candle flicker but the door swings wide and strong hands collargrab my throat and what starts as me screaming through my backbone blasts out my ass as a loud fart and Im yanked from the dark confession hush hush quiet and big man eyeglasses and eyes are inches from my eyes. A guy dressed black. Air dangling me so solid neckholding me and not letting me down not no how and definite. Not fa nuthin.

For a priest. This guys visegrip hands hold me by the throat for hard quick seconds as my feet do a fast dangling air dance that gets me going no where except two more farts. And as he shakes me my brain rattles against my headplate and he puts me down right there on the floor in the back of the church and Ross shouts from behind the curtain inside of his confession box, Jate. Jate. You all right? Answer. Answer me.

As FathaLuis turns to Rosses voice Im rolling on the floor coughing up a choking storm and Rosses head pops out from behind his curtain and Ross sees FathaLuis and Rosses face disappears again behind the velvet green.

Then FathaLuis opens Pruneys confession door that has a curtain yanked back and Pruney been watching my torture all along. Here comes Pruney being pulled by his ear. That big giant preece with a mustache and a whitecollar dressed all in a blackrobe is smacking Pruney backside Pruneys head and carrying on in Portuguese that Pruney is talking back to him in. Not backtalk talking back. Not that kind of backtalk. But answering questions backtalk. The Father is all big eyes. Looked like his lips just dragged hard on a cigarette butt. And preece hands on his preece hips. And FathaLuis is dressed in a long black preece nightgown. Pruney is pointing Ah-Lady-a-Fatama. Michael ArchAngel. And the Stations-a-the Cross. Pruney. A blue vein bulging up the side of Pruneys throat. And Pruney about near crying. Bulging blue vein and Pruneys face all fat with throbs and eyes looking like he seen the Hooglies. The Father shoulder holding Pruney. Gentle. Shaking Pruney. Then giving Pruney small pats. And a hug.

While FathaLuis is Pruney going at it. FathaLuis says, Whoever is in that other confessional better step out right now.

Ross comes out his confession. His cheeks slap the floor and his eyes shout. Run for it. So I turn. And direct in front of me.

The old lady who was praying AhLady-a-Fatima.

Im freezed solid.

Scared stiff.

And my feet wont do anything near like skedaddle.

That old woman was like so many of the Portuguese old ladies in De-Gammas Bakery or SousasShellfish. Short. But taller than me. All in black.

A blacklace kerchief on her head like a real fancy fishnet. She bowlegged. Her hands holding rose ree beads and her chin with a few whiskers. She puts her arms up in the air like shes shooing away a dog and Im going nowhere. Bad enough getting caught in the confessions. No way am I making anything worse by getting in a what all mixup with a church old lady.

That old lady is talking Portuguese. Arms in the air. And FathaLuis calming her.

And FathaLuis helps the old lady light a candle. Sets her on a kneeler beneath the feet of crucifiedJesus. FathaLuis turns to us and says, You guys. Outside. Now.

FathaLuis goes out the big front streetdoor.

Then Pruney does something absolute crazy. Maybe even mental.

Pruney reaching into the stonefont holywater. Squeezes the holywater ocean sponge. Wipes his face. Puts the ocean sponge back in the holywater font. Blesses himself with wet fingers and says with frustratedness to Ross and me, Eecoodeesh. The calm before the storm. Ah NorEasta. Lets go get our pennants.

And why Pruney thinks hes gonna be flag waving in a blizzard is beyond me but when he puts his hands in his back pockets. Is he gonna pull out a white handkerchief and do the sign of surrender or get lost in all the white? Which. At this point is prettgood idea. Lets face it. Ross and me twelve years old. And Pruney being runt fourteen. We should. As Dad would say, Quit while we're ahead.

And as Pruney and Ross go to the doors. I turn one last time. And even through the dark of his corner. Michael the ArchAngel. His sword raised high ready to chop off Lucifas ugly head.

Other side of the church.

AhBewdeeful Lady-a-Fatima. Floating on her cloud. Smiling.

And if it werent for that glorious smile on her beautiful face. And Pruneys possible quit while we're ahead white pennants flagwaving surrender. Never could I have followed Pruney and my brother Ross down those front stairs past the Portuguese old lady at the kneeler lighting a candle under the feet of frontdoor crucified Jesus.

Nope. Jesus give me the Hooglies.

The big priest choke give me the Hooglies.

Not ta say. But. AhBewdeeful Lady-a-Fatimas smile. She gave me the brave to walk through those door. Back onto LandStreet and into our small town of Sowams.

• • •

So Pruney and Ross and me are pushing that heavy front church door open. Letting out all the big church quiet and letting in the LandStreet traffic noise. And there at the bottom of the steps and standing near our bikes on LandStreet in the wide open air is Mom and Dad talking to FathaLuis. Whoever woulda thought such a thing? Mom and Dad walking around the NorthEnd being neighborey and they walk into the thick of our storm.

And Pruney walks up to Mom Dad and FathaLuis. Runty Pruney. Instead of pulling out his surrender handkerchief pennant. Runty fourteen year old Pruney shoves out his hand for shaking like FathaLuis and him are best of old buddies. And FathaLuis just looks unimpressed at that outstretched dirt fingernailed calloused Pruney hand and says, How do you expect to become a top shelf altarboy pulling stunts like that in there? A house of God. That building is a house of God and you boys treating it like its the PortugueseSocialClub.

Pruney says, FathaLuis. I thought you was gonna be ta your sisters house NewBedford for Thanksgivin? Eecoodeesh the two-a-yous here.

And before FathaLuis could answer. Pruney turns to Mom and Dad. Ross and me. And Pruney says, FathaLuises sister is one heck of a good cook. Took me to his sisters house NewBedford last Sunday after mass for lunch. Said she was gonna cook Thanksgivin for you today dint she FathaLuis?

FathaLuis doesnt answer Pruney direct. Instead he just hard stares. But then makes a face like loose front tooth sucking. And FathaLuis. Shaking his finger says, Me you should not fear Pedro. Its God.

This is difficult. Figuring whether FathaLuis being mean to Pruney or whether FathaLuis just being a grouch like MistaCogg sometimes. A grouch but in a good kind of way. And Dads thinking the same thing because Dads looking down. Not the kind of downlooking that is afraid of something. Like Ross and me will do if Dad is griping about whatever. But the kind of downlooking Dad does before he kicks a rock or busts a trashcan when he says he just needs something to kick.

FathaLuis put his hands on Pruneys shoulders. And all on a sudden Pruneys face gets all pruned up and his two eyebrows become one line of scrunched up hair and Pruney one eye squints Popeye. And Pruneys face is full of PruneyMendez worry.

But then Dad speaks up and says, Im not one be teaching my boys fear the Lord. But you can be certain FathaLuis. Im not the least bit happy these shenanigans. Their mother and I will stand by any appropriate make-goods. Anything Father. Work be done in church. The parking lot or your yard. Leaves to rake? These boysll work. An aftanoon or two. Or three. Windows. Trash. Whatever. Put em to work. My boys. And their friends. Be thinkin twice before they disrespect anything or anyone again.

And of course Moms nodding her head yes in total agreement with Dad. And Dad asks, You boys understand what Im sayin? You guys apologize and stay outta churches you dont belong. Understand?

We all three say, Yessir. SorryFathaLuis.

FathaLuises smooth hands on Pruneys shoulders. FathaLuis serious face is eyes real narrow. His big mustache. Black hair. Thick. And lips. Bottom one under his top teeth. And then that bottom lip gets pushed out by FathaLuises tongue. Just as I realize he looks like the photo of that guy in GilOwens SquarePeg. FathaLuis says, I see. Well.

FathaLuis says, Pedro, next week. Why dont you bring your buddies to our altarboy meeting. We'll be serving refreshments. You boys be the clean up committee. Sweep the floor. Empty the trash. Do whatever needs done. A few OurFathers. HailMarys. And a good act of contrition wont hurt you none either.

And FathaLuis says to Mom and Dad, Boys being boys. I was much the same when I was a kid. Was my sister kept me on the straight and narrow. Soon as she comes out the church we'll be to driving to NewBedford. She is a good cook.

Dad reaching for Moms hand with a smile swipes her strand hair behind her ear. Mom is more beautiful than AhBewdeeful Lady-a-Fatima. And beautiful Mom says to Ross, Your dad and I are walking uptown. You boys go on home.

Ross says, Football. The marsh. Everyones meetin for a game. WillieD. Mush. Zeebo. Rest-a-the guys.

Mom says, Jate no football. But you Ross? Sure. Just be careful. No tackle.

Then she turns back to FathaLuis and says, Sorry. Us meeting this way.

And FathaLuis says, Have often to remind ourselves. Our Lord was once a boy. God came into the world a child and even he too made some temple mischief.

Both Mom and Dad. Heads nodding up and down. Yes. Shake hands with FathaLuis. And leave for their uptown walk.

Ross and me on our bikes.

Pruney lags back talking FathaLuis. Something about next week altar-boys.

Ross and me shove off leaving everyone distant.

Dad turns and shouts, Turkey. Two. Dont be late.

When I look back. Its Mom and Dad walking up the street. And standing top the stairs. FathaLuises sister who. Before in church. Had lit a candle and sent a prayer to heaven.

At the bottom of the steps. Our pal PruneyMendez. Shaking hands with the sisters brother. A priest.

A priest looking like the picture of a guy in GilOwens antique shop.

A blackrobe priest.

A priest with his hands on Pruneys shoulder.

A priest. Who God would strike dead on the spot if the priest ever told. Secrets that he knew.

Next time I saw FathaLuisAlegria he was a hand on my shoulder. And smelled like a thick neck with the aroma of Moms lavender seeds. Ernest Hemingway. Looks just like the picture of Hemingway GilOwen has in the SquarePeg. Hemingway. A big guy. Cool combed back hair. And a mustache that says Im a man and dont you forget it.

FathaLuis shook my hand. His fat fingers. Gripping my shoulder. Then he pulled me into his stomach. My face into his belly. And he slapped my back. The way the Portuguese men do when they like you. Lotsa men do that. Lotsa men. That slap on the back thing. My dad did.

But FathaLuises assistant. His deacon.

Marteem Silvia dint do that.

Wasnt his style.

Wasnt his way.

Marteem Silvia. Smoking a cigarette. Drinking a glass of wine. While FathaAlegria was all hand shaking and holding shoulders. Giving big hugs and making us all feel okay even though we werent. As Pruney said, Membas-a-the parish.

But because we got caught in the confessions. And according to Mom and Dad. Our need for making things right. We were Pruneys guests. We were welcome. More than welcome. Brothers in Christ was how FathaLuisAlegria put it.

We had gathered in the church basement.

FathaLuis. Sitting in the back.

Marteem Silvia addressed us.

Boys. Students. Gentlemen. As you begin your preparation for altarboy training. Youll. No doubt. Have questions and concerns. Curiosities and challenges. Lord knows. Im terrible inept at solving any of lifes problems. Thats why Im here just a deacon and not official like a priest. But this man. This man sitting behind me. FathaLuis. FathaLuisAlegria. During your preparation. Here in your parish. This man. FathaAlegria. Hes the one for you to see for all your concerns. Boys. May I introduce FathaLuis. FathaLuis?

Thats when he stood.

Thats when ErnestHemingway stood.

Thats when ErnestHemingway the guy who choked me in the neck stood. Walked to the front of the room. Cleared his throat. And spoke.

ErnestHemingway spoke in Portuguese and I understood nothing but it dint for real matter because FathaLuis was. So? His voice? His face? His expressions? Watching him felt good. Hands through his black hair. Finger to his lips. Walk left. Walk right. Wag his index finger. No. No. No. Everyone laughing. Back tracking. Tiptoes. To his left. Drop flat on his feet. Hands behind his back. Rocking his big giant body back and forth. Right open palm on his heart. Eyes up. Left open palm. His forehead. Everyone laughing again. Him bolt upright. Real quiet. His voice. His eyes looking everyone in their eyes. Everyone in the room. Connecting. Moon eyes. Pie face. Pinching nostrils. Thumb and index knuckle. Index finger stabbing. Stabbing the air. Hands on his hips. Everyone quiet. Stand. Bow heads. Sign of the cross. Say a pray. Sign of the cross. Meeting over.

Cookies. Crush orange soda. Not Nehi orange like what CapnJack woulda had. Crush. Good stuff too. More introductions. Handshaking. Necktie guys. Sweaters guys. Backslappers. Lotsa Portuguese language. Some English.

Then the smell of lavender.

Visegrip fingers on my shoulders.

And ErnestHemingways Im a man and never forget it mustache.

In my ear.

Whispering, You boys dont be strangers.

Stop by again.

Real soon.

19
On the Q-T

The north end of Sowams was for real a very noisy place. That is after seven in the morning till about seven at night.

The AmericanLuggageMill factory cross the railroad and a few blocks away from our BaggyWrinkleLane was always windows open and clacking and hissing. Clunking and buzzing. Sometimes. You could hear announcements over the intercom. Sometimes in English. And sometimes in Portuguese. But most of the clunking and the clacking ate up the talking so that what you for real heard was just a steady clacka clacka hissing.

The wintertime was noisy too. Youd think with the cold theyd close those windows. But the windows stayed open all year round. Not that it was cold inside. No way. It was hot. MistaCogg said in the winter most of the clunking and clacking and hissing was steam pipes firing up and blasting more heat than those workers could possible stand.

Said, You gotta love the iron knee.

And I dint get the iron knee part.

Probbly like a plate in the head except for the leg.

But GilOwen said, Thats the U-S of A.

Said when he had returned from a Florida winter vacation. He looked down from the airplane and saw a fat mother pig on her side with dozens of piglets suckling off her teats. Except he said it was a factorymill and an immigrant neighborhood. The American Dream.

I dint get that America Dream praspective for nothing. Especial about the iron knee. Or was it ironing? Mom sure hates doing that. But. The factory mill part with little piggies sucking teat. That sure was funny. GilOwen. Such imagination.

Irregardless.

The Quequeshan neighborhood GilOwen was talking about was hid away from the rest of the NorthEnd. It was a three sidestreet cluster. Alleys really. Each alley tangling the riverfront running along WaterStreet and knotted in a worker house huddle across from the mouth of the Queque-shan at the base of the smokestack and bell tower and ending as a ship-ping dock warehouse. I never woulda knowd. Till delivering papers with Pruney. About the bookie joint owned by Whimpy BugEyes McPherson. Who. Pruney said. Was the real big boss of Sowams. The guy in charge of everything.

Before then. I dint even know about being in charge of towns. Be-ing the boss. Or what a bookiejoint was. We werent allowed by Dad. Or Whimpy. To go inside the bookiejoint. We was always giving the newspa-per to Zompa TheDoorGuy Galucci.

And then Zompa TheDoorGuy Galucci would take the newspaper inside.

In the summertime. The door would usual be open and we could see the inside guys playing cards and smoking cigarettes.

But sitting on the stoop waiting. Would be. Always. ZompaGalucci.

Zompa TheDoorGuy Galucci was real nice. And he was big too. Not like BobbyBrayton giant big. But more like a creamfilled donut. And on the usual. He was quiet. Sometimes ZompaGalucci wouldnt say nothing except, Hey boys. And other times ZompaGalucci would ask questions like, Hey Prune kid. How many papers ya got on yuh route?

Or, Hey kid. How about you goin over to FatFingaPetes and gettin me a cobbagoul sangweech with some nice mozarell an a Coke? And get the bote-a-youse one while yuh at it.

Then ZompaGalucci would give us a five dollar bill that he said was tree dollars and then he would say, Keep da change.

Sometimes ZompaGalucci would ask, Whos yuh ol man?

And when Pruney would tell. ZompaGalucci would say, A portagee huh?

Once when Zompa TheDoorGuy Galucci asked me, Whos yuh ol man? I told him. And he. Reaching at me. Grabbed both my wrists. His grip. So hard. My own heartbeat sinked into the flesh of his firm. But his fingers soft. And he looked at me with strawberry jellydoughnut cheeks and a fist of curls hanging between his eyes and he asked me, Clara Lee Rossi yuh mother? Chrice. Terrible ting dat truck hit your head. But lookatcha. All betta. I memba you and yuh brother. The bote-a-youse. At da beach.

And Zompas eyes were all glitter in a hazel soup and he yelled back into the bookiejoint, Hey Whimp. Dis heres one-a-Tavinos boys.

When ZompaGalucci yelled that. I seen Whimpy BugEyes McPherson sitting under a old floor lamp with just a light bulb and no shade look up from the big stuffed chair that he was always sitting in. And Whimpy BugEyes McPherson who I never seen before give me a look like he too knew me. Like he knew all my life who I was.

When I asked Pruney, What those guys in the bookiejoint do?

Pruney said it was horse racing and numbers. Which of course was all plate in the head to me because. Far as I could tell. There was no horses in Sowams and whenever numbers were mentioned. I was all plate in the head big time confused.

But anyways. The AmericanLuggage tractortrailer trucks would go into the millgates down near the Barrington bridge and leave up QuequeshanStreet right behind Whimpys. Sometimes. When the drivers went into Whimpys. ZompaGalucci and some Whimpys other guys be unloading luggage from the AmericanLuggage trucks. And then Zompa-Galucci and Whimpys other guys would be putting that AmericanLuggage into their car trunks. Whimpy BugEyes was first place those AmericanLuggage truck drivers made delivery. Which was strange because those AmericanLuggage truck drivers for real dint truckdrive very far to the loadingdocks to make their first delivery. I mean wouldnt it been easier if ZompaGalucci and the rest of Whimpys guys just went over the loadingdocks and picked up the luggage themselfs?

When I asked Dad about this he told me, Never you mind what those guys are doin. You keep your nose clean. You keep it under your hat. You keep it on the Q-T.

Which Dad said spelled quiet in shorthand. And if Q-T was a short way to spell quiet then. I was all for it. Because. As you know. Never did I like spelling words the long way very much.

So kept on the Q-T. Thats what we did.

The Q-T.

The PowaHouse.

We kept that on the Q-T.

And what we did in the PowaHouse. That was the Q-T too.

Then there was that one time we let something on the Q-T slip. Not me. Ross. Considering Ross used to talk with GilOwen about stuff a whole lot more than me. There was no blaming for Ross messing up. And. Not ta say. But. Im not sure Ross did mess up. Pruney wasnt upset. Pruney actual told Ross. Thanks. You tell GilOwen. And your dad. I said thanks. Thats what Pruney said to Ross and me both separate.

Then Pruney never said nothing about it ever again.

What it was. Was this.

Pruney become like Kay in MissusCoggs *SnowQueen*.

Pruney become undifferent.

Pruney stopped coming over.

Stopped coming over our house like he use to.

Oh. He'd spend a sometimes. Few hours. Friday or Saturday nights. Or a late Sunday afternoon. But not all the time staying over like he did before. What it become was. Gotta work early. Or. The OlMan wont let me. And a couple-a-three times it was even, My cousin SkiffheadEd is sick and I gotta take care-a-Edu on accounta AuntJovita bein sick too.

Then Pruney stopped.

Stopped telling.

Stopped telling us about church and stuff.

But even worse. Pruney werent no more his wordmusic self. No more blathers. No more Eecoodeeshes. Or wonder. And amazement. He even stopped singing his favorite radio songs like *Im Henry the Eighth I Am I Am*. And his favorite. *Hang on Sloopy* that he always sung uncorrect wrong as *Hang on Snoopy. Snoopy hang on.*

Instead of being his usual self. Pruney got more like Rosses favorite song. The one about silence having a sound which I dint really understand because how could silence have a sound? How could that be?

But. Pruney prettmuch got silence and stopped telling and talking after Thanksgiving and never even said a word on Christmas. It was like Pruney was in TheSnowQueens far away castle.

Pruney never told us about him being a shepherd at the manger.

Pruney never told us about him getting to carry. All around the church. A fancy velvet pillow with baby Jesus on it while the choir was Midnight-Mass singing Portuguese Hah-lay-lew-yuh. Hah-lay-lew-yuh.

And Pruney never told us that on NewYearsDay he got to swing a big gold cup. Mom called it a chalice. Dangling from chains with incents smoking up the church.

Nope. Pruney dint tell us none of that stuff. Mom heard it all from neighbors when she did her walks around town.

And one time in midJanuary. Mom heard it from Pruneys AuntJovita too. A late Saturday morning. Mom bumped into AuntJovita shopping FirstNationalGroceryStore.

According to Mom. AuntJovita said, Pruney come home sick from Saturdaymorning collecting paper route customers money and he wouldnt be able to carry his afternoon papers and could Ross and me maybe climb stairs for him?

Mom told AuntJovita sure we'd help. And then Mom came home and told Ross and me. But then she immediate left the house to do more errands. And I thought Ross be happy as me to help Pruney. Instead Ross did long faces and scowls. When I. At the kitchen table said, Wonder what kinda sick Pruney got?

Ross shoved his sketchbook aside and said, It isnt Pruney got sickness exact.

Whaddaya mean? I said.

Rosses face like a piece of glass stabbed his lip then quick went away. And again. He picked up his sketch pad. Flipped to a clean page and real calm said, On ice. Probbly slipped. His tailbone. Hurt. Cant bend. AuntJovita give him plenty asprins.

And Ross explained because MistaCogg was Pruneys first stop. We'd meet at the Port n Starboard Shop. And then. All three of us. Do the NorthEnd 42 papers like on the other different Saturdays when we did the route with Pruney just for fun.

Before we left the house. Mom come home and said it was snow flurries and be sure and wear hats and mittens. But after we got dressed. Mom gave final inspection and waved as Ross and me rolled down BaggyWrinkleLane.

The air was quiet.

And the few flakes.

Small.

And riding our bikes in that ease of snow was no problem. And as we crossed LandStreet at the junction light. MistaCogg was in my head saying, Small flakes. Big storm. And I gotta addmit. Felt for certain. This time he'd be wrong. It sure dint look. Or feel. Like a storm. And although it had already snowed a couple-a-few times this winter. This snow. Like all snow. Made me happy and excited.

When we got to Port n Starboard Shop. MistaCogg was already attitude lipped and selling some Barrington people a fake harpoon. And even though MistaCogg told Ross and me to warm ourselfs by the stove. We instead waited outside. And not for long. Because Pruney. Backstiff straight. Like a broomstick up his ass. Come walking down the street pushing his bike. And as usual. He wasnt wearing a hat and no gloves neither. The canvasbagged newspapers in the wire frontbasket were better protected from the snow than Pruney.

At the SquarePeg. GilOwen. Unlike MistaCogg. Was long on questions while Pruney was short on answers. Me and Ross said nothing. But GilOwen stood at the window and watched us trail our way in the snow.

Then GilOwen even stood outside on the corner beneath his flag flying mast staff. And through the thick of ease wind and down falling flakes. Like the poem he said to me and Ross. GilOwen watched us more a long time before he went back in.

Inside SipponsBar was just a couple of guys I dint know. The jukebox was playing *Hang on Sloopy* and Pruney shoulda picked up on the tune and sang *Shake it shake it baby*. But no. Outside Pruney was just standing silent in the snow. And in those weeks. Pruneys stopped talking foolish like he always done. Pruney was hurting. His face pale. His eyes. Closed. And as Ross crossed back from Anunziatas Pool and Billiards. I said to Pruney, Musta been a hell of a fall.

And Ross. With a second scowl he give me that day. Said, Stating the obvious wont make it any better.

But pained Pruney said, Easy Ross.

And Pruney turned to me and said, Isnt so bad Jate. Jus landed wrong is all.

And we walked in the snow saying nothing more.

And for a instant. I knew it was how SnowQueens Gerta felt when Kay had went away.

And on this day snow was making everything beautiful. Not enough for difficult pushing our bicycles. Or for people to shovel their sidewalks. It was simple plain pretty.

During the rest of that January. Ross and me helped Pruney a few more times. And by February Pruney was walking and stairclimbing by himself just fine.

And now. As I look back on those days. Ross was doing more scowls and said my plate in the head made it difficult for me to open my eyes.

And I didnt understand that because the night Pruney and Ross talked to Dad was the day in early February when Ross and me. Without Pruney. Went to the LyricTheater for the afternoon show and seen. With our eyes wide open. The greatest movie ever. *Lawrence of Arabia*. But I cant tell about *Lawrence of Arabia* because. For now. I gotta stick with Pruney. I'll save telling about *Lawrence of Arabia* for later.

Anyhow. That night Pruney did stay over our house. And that was kinda strange because he come over very late. It was his last time. And all through me telling Pruney about the movie. He just dint care. Said he needed to sleep. Ross gave me no support neither. Ross was quiet too like Pruney. And after we did fall asleep. I woke because I hadda take a leak. And Pruney wasnt on Pruneys Island. And Ross wasnt in his bed neither. And I could hear voices in the living room.

The voices were Pruney.

The voices were Ross.

The voices were Dad.

The voice of Dad was saying, You boys did right tellin GilOwen. And GilOwen did right tellin me. And Pruney. Dont you worry he'll never be botherin you again.

GilOwen bothering Pruney? Why would that be? But had to piss so real bad and figured Ross. Or Pruney for that matter. Would tell me everything plenty and soon enough. And by the time the toilet was flushing. Ross was back his bed. And Pruney was laying on Pruneys Island so I asked, Whats up?

Ross said, Pruney and Dad. A talk. Thats all.

Bout what?

Pruney said, Dont wanna talk bout it. Jus wanna sleep. Gotta help Digga. Funeral parlor. Bottles in the mornin.

And we all just lay there.

No big deal.

But it was a bunch of more undifference none the anyhow.

Prettsoon. Ross and Pruneys breathing told me they was asleep.

Pruney on his island.

Ross in his own bed.

And it wasnt long after. Sleep come to me in my bed too.

All of us each on the Q-T. And good.

For the most part. Sowams was a very quiet place. Except for the AmericanLuggageMill factory? Not much noise was heard around town.

But by EastaSunday. Something would be different.

Thered be no more sounds of silence.

No more Pruney and Ross giving me undifference.

Something on the Q-T would make the loudest hush of all.

Make lotsa loud Q-T.

Everybody in Sowams would, *Shake it shake it Sloopy.*

Everybody in Sowams knowin what was goin on.

Gonna know the scuttle.

Gonna know stuff.

Everybody in the know.

Everybody knowin stuff.

Singin not singin *Sounds of Silence.*

Everybody that is.

Cept plate in the head slow me.

III

Holy Week

20

How Come You
Gotta Go ta the Dogs?

The next morning. Which was Sunday. Pruney was gone before I awaked.

Ross and Mom were making breakfast. And Dad was in the livingroom reading the Providence Journal listening to Caruso doing a opera. When I went into the livingroom Dad folded the newspaper. Lowered the hifi volume and said, So what did you think-a-*Lawrence of Arabia?*

The best. Especial the part where just before they blow up a train. Lawrence of Arabia gotta kill his friend cause the guy catches one in the belly and Lawrence of Arabia cant leave his friend wounded so Lawrence of Arabia shoots his friend in the head and then this other guy who is also Lawrences friend sinks in the quicksand and they cant do nothin to rescue him. They just watch him sink.

And Dad asked, Do you think Lawrence of Arabia felt bad about not being able to save his friend?

Sure he did. But there was just no way.

And Dad asked, What do you mean?

And I said, Blastin cap in the boys belly exploded. Train comin down the tracks. That kid sufferin. Lawrence hadda act fast. Gun to the head cause they was pals. Hadda do it Dad. Lawrence just hadda.

Dad sat back in his chair and looked out the window. Seagulls circling around in the sky over the AmericanLuggage.

I love that movie Dad. I for real love it.

And Dad just kept staring at the circling seagulls. Wasnt a cloud in that sky. Only clouds were Dads eyes.

Then Dad said he had seen that movie a few years ago when it first came out and now he wanted to see it again. So I asked, Can I see it again too?

But it was like Dad dint hear a word I said. He was lost in a fog that wasnt really there. It was all blue sky.

So again. My question. And then. Just like that. Dads eyes got cleared. And he smiled and said, Maybe.

Dad said, Maybe next Saturday night. Take you and Pruney cause Ross and Mom are goin Providence for Easta weekend with your AuntBeni.

Which was fine by me because AuntBeni was a bit too particular about things. AuntBeni hated dungarees and sneakers and BobDylan and she always wanted Ross and me to wear khakis and loafers. She also talked a lot about art. Especial what she called, Italian Ott. And Ross was way more interested in that art stuff than me.

Anyway. In the afternoon. Mom. Dad. Ross and me. Because it was early April. We bundled up good with winter coats and mittens and extra sweaters and wool socks and stocking caps and we went for a long drive to Newport where we spent the rest of the day freezing off our noses. Fighting the new arrived Boreas wind. Looking at the tide pools. Getting again warm in the car. And finally going to Dads favorite seafood shack. Bolios. Where we ordered two baskets of bigbellied Ipswich fried clams. A couple of stuffed quahogs. And four bowls of steaming hot cioppino with crusty Italian sourdoughbread for dunking.

And Dad told us that cioppino was a Italian SanFrancisco word that meant all the fishermen would chip into the pot with some fish to make a stew.

But Mom said it was from the Italian word ciuppin what described the stew.

Ross said that. Either. Or. Cioppino was the best kinda soup in the whole wide world in the winter.

And. Not fa nuthin. I agreed.

Out the window was late afternoon and the sky had clouded except where every now and then there was a break and the sun would be streaming through. And if Pruney had been there he woulda said, It was the fingers-a-God reachin down.

Besides talking about cioppino we wondered if the weather would ever for real turn into spring because winter just seemed to be hard holding on and letting go not fa nuthin.

And as we dunked bread and let cool our soup. We watched ocean waves and merchant ships rise high in the Atlantic.

Then fall.

Then rise again.

And fall again.

Then rise again.

And the ships rolling into NarragansettBay.

Wind and waves blowing white across the bows.

And reaching.

Not too for so far.

Providence.

Before we left Newport to head back over the MountHopeBridge to Sowams. Mom and Dad did a thing they never before did with Ross and me.

They took us to church.

As we were looking for a sidestreet parkingplace. Mom explained today was a special Catholic church day. PalmSunday. And that we were gonna visit the church PresidentKennedy and Jackie got married in. It was right there on the corner. SaintMarys. And Mom pointed across from where we were standing.

And sure enough. There was a big brown stone church with a real high steeple. Not two round steeples like Pruneys church. Just one. But this steeple was higher than Pruneys. And not round tops. But a point. With a real nice cross on the point top too.

And Mom said it was a IrishCathlicChurch and she always wanted to visit here. The place where, A dreamboat weddin had been.

And Dad rolled his eyes. Like Ross or Pruney always did when I dint understand the stuff they was telling. And Mom hit Dad on his shoulder. Then Mom. Grabbed Dads hand. And Dad pulled Mom into his arms and gave her a big kiss and said, Someday youll be gettin that diamond ring I swear.

Mom told him not to swear because we were going into a church. Mom took off her stocking cap and pulled up the navy blue blue scarf from round her neck and put it on her head. She looked like Lawrence of Arabia. Dad pushed aside some of Moms hair with his fingers and smiled. Then Mom tugged Dad. Ross and me together. And direct above the doors was a circle with a cross in it. And Dad pulled on the black handles of the tan colored doors. Creaking came from big black hinges Mom called ornate. And the four of us hugmugged into the PresidentKennedy wedding church in downtown Newport RhodeIsland.

As the big oak door closed behind us and left us in the dark. A enormous stained glass window on the very back wall above the altar glowed

with so many reds and greens and yellows and blues it made me think of
Sears window color TVs and I hoped someday soon we'd get one.

And those beautiful window colors danced all over the center aisle.
And I gotta addmit. As we were walking up that aisle with all them television colors reflecting on us and everywhere. I on the sudden knew how
Scarecrow. Dorothy. Lion. And TinMan must of felt when they were going down that long hallway to visit the Wizard of Oz. Emerald City. Because. Even though I had only ever seen the movie in black and white. I
knew. The color Mom told she seen it in. When she was a girl. Just had
to be like this.

PresidentKennedys wedding church was real impressive. And although
that PresidentKennedy wedding church dint have painted ceilings with
lotsa Bible people all over the place like Pruneys PortugueseCatholic-
Church. What that PresidentKennedy wedding church did have was high
ceilings Dad called vaulted. There was lotsa arches with unlit ceiling lan-
terns hanging from chains. My neck was hurting from looking up. And
just when I was getting dizzy. Dad was along the entry place of the pews.
Feeling with his hands what he called, Elaborate scroll carvings.

These pews werent low at the aisle like in Pruneys church. But were tall
and gave a feeling like if you went into the pew. You was going through
a gate of some important entrance. And they sure was carved nice. So
smooth to feel. Arches and crosses. Like what was all over the rest of the
church everywhere you looked.

Not ta say. But. As nice as the PresidentKennedy wedding church in
Newport was. In some ways. It was just like Pruneys PortugueseCatholic-
Church in Sowams. Crucified Jesus hanging over the altar. Lotsa candles
flickering. 3D stations of the cross on the sides. Confession in the back.

Them preececlosets made Ross and me laugh. And our laughing made
Mom say, Whachya boys gigglin at?

Ross covered fast and said, The ott. Pruneys church got frescos. Plus
his statues have color. These statues are all just plain wood. Look at Jesus
above the altar. At Pruneys church. Jesus has blood all over. Especial on
his face. And another thing. Here theres no Michael the ArchAngel and
no AhLady-a-Fatima.

Mom said, At this church there is thee Ammaculate Hott-a-Mary who
is the same Mary as AhLady-a-Fatima but the Ammaculate Hott-a-Mary
story is a little different. And there is SaintJoseph her husband. And Saint-
Patrick who the Irish just adore cause SaintPatrick chased the devil outta
Ireland.

Dad said, Thought it was snakes?

Mom said, Same thing.

I said, Tween SaintPatrick and Mikey 2A's. Devil dont stand much a chance.

Dad said, Youd be surprised.

Mom said, Look close. The ott is bewdeeful. But not a distraction. Next week is Easta. PassionWeek. And all these wood statues will be covered with purple cloth. Durin PassionWeek. Everyone focuses on the pain-a-Jesus and not the statue bright colors. Or the happy things in the world. Then durin HolySaturday services. The purple cloths will be taken from the statues. And therell be lots-a-Easta lilies cause Christ has risen. And everybodyll be happy again. Course the next mornin. Easta Sunday means fancy clothes. The men extra handsome. And the women? Very pretty.

And without saying another word. Mom took Ross and me by the hand. Left Dad sitting in a pew. Mom walked us to a side altar under the statue of Mary. Mom lit a candle. Knelt. Blest herself the sign of the cross like Pruney always did. And Mom said a prayer. Quiet with eyes closed. Just her lips moving. I was about ready to take a conniption. She never told us she knew church holy stuff. And to tell the truth. Seemed to me Mom knew just about as much what Pruney called. Cathlicism. As did PruneyMendez.

Then I looked back at Dad and saw a even stranger thing.

Not the wink Dad threw at me. That wink I half expected.

What I saw was Dad kneeling too.

And Dad smiling proud.

Proud of his two boys.

And proud of Mom.

Like PresidentKennedy been.

That day he married Jackie.

Thursday before Easter. School got out early. Was the start of our ten day Easter break. Thursday release was like a early holiday. A happyday before the sad.

MistaCogg always said, Kids and teachers spend as much time outta school as hores spend in convents. And he got that one wrong because what we SarahHaag learnt. Hores live with pirates. And its nuns live in convents.

And also the next day wasnt for real the happy holiday kind like Christmas. And Fourth of July. It was the sad holiday kind. Like MemorialDay.

And VettrinsDay. On GoodFriday nobody was happy that Jesus got killed. Not even JackCogg. But. Not fa nuthin. Lets face it. A day outta school is day outta school. So. You might as well make the best of it. Right?

Anyways. Late Thursday afternoon. I was coming home helping Pruney from his paper route. He was all quiet. Except once when he said, Hurry up. Goin too slow.

When we got to South QuequeshanStreet. Near the firestation. Pruney went to his other job at Sousas Shellfish. Dint even wave goodbye. Just silent stiff rode away.

And my bike tire was rubbing against my fender. And although Pruney was important. Fixing my fender had to get done because a fender rub drives me cocomoco crazy. And while doing that. What do you think I see? Its Dad going into Whimpy BugEye McPhersons.

Me and my bicycle we stopped below the bell tower bottom of QuequeshanStreet. A block down from the firestation. In the alley. And AmericanLuggage trucks all parked. And I was behind two curbside trash cans. Kneeling low on the ground pulling out my fender from my tire and I just happened to look up. I see Dad cross QuequeshanStreet. But Dad couldnt see me. Not from that angle.

Now. What you gotta understand is. Dad never. Never. Went into Whimpy BugEye McPhersons ever before. Leastways never that I knew of. Dad was always telling us, You guys deliver the newspaper and get outta there. No hangin round. No playin pool. No nuthin. You just drop off the paper and make like a tree and leave. Leave. G-O. Go. Exit. Got it?

And Ross argued saying, Yeah, but sometimes ZompaGalu—

Dad would give us the steely eyeball. And repeat, Drop the paper and leave.

And we'd say, Yessir and then we'd keep on the Q-T. The soda errands Zompa had us do and the good tips ZompaGalucci he always gave.

So Dad going into WhimpyMcPhersons was a real big deal. And of course. That got me thinking. Why isnt Ross here instead of on his way to Providence with Mom? And Pruney too instead of working at Sousas? They would know somethings up. Dad standing on the stoop. Head high. Proud as all getup. Like he goes in Whimpy all the time. And the QuequeshanStreet neighbors should care less.

So. Dad knocks on the door.

Of course ZompaGalucci opens it. Right?

And ZompaGalucci is all surprised and maybe even more surprised than me.

And ZompaGalucci is all real loud and laughing, You son of a bitch. Yousonofabitch. Where the hell ya ben? We see more-a-ya kids an that runt Portagee paperboy an we eva do-a-you. Yousonofabitch.

And ZompaGalucci is all his pointing finger in Dads face, ClaraLee done it to ya dint she? Tol ya. I tol ya. Forget yuh rubbers. Ya play. Ya pay.

And ZompaGalucci is all his thumbs and his pointing fingers together shaking, Dint I tell ya that huh?

And ZompaGalucci is all pinching Dads cheek saying, You chooch. But—

And ZompaGalucci is all his hands like hes praying, Respect. Ya did the right thing marryin her. Respect. Atts what I always say.

And ZompaGalucci is all back to finger wagging and cheek pinching, Hey. But thats no excuse fuh ya to be forgettin about chya friends ya bastid. Ya friggin ballbusta. Ya neva stop. Always bustin my balls. Come on inside. Whimpyll be glad.

And the most amazing thing is Dad is smiling. And Dad is laughing. And Dad is hugging ZompaGalucci while me Im laying on the ground behind trash cans watching.

And then ZompaGalucci and Dad go inside Whimpy BugEyes book-iejoint.

ZompaGalucci does one last look round the QuequeshanStreet neighborhood. Hard left. Fast right. Door window reflection. Brushes back his hair. Tightens his belt. Closes the door like nothing happening.

And everythings just QuequeshanStreet all over again.

So. Now theres no way I can just leave. I gotta see whats going on and the only way to do that is to push my bike to Whimpys alley. Lean my bike against the sidewall. Stand on the ballbuster bar that makes it a boys bike. And look in. Of course this is a stupid thing to do. Standing on my ballbuster bike bar because what if the front wheel flips round and the whole bike rolls right out from under me? Id much rather have Pruney here givin me a boost. But Pruneys not here. So I do what I do. Which is fine because my bike is just high enough for me to almost see into the dirty window and through the ragged up curtain with holes.

And through curtain holes at the very bottom of that side window. ZompaGaluccis in the kitchen with his back to me. I cant for real see his face except for a couple of times when he turns because it looks like hes making a sandwich. Or a coffee. Or something. Theres also a couple of other guys that I recognize. But I dont know their names. Playing cards around a table. I cant see anyone playing pool. But I know they are because I hear a break. The crack of poolballs. And someone says, Good shot. And then the balls make that clump clump sound when poolballs fall into the pockets. Of course theres Whimpy BugEyes. Sitting in the big stuffed chair he never gets out of. His hands folded over his stomach. Listening to Dad whos on a wooden slatchair whispering into Whimpys ear. And then ZompaGalucci pulling next to Dad getting in the soft talk too. Zompa out loud says, Fuckin preece. That fuckin preece.

Zompa has said priest. I gotta addmit. The whole thing that Im both seeing and hearing reminds me of what I imagine confession would be but without the confessional. And while Im imagining Whimpy priest dressed in a black robe. Im also at the same time wondering why everybody calls Whimpy BugEyes. I mean his eyes are prettmuch like anyones. If anything. A bit smaller and a bit squintya. More like the eyes of a cat in your lap that you might be petting.

Dad leans real close to Whimpys ear and Whimpys eyes get smaller and narrower. And whatever it is that Dad is whispering in Whimpys ear sure is keeping Whimpy interested because Whimpys tilting his head closer to Dads mouth. Dads lips. Whimpys face getting red. Then redder and redder. A vein like a twisted finger comes from under his jaw and pushes up past his high sideburn and disappears. Whimpys hand. His fingers rubbing that swole vein. Whimpys eyes closed. Loss. Total. Both eyes gone inside his hair slick back head. But then all on a sudden. Whimpys eyes. Flash. Open. Open. And real big. Pop right off his face. And he says, That assfuckin cocksucka. Oh the poor kid. That poor poor boy.

But just as quick as Whimpys bug eyes pop out his head. Them bug eyes go back into his head again. Small. And slanty. Just like before. Whoa. Or as Pruney would say. Eecoodeesh. Thats why they call him BugEyes.

And because Pruney had said any suck words was bad. I knew Mom would not been happy knowing Dad. Or especial me. Was around such cocksucker talk. But leastways we werent saying it. Just hearing it was all.

And then my bike does just what I was ascat it might do. The handlebar spins. The front wheel flips. The whole thing slumps. And ZompaGalucci turns round because he hears my something as Im hanging on the windowsill by my fingernails that are loosing their grip because of all the dust and soot that collects on a outside windowsill and my arms arent strong enough and my face is mashed against the outside wall and so is my belly with my shirt and jacket rolling up and Im hoping not to get splinters all over and I drop onto my felled down bike and the chain crank grinds my ankle I just know be bleeding under my sock. And then Im picking up my bike and running with a ankle limp. A belly scrape. And a fender rub.

Im running up the alley jumping on a pedal with my bum ankle foot doing a kick and a jump over the ballbuster bar landing smack on the seat without crunching my nuts and then Im riding through the American-Luggage parking lot neath the smokestack and belltower between all the trucks past the loadingdocks up South QuequeshanStreet onto Water and I dont think ZompaGalucci or Dad or any of the other bookiejoint guys coulda been in that alley quicker than I got out what with all the speed I had flying past the SquarePeg past the StoneFleetTavern counting thirteen millstones past JackCoggs Port n Starboard Shop and I betchya Whimpy BugEyes McPherson never left the big stuffed chair.

And.

Wow.

Was I ever gone.

Outta there and fast.

There was no way I was going straight home.

Not after what I just seen.

Besides.

With Dad still inside Whimpys. I dint want be by myself when Dad got home.

Lets face it. Me seeing what I saw? Was no telling how I would stay on the Q-T with Dad walking in our kitchen door and me not letting on. I just dint have that kind of fake.

Ross did.

And Pruney too.

But me? Without them?

No way.

Mom always said she could read Johnny on the Spot on the spot. But Dad was prettgood at knowing whats up too. So. Way I figured. I had to hang low for a while and go home when that readable Johnny on the Spot stuff wore off. But I dint wanna hang around all by myself and keep stuff on the Q-T that was busting out hard to be told. And since Pruney was at Sousas picking clams. There was no two ways about it.

I was just itching to get there.

Fender rub or not.

And tell Pruney everything I knew.

• • •

Battered by hurricanes blizzards and gales. Sousas Shellfish Market Bait Shop was a low and crumbly building. At hightides the waves lapped smack against its chunky cinderblock walls. Sometimes splashing right through the wide back doors.

Grizzlefaced MannySousa owned Sousas Shellfish Market Bait Shop and Mom said, MistaSousa looked like he dint know a razor from a razorclam.

And yet MannySousa never did for real grow a beard either. What I mean is a bush beard. Not the nub he all of the time had scratching his cheeks.

MannySousa had yellow eyes where white was suppose to be. Like cigar juice had gone from his mouth and leaked to the place where tears get made. And MannySousa always wore a rubber apron. Black rubber boots. A beat up old Yankees baseball cap with grease on the side curled visor where his fingers always pulled it down. A green and black flannel shirt with elbow holes. MannySousa all the time smelled like fish.

MannySousa never spoke much of anything. He was always chomping a unlighted cigar. And he kept to himself. He never seemed to mind whenever any of us kids came in to see the fish he had on ice. Or to look at the crabs and lopstas swimming in the tanks.

MannySousa was Portuguese. Like Pruneys father. Old country too. So maybe why he dint speak much was because he dint know too much English. But. Even when he was around other Portuguese guys. He still kept prettmuch quiet to hisself.

Pruney dint mind working for MannySousa. MannySousa never bossed Pruney. And MannySousa always paid Pruney under the table. Which meant Pruney dint gotta give money to UncleSam. Or to GovnaChaffee. And I knew Pruneys father sent Pruneys pay to other old country relatives. But I had no idea his father was also giving some of Pruneys money to GovnaChaffee. Made no sense to me. But anyways. MannySousa moped around and never said much. But when he paid Pruney. One thing he always said was, Dis is fah yuh papa.

MannySousa would stick a dollar in Pruneys right hand.

Then MannySousa would say, An dis is fah you. PruneyMendez. My bes workah.

And MannySousa would slap another dollar in Pruneys left hand. And MannySousa would never let on to Pruneys father just how much Pruney was paid. And sometimes. Because Pruneys fat lipped smile came so busting out big. Pruneys cheeks so you wanna pinch em red. MannySousa would slap another dollar bill in Pruneys left hand and say, Buy yaself some icecream. An fah yuh friends ere too.

Something would shine through MannySousa yellow eyes when he'd say that to Pruney. And when he'd point to Ross and me.

Pruney always said, Workin for MannySousa is a breeze and pickin clams is easy. Mosly its unloadin the baskets-a-clams the quahoggers bring in on their skiffs. Hosin em down. And sortin em. Cherrystones. Littlenecks. And the big ones. The chowders. The bulls. Then sackin em all up in burlaps.

Sometimes itd be hard to tell the difference between a cherrystone or a littleneck. So then Pruney would gotta ring them. Which dint have nothing to do with a bell or anything youd put on your finger but instead meant Pruney would try and pass the quahog through a brass ring. If the quahog went. It was cherry. If not. Neck.

Pruney always said picking was easy. Only thing made picking difficult was the cold and the wet. The quahoggers. Theyd always help. Unload baskets from the boats. And sometimes theyd even help with the ringing cause thats where the money was. And they couldnt get paid till the job was done. So lotsa them. WildBill Nolan. Russell StrongArms Sweet. Bobby TheBullRake Brayton. Theyd be drinking whiskey and coffee. And ringing right there. Long side Pruney TheSquat Mendez.

But no matter how much they helped. The quahoggers couldnt keep out the hail. Or the snow. Or sleet and rain running down Pruneys face his nose and neck. Lotsa times Pruney wore hats and rubber gloves. But he always said, Hats make it hard to see. And rubber gloves. Not fa nuthin. Even with rubber gloves my fingers freeze. But without em. My fingers freeze fasta.

Each catch of quahogs was ring sorted and iced.

Necks and cherries. With the other fresh catches. In the display cooler.

The chowders were burlapped and flatbed loaded and when MistaSousa drove to Blounts EastBay Seafood Company where the clams got shipped to CampbellsSoup. I wondered if that artist AndyWarHole might ever consider painting a picture of PruneyMendez instead of those stupid soup can lables that made GilOwen so breathless and proud.

When I pulled into Sousas driveway on my bike. MannySousa was chomping a cigar and rolling out the flatbed loaded for EastBay Company.

Pruney was standing on the side of a RussellSweets skiff and when Pruney saw me Pruney gave me a wave and his PruneyMendez grin that made his cheeks go big and his eyebrows do a lift. Pruney wearing his long rubber apron. Big black rubber boots and fat rubber gloves like MannySousa. Except Pruney wasnt chomping a cigar. And. Not fa nuthin. Pruney dint need a shave.

By the time I parked my bike and walked down to the boat ramp MistaSweet was shoved off and Pruney was heading up to meet me. When we finally made it into the fish market shop Pruney had heard everything about my dad and ZompaGalucci and how Dad was talking to them guys quiet and how I saw Whimpy go BugEyes when he started swearing something about assfucking priests. And when I said that. About assfucking priests. Pruneys hands grabbed a hold of the counter top right in front of the cash register and for a moment I thought he was trying to pick up that heavy thing. The way his hands were shaking while he held on tight. The way his arms were vibrating. And his big blue eyes. Wide like he couldnt believe my story. And I hadnt even got yet to the good parts. So I told how I fell against the outside wall and scraped my belly and messed my ankle on the chain crank but I made the great escape. Not quite like SteveMcQueen. But almost and, Here I am now and what do you think it all means?

And Pruneys face went all white like a cold frost from the shaved ice machine just hit him square. And the way hes still hugging that cash register is the only reason why hes not falling backwards. Even his legs are starting to shake and sink to the floor. Just when Im about to ask him if hes all right? Miss AnnieFanny PogostickLegs from LynnWazzalewskis Dance School walks into Sousas fish market and her eyes are all LizTaylor Cleopatra and her lips are stoplight red like at the junction of LandStreet and Water and Missus AnnieFanny PogoStick is pointing with her pink LizTaylor Cleopatra fingernails saying, Three pounds-a-cod. No. Make that two. No. Make it three. A pint-a-squid salad. Without the legs please. And a halfdozen fresh oysters. Oh. And would you shuck them? I shall make a delightful stew.

And then she puts fingernails to teeth like shes tapping out morse code recipe.

Iced face Pruney is now standing alert and hes bagging her order saying, Yesm.

I just know hes thinking what JackCogg would be saying, Lady. Squid dont have friggin legs and I can give a rats arse you makin a delightful oysta shuckin stew.

But Pruney. Still icewhite and shaking. Gives no sign of redface JackCogg and instead Pruney does MannySousa proud by just attending to the order and ringing up the sale.

And soon as Miss AnnieFanny is out the door leaving nothing behind but the same kind of smell as the expensive perfume in Woolworths. Pruney takes off his gloves. Rubs his face warm so theres again pink in his cheeks. His fingers rubbing deep his eyebrows like hes trying to believe my story. And because his legs still seem a bit wobble. He sits on a cod crate near the ice machine and looks me hard and says, Tell me exact the words you heard Whimpy and Zompa sayin to your dad.

Im not sure-a-the exact words. Those guys were assfucker swearin and cocksucker swearin like they always do when they think us kids arent around. But I. For distinct. Saw Whimpy. While Dad was whisperin in his ear. Go bug eyes. At the same time. Heard him say Priest. And oh yeah. Poor boy.

Pruneys breath was lotsa white winter Hooglies. He covered his nose and mouth like he was warming his hands and for a few moments he was no breath.

And I was GilOwen, Add an e my friend. Breathe.

His breathe come on gradual. And some more color in his cheeks. And the shaking in his arms stopped. The white tooth marks where he was biting his lips was disappearing back into the color of lips. Finally Pruney said. Priest and PoorBoy. Racin ponies got the oddest names. Thems the names-a-two NarragansettPark race horses. I betcha your dads playin ponies take you guys on a vacation.

Pruney tilts his head Popeye squint and asks, Your mom been askin go places? This time a year all women wanna go Florida. What about Easta clothes? She sayin anythin about new clothes for Easta? Fancy necklaces? Bracelets? Rings or jewry stuff?

Thats it Pruney. Jewelry. Mom wants a diamond ring. Dad promised her one at the PresidentKennedy CathlicChurch in Newport.

I explain to Pruney all how we went to church on PalmSunday.

A-course thats it. My brother Digga says easiest way make money is play the horses. NarragansettRaceTrack. Or the dogs in Taunton. You hit it Jate. Priest and Poorboy. Betcha sure hes doin the ponies and the greyhounds. No other reason why you go Whimpys. Everybody knows that.

Yeah, I say.

Yeah, says Pruney.

And its good to see PruneyMendez smiling again because ever since Thanksgiving PruneyMendez hasnt smiled much. I miss the way his eyes light up and make me feel like we're all on a big adventure.

When I ask Pruney if hes gonna come over the house tonight? Another Hooglywhite frost crosses his face and the red in his cheeks disappears and his blue eyes go gray and he says, No. Church. Gotta go to church. HolyThursday tonight. Seven.

A frown comes back on Pruneys face. And Pruney serious says, Soon as OlManSousa gets back I gotta be goin home and gettin ready and you should be goin home too.

And Pruney turns away from me and he starts scooping shave ice on the fish.

How bout I call you in the mornin? I say, Tautogs probbly bitin. Flats too. Leastaways theres always choggies.

And Pruney. Without turning says, Jate. Right now I gotta work.

PruneyMendez with his back to me scooping ice.

PruneyMendez. A fourteen year old who looks twelve.

PruneyMendez. A fourteen year old who looks twelve and who goes to school everyday and gets laughed at because he stayed back in the first grade cause his mother died and his father speaks only Portuguese and Pruney doesnt wear the best clothes.

PruneyMendez. A fourteen year old who looks twelve and who delivers papers all around town on a dump bicycle and everyone knows Pruney because Pruney always calls out everyones name and Pruney waves and everyone always waves back smiling and Pruney dont even care that sometimes everyones laughing at him.

PruneyMendez. A fourteen year old who looks twelve and who washes formaldehyde bottles at the funeral parlor for his brother and sometimes Pruney pukes because formaldehyde smells so bad.

PruneyMendez. A fourteen year old who looks twelve and who picks clams in the winterdead and keeps his hands on the helm when OlMan-MannySousa dories off and errands round the river.

PruneyMendez. A fourteen year old who looks twelve like me and he goes to altarboy churchconfession because he dont wanna go to hell because sometimes Pruney and my twelve year old brother Ross make themselfs feel good and anyone who could possible send fourteen year old Pruney who looks twelve to hell has gotta suck snot from a sick dogs nose and suck it hard and suck some more and now I say GottdamnGottdamn-Gottdamn the way JackCogg sometimes says it because it aint fair that I have a Mom and a Dad and a real good fine twelve year old twin brother Ross and we're all welloff living together real happycomfortable Beachgrit n Sunrise and somethings bugging PruneyMendez and he just wont pal like we used to and I just dont know what to do and fourteen year old who looks like hes twelve Pruney says hes gotta work.

He does too. Has to work now because a rich Barrington guy smelling BostonStore and not like Woolworths and looking like NapoleonSolo *The Man from U.N.C.L.E.* walks in and orders, Three pounds fillet-a-sole. A pint-a-bay scallops. A pair-a-two pound lopstas.

Pruneys all Yessir and serious too.

Im on the sudden thinking what the hells up with HolyThursday?

And goddamn.

Goddamn.

I never swear and I dont understand why Im doing it now.

I walk to my bike wanting to see Pruney smile again. Im certain when I get home I'll be asking Dad, Why you need ta play the ponies? And how come you gotta go ta the dogs ta buy Mom a diamond ring?

By the time I get home Im crying like a five year old and I dont know why Im crying. Im twelve. Dads in the kitchen taking food that Mom made out the oven. And I just go up to him a twelve year old big baby.

A pukey moe moe.

And Dad sets the food on the stove. Then the pot holders. And Dad puts his arms around me saying, Hey whats goin on? Whats the matter?

Pruney, I say. Somethins wrong with Pruney. He wont talk. Or fool around. Or laugh. Or come over like he used to.

And I start the pukey moe moe crying all over again.

Then Dads patting my head one hand and rubbing my back his other and my face is Dads flannel shirt my tears. And my slobber getting all over. He dont seem to mind because its just him and me.

Its all just him doing Shhh. Its okay. Shhhh. Everythins gonna be all right I promise.

He kisses my hair and my forehead. And he wipes my tears with his thumbs and his palms. My face feeling the warm of his belly and the damp of my tears the soft of his flannel. And I gotta addmit, Sometimes its nice being treated like a baby. But then again too. Im real sure glad nobody else knows. What Sowams kid wants to be called a pukey moe moe? Thats strictly Barrington rich kids. Not ta say. But. Theres no denying Im all cried out and Dads shirt is so wet and Dads giving me a handkerchief that he pulls from his backpocket. The handkerchief dark blue with white trim and I dont even check if hes already used it thats how bad I need it and when I stick my nose in. Dads handkerchief reminds me of inside Dads bureau drawers where everything smells like Dad after he shaves and Im embarrassed because if Ross were there and Pruney I just know theyd be laughing calling me a pukey moe moe and telling Zeebo Mush and Wil-lieD I made a swamped up mess.

And Dad watches me blow my nose and after I finish I fold up the handkerchief and hand the handkerchief back to Dad. He sticks it again into his back pocket without even thinking about what I just did.

And Dad says, So youre worried about Pruney are you?

Uh huh. But somethin else too.

What else?

You were in Whimpys this aftanoon cause I saw you go in while I was fixin my bike in the Quequeshan alley down from the fire station.

Okay. So I was in Whimpys. But I wasnt aware that I had to be repor-tin to you my goin ons and whereabouts. Since we're havin a man to man hott ta hott. Yes. I had a visit with some old friends. Had me some favors to ask. Some business take care of.

And I say, Business? What kinda business? Pruney says its on accounta you needin money to buy Mom a diamond ring.

Oh really? And what else does Pruney say?

Nothin.

Havin a hard time believin that.

Well he doesnt say nothin. Just clams up all the time.

Dad does a big breath. No e. Shoulders rise. Belly in. Then he lets out his e real slow. Its a real long breathe. And Dad. Like he knows what I dont. Dad says, Pruney has a lot on his mind right now. Things are gonna get better for him real soon and it would be best to give him some space to breathe.

Thats just what GilOwen would probbly say. Then Dad hands me a plate of baked ziti and a bowl of salad and Dad and me sit together at the kitchen table. And Dad with his hands folded at his chin.

Dad arent best friends suppose to stick by each other?

They are.

Did you and ZompaGalucci use to be best friends.

Not exact. But somethin like that.

But ZompaGalucci called you bastid ballbusta and a chooch.

Its just ZompaGalucci. His way-a-bein friendly. ZompaGalucci enjoys to act Italian. A big shot. A spaccone. And thats the way a spaccone carries on.

What did ZompaGalucci mean for you not to forget your rubbers?

Dad looks me straight and says, Little pitchas have big ears.

No. For real. Whad ZompaGalucci mean?

Dad chews his food real slow and talks with his mouth full and says, Jate. You like surprises dont you?

Mostly.

He puts down his fork. Dad swallows. And Dad says, Jate you listen me and you listen me good and never forget what Im about to say. You and Ross surprised your mother and me. You boys. A surprise. Best surprise your mom and I ever had.

Sure Dad. Tautog n Choggy.

And Dad says, Beachgrit n Sunrise.

And Dad shakes his head and Dad smiles and Dad wipes his mouth with his napkin. And Dad shakes his head again.

And I say, Was it rainin?

And Dad says, Rainin?

And I say, Why on earth would you be needin rubbers to be makin Ross n me? You werent wearin shoes were you?

And Dad says, Well Jate. I guess back when I told you how babies were made. I never told how theyre not made. You see. Not every time man and a woman love each other do they wanna make a baby. Matter-a-fact sometimes dont wanna make a baby at all so they have somethin prevents ingredients gettin together. Over his penis. A man wears. Like. A thin rubber tube. Somethin give protection. Safety. And if he doesnt wear it. A baby. Usual. Gets made.

You werent wearin one? I ask.

Thats right. I wasnt.

Why?

Cause sometimes when people love each other they dont take time to breathe. Theyre too much in a hurry and they just stop thinkin straight.

Lovin makes people sometimes do crazy things doesnt it?

Yes. Yes it does.

Dad puts down his fork. And he wipes his mouth then puts his hand under his chin and rubs his whiskers with his knuckles and I can hear his sandpaper sound. And I get the feel he wants saying something more. But he just stares. Stares hard at me. And he stares out the window. And theres that separation line between his smooth cheeks and his black whiskers because he hasnt shaved today. Then he looks back at me again. Puts his hand down so hes got both his hands either side his plate. He looks at me for a long time before he picks up his fork and starts eating again.

And when he does. Hes real slow. And even though hes chewing his food. He wipes his lips. Jate. Have you ever heard-a-lust?

Dont think so. Is it like rust? What is it?

Dad says, Well. Lust is. Its not rust. Its when you want something real bad but dont care how you get it. Lust can be cruel. Lust can. Often be wrong. Love. On the other hand. Is. Is when you care. Lust and love. They can get mixed. Sometimes. Love. Its. Its such. A thing. You n Ross. Your mom n I love you both so much. We care. You guys know that dont you?

Sure Dad. A-course we do.

And Dad gives me one of his real big smiles and in the next instant of a second the both of us are chowing down and talking about what good ziti Mom makes and I say, Its the sauce.

Dad says, No. Its the ricotta and the mozzarella cheese that she mixes together. She doesnt use cottagecheese like some jabronies do.

We eat seconds. Love that ziti. And finally agree its the sauce. Garden tomatoes Mom preserved in jars last summer and when Mom preserves stuff in jars. She calls it canning. And its cans that get rust. Not jars. So rust aint lust.

And that makes everything just fine.

After we eat Dad says, Lets not clear the table till tomorrow. Lets live like bachelors and go gallivantin.

I say, How about KingPhilipRoad up Montaup?

Dad takes me to FatFingerPetes where we each get a spumoni icecream and then drive to the top a MountHope for to eat dessert and watch the Easter fullmoon rise.

That Easter moon is already prett high up. And from the top MountHope we see the PatienceIslandLighthouse sweeping a complete circle all round the bay and into the mouth of the SowamsRiver. Every minute or so that beam of light catches the top a MountHope and lights up the treetops. The inside of the car. All the other cars parked by the side of the road with people in them who. Dad says are, Probbly mixin lust n love watchin submarine races.

The craziness of the world was what Dad was getting at.

Far as I can tell hes describing impossible stuff. The bay is prettfar away and you could never see a submarine from way up here. Less maybe it was daytime and you knew where to look. I dint wanna say nothing about this to Dad but it seemed to me most of the other people were doing like us. Sitting and talking. Eating icecream. Or looking. Although every now and then. That light beam made it look like some of those people. Mightve been kissing. This one couple in the car next to us were doing a wrestling match to see which one was gonna be the boss of the steeringwheel because they were trying to squeeze together between the steeringwheel and the front seat at the same time. Then they was gone. But what was strange was the car wasnt staying still. It was wiggling. Little bounces. And hands in the air. When the light swept past and everything went dark again whoever finally won the wheel mustve wanted to go driving real bad because the car started up and they drove away all tires screeching.

Just Dad and me.

Every few seconds. A sweeping glow.

To the north. Belltower. Smokestack. Proddastint steeples. The PortugueseCatholic SantoRosario RoseReeChurch where Pruney was being a altaboy with Mikey2A's. AhBewdeeful Lady-a-Fatima. And the confiscated flesh and blood of suffering Jesus.

And the south. Gray with silver sparkles. NarragansettBay. Newport.

And final. Way off.

The black AtlanicOcean.

Sloping direct out below us was MountHopeShores and Dad said, If you look real careful you can see the puddingstonespot.

And then Dad told how it all began. Not just the day Dad met Mom while Mom was reading a book about scrimshaw what JackCogg had give her. But Dad told too how he and Mom wasnt even married but they were crazy in love for each other and how they walked by the railroadtracks to MountHope Shores and went on ahead and made Ross and me anyway. About how a justice of the peace married Mom and Dad at the town hall instead of by a priest at the ItalianCathlicChurch which Dad said he was sure caused, Your Grandma and Grampa Rossi to roll over in their graves. God rest their souls. They were fine people Jate. Real fine people.

Then Dad explained about how AuntBenedeta had been mad at him ever since. And about how the priest and lotsa people at the ItalianCathlic Church had had a attitude toward Mom and him that Dad dint like. Dad said he personal dint care what they thought of him. But, No one was ever gonna show that kinda, Holier than thou attitude toward your mother. Not while Im alive. And not even afta.

Then Dad told about how his Mom and Dad. Nonna and Nonno Tav-

ino came from the old country. Not like Grandma and Grampa Rossi who
came from NewYork. And about how Nonna and Nonno Tavino came
from a island called Sicily. Nonna had a fig tree twig hid in her suitcase
that Nonno eventually planted in Providence. And then how both Nonno
and Nonna died within days of each other when Dad was seventeen from
a disease called T-B that Dad said meant tuberculosis.

Like Q-T means quiet? I said.

Like Q-T means quiet, Dad said.

Dad told how. Before his father. Nonno died. How Nonno and William WillyWhimpy McPherson worked collecting money for a man
named Salvatore Raymond SalRay SanAngelo in Providence at a place
called FederalHill. And how FederalHill was small. And crowded. It was
packed with tenement houses that were filled with awful smells and no
kitchen sinks and no plumbing. Everyone had to do their personal business and take showers at the public bathhouses and there was no fresh air
to breathe except for the air that came from a square hole at the center
of the building. Dad called it a chute. A air chute. But everyone instead
dumped garbage into it. Too many people died of tuberculosis and how
Dads father Nonno made Dad promise two things before Nonno died.
First being that Dad would move away from FederalHill. And second
being that Dad would never work for Salvatore Raymond SalRay San-
Angelo. Or William Whimpy BugEyes McPherson. And thats why Dad
took the first job he could get at the AmericanLuggage. Which made bad
blood between Dad and Whimpy. Which Dad said for real wasnt bad
blood because Whimpy was Irish. But that was beside the point because
Whimpy was always a hot head who called Dad a sucker for working in
a factory because Whimpy said Dad worked for chump wage when Dad
could be working for SalRay. But Dad said he gave his word to his Pop.
And anyway the AmericanLuggage job dint last too long before the op-
portunity come along to work the dredge and make some solid money
with benefits. Dad said he could always hold his head high because Dad
knew he was keeping his promise. And anyways he was never ashamed to
make a honest buck. Although easy money tempted him Dad said he had,
No regrets. Cept bein away from home so much. And anyway. Whimpy
said, Blood is thicker than water. Whimpy dint hold a grudge.

Marryin your mother was the best thing I ever did, Dad said.

And then Dad said when Mom and he got married. William Willy-
Whimpy BugEyes McPherson told him, A couple-a-times I should-a-been
grabbed and tossed into the clink but your Pop took a few raps for me I

will never forget. I owe you kid. I owe you.

As a wedding present William WillyWhimpy BugEyes McPherson told Dad, My hand is always ready should you ever need a fist.

And Dads voice. A broketomb rasp. Said Whimpy made him shake.

They hugged and Whimpy kissed Dads cheek. And then Dad did the same to Whimpy.

Then Dad started the car for us to leave. The PatienceIsland Light house did its sweep and glowed us solid and Dads eyes looked straight into mine and his face fullgray like the Hoogly gravestone. And everything went dark again.

And Dad said, Collar or no collar.

Nobody be botherin PruneyMendez anymore.

21

BadFriday and GoodSunday

GoodFriday morning and I was sitting in Moms garden all plate in the head about them Roman soldiers that crucified Jesus. Those guys. In a most horrible way. Kill Jesus on a cross. Flesh eating and drinking blood? And everyone says the day is good?

What was so good about GoodFriday?

Pruney dint know. But thought it had something to do with Latin language and Jesus coming alive from being dead. Pruney said, Without the death-a-Jesus on Friday. Which was a bad thing. We coulnt-a-had the rezarrection-a-Jesus on Sunday. Which was a good thing.

Then why dont they call it BadFriday and GoodSunday?

Pruney said, Jate. You got a point. But the name EastaSunday has somethin to do with the sun risin in the East an since Jesus is the S-O-N of God. The risin S-U-N became everybodys hope for bein saved from the devil and there you have it. Just like the Wampanoags. Dawn Kids. Plain as day. EastaSunday.

Mom said Easter is the combine of a Angel Sexton Greek godwoman named Esta and the fullmoon representin Jesus come alive again.

With all due respect to your Mom, Pruney said. The moon idea is ridiculous because if it was all about the moon. Then Easter would be on Monday. Which everyone knows is named after the moon. And not on Sunday. Which is named plain clear obvious.

Well. How did the rabbit get into the picture?

Pruney said, Rabbit? What rabbit?

The EasterBunny. Howd he get inna the story?

Pruney said he wasnt sure but he was certain the rabbit had, Somethin to do with when Jesus come outta his tomb in the garden all rezarrected and newbody powaful that Jesus scared the livin daylights outta the garden bunny.

Pruney said, Jesus just walked over to the cabbage patch where that poor bunny was froze stiff with solid fright and said, Hey little buddy. Dint mean to scare you. Want a Hershey chocolate bar? Make you feel better. Rabbits and Jesus could talk together cause Jesus was God. Rabbit said, Sure. The Hershey chocolate was the best tastin chocolate he ever had and would it be okay if he could have another to leave on the windowsill-a-the cripplekid that lived next door? That bunny told Jesus that the cripplekid was always leavin lettuceleaves and carrots for the rabbits and woulnt it be nice if he could now leave the cripplekid a chocolatebar? And Jesus said, Hot diggity. Thats a good idea. And how about I also give you. Every Easta. Supa powas to deliva all kinda candies. Jelly beans n stuff. To all kids. Not just cripple ones. Rabbit said, Cool. So Jesus makin fancy with his hands and he blinks real hard. And Bing. That rabbit become the EastaBunny right off. Thats where the EastaBunnyRabbit come from.

When Pruney told that story Ross wasnt around. But no doubt about it. Ross woulda said something like, It dint exact happen that way.

But me. I liked that story just fine. Especial since earlier a couple of marsh rabbits were hopping out Moms garden. Which at this point in the year. Was nothing but turned dirt and dead plants hoping soon to grow once spring warmed things.

So out in the garden we left some of last nights leftover salad lettuce for rabbits.

Dad was in the house getting ready to run around town in the car to do some errands and had wanted to know if I wanted to go along. I had told him, Staying home. TV. The Dialing for Dollars One O'clock Movie.

Ross had told me today was *MobyDick* with GregoryPeck being CaptainAhab and Ross said he would too be watching *MobyDick* in Providence at AuntBenies and that it would be cool if we was both watching the movie at the same time but in different places. And cool. That would be fun.

So there it was. *MobyDick* movie plans for GoodFriday.

But Pruney said, No way.

Said first of all. Had to serve. Said it was Mass. Or something like Mass at his church. Pruney said from noon to three would pretty much be kneeling and praying. Adoratin-a-the blessed sacrament is what he called it.

Pruney said that from three to four was Stations. Then outta church. Deliver papers. And then afta. Be pickin clams at Sousas. Probbly till six or seven. And then back to church. More keepin vigil while Jesus be layin in his tomb desendin into hell an gettin ready for his glorious rezarrection on Easta mornin.

Wow. Sure glad I instead get to watch TV. Dont *MobyDick* have something to do with the rezarrection of the dead? Dint MistaCoggs say so in his drunk pablabborating with GilOwen? How exact had MistaCogg put it? Wow *MobyDick* the movie and me at home instead of being at church on my knees thinking Lord knows what about Jesus being crucified. Dead. Then buried. Descending into hell and getting ready to open the gates of heaven for good Jews. Arabs. Africans. Chinese. And undergenerous native peoples like American Indians and Australian Aborginines. And furthermore Jesus was also gonna visit a place called Limbo. Get all the dead unbaptized babies. Which Pruney thinks is a especial good idea because like he said, Werent the babies fault they got born before Jesus could kick in solid with his glorious plan-a-salvation.

The thing about the Dialing for Dollars One O'clock Movie was that it never just began with the movie. Instead what it had was this coat and tie guy TomMorgan. Him telling everyone he had a jackpot of money. Then he would reveal how much money was in that jackpot. Say one hundred fifty dollars. One hundred sixty five dollars. Whatever. Then he'd phone-call somebody up. Usual some woman at home. And if she knew the answer to his two questions. She would win the jackpot.

The first question was always something to do with the movie. Like, Could you please tell us who the star of todays movie is?

And second, Do you know how much money is in todays jackpot?

If the woman knew the answers. She'd get all squealed with joy. And she'd get the cash. But if she dint know. She'd get all sad depressed. Sometimes even weepy. TomMorgan would say something nice. Make her feel better. Then TomMorgan would raise the jackpot amount and the next caller would gotta know. That is. If she wanted her hands on all them dialed dollars.

Whenever me and Ross watched the Dialing for Dollars One O'clock Movie. Which. Because of school. Wasnt often. But when we were sick. We always wrote down the amount. And the question answer. Which TomMorgan would always give. Then we would wait for our phone to ring.

But it never did.

It always seemed that instead of calling someone who was ready like us. TomMorgan would always call someone who wasnt watching or someone who was watching but dint know the answers because they just werent paying attention.

Todays question was, Who directed *MobyDick?* And not only did Tom-Morgan tell that it was JohnHuston. But JohnHustons name was on the screen at the beginning.

When the first caller answered TomMorgans question. She said the movie was directed by HermanMelville which made me groan with her kicked by a pigeon stupidness. But she was from Cranston. The West side of Narragansett Bay and we never did hold much against them people because they couldnt even pronounce the name of their own town. They always said Cah-van-ston. Which every RhodeIsland jabroni knew was wrong. But it was like what ZompaGalucci used to say, Some people just dont know from nuthin. And Zompa would shrug his big shoulders and say, Whaddaya gonna do? And go back to reading his newspaper. Or watching the WaterStreet traffic.

And I gotta tell you. That *MobyDick* movie had me watching serious.

My favorite parts was all Queequeg.

Queequeg smoking his pipe in bed.

Queequeg spitting and then throwing the harpoon at the target on the barrelhead and showing he was a good shot to that astounded boat-owner.

Queequeg throwing bones to see his future and with a look of horror on his tattooed face. Going all stiff and silent and not even moving a muscle when the bad guys started cutting up Queequegs chest with a knife and I just then remembered MistaCogg telling GilOwen the Indians name was Queerqueg. Not Quee.

Not ta say. But. There was other good parts too. Like the weird guy named Elijah. The sad faces of the women who were watching their husbands go to sea. One old hag woman even had whiskers on her chin and she reminded me of FathaLuises sister that day we got caught in the confessions. And of course. SarahHaag too. Her with her four A's. Maybe she had whiskers too.

Then there was big FatherMarple. The preacher on a pulpit that looked just like the bow of a ship and. Wow. If we had a church like that here in Sowams. Id go every Sunday.

But best was CaptainAhab who looked a whole lot like a angry Abraham Lincoln. Gosh. CaptainAhab was something. Them eyes. Wicked look in one. Left eye. Seemed always leaking something down his face that even stained his beard. That GregoryPeck bearded CaptainAhab had a way of sideways glancing and talking at sailors that set the Hooglies crawling at the back of their sailor necks and running down to their sailor livers. Leastaways thats what that leaky eye sure done to me.

Then.

During the height of the storm. Which was. A. For real big storm. Blowing and knocking that boat to smithereens. Toppling masts and ripping sheets. And waves dashing them men about. Right at the height of their danger. All on a sudden. Everything started glowing. Spars. Masts. Rigging. Glowing like Christmas lights. And one sailor yelled, SaintElmos fire!

And Ahabs harpoon that hes holding high starts glowing too.

And without the slightest bit of fear or wonder. Ahab smooths his hand over that harpoon and puts out the fire.

And as much as that doing was a sight to behold. I was total plate in the head.

I mean.

What caused all that glowing? And how did Ahab get such power?

22

Knotted Lines

On Saturday morning I slept late then decided to call. On the phone. Everyone and see whos coming fishing. After all. It now being springtime. Flatfish should be biting. And if not. There was always choggies to catch and seagulls to feed.

WillieDs mother said WillieDs still sleeping. Call again after eleven.

Mushes phone. No answer. Probbly meant Mush was with his mother shopping.

Pruneys. His father answered. I said, Hello. MistaMendoza. This is Jate Tavino. Pruney there?

And. Not fa nuthin. But no matter how many few times I spoked to OlMan MistaMendoza. It hasnt been many because MistaMendoza is nightshift. Day sleeper. Its always like hes never before heard my name. Or my voice. And I wonder if even he knows me.

Anyway. OlMan MistaMendoza was talking me in Portuguese and I dint understand a word he was saying and I remembered to use Pruneys real name and repeated Pedro? Pedro? Pedro? Until MistaMendoza final understood and then MistaMendoza did some more hollering off the phone and AuntJovita was hollering. Then next thing theres Pruney. Not hollering. But talking. Talking to me. Talking to me on the phone.

Pruney says, Hello.

I say, Its me. Whats happenin over there?

The phone is OlMan in the backroom hollering more Portuguese and Pruney in the frontroom hollering more louder Portuguese to backroom OlMan.

And Pruney is covering with his hand the part of the phone you talk into but what hes doing doesnt complete block out the sound because hes moving his hand all over the talking piece and instead the hand blocking makes it so some of the hollering is loud. Then quiet. Then loud. And then quiet all over again.

Final the sound is just Pruney on the phone. AuntJovita and OlMan still hollering. But not so loud because theyre probbly in another room.

Pruney says, Hey Jate. Whats goin on?

Fishin. Wanna go fishin.

Pruney says, Where?

Docks. Sousas.

Pruney says, When?

A hour. About eleven.

Pruney says, You have a extra sinker?

Sure. Plenny-a-hooks and sinkers. Even a extra hand line. If you need it.

And Pruney says, No. Just a sinker. Thats all.

Dont forget tonight is *Lawrence of Arabia* with Dad.

Pruney says he gotta talk to me about that.

And then OlMan yelling Portuguese again. Getting louder. Probbly coming out the other room.

Pruneys brother Digga hollering too.

A womans voice. AuntJovita.

Pruney hollering back in Portuguese and Pruney says *Lawrence of Arabia.*

Then a crash and a thud. Like Pruney dropping the phone and it bounces back up because of the cord and slams into the wall.

More AuntJovita hollering.

And blocked Portuguese.

And unblocked Portuguese.

Then the blocked OlMan voice.

Then the blocked and unblocked Pruney voice yelling Portuguese.

Then more blocked AuntJovita voice. But real high and kree kree total mental seagull. And Pruney screaming like hes cussing someone out.

And Pruney unblocked sounding like hes crying and talking with a burnt tongue. Like hes trying to tell me, See you about eleven.

Then the phone goes dead.

And things sound prettmuch normal at the house of PruneyMendez.

Since I had a hour to kill I decided instead of going straight to the docks Id ride my bike up LandStreet and stop at Woolworths. See the Easter bunnies and chickbirds five and dimes always sold this time of year.

The bunnies were all clumped together in a small picketfence corral that smelled like rabbitfood pellets and straw. Some rabbitshit too. But for the most part the bunnies smelled like rabbitpellets. And I gotta addmit. The bunnies were real clean. Or as Ross would say, Adorable.

I pet a black and white bunny under its ears and then pulled those ears back so its eyes looked like a Chinese. Dint pull them back hard or nothing. Just a slow tug that let the bunny know. Hey. Such soft ears. The bunny enjoyed it too. Poked his head up. Wiggled his nose and whiskers like he wanted more. So I pet him again. Wished for a carrot. Such a adorable bunny.

Then there was chickbirds.

Chickbirds running ever which way in a rubber kiddie pool unfilled without water. One sorry chick had one of his guts hanging out his butt and was running around like everything was hunkadory. Only time it acted like anything wrong was if another chick come up behind and took a nip at its ass dragging gut. A couple of the other chickbirds lay around dead. Their tiny wings flipped out. Their bleeding heads stretched long far on their necks. Like those chicks probbly collapsed reaching out for something. Like they were running a race and dropped dead in the act of trying to get over the finish line. Only their heads having made it. But the live chicks dint seem to pay no mine. Dint seem to mind the dead chickbirds cluttering up their running space. As a matter of fact some of those live birds were pecking the heads of the dead birds. The living trying to wake the dead.

And. Not ta say. But. I gotta tell you. While a store clerk was selecting out them frazzled bodies. I almost had me a Hoogly conniption when with my own two eyes I seen one of those dead birds. Bloody head and all. Jump up and start chasing the bird that pecked him.

But irregardless the bad behavior of a few. I always did love the Easter chicks. The way you could hear their cheep cheep cheeping no matter where you went in the whole of Woolworths five and dime. And I was thinking about buying one of those nice chicks too. They were such a deal at only fiftycents each. Not two dollars apiece like the bunnies. But lets face it. I dint have that kind of money to be spending on for bunnies. Or for birds. So I decided just keep looking. Even though it was still early the place was for real crowded with lotsa little kids and all sorts of flowers. Daffodils. Bluebells. Lilies. Which made the store smell glorious. Just dog glorious.

And the Easterbaskets.

You never saw so many.

Easterbaskets stuffed with fake pink grass.

Easterbaskets stuffed with fake green grass.

Easterbaskets stuffed with real. Not fake. Toys.

Easterbaskets stuffed with all the good candies.

Some Easterbaskets stuffed with toys and stuffed with candies.

Trucks. And bunnydolls. Jellybeans. Foil wrapped milkchocolate eggs. Chocolatecovered marshmallow rabbits. Egg coloring kits. Greeting cards. The first two aisle shelves were lined with nothing but all those Easterbaskets and bags and boxes of Easter candies.

My favorite candies were the yellow marshmallow Peeps because you got six for a dime but mostly because you could squish a whole Peeps into your mouth and work it good into a yellow suds goo ball. Then open your mouth and show somebody.

Last Easter. Pruney and Mush and WillieD and me. We all gooed up a whole sixpack of Peeps each.

Ross wouldnt though. Just watched.

But if Ross now been there in Woolworths with me. I know he'd turned his nose at the marshmallow Peeps and instead buy the spotted candy-coated malted eggs. The ones he said GilOwen said were past tells. They were Rosses favorites. And he always kept them in his mouth till the past tell colors were gone.

I asked Ross why he called them colors past tells.

And Ross said it was P-A-S-T-E-L-S and pastels was watercolor paints made from powder and that these two French artists named Monhay and Moni liked to leave a good impression on people so they used them pastels a lot. Pruney said past tell had nothin to do with artist. Or the frogs.

I dont know what frogs had to do with anything but Pruney said, Once you sucked the color off the malted eggs. The color was past tellin.

And he was probbly right about that because Ross never corrected Pruney. As a matter of fact. Ross said Pruney was makin his usual word music outta the most foolish-a-usual things.

Another reason Pruney was probbly right about past tell was because if Ross dint think anyone was looking. You could catch Ross taking the malted egg out his mouth and studying it real hard just to see if the colors had disappeared. And they did. The past tells did disappear because all that was left on the outside shell was smearwhite with very light color fading all round. And when Ross talked you could see some the colors on his tongue. But you had to look real quick because if you straight out asked him to show you. He'd just say no.

Showing wasnt Ross.

Showing was Pruney and me.

Since it was gonna be just Pruney and me at the docks and since Pruney could use a little cheering. I decided to buy Pruney a box of Peeps.

Im talking six for a dime here.

Six Peeps for ten cents.

Imagine that?

From Woolworths I rode my bike through all the quiet sidestreets. Down Mingo on Wildwood. Cut through Baker and Miller. On to Washington. And eventual Water. Some of the houses had yellow daffodils and purple crocus in their southside edging. And in some yards. Lawns and trees were budding fresh green. Air smelled good and I like that no matter where you lived in Sowams. Especial the NorthEnd. You could always smell the river. Salt and seaweed. Boats and engines. Hear seagulls. The river in spring. Clean and clear. Not damp swamp like the summer with thick kelp. Or sometimes red tide sufficating everything.

Spring river smell was clear.

And cool. And cold.

Just like the air.

Just like the water.

Clean no matter where you looked.

Clear.

When I got to the docks BobbyBraytons skiff was just getting into the boat ramp. His skiff with a halfdozen bushel of quog. All sizes mixed. Each basket three quarters full so as not spill on the ride in. You know. Slapslap and chopchop of the boat as the skiffbottom hit the waves. That kind of riding always shook stuff and tossed things around real good.

I leaned my bike against a piling. Grabbed my tackle grip out my handlebar basket and looked down from the dock.

Hey Bobby. Any broke clams for bait?

And with his hula girl and anchor tattoo arms that was inside his sweatshirt sleeves. Bobby TheBullRake Brayton underhand pitched high. Into the air. A perfect black chowda that crashed down on the boards. Split open. Gushed juice spilling out.

With a face all wore like the weatherbeaten shingles on the side of JackCoggs Port n Starboard Shop and a dangling cigarette in teeth brown like the outside of furry old conk shells. Bobby yelled back, That broke enough for ya Jate?

I gave him a wave and a shout, Thanks Bobby.

And thought it strange BobbyBrayton was Barrington and dint live in Sowams.

What was Bobby like when he was a kid? No way could heve been one of those rich kid puke moe moes. Not Bobby TheBullRake Brayton.

Now. One thing you gotta understand about the difference between the Barrington kids and the kids like us from Sowams is. For the most part. Barrington kids used fishing poles. Big money reels. And fished from BostonWhalers or DyerDhow dinghies or runabouts with ten or twenty-horse Evinrudes. Johnsons. Or Mercs.

Sowams kids fished from docks and piers. Trestles and bridges. And we hardly ever used poles. What we used was handlines wrapped round a double V cut piece a wood. Or a pineboard cut like the letter H. What we called a tackleblock.

MistaCogg cut our tackleblocks and showed us how to tie tackle mostly using overhand knotloops that youd string through the sinker eye and of course gotta run your hooks off two or three other overhand knotloops youd tie on the main line above the sinker.

MistaCogg said, The more hooks the betta yuh chances.

But we never did use but more than two hooks one line.

And we dint use nylon line.

Too much money.

What we used was a strong heavy greenline hemp or some kind of twill.

MistaCogg even gave us a old scrimshaw scratch awl. Case our lines got knotted.

Which they did.

Knotted lines.

Plenny-a-times.

Especial when those lines were wet and swolled and what a guy for real would want was use a knife and cut them. Thats when MistaCogg would spit teeth and holler, Slice perfect good tes? Put the gottdamm knife away. Work the somanabitchin knots. Work em.

So I always kept the scratch awl in my tackle grip.

Nothing like that scratch awl when you needed it.

But anyways. What I for real like about our cotton greenline is that the saltwater soaked into it and whenever we opened our tackle grips especial home in the winter. The whole bag smelled like seaweed. Or Narragansett-Bay when the fog rolled in on hot summers days.

And another thing. For bait. Barrington kids used fancy lures. Or pricy sandworms MistaSousa would sell in wire handled pint white buckets stuffed with black rockweed. Or red mermaids hair.

Sowams kids dint have nothing against sandworms even though a sandworm could give a nasty bite if you dint take care. Double pinchas.

Ross said they were called pincers. P-I-N-C-E-R-S. But Pruney said, Same diffrence cept with a H and no matter how you spelled it if a pincer gave you a pinch. It would pinchya. And when that happened. It was gonna hurtchya no matter what.

Anyways. Pinchyas. Sandworms got pinchyas coming right out their asses. Or their heads. Those sandworm pinchyas are on the ass end of a earwig. And I know its the earwigs ass end got the pinchyas. Because earwigs. Unlike sandworms. Absolute got heads. Me and PruneyMendez? We cut off plenty of earwig heads just to see those ass end pinchyas stretch back and try and pinch the knife blade.

And another thing. Those earwig pinchyas work even after they dont have a head telling them what to do. You definitely dont wanna put your hand down on the ass end of a earwig with no head. That thing'll bite you. And make you yelp like a cat alley dog. The simple fact is. Sandworms are not earwigs. Sandworms are worms that live everywhere in the lowtide sand. A earwig is like a real mean roach that has nothing to do with worms. But they both got those pinchyas and the point Im gettin at here is. Who ever heard of buying a sandworm unless youre a pukey Barrington rich kid?

In Sowams we dug up sandworms for ourselfs. And carried them in old Campbell soupcans. Or old paper coffeecups. Seemed like a waste of money paying for something you could just go get without having to be buying. If we had the money? We'd probbly be getting a coffeemilk and Twinkies. Or a Dels Lemonade. Or Sousas Frenchfries with maltvinegar. Or clamcakes. Not fa nuthin. But. Why throw money at the fish? They get to eat for free. All the time. Right?

Anyways.

For bait we most used broke clams. You could always find broke clams on any fish market floor or the ones the quahoggers tossed with a smile and a nod the way Bobby TheBullRake had just done for me.

And while Bobby tended to his catch I headed down the ramp and walked the end of the floating dock. The tide was coming in which was easy to tell because even though it was early spring there was a few Barrington yachts moored from their bows and every kid in Sowams knows the current always swings the boat around so the transom tells where the tide is going while the bow is telling where the tide is from.

But then of course the best tide tellers were the dock pilings and the seaweed and junk on any shoreline. That stuff always let you know what the waters were doing and where the tides were at. Considerating what I was seeing. And from the fact that Bobby was already in. The Easter fullmoon low had turned a couple-a-three hours ago and the Boreas northwind was blowing. Against the current. So as the tide came in. Chops and shakes would also toss the dock. But that dint for real mean nothing except that along with wave laps and wind sounds. There would also be. Halyard slaps. Dockknocks and thuds. Grinds and skiffheaves against pitch and roll and slips. A perfect morning for fishing choggies. And maybe even a fat flat flounder or two.

I sat crosslegged. Palmed Bobbys gift clam. Brung it down hard on the dock and for real smashed it open. Clam milk brine dripped all over my hands. I pulled the meat out and with a sharp piece of shell. Sliced the butterscotch colored neck away from the custardthick belly. Fish love any clam part. Not ta say. But. I was being Rossfussy. Everyone knows its the tough neck that is for real the clams foot. And dont ask me why they call it the neck they just do. Its the foot and neck stays best hooked. Clambellys good for striped bass on a big bass hook. But on a small chogg hook. Clambellys just too soft. And mush. Wont hold. But clam neck. Thats a chogghooks best friend.

I baited two hooks with a joint of slime neck. Careful not to stab my fingers with the hookabobs. Washed my hands in icecold Sowams. Unwound twenty feet of tackle line. Stood. One foot firm on the block. Twirled the hemp overhead and let fly.

It was dog glorious casting and before the sinkers hit the bottom I was working my line taunt whipping water off with each yank and draw of my arms and hands.

By the time Pruney rode his bike right where I was kneeling a halfdozen schmear-a-choggies slimed up the dock with bleeding and flipping.

I hadnt fed the seagulls yet but before I had unhooked my first fish those birds were landing on the pilings and kreeing with the chor of expectation. They knew a meal werent far off and they were all ready for the serving.

Pruney plopped down crosslegged beside me and never said a word.

I was so serious on hooking my next. As JackCogg woulda called them. Little bastids. That when I finally did shoot a look at Pruney. I about near fell overboard.

Pruneys face was all swolled red. His lip split raw. His left eyebrow bulged like a egg youd never find in no Woolworths Easterbasket. Pruney was that screamfroze dead Polish kid in the Hoogly grave and I was MistaCogg gawking.

Fact was. Pruney was slapped up.

PruneyMendez was slapped up real bad.

23
Empty Sky Nothing

Pruney dint say nothing and I was so busy wide mouth staring he just wrapped his bony arms around his pulled up knees and buried his face in his lap. And I should have immediate said, What in all hell happened? But. Way Pruney was hiding his face and holding back steam. Every few moments some of that steam would slip through his busted up lips as a slew of jagged huffs and hisses. All I could muster was, Bought us some Peeps. Want one?

Pruney exploded himself to his feet and Pruney swiped them Peeps from me. Tore open the cellophane. Dug his fingers deep. Pulled them out their package. Bit off the head of one. Ripped others to mush and what with all the bruised dog glory power Pruney had in his body. Heaved that yellow mess. And their package. Into the river.

That parish of gulls that had been sitting on the dockpilings and on the roof of Sousas Shellfish Market. Those birds took to beat all in the air with a splurge of kreeing and choring and chawkling and before them Peeps even made a splash those gulls were further tearing them marshmallow chicks to chum. MistaCogg would have said, Talk about your gottdammed banshee chorus.

Then Pruney spit out the Peeps head.

Spit it out right in the middle of my choggies on the dock.

Peeps head with blood from Pruneys lip.

Peeps head with Pruneys lip blood.

Peeps head with spit fish and lip slime.

Then Pruney dropped next to me. Face in his hands. And Pruney started crying.

Crying like I had been doing the night before about him.

Crying to me like I had been crying to Dad.

Said he hated his, Fucking OlMan father.

Said he hated Digga his, Shit ass brother.

Called AuntJovita, A goddamn holy hore.

And said most of all he hated, FuckinFathaLu.

I never heard such talk from Pruney ever before.

Never.

Never ever.

So I knew one thing for sure. I had about all of watching PruneyMendez being miserable that I was gonna from now on tolerate. I wasnt going to Mom or Ross or Dad or GilOwen or JackCogg or the Ghost of KingPhilip on MountHope for answers.

Today I wasnt leaving until I knew what all was happening to Pruney-Mendez and what was going on.

And Im kneeling next to him and Shhh Shhh just like Dad did to me and although I dont have no handkerchief to give him. I let him slobber my jacket shoulder which I know hes doing because I can hear his slobber soaking and when I know he has me all gooed real good I pull back to let him continue his ranting and blow snot into his fingers then flip it and all the yellow Peeps mess off and wash his hands in the river.

And I say, Pruney. Whadaya mean? Whadaya talking about?

And Im wiping his tears my thumbs and my palms and hes growling up a deep lunger. Wincing because puckering his lip for real hurts. But no matter the pain. He shoots. What MistaCogg called, A wag of flem. Off of his tongue into the Sowams. Sits. Head in hands. And all I see is his top knot of curl hair heaving up and down.

And again Im asking, Whats going on? Tell me. Whats the story?

And Pruney says, Cant do *Lawrence of Arabia*. Gotta do. OlMan says. HolySaturday night service. Big fight over it too. Started when you called. Gonna quit altarboys. But OlMan wont let me.

Why? Why you wanna quit altarboys?

And Pruney says, Promised Ross I woulnt tell nobody. Your dad knows because Ross tol GilOwen. And GilOwen tol your dad. And prettsoon all of Sowams gonna know bout me n Ross n FathaLuis n GilOwen bein some kinda sissapoof queers.

Whats FathaLuis got to do with Ross n GilOwen? And whats sissapoof queers?

Pruney says, Ross and GilOwen dont have anythin to do with Fatha-Luis. But when I went to confession one of the times. I tol FathaLuis. Not only about the PowaHouse stuff. But about me n Ross doin some touchin too. And I gotta addmit. Felt real bad about mentionin Rosses name and FathaLuis tol me I hadda do a pennants and I coulnt never let Ross touch me that way again. And then FathaLuis tol me since I was always whackin off. That him and me. That. We. We hadda pray together for extra pennants. Which I was all in favor for cause I jus know the devils in me and Im gonna go to hell. But Jate?

Pruney looks at me. Eyes sunset fog. Pruney says, Cant stop whackin off. No matter how hard I try. Just cant. Devil got hold-a-me solid. And when I tol it to FathaLuis in confession. He said maybe we oughta pray together and would I like that? And I was kinda not sure what he meant. But said, Sure FathaLuis. And he. FathaLuis. He. Closed out the confession. You know. Turned off the lights. Was real late. We. The only ones in church. Us. And. He. Took me. The sacristy. He. He. He locked the door and said if I dint do exact how he tol me. My father. And my AuntJovita. And your mother and father. They would all find out that. We. The PowaHouse. And then he. FathaLuis. Grabs my the neck. And he puts. His. He puts—

Pruney touches his all lumped up eyebrow egg real careful. Like it might. Any second. Bust open and hatch a Easter chick if he touches it too hard.

Then Pruney says, The week before Christmas. He made me. Made me do PowaHouse stuff to him. And worsa too.

And on the sudden Pruneys repeating, FuckinFathaLuis. FuckinFathaLuis. My hand open palm on his shoulder. And under my fingers Pruneys shoulder shaking like BobbyBraytons skiff engine running low throttle but going no place. And Pruneys fingers touched my fingers. His fingers wrapped around my hand. Pruneys fingerprints. Pruneys fingerprints pressing into mine. And I dint know what to say. So I asked, Whadaya mean worsa stuff? What kinda worsa stuff?

And Pruney said, Dont wanna talk. Again he pulled up his legs and dropped his head and tried to get himself lost in the space between his knees and his lap.

So I changed the subject and asked straight out, Whyd AuntJovita hit you?

And Pruney in a soft breath said, She dint. OlMan did the smackin. AuntJovita tried stop it. Digga too.

But why? FathaLuis is none-a-your fault. Whyd your father hit you?

Cause when you called. OlMan said I coulnt go to see *Lawrence of Arabia.* That I hadda go to serve HolySaturday Church and be a altarboy. And I tol you. I quit bein a altarboy. And OlMan. Bam with his right hand. Then bam with his left. And Digga jumps in grabs OlMan. And. Bam. Digga misses OlMans arm and instead Digga busts my lip. The phone goes flyin and thats when I hung up and its blood everwhere. AuntJovita screamin and beggin em to stop and OlMan hollerin if I dont do HolySaturday Services then Im on the next boat back the Azores.

And when Pruney says that. A plate in the head throb comes on strong. Jellyfish stings down my arm and my fingers claw. Its me having a episode. And I got no legs and I drop to my ass on the dock and Pruney catches my head and handholds it just as I fall back feeling sandworm pinchyas and I pull a deep breath. Somewhere in my head a bit of steel scraping rock and hint of rot clams. Add an e and plate in the head softer and softer and jellyfish sting fading away and my claw just fingers again and Pruneys face is split lip and bigblue eyes and fat cheeks. Winter red purple. Pruneys face staring me hard into focus. And I say, The OlMan.

Pruney puts his arm under my head. And Pruney says, Easy Jate. Easy. Lays his whole self right along side me.

My arm. Small shakes. And a bit unsteady but I roll to my left and manage up and say, Azores other side Alantic. Your father woulnt do that?

Pruney sits up. Holds my shoulder steady and says, Steady Jate.

Jus a episode, I say. But OlMan?

And Pruneys big blues. Tight. Still holding me says, He aint kiddin. Says Im gonna live with my vovo gramma n grampa. And other aunts and furtha somemore OlMan said forget about ever seein you guys again. Your house. Off limits and no more. Whole thing just makes me sick ta death Jate and I hadda get outta there. Jumped on my bike. And. Here I am.

And Pruneys fingers real slow let go my shoulder.

I feel steady. All feels good.

So we just sit.

We sit for a long time Pruney and me.

Sit on the dock.

Watch the seagulls.

Watch the water.

Watch the tide pushing the channel buoys.

Watch the clouds.

Watch the sun go behind the clouds.

Have ya tol OlMan bout any-a-this FathaLuis stuff?

Pruney gives me Eecoodeesh and a prune face disappears into pulled up knees.

What about Digga? You could talk to your brother coulnt you?

Pruney head on knees says, Dagama? No way. Woulnt never unnastan.

But you told my dad.

Pruney. To his knees says, Dint tell your dad. GilOwen did cause-a-Ross.

Well. What did my dad tell you?

And Pruney said, Tol me FathaLuis was never gonna touch me again and I hadda put all-a-this in the past. Forget about it. But. But that was last week. And afta last nights HolyThursday service FathaLuis said he wanted see me durin Easta vacation and I just know that afta tonights HolySaturday services hes gonna say somethin he always does. Hand. Shoulder. Smile front-a-OlMan. Tell Digga how hes so proud of me bein such a good altarboy. And Jate? I cant take no more. No more.

And Pruneys usual beautiful blue eyes are now empty sky nothing.

And I dont know what say. And wish Ross were here because Pruney needs hearing something right and good and Ross is always good at saying something right.

Even though theres sun bright between dark clouds. It dont feel bright. But more what Mom would call, A sorrow.

Its Pruney and me sitting and looking. Looking at the Sowams.

Wind against tide.

Tide against buoys.

Port and starboard.

Red and green. Red right return.

Sun drying salt on our skin.

Bay smell in spring.

Clean of it all.

Seagulls kreeing.

Halyards slapping.

Wind on the Sowams.

The sound of waves.

Such a good thing. A river. When no more. Whats left to be said?

Pretty soon buoys point straight to the sky. The afternoon tide done and not as high as I figured. But we're feeling low as ever and its time Pruney be delivering papers. Paper route always interrupts everything Saturday afternoon.

And I tell Pruney, Before Mom went to Providence she bought a cod from Louie Squeegee FishMan Respeegie and she made fishcakes. And afta we finish deliverin papers. We should eat lunch my house.

Pruney always liked eating Moms food. But it wasnt just that. The food. It was more like Pruney had thrown away something heavy and was now again gonna walk the crushed shells of BaggyWrinkleLane and not worry about where the stuff he threw away landed. It was like all on a sudden Pruney had changed from being a Wednesday ProvidenceJournal to being a Saturday one. Fact being. Saturday papers were always easy to carry. Skinny things. Not fat heavy like Wednesdays. Or Sundays. That were thick on accounta all the advertising inserts.

And between us two. Pruney and me.

Pruneys fortytwo papers were a breeze.

In less than a hour after we left Sousas docks we were winding down with our last papers. Heading for South QuequeshanStreet. Whimpys bookiejoint. And as usual ZompaGalucci was stooping on the front step. Checking out everyone coming and going and I knew he saw us. Probbly soon as we made the turn off WaterStreet. I swear. ZompaGalucci could see around corners. ZompaGalucci could see over buildings. Zompas eyes never missed nothing. Nothing never missed Zompas eyes.

Never.

ZompaGalucci. Watching. Across the street. Birds. And counting pigeons.

ZompaGalucci. Seeing MissusMalloy petting her cat and pulling down shades.

ZompaGalucci. Knowing exact how many cars cruising and people walking.

ZompaGalucci. Telling which gardens on QuequeshanStreet have crocus blossoms and tulip greens and just whose for cynthia bushes already blooming yellow.

Zompa. Cozy. Scarf wrapped round his neck. Wool coat. That thick ZompaGalucci face soaking in the out from behind the clouds sun.

Zompa TheDoorGuy Galucci says, Hi boys. Whats in the news taday?

Zompa never looking at the paper.

Instead. Zompas face is JackCoggs at the Hoogly grave.

ZompaGalucci talking Italian saying, Mannaggia la gawts.

Zompas biting on his fist and again saying, Mannaggia la gawts.

And Zompas got this look that he gets when hes got high blood pressure. His eyes are Whimpy BugEyes McPherson. Zompa disappears into the bookiejoint slamming the door so hard a knot of wind pushes the curls on Pruneys head.

And then the door pulls open again. Its Zompa. But now with some other guy I dont know. Because I never before seen this guy. Because this is a guy that if you seen before you woulda knowd you seen him. What Im getting at here is. This guys a tall skinny guy with a funny hat looking like a upside down meat pie. EdNortons on JackieGleason. But more brim stingy. Not fa nuthin. This guys no EdNorton. The guy. This guy. The guy. He looks mean streets on account he comes outta Whimpys wearing dark sunglasses. And the guy. He looks at me. But only from one side of his head. Like Ahab looking sideways at the guys on the deck. Then the guy. He looks Pruney the same way. One side. Then the guy. He takes off his sunglasses. And here Im not kidding you. The guy. Hes got a scar running middle down his forehead. Splits his left eyebrow so he got three eyebrows instead of two. And that split scar cuts clear cross his left eye. Im talking his eyeball here. His eyeball that doesnt have any color in it. What this eyeball does have is the look of one a Rosses past tell malted eggs after you suck the past tell color off it. You know? That milk smear before the inside chocolate shows through. Thats what this guy has for a eyeball. And that scar doesnt stop there. No way. It cuts full right over his cheek down his jaw and then disappears under his fat left ear lobe. Im thinking. Not fa nuthin. But. For such a tall guy. For such a tall skinny guy. That guy. I gotta addmit. Like a fat man. That guy got clamcakes for ears. And jeez. I wonder how that guy. That guy. How that guy. Howd that guy he get that scar? Is he Ahab? But he dont look like Ahab. Meaner.

Hes ScarHab.

And ScarHab walks over to Pruney. Grabs Pruneys face with one hand. Pruney holding tight the bike grips. Pruneys feet pushing the bike back. ScarHab squeezing Pruney at the cheeks. Pruneys eyes going choggy everywhich way. Pruneys lips all flounder. But ScarHab keeping Pruney put with just enough tight. And ScarHab turns Pruneys face left. ScarHab turns Pruneys face right. Then ScarHab lets go Pruneys face.

ScarHabs fingers go for Pruneys curls.

Pruney ducks his head.

The way Pruney ducks his head.

The way Pruney gives ScarHab a look.

No Eecoodeesh.

No Popeye.

Instead Pruneys doing slit eyes.

Whimpy listening to Dad.

ScarHab raising his hand to Pruney. Not like hes gonna hit Pruney. But more like you do to a stink alley dog that just growled you.

And ScarHab giving Zompa the milk eye and saying, Whaddya think?

And Zompa says, Whaddo I think? Whaddo I think? SalRay dont know from Whaddo I think? Youre here because SalRay dont like Whaddo I think. What he thinks is. Im a chidrool. An atts yuh. Whaddo I think.

ScarHab bites his lower lip. Runs his tongue around his teeth. Pulls his nose. Stretches his mouth. Puts his sunglasses back on and again stretches wide his mouth. And using his right hand. Wipes with his thumb and fingers both side of his open lips. And ScarHab says to ZompaGalucci. English. Italian. Like Mom and Dad do when they want private Ross and me. What I hear is. ScarHab calls Zompa, Echo fatso fineeto.

Youd think with that kind of name calling Zompa might get sore. But all Zompa is. Shrug shoulders. And Zompa. Plain English. Says to Scar-Hab, Then its done.

ScarHab sees Pruney and me are little pitchers big ears so on a sudden ScarHab goes BOO and makes us take a hotta right there on the curb-stone. And ScarHab wraps his thumbs together and flaps his hands. Says, You kids got fuckin wings on yuh backs.

And. Not ta say. But. Pruney and me. We turn around and we look.

No wings. Theres just all of QuequeshanStreet. Nothing going on. Just the usual. Maybe we dint have wings. But we sure did have the Hooglies.

And ScarHab. Real loud. Laughs. Grabs Pruneys bike handlebars. Gives the bikebars a jiggleshake. Slaps ZompaGalucci flat shoulder.

And ScarHab. Even louder. Laughs.

Zompas all red in the cheeks says to ScarHab, Why you always a friggin ball busta? How many dozen times a day I gotta sonofabitchin tell you? Kids for chrice sake. Theyre kids.

ScarHab still laughing.

Zompa still steaming.

But Zompa in the dooorway. Turning. Saying, You boys. Happy Easta.

Two of them ZompaGalucci and ScarHab. The two of them fumbling back into Whimpys bookiejoint.

And I say, Is that ScarHab nuts or what? Whaddya think he ever meant by callin ZompaGalucci a fat echo?

Pruney says, ScarHab aint nuts. Hes wicket wacked out mental. And fat echo? Probbly ScarHab thinkin Zompa a wise guy because Zompa kept repeatin ScarHabs question.

And then Pruney. Outta nowhere. Says hes real hungry. And further some more what hes more interested in thinking about instead of fat echos and wacko chidrools in a bookiejoint are Moms Louie Squeegee FishMan Respeegie fishcakes and could we please lets get this friggin paper route finished for chrice sakes so we can best be eatin?

My fingers snap and I do a *WestSideStory, Cool your jets Daddy O.*

And now its Pruney and me both being a little of mental because we're doing that song Dad always sings and it makes me feel good because. Even with a beat up face and looking like the Hoogly dead Polish kid. PruneyMendez is singing and snapping his fingers delivering the last of the papers on Quequeshan then riding down WaterStreet through the junction crossing at Kelly and up BaggyWrinkleLane for Saturday afternoon fishcakes. Singing, *Dont know what it is but it is gonna be great.*

And Im so glad Pruneys not thinking about ZompaGalucci. Or scar guys with milkeyes and sissapoof queers. And quitting altarboys. Or HolySaturday night services. Or. As PruneyMendez said on the docks through more tears than Ive seen in a year,

FuckinFathaLuis.

24

A Whiff-a-the Sweat-a-Dads Workclothes

Mom left the fishcakes on a pie plate covered with aluminum foil in the refrigerator and a note saying just warm them because they were already cooked. Which we did. Warm them that is. Till they was gold all over and the kitchen smelled good. And those fishcakes were delicious. Especial with tarta sauce smeared. Pruney wanted ketchup with tarta sauce. But me? Im just tarta. Plain. No ketchup. So while Pruneys doing ketchup in his food he drops the bottlecap to the floor and gotta duck under the table to find it.

Just then Dad walked in and he made a real big deal over how he could smell those fishcakes all the way down BaggyWrinkleLane from JackCoggs house. And then. As he took off his TerryMalloy and hung it on a chair. Somewhere between Dad rolling up his shirt sleeves and me catching a whiff-a-the sweat a Dads workclothes. PruneyMendez stood up from under the table. Ketchup cap in his hand and making it tight on the bottle. Pruney looking at the bottle. Right there in the kitchen between just Dad and me. It was wind on the river and saltspray hitting Dads eyes over Pruneys split lip and Pruneys knotted brow.

And its weird because. Pruney putting on that bottlecap. He dint see saltspray hit Dads eyes like I done. Leastways I dont think Pruney did.

Only me.

Then again. Pruney might of knew because he was only focused on that ketchup cap and bottle for just a quick second and no doubt about it. Pruney always saw a lot more stuff than me.

So maybe Pruney did.

Maybe Pruney did know.

About the saltspray in Dads eyes.

But I dont think so.

Only Dad and me.

And I dont think Dad knew I knew because Dad just sailed over his own surprise of Pruneys bruises with all making hes bigtime surprised and happy about Pruney being at our table again.

Dad saying, Well look whos here Mista Pedro Pruney Mendoza Mendez.

Dad giving each one of those names some pride.

Pruney with his curlhead high. And his shoulders throwd back and that all fatcheeked smile that only PruneyMendez could do when he was feeling good and that made everyone around him feel good too and I gotta tell you. In a way I was jealous. Just a little. Not a lot. What I mean is. Not fa nuthin. Pruneys old man never said hello to Ross or me like Dad done to him.

Never once.

Not even.

So Dads washing his hands at the kitchen sink and over the running water noise he says, At the movies tonight. You guys want popcorn? Ju-Ju Bees? Or Good n Plenty?

And Pruney puts his fork down real quiet.

Pushes his plate forward.

Hands in his lap.

Shoulders slumped low.

Real low.

Fishcake and ketchup in the corners of Pruneys lips.

Pruneys upper split lip shaking.

Bottom lip shaking.

Chin shaking.

And when Dad shuts the faucet off the quiet getting real loud with the silence.

Dad looking at me.

Dad drying. This way and that. His hands in a dishtowel. Like he cant get them dry fast enough. Dads salt stung eyes asking, Whatd I say wrong?

My mouth answering, Pruney cant come to the movie tonight. His ol. His father. His father says he gotta do HolySaturday night mass.

Pruneys upper split lip still shaking.

Bottom lip still shaking.

Chin still shaking.

Pruneys blues. Red right returning.

Pruney says, Not a mass. A vigil. Its keepin wait.

Pruneys about to cry again.

And Dads stooping low. Looking Pruneys eyes.

And Dad. Knuckles on whiskers. That scratching sound.

Dad biting his lip.

Dad. Taking a breath.

Dad. Hands between knees.

Dad holding that breath. Adding his e. And final.

Dad saying, Pedro?

And Pruneys eyes? Looking like a pair of wet rusty scuppas.

Dad says, What you last week told me.

Dad says, Its not fair,

Dad says, And its not right.

Dad says, And I try not to imagine.

But Dad doesnt finish because Pruneys trying to keep it all in. Fourteen year old who looks like hes twelve Pruney. Not wanting to be a pukey moe moe in front of twelve year old me. Pruney trying to act like a man. Pruney opens his mouth like hes gonna take a breath and I cant see Pruneys tongue or teeth or nothing just a big hollow opening and Pruneys trying to decide whether to push air out or take air in and he doesnt do nothing except his head shaking up and down. Then. Then outta fourteen year old who looks like hes twelve Pruneys mouth comes the most lonesomest sound. Its sorta the way I imagine a choggy would sound. If choggies could make sounds. Just before getting eated by a seagull.

And Pruney stands.

And Dad stands.

Pruney buries his choggy lonesome into the sweat of Dads workclothes and wraps his arms around Dads waist and Dad runs his fingers through Pruneys curls and I start crying too and wrap my arms around Dad and Pruney. And the three of us. As Mom would say, Hugginmuggin. And Dad saying soft, I know. I know. I know.

Dads face. Whiskers. Kind that hurt like thorns when he kisses. Eyes like he gets when he hears the KingPhilip story. Jaw set like the curves on the StoneFleet Tavern anchor leaning on the millstone.

And I say, Dad we cant let Pruney go to church tonight.

Dad looks me square. Dads eyes like they caught another gust of saltspray he never expected. And this time that spray hitting and stinging him way more then when he first noticed Pruneys split lip and bruises. On a sudden Im imagining Dad saying, Jate. I wanted to keep you from that ugly. You been through too much. Your headplate and all.

But Dads saying nothing.

Just that saltspray look on his face then his knees going wobble. What MistaCogg would say of a guy who dont got his sea legs. And no doubt about it. What I said for real knocked him unawares. Like me being a loose cannon that everybody knows gets a sailor more scared than a straight on hit to the hull.

Dad says, I know. I know. Lets sit. And lets talk. Dads all on a sudden pulling himself to a chair. Dad unwraps Pruneys arms and Dad sits.

And Dad takes a breath. Then again. Then again. Till he breathes without gulps.

And Dad takes a back pocket blue handkerchief and gives it to standing Pruney.

Me? Im using a paper napkin from the table.

And Pruneys face red and wet. His cheeks creased with folds from Dads flannel.

Pruney. Using Dads handkerchief. Tough. And solid.

And Dad. From his seat. Not looking down. But looking eye to eye with Pruney. Dad says, Pedro. Remember last week? Our talk. You. Ross n me. Nothins changed. Nothin. FathaLuis will never be touchin you again. Ever. Those days are finished. Done. No more.

Pruneys got lines in his forehead. One eye open. And one eye closed. Hes touching the knot on his eyebrow trying real hard to believe the stuff Dad is saying. And Pruney buries his nose in Dads handkerchief and Pruney wipes his cheek and his chin but on one side of his mouth he still got the smear of the fishcake. But I dont say nothing and instead ask, Dad, howdya know? How can ya be so sure?

Dad looking at me says, Jate. You remember anything from our Thursday night talk? MountHope?

Dads forehead. One thick eyebrow. And I say, FederalHill. Nonna and Nonno.

What else?

Bad blood between buddies. Zompa. You. No it was Whimpy. Whimpy? I dunno. Dont remember.

Dad said, You remember. Youre doin fine.

Dad looking into Pruneys big blues.

Dad saying to Pruney. You see Pedro. This isnt just. Just about you. Its about Ross. And Jate. The three-a-you. And then some. Lets just say if Jate had a problem and in order to. To. To solve the problem. He needed a favor from you. Would you do the favor for him?

Pruney. Both eyebrows together like Dads nods, Yes.

And lets as well say maybe the police could also solve your problem. Take care-a-things. You know. Do. Take care-a-things. But. Your father. AuntJovita. Your brother. Dagama. They would all. All of them. Gotta. Be. Be involved. And you too. You would gotta. Go to court. Write police reports. Be in the newspapers. And on the TV Channel 10 news. How would you want your problem solved? By quiet doing a favor for your friend or by going to the police?

Pruney said, Doin it for my friend. Quiet. Doin it myself.

Thats what Im trying to tell you here. We all have friends. And friends take care of friends. On the Q-T. Quiet. Secret. Everyone quiet. Understand?

Dad took the blue handkerchief he had gived to Pruney and folded it. Then pulled Pruney close and Dad wiped fishcake and ketchup in the corners of Pruneys lips.

From the edge of his seat. Dad squats to the floor. Dads arms reaching. Both his hands. Up. Each of Pruneys shoulders.

Pruney looking down at Dads whiskers.

Dad looking up into Pruneys big blues.

I promise you. Just like I would promise Jate. Just like I would promise Ross. Just like I would promise their mother. Now listen to me good. FathaLuis will not be bothering you. Or any other boys. Anymore.

On the souls of my wife and my children.

I give you my word.

25

Cant Be Said Dead

Usual when something happens night in a church. Almost any church. Especial a Cathlic one in Sowams. And the Baptist one with the Tiffany. If you look at the church from the outside. The stain glass windows glow like AuntBeni giving a slideshow.

But tonight. For HolySaturday. Pruneys church is all Hooglied because nothing is lit up like regular. Im talking Pruneys church building is dark. The windows are gray. Not even the usual small nightlights on the heavy front doors. Nothing on the twin steeples neither. So dark.

But the parking lots full of cars and something definites going on.

And walking up those front steps. Only light. A LandStreet pole. Car headlights passing opposite directions hitting the church. Stone faces of the saints and angels staring down. Those stone faces of saints and angels are alive. Looking their lefts and looking their rights. Pull open the heavy door. Step inside. Dark forms of people all around. Door closes. Then sounds. A knife blade hitting stone? Spark fuzz busting from dark sounds. Glowing faces. Sparks fading. Metal hits rock. Spark fuzz spills. And someone chants. Whoosh. Flames. And smoke. Right there in the lobby and a bunch of people getting fire glowed and a few people cough and a altarboy holding a cross and flames are snapping and its not a very big fire. Just big enough roast hotdogs.

Its all about as different as Pruney said it would be and a bunch a huddled people wont move no budge because theres for real no place to go so on my hands and knees and its legs and wool pants and overcoats and shoes then a white robe and light getting throwed off from a campfire in a big wash tub top a table. And the priest whos not FathaLuis bowed like hes about to give the campfire a big hug. His eyeglasses reflecting flames. This priest whos not FathaLuis is doing all the Latin chanting.

And I remember when Pruney told Ross and me about that chanting. Said had to do with some King named Gregory. Like GregoryPeck. And now theres Pruney wearing a poofwhite shirt with real poofsleeves over a long black altarboy robe. Pruneys holding the HolySaturday candle. And that HolySaturday candle is taller than Pruney is high. Thicker than Pruneys arm is wide. And the priest whos not FathaLuis is doing more arms out Latin Gregory chanting.

The priest whos not FathaLuis. Grabs. Out of the campfire. A thing like a scratch awl MistaCogg uses to punch holes in canvas. Except the point on this scratch awl glows red hot. And the priest whos not FathaLuis holds that red hot scratch awl by its wood handle. The priest whos not FathaLuis sticks that red hot glowing tip of the scratch awl into the HolySaturday candle. Pruneys eyes real big. Pruney bites his low thick Pruney lip.

The second time the priest sticks that thing like a scratch awl into the HolySaturday candle. Pruney pulls back his head. Stretches back his neck. Pruneys getting his face far away he possible can.

Third time the priest pokes that scratch awl thing into the HolySaturday candle Pruneys face all white and Pruneys head pushed as far back as Pruneys head can get without Pruneys head busting off loose and Pruneys straining so much its the MountHopeBridge wire cables popping out Pruneys neck.

Fourth time the priest pokes that scratch awl thing into the HolySaturday candle Pruneys eyes close and his head strains backwards and sweatbead flames reflect out Pruneys forehead and Pruney biting his bottom lip so hard and shaking his head so much the priest grabs the HolySaturday candle and steadies it but nobody except me. Noticing Pruney about ready to faint.

Everybody staring to the HolySaturday candle.

Fifth time the priest pokes that scratch awl thing into the HolySaturday candle. Wax melts down Pruneys hands and as soon as that melt wax hits Pruneys fingers the melt wax turns white like blisters bubbling on Pruneys fingers with Pruney shaking so much and stretching his head so far back straining his neck so tight sweating tongues of fire so wet the entire HolySaturday candle shakes and when the priest pulls out that scratch awl thing from the HolySaturday candle the priest gotta steady the HolySaturday candle with his own priest hands and Pruney lets the HolySaturday candle go and Pruney disappears into the crowd.

The priest immediate passes the HolySaturday candle thats taller than Pruney is high and thicker than Pruneys arm is wide to the other altarboy.

Back on my hands and knees gonna find Pruney somewhere in the lobby in those legs and shoes and wool slacks and overcoats and finally. Pruney under the lobby vote-a-candle under the lobby feet of crucified Jesus. Pruneys eyes are closed. His arms wrapped around himself. My fingers touch his face.

Up above in the crowd the priest is still Gregory chanting Latin.

Below the vote-a-candle under crucified Jesus I say, Pruney its me. Jate.

Pruney opens his eyes on a sudden and us two hugging under the vote-a-candles under the feet of the crucified Jesus.

Hugging ear to ear.

Hugging chest to chest.

Hugging knee to knee.

Hugginmuggin ourselfs.

The priest still chanting Latin.

Under the vote-a-candles under the feet of the crucified Jesus smoke floats down. Smelling like leaves burning in a street in autumn fall and cloves and apples even lavender its all those legs shoes wool slacks over coats and Gregory chanting priest and the people Gregory chanting back to the priest whos not FathaLuis.

I say, Pruney lets get outta here.

Dont lets leave Jate. Please. Not yet.

We gotta leave. Youre sick ta death.

My ol man kill me if I dont stay.

FathaLuis will kill you if you do stay.

FathaLuis not here.

Not here?

FathaMarchado announced beginnin-a-the service. FathaLuis. This aftanoon. Had a emergency

A emergency?

On the Q-T. FathaMarchado. I heard him whisperin one-a-the men. DivineOrder-a-theHolyGhost. Said a miracle they cleaned up all the blood.

DivineOrder-a-theHolyGhost? Blood?

Yeah. FathaLuises emergency. And DivineOrder-a-theHolyGhost is kinda like a club for the men-a-the church. My father and brother are in it. Theyre here tonight and later gonna be part-a-the service.

My face is showing Pruney Im total plate in the head.

Pruney says, Its on the Q-T. No ones sayin nothin. Theres whisperins bout somethin what happened at the rectory this aftanoon. FathaLuis. Thats why FathaMarchados here.

And I say, Whos FathaMarchado?

Hes the Fatha who. That guy Gregory chantin up there right now. Come from Providence. Never neither before seen him either.

FathaMarchados Gregory chanting starts getting louder. Organ in the church balcony playing. Everyone in the whole church singing. And all the shoes and the legs. Wool slacks and overcoats. They move out the lobby and into the main church area. And Pruney says, Gotta get back ta the procession.

Pruney wipes his eyes and nose on his altarboy poofwhite shirtsleeve. Crawls from under the vote-a-candles under the feet of crucified Jesus. And Pruney disappears into all those legs and shoes and wool slacks and overcoats.

Even though its dark. What makes it so everyone can see is people holding candles that theyre lighting from the flame on the HolySaturday candle. Passing the light down to the next person. And to the next. And to the next. Lets face it. Dont know no Latin. But FathaMarchados singing about someone named LemonChrissy. Every time he sings LemonChrissy everyone Gregory chants back something like Grassy Ass Day O. And since it makes no sense that these people would be cussing in church and since theres a ceiling picture of Jesus riding on a donkey that part of the chant must have something to do with a grassy place where that donkey eats every day and the O part maybe means oats.

And everyone is all singing hal-lay-lew-yuh. Hal-lay-lew-yuh. And a baldheaded altar boy in a all white robe starts swinging a gold fancy can on three chains and real thick smoke pours out the side and smells like nothing I ever before smelled. All the statues are purple cloth covered just like Mom had told. And. Not ta say. But. If never before had I seen those statues. There woulda been no way for me to guess which Bible person was under that purple.

Also if I was one of those statues? Under a purple sheet for about a couple-a-three weeks. It would be total happiness final getting a breath of fresh air.

Then someone front altar sneezes. Pruney standing under a set of three bells connected to a single gold braid rope with Pruney puffsleeve wiping his nose and staring at FathaMarchado. Pruney waiting for a FathaMarchado signal.

Organ plays. People singing. And the incents burner on three chains is clacking. And FathaMarchado turns his back on the audience and looks straight at Pruney and FathaMarchado nods. Pruney yanks that gold braid rope. Bells jangle up a storm. Everybody in the whole entire church smiles. White teeth everywhere. Lotsa sparkle eyes. Bright candles. Everyone singing and Pruneys bell ringing. DivineOrder-a-theHolyGhost men come from the doors either side of the altar stand in a row along the altar rail. Then FathaMarchado gives another nod. And each of the DivineOrder guys goes to a statue. Reaching behind. Finds a sash. Pulls.

Down falls the purple ghostcloth.

Pruneys brother Digga climbs the altar stairs and stands front of the tabbanacle and grabs hold of the sash and down falls the purple ghostcloth.

Its Jesus wearing a white toga and jumping for joy because he just got uncovered.

JumpingJesus. Hand straight front showing off a nail hole. Other hand. Above his head. A red nail hole too. And across his bareskin palewhite chest. A bloodgash.

JumpingJesus and not the tortured body of AhSufferingLord cross crucified.

And Pruneys dad and a couple of other DivineOrder-a-theHolyGhost guys pull the purple ghostcloth from AhLady-a-Fatima and shes more happy than I remember and down comes the purple ghostcloth from the three children. Louseea. Yahsinta. And Fransisco. Then the sheep. Free too from their ghostcloth.

On the other side of the church its the DivineOrder-a-theHolyGhost men pulling the purple ghostcloth from Michael the ArchAngel.

The men looking up.

The purple ghostcloth falling.

People in the front row. All singing stops.

FathaMarchado. Gregory chanting stops.

The baldheaded altarboy with the threechain can smoker. Clacking stops.

Singing on the left side of church.

Stops.

Singing on the right side of church.

Stops.

Just the organ playing and Pruney ringing the bells.

Organ stops.

Then Pruney.

Bells stop.

The church. All on the sudden. Quiet.

Only sound.

Candle flames.

Everybody in church. Stopped.

Stopped and looking.

Looking at Mikey 2A's silver sword. But its red.

Mikey 2A's arm stretched out and on his hand a blooded turkeyneck. And giblets.

Mikey 2A's pointing Lucifer to hell not how I first time remember Mikey.

And the men who purple ghostcloth unveiled Mikey 2A's are wrestling him and Lucifer down from that statue stand.

Bloody turkeyneck giblets fall off of Mikey 2A's hand.

Bloody turkeyneck giblets hit splat the shiny church floor.

One DivineOrder guy steps on the bloody turkeyneck giblets. And the DivineOrder guy slips. Loses his balance. And then. For a moment. Mikey 2A's and Lucifer are flying.

Flying through the air.

But not really flying. More like falling. A tumble. And everything up is down. Down is up. Angels head is upsidedown and devils head is downside up. Wings and halos and devil horns. Mikey 2A's sword slicing heaven. Lucifers eyes rolling up. Devils eyes twisting skyward and Mikey 2A's eyes swirling top his skull. And the first thing that hits the floor is the tip of Mikey 2A's right wing. Then his arm. And final. His blood hand red sword.

The whole church pulls a breath.

Then.

Smash.

Plaster on the floor everywhere. Exploded full weight Lucifers back busting Mikeys knees Lucifers skull. Broke arms. Broke sword. Broke heads. Broke wings. Broke feet. Broke Lucifer devil horns. Serpent broke tail. Halo rolling around like a tiny hulahoop. All those devil broke angel parts top of the poor guy who slipped on the splat of the turkeyneck giblet.

And everyone shoving out the front rows like the MobyDick sailors diving from their boats and shrieks of Portuguese to help the poor fallen guy. A man on his back making. Like Pruney always does. The sign of the cross. And a fat lady stepping over a skinny one. Two guys side leaping over the pew divider. Arms swatting air. AuntJovita hand waving hollering Pedro Pedro. Pruneys brother Digga on one the pews his head darting to the left and then to the right and a cigarette stuck in his lips not lit but there none the anyhow till he swipes it out just before he. Towering over everyone. Jumps back down and again crowd lost and gobbled.

Threechain smoke burner baldheaded altarboy on his hands and knees heaving a braying grassy ass day oats donkey and every time he heaves Im expecting splashes out his mouth but the only out his mouth thing is growl gut wretches filling the church.

And a front row lady. Heavy red makeup cheeks. Black fur collar. Yellow wool coat. Faints into arms of big HolyGhost guy next to her who astonish looks where he gonna set her in the pew because everyone else spreads out and makes room. Someone raises her legs and her dress slides up and theres garters with the nylon stocking tops and another lady pulling that dress back down. And is that a girdle? I gotta addmit. Yes. A girdle. Just like Moms.

Dryheaving baldheaded altarboy with the threechain incents burner final splash pukes meat colored chunks. And a whiff of that gush barf mixed holy smoke mixed body smell mix makes my stomach oh God fresh air. A DivineOrder-a-theHolyGhost guy announcing Portuguese and English everyone stay seated remain calm.

Pruneys old man helping the splash puking altarboy. And someone wiping puke. And wheres Pruney? Statue dust haze and rising holysmoke at the crowd edge near hunks a plaster. And Pruney tossing his altarboy uniform a heap on the floor. Theres people in the aisle. Wet wool and sweat. Incents and vomit. And Pruney squeezing through historicals towards the front altar is holding. The black handled flat gold pan. The shining rescue plate of Jesus. With on it. The dark raw turkeyneck and giblet meat.

And enough of this HolySaturdayNight Easter Portuguese SantoRosario RoseReeChurch. Lemon Chrissie. And Grassy Ass Day O and the DivineOrder-a-theHolyGhost. Im gonna grab Pruney and the two of us will get the hell out.

When I squeeze to Pruney through the crowd. Pruneys face is Hoogly crypt.

His voice solid steady says, Your dad Jate. ZompaGalucci. ScarHab.

Pruney shows me the redmeat on the black handled gold rescue plate.

Pruney passes the black handled gold rescue plate to FathaMarchado.

FathaMarchado right hand. Reaching under that rim shim gold plate. Raises it center. Heap of turkeyneck and giblet meat.

FathaMarchados mouth.

Shimmering.

FathaMarchado eyeglasses.

Shimmering.

FathaMarchado bug eyes.

Shimmering.

FathaMarchado white robe. Blood. Because Pruneys wiping clean his fingers.

And in a uncorrect breath that aint no breathe.

On that JesusChrist gold rescue plate.

There aint no turkeyneck and giblet meat.

PruneyMendez just handed FathaMarchado someones dick.

PruneyMendez just handed FathaMarchado someones balls.

Its LandStreet again and Pruney is getting into the back seat of AuntJovitas Valiant. And that car pulls out the church parking lot like a Seekonk speedway jalopy. Pruney sees me through the fogged rear window and his face is all blurr and his hands show me call on the phone.

Or maybe is he gonna call me?

Either. Or.

Pruneys going home with AuntJovita. And lets face it. Things could be a lot worser. Not fa nuthin. But. Someones dick and balls? Police coulda been asking Pruney questions.

I work my way through the crowd at the bottom of the churchstairs.

At the top. Still wearing the blooded white robe is FathaMarchado. And Pruneys old man.

Theyre shouting at each other Portuguese. Waving their arms. Sirens wailing from way uptown above all their gabbering. Pruneys brother Digga lighting a cigarette yelling back at his old man and then yelling even louder at FathaMarchado.

All around this craziness fog and a heavy mist rolling in. Fullmoon glowing inside the clouds. Mist glows beneath the street lamps. Like Ahabs glow. No. Lucifers. And the headlights of a passing car spin mist like snow then in the red backlights that mist is red Lucifer tongues and those red tongues low on the lick.

But then the next set of headlights spin flying white ghosts. Not the HolyGhost mind you. The ice dead breaths of the devil. This HolySaturday Lucifer breath was working its way into everything. My hair. My face. My plate in the head. Even into the fat knuckles of each of my fingers.

No warm anywhere.

Piss shivers and cold all over.

And walking past the cemetery is no help neither. And for the umpteenth time in my life I know the Hooglies arent just MistaCogg talking. And I do his mutters.

Doglick breath

Sign of death

And from way up LandStreet the scream of sirens grow louder and louder. By the time a cop car. Two fire trucks. And the rescue squad. Pull into the front of the church. Im beat feeting around the corner of KellyStreet. And I wondering is Dad hearing all this commotion from inside the LyricTheatre? Is Dad thinking the AmericanLuggageMill is on fire? Or our house is burning to the ground?

Maybe the *Lawrence of Arabia* battle scene noises are drowning out all the street commotion. The battle where Lawrence. Like a crazy man yells. Take no prisoners. And then gets his arm all bloodied up from shooting anybody he can land a bullet into. That battle scene would killed the quiet outside church noise real good.

Somewhere in the dark a KellyStreet between my footsteps the insane *Lawrence of Arabia*. Mikey 2A's. Pruney. The Hooglies. The railroad tracks. GilOwens and MistaCoggs. Up the crushed quahog shells of BaggyWrinkleLane. Past weepinwillow and the piazza door incantanating shakes all over. Another quick doglick breath and even add a couple-a-three LemonChrissies LemonChrissies but what with my spazzing and fingers so cold and so wet the doorknob barely turns. So I huff Lemon Lemon LemonLemonLemon into my hands and work the slippery thing the right way. You know. Correct. And final on a solid LemonChrissie the door opens and at last into our kitchen. Straight for a kitchensink towel. Grab one off the rung and wipe my sopping wet plate in the head dry.

In the living room. The dark that isnt ever real dark is doing some amazing things. The pale yellow of the across the tracks street lamps. Steady pink from the AmericanLuggage sign all mix up with the emergency trucks and police cars flashing their red what is visible in the NorthEnd fog. Me. Alone. Near spazz. I turn on the gas heater stove and listen. The blue flame pilot makes that wallop sound the way that blue flame pilot always does when it catches the invisible gas. Busts into orange flame. And then busts back into quite hot blue.

Then sit. Just sit. Sit in the dark. Sit in the living room dark that isnt ever real dark. Sit in the not so real dark listening. Listening to the sounds of the metal gas heater stove as the flames lick hot. Creaking and crackling. Creaking and crackling.

Way deep in my metalplate head. Listening again. FathaMarchado Gregory singing about LemonChrissy and GrassyAssDayO. And all the men coming from out the side altar taking off the purpleghost cloth from the covered statues. And Pruney rang the bells when FathaMarchado gave him the look. Pruney telling me ScarHab. Zompa. Your dad. Then Pruney handing FathaMarchado the rescue plate of Jesus with the dick and the balls.

Sitting there in the living room.

Blue flames in the metal gas heater stove.

Heat rising through the crisscross grate.

Heat rising and turning the heat catcher wheel ringing ting ting ting off of Moms *Made in Italy* top of the stove angel chimes.

Yellow pale across the railroad track street lamps.

Pink glow from the AmericanLuggage sign.

Red and yellow emergency trucks and police cars flashing in the North-End nightfog.

My plate in the head truck accident. MistaCogg saying, Be careful of the machines. He dont call them cars. Louie Squeegee FishMan Respeegies truck. The smell of fresh provolone. Striped bass. Eels. Flounder. Swordfish steaks and cod roe on ice. Ross and me running across. But me stopping to pick up the crab claw that the seagull just dropped from the sky. And turning to show Ross and Mom. The brakes sound from the truck. The cool air on the warm blood that MistaCogg said was my brain poking out my head. The plate the doctors put back instead of my skull. Pruney using GilOwens cherrywood bowl. To show Ross and me why a cherrywood bowl be better than a stupid old plate. The way the total right side of my body was all froze up that whole first year. And then how it started working again except for the sometimes shakes and me staying small and runty and not growing fast like Ross.

All the times not remembering things too good. And me having episodes.

And for a long time the living room walls blur around me.

The outside lights from the up the street fire trucks.

The whole room dark to red. Dark to red. Dark. Wish Ross had been with me in church to see all that stuff then. Be in the living room with me feel all this stuff now.

My fingers and my arms that jellyfish stinging hurt makes my hands shake. Plate in my head pain is coming on strong. Might forget big chunks of this HolySaturday nightstory when it comes time to tell.

Then the phone rings. A tremble of pain from my arm to my head.

Stretch fingers.

Make a fist.

Then stretch my fingers again but this time more way wide.

The phone rings seven rings before I pick up.

But I dont say nothing.

Nothing at all.

Quiet.

So is the phone.

The phone all quiet and empty.

Then. Through that empty. Pruney says, Lo.

No one shouting like usual in Pruneys empty.

Just Pruney and me.

Pruney and me on the phone.

Pruney and me reaching through the empty.

Me saying, Your face. At church. Not too so swelled up.

Pruney saying, Yeah. Well.

Me saying, Uh huh.

Pruneys end long on empty. Here its just ting ting ting from the living room stove. Does Pruney hear the stovetop angels too?

Finally Pruney says, When your dad gets home you tell him I called.

My dad?

Your dad. Jate dont you memba nuthin what he told us this aftanoon?

Blue flame sounds. The metal gas stove. Ting ting ting. Angels *Made in Italy.*

You want me to tell my dad you called and thats it? No what for?

Pruney says, People coming inna my house right now. Gotta hang up. Holy shit. A cop too. When your dad gets home you tell im Im on the Q-T and I know nuthin. You gotta member that Jate. Tell im Im on the Q-T and I dunno nuthin. Got it?

Got it, I repeat. Q-T.

And Pruney hangs up.

More listening into the phone because Pruney might pick up again. The black plastic phone piece hard against my ear. The voice holes too. But cant feel Pruney.

Just lotsa the empty. Plate in the head empty. And arm jellyfish sting fading.

Lotsa plate in the head empty coming through the voice holes.

And then nuthin.

Nothing except angels.

Angels *Made in Italy.*

Our stove top angels.

Ting ting ting.

Easter Sunday morning under a bedquilt. But still in my HolySaturday night clothes.

Dad was talking on the telephone in a voice meant he dint want me to wake. Or hear anything he was saying. His voice down low. But in a few moments loud enough for the Andriozzis across the tracks to hear him. Then back soft and louder whispers and louder and softer and its Goddamn ZompaGalucci a couple of times. Then silence. Not ta say. But. What does ZompaGalucci got to do with anything?

Again Dads voice, Only suppose to lean on Alegria. Take care-a-business. Ten oclock. Afta services. Not late aftanoon passion play for the entire friggentown for chrice sake. Thats why I was at the movie. Sorry. Sorry. Im sorry. What else can I say? But Jate. Yes. Yes. Jate was there. Cant be. Cant be said dead. Missing. Thats what Im trying to tell you. Yes. Uh huh. The three of us yesterday here eating lunch when. The whole thing. Now? In bed. Who knows?

Then Dad got real quiet again and its Mom hes talking to. Dad saying he loves her and him and me will be at AuntBenies house around noon.

A FederalHill trip would normal make me excited. And the news for certain got me outta bed. But I gotta tell you. This morning my feet were a ton of bricks and my legs worked extra hard to get me from the bedroom to the kitchen.

Dad was seated at the kitchen table with his mug of coffee and a tray of Moms new made coffeecake. Some last week biscotties. And Thursdays crossbuns.

Dad said, Well good morning Giovanni.

And Dad poured the MaxwellHouse and stirred in some cream. Dint exact look at me. But his coffee. The little whirlpool. His spoon.

What time did you get home? I asked.

About midnight, Dad said.

And?

And what? The movie? Did ya like it?

Course. Thats why a second time.

Dad had put my mug next to the coffeepot on the stove. And I poured myself a full cup of MaxwellHouse but left room for cream. When I sat back down Dad looked up from his cup. He dint have anything in his mouth. But the way his jaw was working. Looked like he was trying to bite something wasnt there. A frown crease forming the letter A above his nose on his forehead. Dads chestnut browns looked. Bleared. And tired. But then those bleared eyes got fast unbleared and stared direct in my eyes and Dad said, Last night wasnt suppose to happen like that.

Like what?

Like whatchya saw last night.

And for a long time *Lawrence of Arabia* was flickering off the plate inside my head. Dad eating popcorn watching *Lawrence of Arabia*. That boy drowning in the sand. Lawrence shooting the other boy. Blasting cap. Belly wound. Bullet to the brain.

Then a shimmering, You mean you heard? About Mikey 2A's dick and balls?

Dads eyes followed the full of my face down my shoulders to the whole of my arm which was twitching just a little. He stared there for a long time and scraped his knuckles against his chin whiskers. He rubbed those knuckles and said, Jate tell me. Church. You and Pruney. At church. Everything you remember. Church.

So. I told. The campfire inside the front door. And the HolySaturday candle taller than Pruney and thicker than Pruneys arm wide. Pruney under the vote-a-candles the feet of crucified Jesus what is also the front of the church where you first go in. Pruney called it the vestabull. Pruney scared about the way the new priest that wasnt FathaLuis was sticking the candle with a hot poker awl. And Dad was staring so hard at me. All on the sudden. Couldnt remember nothing. And then Mikey 2A's and Lucifer flying through the air. And Pruney scooping off the floor with the gold communion plate a turkeyneck and giblet but then knowing what they for real was and Pruney wiping the blood all over the new priests white robe. And then. Outside. A awful fog. And when home Pruney called because he wanted to talk about being on the Q-T. Thats what he said. Tell you he was on the Q-T. Then me falling asleep and nothing else.

Dad did a long sigh like cooling off his coffee.

And he wrapped his fingers around his cup. And there was just something about them fingers holding tight that mug that made my own fingers shake. Made my head shake too.

Dad? Why would Pruney tell me. He and you was on the Q-T? You dint have nothing to do with putting those privates on Mikey 2A's hand did you?

And Dads fingers grabbed even tighter that coffeecup and he brought it steaming to his lips. Drank slow. Put it back down. Pushed it aside.

Then after some quiet he said, No.

His hands. Flat on the table. His fingers. Spread wide.

My own fingers going like a claw and Dad hands up from the table pulling my hand into his. Both his hands holding mine and my claw melting flat in the firm of his warm.

And after some more quiet he said, But Jate. Lets. Lets give it all a rest for now. Its not a good idea you talkin about this with anybody. Course by now all of Sowams knows what went on in that church last night. It sure as hell is no secret. But what Pruney means by being on the Q-T is that some said things are best said unsaid. And the less this thing is said. The better off for everyone. Even in your writing.

But Dad, I said.

And slipped my hand from Dads hands. And Dad said, When you say two plus two. You dont also need to be telling four.

Can Ross n me talk about it?

Of course you can.

Pruney too?

If Pruney wants. Let Pruney talk it first. Otherwise. Let it alone. Capice?

Sure. Dad?

Jate?

Whats GrassieAssDayOats mean?

Grassie Ass Day Oats? Grassie Ass Day O? Deo Gratias? Deo Gratias. Why? Why you wanna know?

The preece a bunch of times said it last night.

Thanks be to God.

And LemonCrissy?

Huh?

Whos LemonCrissy? The preece with the candle kept calling Lemon-Crissy.

Jate. Its all Latin. The priest was probbly saying Lumen Christi. Lumen Christi. Light of Christ. Mom knows this stuff better than me. But John.

Jay Tee. Johnny Jate Tavino. Listen. This. This thing is probbly gonna be
on your mind for some time. And you might forget. Or confuse. Certain
things. Plate in the head as you often say. But also you might remember
things too. Other things. So. So. Promise me. You ever remember. Things.
Things you wanna talk about. Just come and ask. Nows not the time. But
when you get. Older. You'll. You'll probbly have. Have more questions.
Time. And distance. Focus. Put things focus. And. Funny how. You never
get such an up close view as when youre far away. Believe me Jate. Someday all of this. All this. This. This thing. This thing will make sense. But
for now. Give it a rest. Let it go. And give Pruney a rest too.

You mean not hang out with Pruney no more?

No. You guys still be pals. What I mean is dont ask questions. Let him
tell what he needs. When he needs. Maybe soon. Like he did yesterday.
Then. Maybe never again. Pruney may never wanna talk about this thing.
And because Pruneys your. Your pal. You gotta respect what he wants.
And that goes for Ross. Ross will be hearin these same things from me too.
You both gotta follow through. Understand?

Sure Dad. I understand.

And. Not ta say. But. In my head its MissusCogg. And MistaCogg.
And GilOwen. All telling me. Strong stuff. GilOwen saying, My headplate being a gift. Praspective. The relate of things. The mind like two
strong wings. Time and distance. Praspective. And I dint ever remember
thinking this sorta stuff before. It felt good.

And Dads eyes foggy. And I say, Dad. Its like *TheSnowQueen* and
asquantum. Kay and Gerta bestfriends. No matter what happens to Kay.
Gerta never gives up. As for asquantum. How many ways we call it? You
all have your own words. You say asquantum. GilOwen says chataqua. For
JackCogg? Its gammin or shootin the breeze. Moms always pablabboratin.
Well. Me? Its reachin Montaup.

And Dads eyes still a bit of fog. Not clear when he knows exact a
thing.

So I said, Even with the wind across the bow. We're never on the rocks.
Are we? You and Mom make that boat get where we wanna go.

Dad said, Reachin Montaup.

I said, Just like story tellin.

And Dad said, Thats a different way a lookin at it.

For the first time. Understanding was in me. And I asked, Praspective?

Sure, said Dad, Praspective. Reaching Montaup. Thats good.

And Dad cupped his handpalms on my jaws. The coffeecup warm on the cold of my skin. And he looked me long and hard. Hazel in his eyes. Clear. The lick of his lips. Strong of his chin. Jate, Dont ever let anyone tell you theres wrong with your head. You just go right on takin your own sweet time thinkin things through.

Then he squozed both my cheeks and held them.

Promise me one thing MistaReachingMontaup. No more ZompaGalucci. No more Hes your buddy. No more Hes your pal. You and Ross stay away from him. Away from Whimpys. You are to have nothing to do with that place ever again. Stay out. Or so help me.

And he jiggled my face and let go of my cheeks.

And the way Dad said, So help me.

A glint of sparkles in the clear of his hazels.

TheSnowQueens power.

Mikey 2A's sword.

FathaLuis glasses glint.

And Hooglies real bad.

What about Pruneys paper route?

And Dad said, You stick Whimpys paper in the fence across the street. Zompa will get off his fat ass and fetch it. Remember. When you get to Whimpys. Stay clear. No more Zompa. You hear me?

Yes Dad.

And another thing.

Whats that Dad?

You keep reachin Montaup strong. Promise me.

Promise.

And one last thing son.

Whats that?

Happy Easta.

Happy Easta you too Dad.

IV
Blizzard

26
WibWob

That afternoon Dad and me went to AuntBenies for Easter dinner. After her wonderful food and lotsa AuntBeni hello and goodbye kisses. Dad drove Mom Ross and me past the wood streetcarts with the fruit and the chickens and the rabbits in the crates. All the shops and stores were closed. But the carts and stuff were parked on the street. Some with canvas over them. Some. With the rabbits and the chickens. Were left open air. Dad said no one would bother them. On FederalHill if any character stepped outta line. It would be better for the character if the cops got him first rather than the guys connected with the pushcarts.

Dad said on FederalHill. Cops hardly ever get the robbers first. Always its the pushcart guy and the streetfolk one step ahead of the law. Behind it too.

Dad showed us the tenement house on the avenue corners of De-Pasquale and Atwells. Where Nonno and Nonna lived. And died. Then he drove over a street or two to SalRay SanAngelos house which was big like a mansion and Dad showed us the fig tree that was growing real huge over a fence that was crowded thick with beautiful yellow for cynthia flowers and he told us about how NonnoTavino planted that fig tree from roots Nonno got in Sicily. Then how Dad. After he met Mom. Rooted a sucker from that tree. And from it. Grew the fig tree that was now winter wrapped and growing in our yard in Sowams.

By the time we were again driving down KellyStreet and turning at JackCoggs house into BaggyWrinkleLane I hadnt yet the slightest chance to tell Ross the what alls of last nights going ons. So. I said to Mom and Dad that Ross and me were gonna take a walk to the bridge.

And Dad said, Dont jump.

And I said, We wont.

And Mom slapped Dad on the shoulder and then Mom said to Ross and me, Look. The sun is a giant sugar cookie dippin behind the AmericanLuggage and the sky is a cappachino topped with high clouds.

Mom said, Poor crocus and for cynthia and midApril EastaSunday. Dead-a-Januarys returned. White breaths a sure sign. Weather smells like snow. Feels it too.

And it did. Smell and feel like snow that is.

But I wasnt thinking about Mom talking sugar cookie cappachinos in the sky or the weathersmell just now. As Mom and Dad went into our house. Someone was riding a bicycle wib wob over the not too far away KellyStreet railroad tracks.

Wib wob and zagging.

Wib wob and smooth.

Ross threw a once real hard wave.

All the way down BaggyWrinkleLane in the slate black spring air like January all over again. Waving back soft in a sad way. Come riding through the tiny ice crystals flying in the sky. PruneyMendez.

We ran down BaggyWrinkleLane to meet Pruney and stop him from coming into the house because Mom and Dad would do a big fuss. Especial maybe Mom. Which on the usual Pruney woulda liked. But first. We had to make sure Pruney was okay. See if he'd be comfortable under the dig of it all.

When Pruney pulled up all bare knuckle froze, he said, Where you guys been? Called twice this aftanoon.

Pruney sat on his bike with his leg extended like a kickstand. He dint have on a hat or gloves. Just a hooded sweatshirt and a windbreaker. His knuckles red. His ears purple blue. And of course his fat red Pruney cheeks. When Pruney talked. His breath puffed and rolled between Ross and me like last nights devilfog. Pruney said, You was in Providence. But I thought you both woulda been home ago hours.

AuntBeni had us in for Easter dinner and dessert and Dad FederalHill played tour guide stopping every corner he remembered about growing up and telling us about Raymond SalRay SanAngelo.

Ross who had got from me only bits and pieces wanted to hear everything he church missed said, Lets get outta here and go the trestle where we can talk.

We put Pruneys bike by Moms birdseed hopper on the lee underneath the weeping willow. Cut through the dead of Moms garden. Scrambled the railroad berm. Past CrescentStreet direct in front of the aqua blue aluminumsided Andriozzi house and walked the rails till the dirt beneath dropped off and instead of firm ground below. We were checking each step on trestle ties above the surge and swirl of the SowamsRiver.

The cold of steel railroad track underneath felt good. Especial after the hot car seat for so long.

Now we sat rail sitting. Listening to the outgoing tide rushing through the pilings. Pruney said, Eecoodeesh Jate. Last night. Huh?

Dad says shoulnt be talkin bout it no more. Les you bring it up first.

Well arent I thats what Im doin?

Guess so.

Ross said, Fill me in. What happened?

So Pruney and me give each other a look and although Pruneys shivering cold hes busting to tell Ross. And Pruney tells it real slow. But with stutters. Not like his usual way of breezing all bluster in a PruneyMendez blather.

When hes finished his shoulders and his lips are shaking but his teeth are not chattering. Hes just whole body shaking and doing a deep inside him hum.

And Ross takes off his own coat and wraps it around Pruney.

Only sound is the tide under the trestle.

I ask, You think FathaLuis is? FathaLuis is dead?

Pruney shakes, Hes either that or. Some hospital.

Ross said, FathaLuis not in any hospital. You can be sure on that.

How?

Think. FathaLuis goes a hospital. They ask, Howdya get yuh dick cut off? He isnt gonna say, I was makin sausage and my dick got caught in the meat grinder. Or. I was shavin and the razor slipped out my hand. No. No way. FathaLuis is dead and probbly the only two guys know where he is. Is. ScarHab. And ZompaGalucci.

For a long time we just listen to the whirlpools and the trestle. Boreas winds gust. Die. But then heave again. From Pruney comes a Hoogly whimper. Ross stares into the water. Stares into these Hoogly breaths and whirlpools and said, Queers. FathaLuis. GilOwen. None-a-this be happenin if it wasnt for queers.

I say, You thinkin GilOwens like FathaLuis?

Inbetween the gusting wind and the slosh of whirlpools. Im not sure what Ross says. But his lips are moving and he keeps looking at the water. Not at me. Or Pruney.

Pruney says, I hate FathaLuis. What FathaLuis did. But never wanted

FathaLuis dead. Not like what ScarHab and Zompa done. And GilOwen no. No way.

For a long time only sound is SowamsRiver slosh gulping and the Hooglies. Ross and PruneyMendez both lost in the Hooglies. And finally through them Hooglies Pruney says, Yeah. I hate FathaLuis. But. He was my friend. My best friend. Cepting you guys-a-course.

Ross said, Pruney. You may-a-been a friend to FathaLuis. But FathaLuis was never no friend to you. Was only himself he was thinkin. Remember what Dad said. Lust. Not love.

Pruney blew into the fists of his own shaking hands making a hollow sound in the tight of his curling fingers and thought long on Rosses words and final Pruney said, OlMan sending me back NewBedford first thing in the mornin.

Big diamond crystals filled the low night sky.

Rosses bare fingers grab Pruneys right shoulder.

The air filled with *TheSnowQueen* snow. Glass sparkles. Not flakes. Swarms of spinning ice. Cold dust. Someones breaths. Frost tears.

Pruneys dark fingers lock with Rosses pale and Pruney says, Gotta stay NewBedford with UncleFahvish till who knows when forever.

We'll deliver your papers, said Ross.

And Pruney said, Sall so complicated.

Im thinking Kays Eternity.

Roses bloom and cease to be.

Hooglies moaning.

And Ross said, Mom and Dad will allow us. Jate and me. We'll do it Pruney.

You guys keep the money like the routes yours, Pruney said.

Its your route when you return, said Ross.

Whirlpools gulp and nightsky sparkles and streetlight sparkles cold winter night.

The sound of snow. Hisses in the swales of marsh grass. Milkweeds. Rosebriars. Bullrushes. And straw. The sounds of trestle Hooglies. The breath of sky. Strong wind. Then nothing. Then strong wind again.

At the house Ross takes off his mittens and gives them to Pruney.

Pruney refuses. Then puts his hands inside them. And hes glad. Especial when Ross tells Pruney, Keep the jacket too.

Ross and Pruney hugging goodbye.

Gertas tears melting Kays ice heart.

Everything ugly was beautiful. Especial when Pruney hugged each of us and said, I love you guys with all the bottom-a-my hott.

Pruney touched my face and he said, Dont let your plate in the head get cold.

And that made me take off my stocking cap and put it on Pruney and pull it down over his ears. We laughed and Pruney said, Thanks Jate.

Then he took off a mitten.

His fingers touched my fingers.

They pulled away.

And it was just cold night.

27

TempestTongue Inside the Veil

Such a Easter storm blizzard we never did see. Mom said the only sensible thing to call it was the EasterBlizzard of 66.

The weeping willow tree branches thrashed against the kitchen walls and the Andriozzi TV antenna across the berm that I couldnt hardly see whipped and pitched. I had no problem imagining our antenna above our heads doing the same wild things.

On the radio. SaltyBrine said Southen NewEngland was tight in the grip of a prime NorEasta and the most sensible thing anyone could do was stay home. Stay off the roads. And stay tuned for further reports.

Those further reports just kept pouring in.

Small craft warnings changed to gale warnings Eastport to BlockIsland. CapeCod. Cuttyhunk. The Elizabeths. Nantucket. The Vineyard. And all of NarragansettBay.

When Mom said she had doubts about letting us go into the storm. Ross immediate groaned, Pruney probbly by now got twentybucks in his pockets doin door ta door NewBedford shovelin.

I said, We gotta deliver those papers. You woulnt want Pruney fired? Last night both you and Dad said Ross and me hadda deliver Pruneys NorthEnd 42 come hell or high water.

Mom said, With the Easta fullmoon tides. Highwaters already here. And. Between praverted priests. Savage men and my disgust. You can bet your bottom dollars. Sowams too is havin a taste-a-hell.

Mom pushed back the kitchenwindow curtains. Turned. Stood direct over Ross and me and said, Your father had to leave this mornin. So I wanted to keep things easy. But I havent even begun to speak my mind.

And I gotta addmit. Sure couldnt remember the last time Mom was so upset. She went to the livingroom baywindows. The incased plumb weights that Dad showed us when fixing a baseball broke window were knocking against their jambs and the outside wind was shrieking low and moaning.

Then the telephone rang.

By the way Mom was asking, Really? About three times in a row. I knew it was Dad. Then she said we were fine. And added, Long as youre safe thats all that matters.

When she hung up. She sat down. Covered her face and rubbed her forehead. Then she looked up. Like she was noticing Ross and me for the first time and said, Connecticut. Just past NewLondon. Stuck. Turnpike closed. He and his pals holed up in Howard and Johnsons. Plenny-a-coffee. Lotsa time. Snow easin. Probbly turn to rain. Said. You boys keep your word to Pruney. Be careful and be home by dark.

And then Mom said, Since your dads enjoyin menu cooked restaurant food. I'll cook anything you want. Special orders each-a-you.

Ross said, BunnyEggs and Italianbread cinnamontoast.

PinkPancakes for PalePeople? I asked.

Mom said, Yes yahooties.

We laughed and prettsoon the kitchen smell was coffee. Bacon. Biscuit. Butter. Eggs. And maple syrup.

And although I dint want any of Rosses BunnyEggs what Mom made special for him. He asked me for a few PinkPancakes and I said, Sure.

He helped hisself to two.

Between the three of us. And the EasterBlizzard. It was a good fancy breakfast.

Especial when. Our bellies full. And Mom. Her right face cheek against her coffeemug and steam of the drink floating up her forehead and into her hair and we just sat and listened to the wind scream and the house shake. We quiet sat like that for a long time. Quiet till Mom put down her coffeemug and on her cheek a mug print glowed red and she touched the red with her right hand fingers then brought her left hand fingers to the other side of her face. Fingertips wet. And she sat ten fingers holding her face in her hand.

Ross got up and stood by her and she wrapped her arms around his shoulders. And when I stood she pulled me in too. And wouldnt let go even though Ross was saying, Are you crying? Whats wrong Mom? Whats wrong?

Its all. Life. So fast.

And I said, SaltyBrine radio said probbly a foot by noon which is just twenty minutes.

And Ross threw me a look that was either. Be quiet. Or. You beat me to it.

Not wanting him to steal my comforting of Mom I just continued and said, Blizzards only snow with a bit more wind than usual. Thats all. Maybe turn to rain too. Heck. Not even any traffic out there cept snowplows and what with their chains. We'll be hearin em three blocks away.

Mom said it wasnt the blizzard. Or the paper route. Or Dad being stuck at Howard and Johnsons in Connecticut. Or anything else we should concern with. Go out there and have fun. We are ourselfs such mysteries.

Then she pulled Ross and me close and made both of us promise we'd do snow angels and she looked us in our eyes. We looked into hers.

The dark.

The rich.

The burgundy brown.

The red puffs of crying.

And I said, You know Mom. Youre awful pretty.

Mom pulled Ross and me tight into her tears.

And on the sudden. Outta those tears. I was discovering brave.

Gertas *SnowQueen* brave.

A Mom sending kids from the table.

Into the what all of who knows whats out there.

Somewhere in the world.

Before leaving our house one last look out the north bay window made me not believe what couldnt be seen.

No aqua blue aluminum sided Andriozzi house.

No redbrick AmericanLuggage mill building.

No A-M-E-R-I-C-A-N L-U-G-G-A-G-E roof sign.

No BaggyWrinkleLane.

No railroad tracks.

No crocus for cynthia flowers blooming.

No KellyStreet.

No marsh.

No nothing.

Just wind. And whole lotsa white.

Socked in, MistaCogg woulda said.

Mom said, Its the nature of things.

And the wind was the wind because everything still held and the window weights knocked inside their jambs and the house tried real hard to bust the roof from the side walls. The snow sounded like sand hissing through a screen and ice pellets smattering the glass just like SaltyBrine on the radio said. Snow turning hail and sleet and back to snow again. And the only thing clear outside the livingroom windows was the EasterBlizzard not giving up and blowing out any sure time real soon. But I wasnt saying nothing to Mom. Or Ross either.

No way.

And now Ross and me were ready to go all the way uptown to get Pruneys papers.

Ross was tying his bootlaces.

Underneath our dungarees and flannel shirts was both our long underwears. Scarves. Hooded winter jackets. Mittens. And stockingcaps.

When we were all set. Mom said she wanted final inspection. First thing she did was flip my hood and pull the drawstring tight. Then wrap another real long plaid scarf around my face. And tie it in the back. And youd think the wool itch and scratch woulda been a bother but I real liked the rust reds and tan golds and forest greens and black twing crisscross of it all.

Ross complained saying he dint want the hood because when he turned his head. His head would turn. But not the hood.

Mom said, All right. But Ross had to wear a wool scarf across his face because that wind. Without the scarf. Would tear his cheeks like cold needles on a babies cold cooly cheeks.

Dont know why exact. But whenever Mom used the word cooly. It always made me feel blushed up. And I was glad that when she said it just now that my face was hid from anyone seeing me. While I was blushing. Mom was finishing Ross and when done. Ross looked like a bank robber. His face covered. Except for his eyes.

Mom said, Dont do LandStreet. Tell me sidestreets youll take to Tassars.

Ross. Through his scarf said, Like sailboats. We'll be runnin with the wind. Make it halfway past the cemetery. Tack starboard at the cobbler shop. And then clear up UnionStreet. Wildwood and Mingo. Slice through Liberty. Cut cross to Church. Then Miller. Sloggover the town common. And wind up at Tassars store to be packin our news bundle. And gotta come back deliverin papers doin Miller and Water and eventual Quequeshan.

Mom added, You boys be careful-a-the snowplows. Watch for ice on the powerlines. Dont touch. Or go near. Anything on the ground electric.

Be careful. And. I love you.

She kissed us both solid on the top of our noses right between our eyes.

And with that we humped across the kitchen and stepped into the breath and holler of it all. And no way. Could I ever in a million years. If I hadnt of previous known. Been convinced. That yesterday was Easter-Sunday.

Two foot of snow covered our walkway with drifts pushing six feet against JackCoggs house. When we hit LandStreet and out from the protection of inbetween the KellyStreet houses the wind grabbed hold and shoved like fifty pair of hands heaving us past the junction light of Land and Water. That hanging stoplight swinging through the air with its yellow red and green all snuzzled under a plaster of white.

The cemetery too was about disappeared. All them gravestones looking more like frostafreeze icecream cones. Even the Hoogly cigar for gifts was fluffed up white and bewdeeful. And I knew if our feet werent sunk deep in the four feet of sidewalk snow banks. We woulda been keeled over like marsh grass planted in cement. The sidewalk snow was so deep because. Not only what the storm was dropping. But also what the snowplows were pushing from the road. Plate in the head obvious right off was there was no way we'd be able to hike the sidewalks over snowbank crud all the way uptown. And the only real way was walking in the LandStreet gutters and taking the side streets exact as we had told Mom.

And. Not ta say. But. That all sounds pretteasy. Believe me when Im telling you. We couldnt see nothing more and five six feet in front of us and if we had not of done that walk a million times before. Thered be no way.

But the wind was at our backs making us like spinnaker kites which is the way MistaCogg always said was the best way to get to any destination. Especial to a port in a storm. Which. Not fa nuthin. Seemed to me exact what Ross and me was doing.

As we cross wide LandStreet into narrow Union. Ross mitten hand pointed. Said, Must be ten kinds-a-snow fallin from the sky. Silverdollars. Pinwheels. Lacedoilies. Goosedown. Clouddust. Moonjewels. Hogsbreath. And pearlfrost.

Best I could do was, Fishscales and dandruff. Shellflakes and sleet.

Ross says he thinks shellflakes is prettgood. And fishscales too. But when he kept rattling off more names. Lacefringe. Coldsmoke and iceflames. I knew he was just trying to make me feel good even though there already was a few things to feel good about. Like the noise. That song. The noise sounds of all the silence. Crunch of snow with each footstep and slide. A snowplow rumbling and its chains all a chink chink chinking. The high whirring of some stuck in a snowdrift car. Tires whirring higher and higher till it sounds like the whir prettsoon be shattering glass.

But my favorite blizzard sound was the chattering of birds that find a seed feeder along someones windowsill or froze birdbath.

Theres always ladies with nothing to do except sit at their windows and feed the birds. Two pence a bag. You could always count on. Right outta *Mary Poppins*. MissLydiaRogers. Too old to do her embroidree art. Sitting at her window staring at birds. Finches. Sparrows. Pigeons and such. And today. Honest and God. A cardinal. Which sets my heart pounding because theres nothing like a red flame flashbusting against white snow.

Its a funny thing how youd think theyd be no way a bunch a tiny birds could be surviving such a storm. But there they all are. A dozen or two. As much surprised by our boots crunching as we are surprised by them. Those birds all on a sudden busting in the air mixing wing flutter and beak chatter with the sounds of the swirling and tossing in a snowdrifts and you wouldnt think you could hear such mixing a noises but you could. And I for one thought it was glorious. Dog glorious. And Ross said he liked it all too. But MissLydiaRogers. Blanket wrapped behind her window. Barely shaking us her finger because of us scaring off her birds. But we waved and she almost waved back to us too. And I sung, *Come buy my bag full of crumbs.*

Then the sound of crashing icicles. Roof avalanches and tree sighs. A roof avalanche. The sudden whooshing of snow from the roof slates to the ground. First like sand sliding off a dump truck bed and hitting hard pack ground. Ross and me stepped careful of roof avalanches near the older buildings. Town hall. The Brown University BaptistChurch with the Tiffany stainglass window set by PaulRevere. Steep roofs and slate shingles? A ton of snow could bury you kah plump fast into the ground. Jeeze.

On the other hand. Tree sighs was something all together different. Tree sighs was gracefilled. More like the sifting sound of white sugar and flour.

And similar to them trees peaceness. Ross and me proceeded. Fast and comfortable. I mean the wind scoop slapped us up and shoved at our backs so much. Not ta say. But. If we were wearing ice skates we woulda been gliding along Mom would say, Like nobodies business.

It was just as Ross had told Mom. We was, Running with the wind.

And I noticed, Not reaching.

And similar like them trees too. We took the cold and the snow. Neither of them at our backs was bothersome. When I lagged behind Ross I laughed about how the rear of his entire everything was white plastered snow from his boot heels to his stocking cap fuzz ball. Like me. He wore the neckscarf knotted at the back where Mom tied it and unless he took that off nothing was going down his neck anytime way too soon.

And everywhere Rosses ten different snows drifted. Not just on the north face of things. But wherever the wind scuttle whipped. Eddied. Bluster bobbed and frothed. Windbared cobblestone. Car hoods and headlights. Some yards had three feet a snow and yet a alley between two tight squozed garages might be nothing but what MisstaCogg would call a skosh blowing through a bramble bottom with all brokegreen bottles and bullthorns.

Two or three times we seen snow squalls like that *Wizard of Oz* tornado. Excepting these ones were small. About the size of us. White and amazing. They come outta no where. A wind howl or a storm scream. Touch down on a snowdrift or a yardflat. Spazz around first there. Then here. Pick up snow and fling it like the center of a cottoncandy spin machine spinnin out spun growing bigger and bigger then yanking way over and beyond and I spin around after the thing but quick as it come it went gone into nothing but falling snow.

Ross said those gotta be snow devils since there was such a thing as snow angels. And if those devils were any bigger? Then they could probbly do lotsa damage.

And I gotta addmit. I agreed with him saying, Suppose the whole storm is for real just one of those squall things only its so gigantic we cant see it because we're in it?

Praspective, Ross hollered.

I knew he was right.

Ross and me kept going till we were cutting through the Methodist Church alley that was fourfoot a roof avalanche slag. Solid to walk on. But nervous making because what if another chunk broke loose and slid?

Ross told me to go ahead first because what if the roof slag did let go? At least he'd be there to rescue me or call for someone for to help.

And I said, Can take care-a-myself jus fine.

Countin on you ta take care-a-me too. Someones gotta go first.

So I walked atop of all that ice and some chunks of roof slate. That ice cracking beneath my boot soles and at one point me tripping and falling.

Ross hollered, Get up. Keep movin.

Which I did till a rumbling and a roar made Ross holler, Run.

And we did a *Combat* charge.

And direct where Ross had been standing crashed a heave of snow and ice and more roof slate shingles some green with moss and we kept doing *Combat* running from that alley till we were over a plow heap and clear in the middle of ChurchStreet.

And we gawked each other through ice crystal wind and breath huffs.

Ross. Face red and sparkling. Turns to study the slide.

We're on the town common between the face of Sowams highest church steeple and polished granite pedestal with the black cannon plastered northside white standing high to the dead soldiers of all the wars. That acre of town common. All clean powder. And for a long long time we just stood and caught our breaths.

Without even talking. More like we was reading each others minds. Ross and me fell backwards into the clean of that fluff making good on the promise to Mom. We made our wings and were flying.

The wind sliced and blew cold cross our noses and our eyes. Thick snow flakes big and little. Sprackled and laced spun from the sky. And I knew what the Mikey 2A's statue feeled just before he smashed to the floor.

I wished we coulda somehow carried him here.

And let him ease.

Roses bloom.

Into the snow.

Into the sky jewels with Ross and me.

And with. It goes without saying.

Pedro Pruney Mendoza-Mendez.

A snow angel in the town common during the EasterBlizzard of 66 is the closet I ever come to feeling holy and good the way Pruney was always trying to get by going to church. And I dont know whether it was the huge Methodist church to the north of us blocking the blizzard. Or whether the storm was actually going calm. But as Ross and me fell back into that snow. All on a sudden. Under that sky pointing cannon. We was seven years old. And Ross n me at the Morris Benjamin & Richards funeral of MissusCogg and so many times she told us *TheSnowQueen* and now laying there in the sweep of the storm just breath feeling the clean of the flakes as they settled on my eyelashes and forehead eyebrows and chin the way the melt dripped slow into my hair and rolled down to my ears. It was like taking a bath and being put to sleep both the same time and I just wanted to lay there in this rest. What I hadnt felt in such a long while. Breath.

But we shall the Christ child see.

Ross was feeling prettmuch the same way too because. Although I was thinking *TheSnowQueen*. He was saying out loud those words from that poem GilOwen had taught him about shaking *harness bells* and *promises to keep*. I knew he was adding his e. And I also knew we both had to climb out our angel clouds. Get moving. Do those papers for Pruney.

Before we walked away we stood looking at our wings. Wings where we flapped. Pruney altarboy robe where our legs clipped back and forth. And as far as snow angels go? Ours were prettgood. Excepting for where we tracked to our laydown.

Now more tracks leading out.

I said, Those snow angels coulda been a lot better if we somehow had flown to this spot where we made em stead of havin walk here like we did.

Said, Imagine snow angels without comin and goin tracks?

And Ross said that would be like being a real angel because you got straight off to be with God without ever having to first live on earth. Ross said that living on earth was sorta like leaving tracks and he for one wanted to leave tracks. Said he dint want his angel without the tracks that led him there in the first place. That being a angel straight off was stupid because then what would a angel be reaching for?

I said, Amazing.

Ross said, What?

I said, That word. Reaching. I claimed it yesterday mornin.

And I told about my yesterday reaching Montaup with Dad and then about how Dad said under no circumstances could we visit ZompaGalucci no more and although Ross was disappointed he said it was amazeful how he and me could be so the same and yet so different.

And by the time we finished talking God. Snow angels. Twins. And such. The town common with the Methodist Church and Moe B. Dicks Funeral Parlor was a full block behind as we were crossing LandStreet. Into snow flying sideways wind. And we entered. Stomping packcrust off our boots. George TheSheiks Tassars Newspaper store. Smack dab. In the center of Sowams. That we. And everyone else. Called. Uptown.

As usual. George TheSheik Tassar. All fine groomed silver hair vested up and serious sat behind the glass cigarette counter with the brass cash register right there in front of him. As usual. When we entered. TheSheik looked at us through blackrimmed eyeglasses and the squint of his eyes. The two lines creasing his nose with that slow chin draw nod that gave us his approve to go back of the store and sit down.

Waiting for papers at George TheSheik Tassars was as about as relaxing a thing a kid could do. Especial on a day when the delivery truck be late on account the storm.

A bunch of the big kids werent there yet. So Ross and me. After we shook off and unbuttoned. Climbed right up and sat on the workbench.

And between the smell of the smoke the damp of the floor and the usual smell of magazines and print we with our backs firm against the rear wall watched the outside blizzard and the LandStreet people struggling by in all that wind and storm.

Every now and then the door would bust open and a customer would stomp and stare like he couldnt belief that he was inside and saying no sign of letting up fumbling with gloves pocket change and bills his snow covered hat a swipe of the palm to his hair then back to the buttons on his coat then his pack of Winstons that he came in for then matches and a light and more bundle his clothes back up. Stash cigarettepack safe in a inside pocket. Then back. Once again. Into the smush of the storm.

Meanwhile. Two or three other. Big guy paper boys. Fourteen. Fifteen years old. Hustling. Coughing and pushing their way to the back for to be waiting with us. The twelve year old guys. Snow melting now and seeping deep into our cotton longjohns and dungarees and the place getting warm and smelling like some BrillCream and wet newspaper sogg and all of us guys waiting and the truck now a hour late and SleekaJoePalmari flipping through a *Playboy*. The tits of pictures gives me a boner and the big guys who is I recognize straight off. Johnny Konks Duffman. And SleekaJoe from the East end of town. SleekaJoe sees me staring at the *Playboy* and says, Rumors all over Sowams. Too bad you and your runt portagee friend are queer for each other because otherwise you might enjoy a piece of this cooz when you get hair on your teenabopper balls.

The back a SleekaJoes head. Ross standing on the bench with a leg swinging out that catches JohnnyKonks slack jaw while JohnnyKonks laughing his own ignorance and SleekaJoe jumping on Ross and Im under the counter because plate in the head and GeorgeTassar is in the middle it all cuffing JohnnyKonks and Ross and George TheSheik peeling off his blackrimmed eyeglasses saying low as the damp on the floor, You boys got something to settle take it outside on the curbstone. Otherwise. In here youre businessmen. Understand?

Yessir, says Ross.

Yessir, says JohnnyKonks who bloody lip and fast as all hell broke loose now quiet and waiting and everything hot damp and clammy sweat. Playboy tits turning.

SleekaJoePalmari says Faggot. Real soft so MistaTassar dont hear. Faggot.

And the other paperboys. Bigger guys. JohnnyKonks and SonnyColetta and JimMartin. So so under their breaths. Mocking Ross, Bite the bag you queerjob preece twat blow me shitass dicklicka suckboy.

Bite the bag.

And blow me.

And I gotta tell you. My twelve year old twin brother Ross dint get down from the workbench counter and give up his place for fifteen year old gooney SleekaJoePalmari. SonnyColetta. KenPickring. RickPetruchi. LB Stanlee. Or any of the other big guys. He gave JohnnyKonks the same steel eyeball that Dad all the time gave us when Dad wanted his way. And as a matter of fact. Ross shoved open a space and told me to sit up there with him. No one said nothing against it so I climbed up and settled in. And then right off the whir of gray and yellow flashed in the front window. George TheSheik Tassar was on his feet. OlMan charging. And pulling open the door. All of us paper boys chain gang heaving back the newspaperbundles from the truck past *Popular Mechanics Archie* and *Playboy* to the quick growing bundle piles on the back counter where we about twenty boys had been waiting.

Before the bundles were all heaved in MarcelAlmador was already counting and clipping and sorting. Guys grabbing their stacks and stuffing canvas carrier bags.

SEA of WHITE FLOODS NEW ENGLAND
Easter Blizzard Packs a Wallop
Cumberland Farms – First National – Almacs: No Bread. No Milk
Chafee Pledges Investigation into Ocean State Emergency
Foster/Glocester Schools Open for Shelter

Ross and JohnnyKonks sorting from the same bundle and in the breath of a tree sigh we were papers packed. Hats back on.

This is your mitten not mine.

Wheres my plaid scarf?

Hey youse guys.

Bye.

A nod through cigarsmoke from MistaTassar.

A tough ass nod from SleekaJoePalmari and our NorthEnd 42 newspapers in the bag not yet slung over Rosses shoulder we are out the door and into the gale.

Theres alot a things that can make smooth sailing go bad and like MistaCogg always said, The time to get ready isnt when youre ready. And as soon as I stepped outta MistaTassars I shoulda went straight back in to square my rigging and trim things fast. I forgot something but dint know what. Ross was on the quick. Straight off. Head to wind. Bow pitched over the wave of the snowplow berm and putting into LandStreet strong and I wanted fast to catch up with no lagging so over the slag I climbed too but my left leg sunk up to my balls real deep. Snow inside my boot. Ice scraping the inside my pants. Long underwear bunched against my knee. Slush gainst my bare leg and my leg pulled out the buried boot and with bare hands I reached into the hole and yanked up my snow filled boot. By the time I emptied the boot and shoved my wet foot back. My fingers and toes were already froze and Ross was a blur in the bite of the wind.

Ross couldnt hear me yelling because Hey wait up in the screech of that slant maybe sounded like a seagull creeing over the wide of the ocean just when you stepped out from the shelter of the dunes.

The storm got more strong and definite the temperatures dropped because now the wind was roars that came from five directions all at once.

I tried running after Ross who thought I was right behind him because Ross woulda never left me stuck with no boot on. But instead of running I fell flat on my ass because even the road pack was slick pond ice. And all north and south of LandStreet the snow was spindrift slithering road snakes and swirls and wisps and lisps of snow what MistaCogg called horecrawls. Horecrawls so strong that each time I tried to stand they would snap me back down. Now I couldnt even see Ross. Just a blind of streaks that were needles stabbing my eyes. And the blink blink yellow of snowplow beacon coming up behind me and the chink chink of chains biting road pack.

I was on my feet. Then on my knees. And on my butt in gutter glaze again.

The snowplow.

The lights.

The chains.

What I see between the fingers of my own hands blocking sting snow and shave ice from biting at my eyes is Ross whos looking like a ghost on bad reception TV and he pulls me up to my feet and the two of us heel to the snow curb fallback like snow angels and the plowblade rushes past and the sandspreader sprays and we're covered to our chests in a wake of streetcrud and roadskree.

And both us. Faces up. Spitting sand and salt. Flip to our bellies and crawl over the snow heave on to the sidewalk. And shove into the alcove of the FirstNational food store. Ross hollers above the wind, Whaddya nuts? You gotta stay with me.

And I notice, Where are the papers?

And Ross hollers, Berm in front of Sears. Stick with me.

And both of us again heads to the wind beating through the blow.

And when we get to Sears the color TV window is reflecting blue and green and red flying snow reception blizzard bad that I couldnt tell what program was on. And Ross says, Quit looking TV and help me find the papers. Must be buried. Snowplow.

Sure enough. The only give away of papers is just the sling strap crimping out the snow bank. The delivery bag is street slag and newspaper all wadded together like someone poured froze up slush all over them and by the time we dig out the bag my fingers are blue and Ross hollers, Where your mittens?

I holler, One in Tassars. Other? The road.

Ross hollers, Put your hands in your pants. Warm em with your dick. I'll carry the papers. Stay behind me.

We're back into LandStreet and Ross has the carrier bag strap over his forehead. Nose to the road. Eyes to his feet and papers on his back. Only way I can move forward is both hands choking my ball sack. Left shoulder and topknot to the northwind. Eyes and nose facing south. Which Im telling you means Im walking forward but looking backwards because my eyes and ears and cheeks cant take but five seconds more being sliced to the bone and I just know the only way we might make it back to BaggaWinkle is by the feel a the street. And the know of that is going fast because my toes are already froze and I cant feel nothing except if Im slipping or if Im sliding and for the most part Im doing both. And to keep from falling I take my hands out my pants and keep them balled fist tight and pulled back as far inside my jacket sleeves as they can go using my arms for balance but feeling more like a seagull with a broke wing. And my eyebrows are plastered with snow and the wind through my stockingcap and the tops a my ears so cold theyre burning and that center spot on my neck below my chin feels like I just got slashed with a razor blade and as clear as a photograph I see my scarf still laying on the counter where I was sitting at Tassars and Mom was right. Without that scarf my cheeks are all baby cooly raw and even now that word makes me smile but for real there is nothing funny because Im feeling so cold and miserable.

Ross just keeps plowing.

Im right behind and we make it to the corner of Land and Mingo and duck beneath the LyricTheatre marquee and the door swings open and JoeMahdahlesski is holding his hat and says, You boys got a extra from you paper I can buy? What the hell in a storm like this ya doin? Why look atchyas. Wheres yuh scarf? Wheres yuh gloves? Why if you boys dont from this storm get in. You'll catch yuh deaths. The bote-a-yous.

And Ross pushes me inside.

And although I wanna answer JoeMahdahlesski and tell him weve no extra papers to sell. I cant do it because my mouth wont work. And my arms wont work. And my fingers wont work neither. And I cant figure on it.

Ross turns and faces me. From the top of his hat to his eyebrows. Froze ice. His cheeks. Something between blue and red. Not exact purple. His earlobes lopsta boil red. His face sleeted. Wet. Dripping. Sopped. From the top of his scarf to his jacket. To his pants. Plastered snow. Like he was sprayed with the fake snow they use on the Sears Christmas trees. Excepting on Ross the snow is all real and beginning to melt in the warm of the box office lobby with old popcorn and candy and JoeMahdahlesski standing in front of the sign.

Coming Soon: Another Classic Returns
To Kill a Mockingbird
One Week Only: Now Playing
Lawrence of Arabia

JoeMahdahlesski says, Hey boys I hate to push yiz outta here. Butchya meltin what I just mopped clean all over my floor. I gotta lock up. Youse go on home and forget dose papers. Deliva in the morning. Jesuschrice. Dat Arab camel jockey Tassar oughta know betta. Youre kids for chricesakes. Not the U-S-A post office. When ya cross the street stay on the sidewalk.

And JoeMahdahlesski opens the door. Ross and me step back into the cold.

And JoeMahdahlesski plops the delivery bag soak filled NorthEnd 42 at our feet. In the lee underneath the marquee. Lotsa snow devils and horecrawls whip past but for the most part the sidewalk in front of the Lyric is swirl swept bare.

Ross just stands and stares at me and says, Hows your plate in the head?

Cold, I say. Real cold.

Ross takes off his mittens and peels the ice from my eyebrows. Some ice chunks break. Some stay stuck. And some chunks sorta melt from his touch that feels real good. Those warm fingers. Melting my face and the ice dripping cold tears down my cheeks. And Ross uses his knuckles to wipe away all that water. Holds my chin in his palm and he smiles. Ross says, Lets make it down to the SquarePeg. GilOwen. Warm up and dry.

But my lips do nothing. Only my tongue says, Okay.

Again. Bag strap on his head. Ross pitches forward. Leads right shoulder and heaves to the wind which is gusting through between houses. Driveways and yards.

In the foam of it all I know we are crossing UnionStreet then Wildwood and Mingo with the SquarePeg. Dark and locked black. No light. With almost a half mile to go. Straight beating to the wind before FatFinger Petes which would not have been the case. If Dad had not of made us stay away from Whimpys.

And the new not allowed. ZompaGalucci.

It was *Lawrence of Arabia* cepting instead of it being hot sand it was cold snow. And I kept waiting for the part where one of us was gonna get sunked in the quicksand but the quicksand never come. Instead it was all the walking in the desert scenes and right now we were huddled behind a sand dune snowdrift.

In the SquarePeg enter way. We both knew soon as we left SquarePeg protection we again be head to fury beating to the wind. No break. No shelter. Full front. No reaching. Face on.

I dont think I can make it, I hollered to Ross. I hadnt felt my feet since the LyricTheatre and my hands were like they got bit off by sand sharks and I was tucking tore stubbs beneath my sleeves. Usual when plate in the head came I could tell. My arm all jellyfish sting and my fingers getting clawed. But now I couldnt feel nothing except finger pain and the steel plate frigid frost to my brain.

We gotta keep goin, Ross hollered back. Im leavin the papers and headin straight home. Lets do it. Stay right behind me.

Rosses face all iced up like a tackleblock froze with the spray of bay waves. His lips no color gray and I couldnt for real see his eyes because of my blur and because of his ice from the pull of his hat to the tuck of his jaw.

A huge gust of wind hit the SquarePeg sign and the storefront windows shook rankling grunkles. Ross said, Now. We gotta go now.

And I thought, Lawrence Arabia reaching the city. Acaba.

And Ross and me bent around the corner of Mingo and Water facing full the stormblow and blizzard.

Ross made the corners of Water and Sisson. StrongRoss the faintest blur in the boldest stir of swirl and cut. Snow keeps on biting. BigRoss. Way ahead of stunted me. Ross. Gone. Disappeared. No more. Just white. Lotsa white and a growing gray. Late afternoon gray. No snowplows. No beacon warnings. Or snowchain chinking. Just the wind. Low and loud. Growls and roars. Rolls and tears. No breath. No tree sighs. Only the steady ache of something so sharp its dull. So loud it disappears in the big of its own self. WaterStreet is waves of white folding white through the air like the veil on the head of Ah Lady-a-Fatima. TheSnowQueen with a crown of ice crystals and those waves of folding white dancing long fur coat. And through those waves. The blur of trees. The cut of roofs. The shapes of houses. Behind the veil was rippling curtains. One after the other. Opening and closing all diffrent times. And then out from behind one of those rippling curtains TheSnowQueens legs from deep thick fur coat. First one leg. Then the other leg. So beautiful and bewdeeful. Her nylon stockings? She held those nylon stockings to my eyes. And thats what I was seeing. All of WaterStreet through the veils and nylon stocks of AhBewdeeful Lady-a-Fatima? And the ice crowned fur coat of TheSnowQueen? I wasnt walking anymore. Feet sliding one foot then the other. My knees not bending. And my feet not feeling. Plowing. Thats all I was doing.

Plowing.

And then I wasnt anymore plowing.

Sitting.

A big snowdrift.

Angels.

AhLady a FatimaSnowQueen waving nylons in front of my eyes telling that Ross poem when we were making snow angels on the common and their voices was kisses in my ears and their breath was snow feathers on my eyes.

It was glorious.

Dog glorious.

I wished PruneyMendez had been there with me. Not for the quiet. Not for the way the fine cold wrapped around me and made me warm. Not even for the lovely dark and deep. But I wished PruneyMendez had been with me because with each of those Ladys breaths I could see Gerta and Kay skating on the mirror of reason. And Louseea. And Yahsinta. And Fransisco. All floating on their own little clouds and praying with their rose ree beads. They all jumped from praying to playing. They were skating. Then swimming at the beach. Then cloud floating again and throwing little snowballs. The gentle waving of the nylon veils. The weather dint seem to matter nothing. They were all five kids having a swell time. And I took a deep breath. Smelled land where there was no land.

Added my own e.

And knew I had found the place to make.

All of Pruneys hurts go away.

That is.

Until.

ZompaGalucci. Slung me over his shoulder.

And carried me through the blizzard.

Into the thaw of Dads absolute forbidded zone.

The bookie joint of Whimpy BugEyes McPherson.

28
The Inside Storm

Even inside Whimpys. The blizzard kept pounding. First. Because Zompa couldnt close the door. Snow heaved like a beached whale so the door couldnt be shut. Just about impossible. And second. The hurt of the blizzard. Im talking real pain. That kind of hurt starts at the thaw.

Zompa said, Goin from life ta deaths painful. But dead ta life? Bah fongool. That hurts like a bastid. You bettchya ass. Not fa nuthin. Like a friggin ballbustin bastid.

Zompa breathing was all strain. The strain moored boats put on dock lines when the tide shifts. Not groans or huffs from his mouth while hauling me. But something tight and strangulating. I wanted to tell him, Add an e for Gods sake. Cause. Not ta say. But. Somethin deep inside-a-yous about ta bust.

Yet nothing could have made him quit. Not the pace he was going. Wind pushing hard. ZompaGalucci pushing harder. He stomped his way through the opendoor snowdrift and dropped me on a old couch under the window I had looked through on HolyThursday when I seen Dad talking him and Whimpy.

Then. Opposite my frozelegs and frozefeet. Zompa about collapsed on a stack of newspapers piled high as any chair. Took off his snow covered ElmaFudd hat with thick wool earflaps. Tossed it. Snow and all. Into the sink. Then he tried unzipping his coat. Even though the door wide open. Something kept on twisting his face and grabbing his shoulder like a Hoogly was pulling him into the night and Zompa had no intention of going. But for a long time that Hoogly was winning. Pulling Zompa. But then. Zompas eyes got squints. Then bug eyed like Whimpys. And then like the Polish kid in the Hoogly crypt doing a MistaCogg monks scream. All teeth. Clamped. Mouth stretched from his clamped teeth. Top part of his face getting pulled off his skull. It was like even me could feel Zompas teeth hurting.

Zompa did a leftside heave. Then another. Then a shudder. Then deep breaths like Zompa was saying, No way. I aint stayin in no flesh eatin stone. No cigar for gifts for ZompaGalucci.

Zompa took more deep breaths. Breaths. Breaths. Breaths. His mouth all tongue he was trying to spit out. And his chin disappearing into his neck and cheeks because his eyes needed all the room. His eyes. Not bug eyes. But huge dark center spot fists.

And then something giving. Zompa doing breathing.

Breath. Breath.

Finally adding e's.

Breathes.

And his tongue now back inside of his mouth. His neck. Those bulges each time he swallows. His cheeks again fat. Not bloat. His eyes soft grapes inside his fists. Not just the fists anymore. Grapes. The green kind. Those grape eyes beneath a calming brow. And his face no more that monk trying to scream. But instead. Zompa.

ZompaGalucci again.

Add an e.

And Zompa. Wobble legs. Flesh fingers gripping the counter. Sweat on his face.

Struggles. Stands. Leans against the counter top. Pots and pans and dishes. Coffeecups. He rolls to the stove and a pot of what smells like a sauce with sausage and peppers. I could tell because the red around the rim. And then ZompaGalucci. Lotsa slow deep breaths. Then fast ones. Panting. Tastes the sauce with a wood spoon just like Mom always does. Hand to heart. Probbly not to spill any sauce on his shirt. All on a sudden Zompas not in no April spring blizzard but instead in a October Sunday Indian summer afternoon. Purple grapes. Colored leafs. Honey gold leafs. Sunburned skinned leafs. Leafs the color of pumpkins. Dried corn. Red peppers and basil sauce. Zompa is in autumn leafs. And horecrawls and snowdrifts are months and months away.

All of Zompas thick ropes and tight muscles in his face now again fat cheeks. Red from the sauce. And like a baby going, Goo.

But me. Im all the shivers and cant catch the autumn leafs. Not fa nuthin. Im like those winter oak leafs outside in the blizzard. Chattering and shaking on the branch. No pine tree sighs about me in any way shape or form. No autumn color neither. Any doctor seen me woulda said I was convulsing from combine plate in the head and a serious case of the ice jeetas. Which means I sure am frozed. Most because the door is still open and even though Im inside and on a couch. That open door with the wind whipping through. Horecrawls swirling. Hooglies flying. And a snowdrift whale blocking the door from being shut. All that winter inside makes me colder then when it was just the outside blizzard. Ah Lady-a-Fatima. SnowQueen. And me.

Zompa says the sauce needs more wine that he pours from a halfgallon jug.

Stirs.

Tastes again.

He turns down the gas till the flame gets blue.

Then. Zompa puts teakettle water on. He says, Gonna be chicken bullion broth. Or hot chocolate. If they have any-a-bote in the joint. Or do I want a expresso? And maybe too a shot-a-bucca? Getchya thawin quicka. Considerin yuh circumstance.

Then Zompa takes some deep breaths. Touches his chest again bearing down hard his teeth with his mouth doing a wince. Grabs a snowshovel leaning left the doorway and swats them horecrawls and they heave out through the open door a huge swimming snowdrift.

Four or five hefts of that shovel make the white whale disappear. And with a effort hard against the wind and horecrawls and Hooglies that keep blowing. Zompa closes the door. Fin eato he says. Breathing hard as he was when he carried me in.

Zompa is front of me.

Him heaving like the beached white whale he just shoveled out.

The shivers still got me. And you know? Those froze meatballs porkchops Mom pulls from the freezer before dinner? The way they look with the meat blood gone rust gray and no sooner the froze meats hit the kitchen warm air than those froze meats grow frost crystals and ice fur? And if its flank steak. Or a chicken thawing. Ross or me will wanna put our handprint on the frost fur? Like we are branding the froze meat with hot iron fingers. Im certain frost fur is growing on me when Zompa pats me and says, Can ya feel yuh feet kid?

Nothin below my knees. Plate in the head hurts too.

Then ZompaGalucci. One hand his heart. And one hand reaching in his pocket. Pulls out a *WestSideStory* switchblade he slaps open snap faster than a blink.

Zompa grabs at my boots. Knife in hand. Zompa cuts my frozed up bootlaces.

No one singing *TheJetsSong.*
Wheres Ross?
No one singing *Somethins comin something good.*
Wheres Ross? My teeth all ice jeeta morse code dots and dashes. Zompa pulling off my boots. My feet. My brain. My eyeballs. Everything sticking banged up plate in the head froze.

Thawing pain shooting feet to head. Ahabs leg getting bited off. Nails in feet of crucified Jesus.

Zompa grunt. Zompa huff. *Lawrence of Arabia.* Take no prisoners. Teakettle whistling. FathaLuis screaming. Ah Lady of Fatima watching. Mikey 2A's reaching. Front door blowing open and horecrawls swirling with the snowdrift whale. Ivories sinking in my flesh. Snowdrift snapping off my ankles. Big teeth. Froze bone. Zompa grabbing at his heart going for the door. Horecrawls whipping around Zompa. White whales. Sharks. Hooglies. Feet of crucified Jesus. Monks scream. Cigar for gifts. Eecoodeesh. PortugeseWow. Praspective. Everything black.

Zompa.
A hurricane candle.
A soup bowl.
Zompa.

One candle near the stove on the counter top. The other on the small table next to Whimpys big stuffed chair. Candle flickers. Shadows reaching about the room. Pool table in the corner. No one breaking balls. Opposite me the big old stuffed chair of Whimpy BugEyes McPhersons. But no Whimpy BugEyes McPherson. Above that. A chalkboard. Narragansett Raceway whitechalk and a yellowchalk list beneath. Then another board with the same kind of things listed yellowchalksmudged Taunton Dog Track. And Foxboro Trotters.

All around the room. Old newpapers smelling the place of Tassars newspaper store. Except Whimpys place got a stronger smell of cigarette and cigar stale. Next to Whimpys chair. A big old radio. Kind I seen in olden day magazines with a entire family gathered and listening. Dad said like TV shows. But without the pictures. *The Shadow. The Lone Ranger.* Or *Sargent Pressing on the Yukon.*

Me on the couch. ZompaGalucci sits close in a slat chair. Candle glows Zompas face gold and rose and snowmelt and sweat round his eyebrows and cheeks. Candle reflects Hooglies and flaming eye sockets. Bowl of steaming tomato sauce. Zompas offers a spoonful. Swalla dis kid, he says.

Sgot polenta in it. Do ya good.

The mush to my lips. Warm spreads. Throat to belly and my no more not so aching feet warm in my toes. I do a wiggle Zompa sees and says, Good.

Zompa does me another spoonful.

And another.

And that tomato sauce and polenta just as good as he said.

Maybe even better.

Its not so hot to burn my mouth. But just warm enough to put the candle glow of Zompas face into the ice block cold of my belly.

Zompa feeding me three more gulps.

On the third I have a immediate thought. Ross. What about Ross?

Zompa answers, He assisted on goin for yuh Mom. Told him stay here. But I aint worried. Hes in primo shape. Its you we was worried for.

Yeah. But he? And she? Maybe? Are they stuck like me? Even Dads somewhere in Connecticut. Stuck.

And Zompa says, Your Dads not stuck. He called yuh Mom just before the powa went out. A snowplow. One-a-SalRays boys. State driva. Guys gonna take im from Providence all the way to Sowams. Soon as he gets in. Yuh Moms gonna send im here to get ya. So sit tight kid. Yuh ol mans comin. And you? Ya got wings on yuh back. Enjoy the storm.

I say, Wings? When he gets here my dads gonna kick my butt. Said you was off limits. Jeeze. Hes gonna be sore.

What sore? Ya got saved from catchin yuh death. Wise up kid. Yuh ol man knows the deal. Yuh dads just fine. And yuh brotha probbly too. You and me bote gonna sit. Im pooped. Ya aint exact a five pound sack-a-potatoes no more. For chrice sake Jesus. I memba when the bote-a-yous. You and yuh brotha. Was as big as a loaf-a-twin bread. Ya think taday was the first time I carried ya? Not fa nuthin. But. I used to hold ya bote down at the beach. ClaraLee be down there every day wid yous kids since ya was two weeks. A couple-a-pair-a-cheese calzones. Youse guys. Adorable. Them wuh the days.

How come Ross n me dont ever remember you from the beach?

Disabled. A hott condition. Dint nobody tell ya? I got me a hott condition. Took me a hotta years ago. Unbafrigginleevable pain like you woulnt bahleeve. Hurt like a bastid I tell ya. Menegga la gawts. Ben on disability fa years. Hott attack. Years ago.

How about before?

Before?

When we come in a while ago just now. You have a heart attack? Take a hotta? Back when you carried me through the door?

Not fa nuthin kid. But. Ya think ZompaGalucci. Cause he got ol man pains. Cant toss ya round? Ya know what yuh friggin hottattack got? It got stugots. Hottattack? Eh.

And I realize Zompas not for real upset with me. Its like Dad once said. Thats Zompa just bein Zompa. So I just go along with Zompas joshin and ask, Is that why I know you only from the paper route with Pruney?

And Zompa says, Pruney? Why you and not that little runt portagee deliverin papers taday?

NewBedford. His ol man wont let him live here no more on account-a. On account-a. On accountawhat ya done to FathaLuis.

What I done to FathaLuis? That what someone told ya? FathaLuis done to hisself. Who told ya what I done to FathaLuis?

My dad said—

Yuh dad? Yuh dad said. Yuh dad said what?

Said, Friends help friends and some things stay on the Q-T. Thats what Dad said.

Well, yuh dads sayin right. And rememba BenFranklin somethin else kid. If we dont stick tagetha theyll tagetha stick us seprit. And we aint gettin stuck. Capice?

Not fa nuthin. Not really. But Zompa?

Yeah kid?

My dad says you and him used to be best friends. Were you?

Truth?

Truth.

I was more frennly widdchya mom.

For real?

A-course for real. I moved to Sowams from NewYork when I was five. She and me went all tru school tagetha. Yuh mom and me. Firs grade ta high school. Dint she neva tell youse?

No.

No? Well let me tell ya somethin. If it wasnt for me? Yuh Mom n dad would-a-neva twelve years ago met.

For real?

Whaddya keep askin me for fa real? Ya think me? ZompaGalucci. Gonna lie ta ya? I knew yuh Dad from up Fedral Hill. Salvatore Raymon SanAngelo. SalRay was the big shot those days. Now too. Not fa nuthin. Dont get me wrong. Anyways. Yuh pop. Before he was yuh pop. SalRay was whatchya call yuh pops paisano. His gombah. His padrone. Anyways. Yuh dad used to come down from Providence all-a-the times. EastBay errands for SalRay. I worked for Whimpy. Who was. And still is. The main squeese-a-the EastBay juice. And this one time. Yuh fatha. Yuh ol man. Yuh ol man before he was yuh ol man. Yuh fatha. He come down from Providence and I say, Lets go CrescentPark ShoreDinnaHall. Some chowda. Clamcakes. Maybe a lopsta. And then the midway rides. And he says, Sure. Why not? So we get there and I see this gal I know from Sowams named MaryMartha Lorienzo. A real sweet hott att one was. Was with her sista Dolores Chubby Lorienzo and their friend ClaraLee Margherita Rossi. Yuh motha. So me. I take yuh dad whos a complete stranga ta these gals ova to meet em. And yuh dads got this Octoba plaid wool. What he used ta call TerryMalloy jacket on with its MarlonBrando collar up the way in at *On the Waterfront* movie. And mind ya. This is the first time these ladies are meetin him. Yuh dads a total stranga. And before I can even innaduce him ta the girls. Dolores Chubby Lorienzo says to yuh dad, Put that collar down. You look like ya belong up on FedralHill. And she reaches ova and puts his collar down. Now heres duh ting. None-a-these girls yet knows yuh dads name cause I aint even like I said innaduced him yet. And yuh dad says. He says. I am. I am from FedralHill. And then yuh motha looks back at Chubby Lorienzo. And yuh mom says, Chubby. Leave him alone. I like the collar up. And ClaraLee Rossi reaches ova and puts it back up. And then. This is the clincha. She. Yuh mom. She takes from her lapel. A Holy Virgin Motha Mary Protect Me Pin. And pins it on ta yuh fathas TerryMalloy mickwool collah and innaduces herself ta him and. Ah madone. They spend the res-a-the night doin the midway tagetha. Ferriswheel. Carouselhorses. Cottoncandy. Games. Prizes. The whole shabang. Straight. Place. Show. Dailydouble. And the quinella.

The vanilla?

The quinella. Quinella. Its a racin thing. Not ta say. But. Ya wanna learn the friggin dog track or let me shut up for a minute soze I kin finish my story?

Your story.

Well. Yuh motha shes gonna be goin home with her friends and yuh fatha wants can he see her again and she tells yuh dad be at SowamGreenhill townbeach in the mornin and can he meet her there. And when he shows up. Its a friggen bewdeeful September. Foileeage startin early in the trees. The colors. Day. And shes in her chair readin a book. And they see each otha the next day and the next night. And bah-da-boom. A couple-a-nine months later. A dozen years ago. The rest is. As they say. Double or nuthin. Youse guys. Histry.

Beachgrit n Sunrise, I say.

Beach who and sun wha? says Zompa.

I sit up on the couch and rub my feet. My hockey socks. Knit wool. Damp. The warm of Zompa and his story.

Zompa? I say.

Yeah kid?

Is FathaLuis ever comin back? Is FathaLuis dead?

And Zompa give me a look like a dark cloud just hit him in the face and his two eyebrows close together and he says, Listen kid, thats a thing ya need to be forgettin. Ya dont eva wanna talk about. Unnastan? Some things. And theyll be othas in life too. Ya gotta leave em alone. Its like that friggin fat Krauht on *Hogans Heros. I say natheen. I see natheen. I know natheen.* This is one-a-those nothin things kid. Anyways. What he done ta yuh little portagee pal whats his name Pruneface. Praversions-a-what-God attended. Irregardless. The world dont need another pansy. His kind aint right. Know what I mean?

Pansy?

A friggin faggot. A homo. Jeeze, I gotta spell it out for ya? FathaLuis was queer.

And Zompa wiped his blue lips with the back of his fat wrist. He stared hard in my eyes. Cheeks shaking. Thick nose making me think of white eggplant. Zompa with wrinkles on his forehead. And his hair. Thick curls like on PruneyMendez.

And I said, But Pruney dint think what ya done ta FathLuis was—

Zompa says, FathaLuis. FathaLuis. I dont wanna hear nothin no more about FathaFriggenLuis. Trust me on iss one kid. That preece got what he deserved. He most definite werent the kinda guy yuh—

And before Zompa could finish.

The door busts open.

Its Ross stomping white whales and horecrawls.

And direct behind ice frosted Ross. Not Dad who we total expected.

But GilOwen.

Right then and there.

Zompa TheDoorGuy Galucci seen the Hooglies.

Who woulda thought such a thing? ZompaGalucci ascared of GilOwen. It sure as heck wasnt Ross who give Zompa the Hooglies even though

Ross did about make Zompa and me both pull a stroke when Ross flung open that door. Wind. Snow and all. Zompa recovered fast. But it was big GilOwen. JohnWayne style. Saying, I come for the boy. That made Zompa TheDoorGuy Galucci grab his heart. Stand up. Sit down. And grab his heart all over again.

In candle darkness. GilOwen. And Ross too. All covered in blizzard snow. Zompas words. The praversions. The queers. It was something scary. And something deep ugly. Troubling me and him bad. But no matter Zompas pale and my being ascat. Only thing I could do was ask Ross, Still snowin?

Even worse than before, said Ross. Nothin and nobody on the streets. Not even the snowplows. Lights are out. Big wind.

And sure enough. Whimpys windows. Whimpys door. Moans and shrieks of Hooglies everywhere through Whimpys walls. A sudden gust for real shook the joint. And Zompa. Ross. GilOwen and me. Held our breaths to give the outside storm its due.

And Zompa turns to GilOwen and says, I gotta hand it to ya princess. Ya got brass balls comin in here like this place is yours.

And GilOwen says, Zompa? These boys. Home. Need to get going.

And Zompa says, And you wanna take em.

And GilOwen says, That is enough.

And Zompa says, Not hoddly the beginnin.

Zompa turns to Ross and me. Ya boys think FathaLuis the only man in town wants boys?

At the same time GilOwen shoving me my no lace boots that I could hardly push in my feet the hurt being still so bad. Then GilOwen gives me my coat. My hat. GilOwen fingers brushing my shoulders. Fixing my collar. Anything keeps his hands moving. GilOwen also says, Zompa. Thank you for your help. We are now going.

Which ZompaGalucci stands looking up to GilOwens chin and Zompa says, Dont thank me ya bella donna homo. Anybody takes these boys home to their mom sgonna be me. What is it ya once told us in class? Watermelon fa pleasure. Boys fa ecstasy. Boys fa ecta— Ya sick bastid prevert.

GilOwen being Queequeg staring death in the face says, Its like everything else youve twisted Zompa. What was I ever thinking? You understanding the ancients and Melville?

And GilOwen lifted me up in his arms just as if I was a littler kid. And GilOwen with voice quiet strong said, Youve had your distorted say in court ZompaGalucci. And they listened. I was. No. I am. Fired. Now get out of my way.

And even though it was winter. And even though GilOwen had on lotsa winter clothes. Bay rum all over. Smell of summer. Smell of good. GilOwen and the power of his arms hefted me to his chest so Im looking over his shoulder.

And as we headed for the door Zompas left cheek shook and his enormous right side sagged. He slapped his forehead and sweat spray flew everywhere. Then his whole body went for to block us from leaving but stopped sudden because Zompa knew by knocking over GilOwen he woulda too knocked over me and Ross. Instead. Zompa grabbed the snowshovel from the wall. Heaved to whack GilOwens back. But. Zompa one hand. Clutched his own chest. And Zompa fell to Whimpys chair.

And the gusting wind. So loud. Again the whole building shook. Shrieks and moans. Rattling jambs. And snow blowing in as we was going out. Only me. From over GilOwens shoulder. Saw Zompas twisted face go bug eyes. Zompa. One hand holding tight the snow shovel. And his other? Going for his own heart.

For the second time. I seen Zompa take a hotta in the night but Im on the Q-T. No sounds except howling wind. Zompa in Whimpys chair. Zompa reaching through the spindrift. Horecrawls and Hooglies whipping around Zompas twisting feet.

When FatFingaPete and the other QuequeshanStreet neighbors found ZompaGalucci. It was only after they dug their way through the snowdrift in the open front door.

Some said the drift ended at Zompas feet.

Some said the foot of Whimpys chair.

Others say it was the pool table and Zompa was halfway buried to his belly.

Either.

Or.

Zompa TheDoorGuy Galucci was froze stiff dead. One hand gripping around the shovel. And the other open. Filled with snow. Palm up. On his lap.

Most everyone said Zompa never knew what hit him.

But I knew different.

And even though he wasnt there at the time.

So did Whimpy BugEyes McPherson.

When Whimpy McPherson gave final words on the matter and ended all debates and investigations from QuequeshanStreet to the police station to the SquarePeg through all over Sowams. I finally understood. Especial for GilOwens sake. And for Pruneys. And Ross. What Dad and Zompa-Galucci meant. When they. Both. Different times. Said. Some things are better said unsaid.

And the way MistaCogg. Imitating Whimpy BugEyes McPherson. Both hands smoothing back his own MistaCogg hair. Pulling up his own Mista-Cogg pants at the waist belt. Tugging snug his own MistaCogg zipper. Side mouthing.

MistaCoggs Whimpy. Telling of Zompas death. Went,

Took a hotta. Sure as holy shit hell.
Musta hurt like a friggin ball bustin bastid.
A bastid I tell youse.
A friggin ball bustin somnabitchin bastid.

V
Reaching

29

Edge of the Point

When a springblizzard thaws.
  Youre gonna have runoff and mud.
  Mud.
  Mud.
  Mud.
  Slop.
  Gutterflow.
  Saltstains and sand.
  Crud.
  On yuh shoes.
  On yuh carpet.
  On yuh pants.
  Everywhere.
  I mean. Where ya gonna play baseball?
  Fly a kite?
  Do stuff in the street?
  Tsawful.

Sometimes on warm nights Mom would meet MistaCogg bumbling atop the railroad tracks and give him a steady to his house.
  MistaCogg lipped up with a attitude doin drunk down KellyStreet.
  Mom saying, MistaCoggs lonesome angry at the world.
  Sometimes theyd sit in the swing under the grape arbor and do black coffee and talk till stars shined strong and the night warm chilled.
  This one time?
  Mom come in our house and says, Talks only to himself. For himself. To what himself is. Mysteries. So many mysteries. Through all life. We

answer only to the mysteries of ourselfs.

There were a few times Mom said, Hes total outta touch and gone loon.

On those times. She would go into our house and phone GilOwen while Ross and me stayed outside watching MistaCogg being angry at the world. MistaCogg who stood front of GilOwens house hollering, Sodomites. Bastids. Cocksuckas.

Mom coming outside saying, Boys go inside.

Me n Ross disobeying and following Mom into BaggyWrinkle night. And in that dark. GilOwens front door light. Switching on. And MistaCogg hollering like Im telling. And GilOwen and Mom talking MistaCogg quiet. And GilOwen and Mom escorting MistaCogg to the glider swing.

Ever gentle GilOwen.

MistaCogg taking a swipe or throwing a jab and shouting, Somnabitchin cocksuckin pinkeel mothafucka faggot.

Mom saying, Shhh. Shhh. Shush.

GilOwen putting MistaCogg on his swing.

MistaCogg getting calm but then again jabbing. Tripping off the swing and stumbling to the marsh. MistaCogg falling to his knees. Going face down. Lifting his head and calling his wifes name.

Then MistaCogg holding TerrorFirmer.

TerrorFirmer in his hands.

TerrorFirmer in his heart.

TerrorFirmer.

His last friend on earth.

One Saturday afternoon. I finished the paper route early and figure I would race the turn of the tide. Fish. Then explore the marsh with Ross.

Mom said Ross was already out there. He had come home early from the SquarePeg and had gone to do artpainting and for me to meet him off the point. I knew where she meant. The place where tide boulders came visible. Where the sogg banks fell steep and the channel cut sharp.

As of late. Ross was quick to head off and do stuff without me. It had actual been a long time. About six or seven weeks. EasterBlizzard. That Ross and me done anything for real together. Usual. Searching the springtime swhorls of marshgrass was one of our favorite things. And I had been looking forward to doing with him it. Especial because of the storm. There was no telling what cool stuff might be out there. Smashed hulls. Logged buoys. Broke traps. A tackle box with lures. Oars. Some with locks. Some without.

Two years ago. When we were ten. We found a life preserver that said Prudence Island Ferry printed on the bottom. But last year. All we found was junk. However. Yesterday. LilMushGahdoo had heard from skinny Nancy MillardWillard who was told by Jerry BeatinEaton. At school. About a dock section from Sousas drifting off during the blizzard and Ross and me figured chances was as good as any that dock section went Kickimuit left and had gone HuckleberryFinn raft like. Under the bridge. Under the trestle. And was now somewhere on the marsh. Probbly in waist high straw and knee low eelgrass. Or maybe between a boulder and forests of sevenfoot bullrush.

So I grabbed my fishing gear and trailed the ditches and lepted my way across the sogg to the channel drop point. There was Ross. Easel up and doing his art. I put down fifty feet or so away from him to let him have his quiet and at the edge of the point. Grabbed me a knuckle of bait mussels. Rocked smashed them open. Baited my hooks. Sat on a boulder. Cast off and had me in no time a small bucket half full of flopping choggies. Two flatfish. And a good size tautog.

Outside the bucket a few fiddler crabs had crept out their sogg holes and were now digging their big fiddleclaws into the. Put aside. Mussel bait orange flesh.

Meantime Ross had folded the easel legs but kept the artpainting locked on it.

He carried his stuff to where I was at the boulder.

Ross leaned the canvas. Wet paint up.

Just finished Moms birthday present, he said. Now needs dryin.

Such a beautiful painting. Swirling yellow red marshgrasses and wave cresting blue waters with distant low clouds. And rising behind them with more clouds. MountHope. Not ta say. But. Mom was definite gonna love it.

Of course Ross ignored my appreciating. Instead. He immediate got a stick and poked them fiddler crabs and they raised their violin claws and flashed their bead eyes.

And because he was doing that a long time and not saying nothing. I final said, Ross? Is somethin botherin you bout as much as youre botherin them fiddlers?

Ross said, Nope.

The marsh breeze rippled the cove. A rush of mallards flew low overhead. Landing. Far off. Water splashing.

In that pure marsh beauty I said, FathaLuis. He done Pruney. Maybe GilOwens doin. You know. You?

And Rosses eyes all slant and his jaw clamps. He stands straight. Grabs his paintbox. Easel and painted canvas. Looks me. His mouth saying words but no sounds come out. His eyes. Tears? But maybe the wind. And off he runs onto the swhales of marsh sponge. Jumps a ditch and disappears into thatchstraw and bayberry.

I follow. Pulling my fishtackle and bucket. Into them tall reeds. And theres Ross. Wet artpaint canvas to the sky. Ross on the dockboards. Piece of straw in his mouth. Full out relaxing on MannySousas raft. Late afternoon sun slant. And Rosses artpainting. A sky wonder. Laying in the grass.

Bewdeeful, I said.

Dint even lose a float barrel, says Ross.

Im talkin Moms birthday present. Your KingPhilipsCove paintin. Its cool.

This raft is way more wicked cool, says Ross. Not even sunk in the sogg.

And he spits a bite a strawtip and says, Youre a stupid jerk you think GilOwen ever put wrong a hand on me.

And with one foot crossed over his knee and him strawstem picking his teeth Ross says, But somethin bout GilOwen has been botherin me-a-late.

I said, What? Whats he doin?

Ross says, What hes not doin.

Whaddya mean? And I push aside the fish bucket and full stretch on the raft. My feet next to Rosses head. Rosses head next to my feet.

Oh, says Ross. No GilOwen just bein GilOwen. Ever since Zompa. Things are different. And I miss him.

You miss Zompa?

No you plate in the head retard. GilOwen.

Dont gotta be cruel.

And somewhere far off a Canada goose honks.

Ross says. That blizzard night. Direct in front-a-us. ZompaGalucci called GilOwen a queer. You think GilOwen dint care what we were thinkin? He for sure did. Remember that time you tol about? MistaCogg makin. In his shop. GilOwen cry?

Yeah. A-course. Why?

Well. That aftanoon. I was SquarePeg paintin. When GilOwen got back. GilOwen woulnt come inside. Just stayed. Leanin against the flagpole. Outside. In the rain. Shoulders heavin. Afta you told me. Made complete sense. He was ashamed.

And Ross sits up. And his eyes. Moms chestnut burgundies.

And Ross continues, Worse though is what I since GoodFriday watchin *MobyDick* thinkin. That movie minded me-a-how MistaCogg tells the book and MistaCogg is right. *MobyDick* is about queers. Its like Pruney says, Devil got hold-a-queers somethin wicked bad. And the only way for Ahab to kill that devil is to kill MobyDick who just turns around and kills Ahab. Same with ZompaGalucci.

And Ross spits bits of straw. Looks down at me and says, GilOwen doesnt have a mean spirit. That ugly. That Zompa mean. GilOwen never hurt anything or anybody. GilOwens bout the most decent guy in the whole world but all he ever hears is devils in him and people puttin on him blame.

And I said, Blame? Whos blamin him?

And Ross says, You. Askin me if he did wrong. Been goin through that his whole life. Zompa blamin him schoolteacher stuff whether its true or not and Mom says its not. Not a bit-a-truth. Just Zompa bein Zompa. But. GilOwens teacher job. Ruined. Words. Cruel stuff. Sure Zompa was nice. Like Ahab nice to his sailors. But in the end. That ugliness? Well. It turns around and kills Ahab and ultimate it killed Zompa too. But regardless. There it is. Queers an easy blame. You asked me if GilOwen was doin me like FathaLuis done to Pruney. And I told you no. Never. But what does get done is words. Zompas mean words. MistaCoggs words. Yours and everybodys stupid words.

And I said, But that night on the trestle. You said maybe GilOwen does like FathaLuis done to Pruney.

You are such an idiot.

Pruney told me. Him and FathaLuis. They did PowaHouse stuff.

Yeah. And a whole lot worse. But thats not GilOwen.

Well nobodys tellin me nothin.

Pruney dint want. All. You. The details. To know.

Why?

Cause Pruney thought ass rape fuckin is too --

Ass rape fuckin? What is it?

A pair of swans overhead. The open and close of their wings. Rosses mouth twisting. Rosses eyes. Moms burgundy brown. Little bits of purple. Glints of sun. Deep worry. Rosses bewdeeful eyes going dark. Real dark.

Sudden. A fish flips in my bucket. Rosses eyes. Ahabs lightning har-poonglow. Ross picks up the spazzing tautog squeezing tight the squirm-ing fish and Ross tighter squeezes till the fishs eyes bulge and the fishbelly bloats and Ross does a horror yell and pushes his pointing finger into the tautogs tiny swolled asshole.

And a gush of gullet.

Screaming Ross tears out the belly.

Tears out the gills.

Tears out the guts.

Then Rosses blood drip clawfinger pokes out the fishs mouth and Ross rips the bottom jaws jagged from the togs split head.

And.

Breath.

Breath.

Breath.

Ross says, That. Thats ass rape fuckin.

And he heaves the slime mess. Wib wob.

To the quick clawing fiddlecrabs.

And.

On mistake.

Bloodguts and splatter. Moms Happy Birthday present.

30
Past Montaup

May and June meant things were green. Broad chessnut trees. Snow white blossomed clusters. And in each breeze. Those blossoms were wedding confetti. In the air. And curb strewed on every sidewalk in town.

Most of the folks were walking and wiping their heads and saying stuff like, Summers comin on early. Pussawillows big as thumbs. Dogs already losin their coats. Gonna be a hot one this year.

Full tulips and lilac bushes had all-a-the kids picking flowers and cutting lilacs for classrooms even though the school principal would lecture saying, Lilac pollen gets students drowsy. Keep lilacs in the gardens. And not to school. Please.

But no teachers I knew never away turned a armload of spring. And no lilacs I seen ever made students fall asleep. Some teachers for certain did.

Made kids fall asleep. But not the lilacs.

The lilacs-a-Sowams.

Everyone loved the lilacs in spring.

Pruney had left us for NewBedford the day before the EasterBlizzard. And we hadnt seen or heard from him since. Although the calendars definite said late May. RhodeIsland disregarded calendars and pretty much did things its own way. Winters sometimes left late. And summers just as more often arrived early. And although everyone always acted like it was the first time they had ever seen such a thing. Everyone also knew. Thats the way weather is. Thats just the way weathers gonna be.

But MistaCogg? He called the weather queer.

And for me queer was like barnacles on a stick being poked through my ears. Not the word itself. But the way JackCogg said the word. And. Even the way he said it was. For real. No big deal. He was just being Jack. CapnJack. MistaCogg. Dint even raise his voice. Dint even look up from the raw tree pole clamped in a vise onto what he was locking a pivoting splay barb like Id seen him do a hundred times before. Missouri Meerschaum in his mouth. BorkumRiff curling around his head. Glasses off the tip of his nose. Just said, Sall might a bit queer.

He talked about. Like everybody else. The weather.

I said, MistaCogg?

Hmm? he said. Flipping up the barb paying me the slightest no never mind.

Whats queer? I said.

And MistaCogg stopped. Looked me over his eyeglass rims. And MistaCogg said, Late May. Ninety degree. Three days in a row. Hell. Theres snow piles. Size-a-VolkswagenVans. Huge snowbanks still melting round the perimitta the StoneFleetTavern. No ones seen the millstones since EastaSunday. Even rumor theres only twelve. Sayin snowplow pushed one inna the drink. Such a thing. Donchya think that ratha odd?

I said, Yessir. But thats not what I mean.

CapnJack stopped. Stopped what he was doing.

Stopped what he was doing and sat.

Sat on his chair and crossed his legs. Crossed his biscuit ankle good leg over his biscuit ankle bad. Left over right. Stared out the window. Puffed his corncob. And said, Jate whats on yuh mind?

Nothin, I said. Just came in to get me a Nehi. Its okay init?

You gonna clean me out?

No sir. You put in a full case. Other day.

So what ya got goin?

Well nothin. Just wonderin stuff is all. Ross. Ross is way smarter than plate in the head me. And good. Hes good too. But that word? Queer?

And there it was. Feeling tough in the talk and rough in the ears. But I kept on.

I said, Queer. Just aint all. That. For me. Queer.

And MistaCoggs ears got twitchit. Him scratching underneath his cap and on the sudden him on his feet inspecting that pine pole looking for insects hiding underneath splinters and bark. MistaCogg his palms up and down the length a the thing feeling for both smooth and rough then grabbing the shave lathe and swiping curls a pine that smelled up the place real nice and it reminded me of the smell of Pruneys Holy Rosary Portuguese-Catholic Church. Our Lady of Fatima. And more particular Mikey2A's tossing the devil outta heaven.

Then MistaCogg sat. Puffed his cob. Crossed the good leg over the bad and then uncrossed it. Lots a BorkumRiff round our heads. Smoke smell real good.

MistaCogg said, How old now you n Ross?

Be thirteen. June nine. Real soon.

And MistaCogg repeated sorta whisper, June nine.

MistaCoggs eyes. Tired. His face. Lotsa whisper lines. And his skin. Weatherbeat shingleshakes of his shack. And yellowteeth real hard on the blackbite of his pipe.

Then taking that pipe from his drycracked lips MistaCogg said, You know Jate? Aint my landscape.

I said, What? My birthday?

Naw. This stuff. Not my landscape.

Okay.

And MistaCogg. Looking for tools? Turned away. Gived me his back. Then. Pulled. From between toolboxes.

A framed MissusCogg embroidery?

MistaCogg stood in my way.

From Per	*here need not be*
Wisdom	*emory*
—Dante	*ossetti*

MistaCogg arms shaking.

And then MistaCogg slipped the framed art back from where he got it. MistaCogg leaned into the wall. Held himself steady against the wall.

Breath.

Breath.

Add an e.

Breathe.

Breathe.

Shakes stopped.

Then MistaCogg slow turned again to me and poured himself a brandy.

And again. But almost a whisper. MistaCogg said, Queer. Zall a might bit queer. And Im meaning here Jate. Odd. Just plain odd. The way-a-the world. That word n me? A big piece-a-work. A big ol piece-a-knottypine-wood that needs a lotta work.

He did his shot and he wiped with his wrist and shirtsleeve.

Booze eyes stared like he knew secrets. Like that embroidery had just told him stuff. FathaLuis. Pruney and Ross. The secret of me. And the secret of the other guys. And I wished I had kept my mouth shut and not asked MistaCogg nothing.

Absolute strict.

On the Q-T.

I finished my Nehi. Went outside and stuck the bottle in the empties-case. It emptyrattled the other empties.

And MistaCogg loud said, One for the road. Get you another.

And his so sudden shout bout near made me take a hotta.

But I took a Nehi. And went back inside the shack. Said thanks.

Once again MistaCogg crossed his legs. And he hard watchedme untie my pack and stick the Nehi between all my busting out pages. Notebooks. Scratch scrawls. And at the pack bottom. I found me a pen. Scribbled page top. Pen worked fine.

And MistaCogg said, Hows that book coming?

More work than expected. Never woulda started had I knowed.

And I shut the spiral.

MistaCogg put out his hand and said, Gonna need a churchkey.

He dropped a bottle opener into my grip. I tied the flap. And slung the pack over my shoulder.

MistaCogg said, Jate. Regardless-a-my spats with GilOwen. I-I-I-

And MistaCogg choked on his own gutjuice and sawdust.

And MistaCogg hard palooeyed to the woodburning stove.

And in the immediate quiet I said, You shoulda never all them times said mean stuff.

And MistaCogg looked down. Did a breathe. And said, Youre right Jate. GilOwen dint deserve none-a-mos-a-what I give him. None.

I said, GilOwen is a good man.

And MistaCogg stared.

Old tired eyes stared.

MistaCogg said, Worlds full a pigeonkicked idjiots like me and some-a-us are tryin get a handle on things bigga than ah bit-a-mind can wrap round.

I said, Thats three-a-us.

MistaCogg said, Howszat?

Ross n me too. Just tryin to figure on stuff is all.

And so much stuff was going through my headplate.

Stuff I dint know how to say.

I needed to sit in the sun. Do some more thinking.

Write immediate solid thoughts. We are so many mysteries.

I pushed my pen into my dungaree left side pocket.
My pen. The daggerboard. Dads skiff.
And chestnut blossoms flew.
The wind from the west.
Pages.
Sheets.
Sails.
Pointed my bike south.
SowamsGreenHills.
TheHooglySpit.
KingPhilipsStrait and Narrows.
MountHope.
Montaup.
Wind crossed my bow moving me forward.
Sailing.
Riding against the tide.
Far past those rock shores.
Beachgrit and Sunrise.
MistaCogg stared out the window.
Watched.
MistaCogg watching.
Watching.
Watching me and all of WaterStreet.
All-a-WaterStreet and his world going by.

Deepest Gratitude:
Barbara K. Richardson.
Difference. Wisdom.
Encouragement. Generosity.

Highest Regards:
Mike Medberry

Lou & Alexandra Florimonte. Maria Tish. Carrie Ure. 2nd Floor Danni.
Joy Erman. Laird Erman. Mike Dean. Star Odom-Hamilton. James B.
Richard Odom. Christine Fadden. Jaclyn Martinson. Mitch Wieland.
Sage Ricci. Mary Ellen McCanna. Robert I. Mc Leod. Nicola Potts.
Larry Young. Darlene Matson. Ryan Blacketter. Joe Rogers. M. L. Selvig
William Bill Thompson. Orlando Vitullo. Jem Wierenga. Steve Arndt.
Scott Edward Preston. Joanna Rose. Patrick McCarthy. Diane Ponti.
Ed & Nancy Sebor. Brother Schmoseph. Ellenora Ellie Karapetian.
Thomas Van Slyke. Mary Schneider. Charles Brandt. Cheryl Thomas.

Keith Murray
Uncle Ray
Joseph Allen Tetlow, SJ

The IcePond Gang:
Sharon & Dicky; Gail, Willie, LilSis & LilJoey; JoeyS; Zeb; GailC;
DeeAnneM & JoeyM; Gregory & LilFrankie; Debbie & Denise;
Kevin & Cooper; Michael, Paul & Philip.

Bonnie and Ed Mudge:
Your friendship on Day Island in Tacoma Narrows made all the difference.

Frank McCourt and Gay Talese:
Thanks so much for inviting me to walk with you.

And finally:
Tom Spanbauer and his Cannon Beach Haystack classes.
Heartbeats always to Gina Shalanic. Colorado-Rick. Gregg Kleiner.
Ellen Michaelson, MD.

Most especially to all Dangerous Writers at Tom's Portland table.
Then. Now. Future.

And:
*The Call of the Wild. The Adventures of Huckleberry Finn. Moby Dick.
Of Mice and Men. Sometimes a Great Notion. Hamlet. Dalva. "in Just."
Legends of the Fall. Beloved. The Man Who Fell in Love With the Moon.
Flowers for Algernon. "The Body." In the Wilderness. The Color Purple.
Fall of Frost. Blood Meridian. Rope Burns: Stories From the Corner.
To Kill a Mockingbird. I Should Be Extremely Happy in Your Company.
Angela's Ashes. Christ in Concrete. O Pioneers. My Antonia.*